THY
BROTHER'S
KEEPER

THY BROTHER'S KEEPER

A NOVEL

by R.C. Sproul

Wolgemuth & Hyatt, Publishers, Inc.
Brentwood, Tennessee

Wolgemuth & Hyatt, Publishers, Inc.
P.O. Box 1941, Brentwood, Tennessee 37027.

Printed in the United States of America.

ISBN 0-943497-37-X

To Johnny—wherever he is
and whatever he is doing.

Second Samuel 1:26

"Esau my brother is a hairy man,
and I am a smooth man."

Genesis 27:11

ONE

There is a mystical blackness to a church sanctuary at night, an ebony drape that falls upon the heart like the dark night of the soul. The vibrant sounds and colors of Sunday morning evaporate in the shadows of an evening service. It was Wednesday night, the eve of ashes signaling the beginning of Lent, that dreadful forty day period marked by somber vows and frivolous abstinence from chewing gum, cigarettes, and other external marks of a forgotten piety, all dedicated to the commemoration of the grand passion of the Christ.

The sanctuary was filled with supplicants, some there for holy observance, others beset by curiosity to hear the visiting speaker, the Reverend Doctor Richard Evans. The presence of Evans made the event a mixture of the sacred and the profane, the town turning out not so much to hear a sermon for the edification of their souls, but to view a performance by a hometown boy who had risen through the ecclesiastical ranks to become a religious celebrity. Now in his early forties, Evans was a national spokesman for Christianity, a religion some believed was gasping its final death rattle before succumbing to a torpid spirit of secularism which decreed the death of God and the irrelevance of the church. Evans was a walking anachronism, a medieval knight tilting his lance at Aquarian phantoms, a throwback to centuries past, preaching an orthodoxy so lucid that it sounded almost new.

The ministerial staff of the affluent Briarwood Presbyterian Church had noted early Evans's penchant for the conservative. As a seminary student he was cautiously tolerated by his spiritual mentors who took pride in their reputation for being the most progressive of the liberal ministers in the district. Their tolerance soured when it became apparent that Evans's zeal for orthodoxy was not merely a youthful phase of idealism but was hardened in

1

his brain like a calcifying plaster. He was a maverick to the system and an embarrassment to the congregation until his fame grew to such proportions that his views no longer mattered to the hometown folk. The prophet now had honor and his own country wanted to bask in its glory.

Evans sat alone in the first pew at the front of the sanctuary. He understood the political nature of the invitation to speak in his home church. He had been ordained for fifteen years and had preached from the pulpits in a hundred cities across the land, and now spoke to millions on national television. But for a decade and a half he had been in exile from his own church, banished from the nursery of his faith.

The congregation was filling in the pews behind him but he dared not glance back to survey the crowd for familiar faces lest his own face betray the acute anxiety attack that had him in its grip. There was always the tingle of adrenaline and the rumbling of his stomach before he spoke; but he was a professional, a veteran who was not supposed to be paralyzed by fear or intimidated by an audience.

His eyes lifted to the chancel, moving automatically to the stained glass window above the altar that depicted the serene presence of Christ in the midst of benign and docile lambs. As a child growing up in the church he had been tranquilized by the scene in the window. It was a respite from boring sermons droned by preachers of another era, a focal point for meditation in the dull moments of the liturgy. His spirit sank as he realized afresh that the scintillating beauty of stained glass is extinguished with the setting of the sun. Without its effulgent rays piercing the translucent panes, creating the magic of dancing prisms, the stained glass is mute. The gray lines of lead separating the panes and chips of glass offered the only contrast in color to the almost solid veil of black. The night blotted out the figure of Christ, snuffing with it Evans's hope for consolation.

Evans sat upright, ramrod straight, giving no hint of his uneasiness. He assumed the air of one who had everything under control, exuding a quiet confidence that he was master of the moment. There was no fidgeting, no nervous shuffling of his feet nor anxious wringing of his hands, though he was glad no one was grasping them to feel the clammy sweat that silently oozed from his palms. Hidden from the congregation were his deep brown eyes, now marred by a glint of black, where a pinpoint circle formed a tiny vacant tunnel that burrowed into the recessed chamber of his brain, inviting the beholder to gaze into the torment stirring at the end of the tunnel. It was a hollow point of fear detectable only by a person gifted with the ability to read the subtle nuances of the eyes, the windows of the house within.

Dr. Evans maintained the balance of his head while shifting his eyes to the pulpit, fixing his stare on the heavy satin cloth draped over the front edge, cascading down to its snow-white fringe. Embossed in the center of the cloth were the letters IHS, borrowed from the ancient standard borne by Roman Legions under Constantine. *In Hoc Signa. In This Sign—Conquer* was the mystical interpretation the emperor gave to his dream of these letters, the first consonants of the name of Jesus. Tonight the pulpit cloth was purple, the rich symbol of royalty and blood. The symbol would hang there until Good Friday when it would be exchanged for black for a few short hours before yielding to the albino cloth of Easter morning.

The hardest part of speaking was the interminable wait through the organ interlude and the opening minutes of the liturgy. Evans linked the feeling to the moment in the locker room before the opening kick-off of a football game when nervous energy attacks the bladder making frequent visits to the restroom a necessity. He smiled to himself, remembering the comic sight of gridiron gladiators marching to the bathroom, spikes clacking on the slippery tiled floor, and the awkward gyrations required to adjust the padded uniform pants to make the normally simple process of relieving oneself possible. The first blow of contact on the field released the nervous energy to flow with the rhythm of the game. For the speaker it was the first words from his mouth that transformed the adrenaline from enemy to friend, provoking the edge of emotion necessary for aggressive speech.

The dreary interlude, a dirge of mournful mood played in a minor key, was coming to an end and the host pastor rose from his throne-like velvet chair to intone the invocation. Evans was glad that a midweek evening service did not require the formal gowns of classical Scottish Presbyterians with their flowing sleeves hanging from the elbows in great folds of heavy fabric and the neck adorned with Geneva tabs, the starched white collar accented by the inverted vee pointing from throat to sternum. He preferred to speak attired in a business suit, unencumbered by the formal garb of the clergy that never quite fit his body or his psyche.

His style was Ivy League, the standard mode of tradition that married his wardrobe to his theology. Evans loved all things classical from the Chippendale chair and the Queen Anne lowboy to the Brooks Brothers suit. Eschewing the passing fancy of fashion-designed garments Evans stayed with the substance of tradition, committed to the clothier whose tailors made the suit for Abraham Lincoln's inauguration day ceremony. It was the style of the patrician, the elitist who transcends the fickleness of the *nouveau riche* and the ostentatious apparel of those oriented to the theatrical. Evans's choice of clothes was a matter of honor to him, a vow to the venerable, an oath to the uniform of rank, no less precise in its accoutrements than the insignia attached to the shoulders of a military officer. His pants were cuffed exactly one-and-one-half inch, to be maintained in season and out. There was a vein of arrogance about the stipulation that no tailor dare transgress. The rule was as sacrosanct as the Ten Commandments with the man; he would wear cuffs on his undershorts if he could find a clothier who made them.

Tonight's suit was a charcoal-grey worsted, complete with vest, and silk foullard tie of subdued hue of burgundy, matching the color code of Lent. He could easily be mistaken for the president of a bank or a Yale Law School graduate who had reached the summit of senior partner. The clothes were designed to give a look of distinction, the image of the senator or statesman, but somehow they didn't quite fit the features of the man. His build resembled that of a pulling guard, poised for brutal attack. His shoulders were broad and muscles rippled in his back stretching his jacket to an awkward angle pushing up the back collar to gather clumsily away from his squatty neck. His complexion was swarthy. A hint of olive revealed the Slavic genes mixed in his bloodline from the ancestral roots of the Balkans, but the angular features of the Serbs were softened by the Irish strand of his heritage. The athletic body gained a touch of distinction by the graying temples and splash of silver on his forelock.

The final stanza of the hymn was sung and Evans listened to the host pastor recite the honored guest's credentials. Glowing introduction with hackneyed superlatives made Evans uncomfortable and impatient for their termination.

". . . We welcome tonight, Dr. Richard Evans . . ."

Evans rose and moved quickly to the pulpit, feeling the gaze of the congregation on the back of his neck as he mounted the stairs to the elevated platform.

Some men capture an audience before they utter a word. Evans possessed that presence, the aura of charisma that communicates power by a glance of the eye, and leadership by a manner of standing. His eye contact commanded attention, filling the sanctuary with a current of electricity.

A single recessed spotlight high above the pulpit shone directly down upon Dr. Evans as the ushers manipulated the rheostats controlling the sanctuary chandeliers to the lowest setting of dim, leaving the room bathed in the ambience of a theatre with the solitary figure of an actor isolated in a poignant moment of soliloquy. Evans spoke, his initial lines falling like the verdict of guilt upon the anxious ears of a prisoner.

"The king . . . is dead . . ."

No one knew the identity of the king or his place in human history. No matter. Already the congregation was stunned by the drama of the death of the monarch. Those who had regard for no sovereign, who despised royalty, were made to feel like grief-stricken peasants at the funeral bier of their benevolent king.

Evans's pause was calculated, perfectly timed to excite the imagination while giving him the microseconds necessary to dart his eyes from face to face around the congregation. The indefinite mass before him came into sharp focus. The passing years could not mask the familiarity of some seated there. Impulses of recognition flashed through his brain as certain portraits stood out in the crowd. There, with whited mane was Mr. Lopat, his high school baseball coach, Mrs. McGraw his third grade teacher and the widow Doberman who ruined a childhood football game for him once by calling the police. There was Ted Branowski, the shoemaker and Frank Hartwell, the local hardware merchant.

They're all here. They're staring at me.

So disconcerting were the glimpses of recognition that Evans almost held the pause too long. He spoke with no prepared manuscript, no structured outline, no scrawled notes. He wanted nothing to impair the purity and totality of his rapport with the people. This manner of speaking demanded intense concentration, as the mind must prepare the mouth with ideas running at a precise rate ahead of the spoken word. The style made no provision for a wandering mind, the quickest route to stumbling speech. He recaptured the pause not a second too soon and said it again with a slight change of intonation.

"The king is dead . . ."

Johnny sat alone at the end of the bar oblivious to the haggling going on five stools to his left. He tuned out the cheap hooker who was making her move on the already inebriated millworker she had targeted. The woman's movements were mechanical; she was tense, as tight as a piano wire. She was desperate for a score. She had already lost the battle with age, the cruelest foe of her profession. Failing to conceal the truth, the heavy layers of cosmetics merely cast a garish look on her face. She was stale, like everything else in the place. Her presence was consistent with the faded decor of the room. The mirror over the bar was permanently clouded by the residual elements of lingering blue smoke that a grease-caked exhaust fan could not dispel.

Johnny was usually garrulous, lightening the mood of the dingiest bars with his infectious laugh and mischievous Tom Sawyer grin. Tonight he was pensive, fixing his eyes on the glass in front of him, idly stirring the plastic stick in his Scotch round and round as though churning a cauldron searching for mystical augers of the future. Perhaps in the smokey liquid he could catch a vision of the type normally reserved for crystal balls. He glanced nervously at the clock and winced as the sweeping second hand was pushing for a decision. If he was going to follow through with his pilgrimage he would have to get moving. He drained his glass and softly called to Gil, who had enough experience as a bartender to keep his distance when Johnny was like this. Gil reached for Johnny's empty glass and said routinely, "Another round?"

"Not now, Gil. Tell me, why would a church be having a service tonight? It's Wednesday."

Gil's eyebrows lifted at the question, framing the smudge that was still visible on his forehead imposed by an earlier encounter with his priest. "It's Ash Wednesday, Johnny, everybody goes to church on this day."

"What the hell is Ash Wednesday?" Johnny was annoyed by Gil's sudden sanctimonious air.

"It's the beginning of Lent. You know, it's the time when people give up their bad habits and vices. It's great for the soul but lousy for the liquor business. What's up, Johnny? Why are you asking?"

"I was just wondering. I heard about a guy who's preaching over at the big church in Briarwood tonight. No big deal."

Johnny pushed some wrinkled dollar bills toward Gil and eased himself off the stool.

"Catch you later, Gil."

Johnny switched on his grin and affected a springy step as he moved toward the exit. He gave the whore a good natured slap on the rump when he passed her and coupled a wink with his grin. "Hey, Mona, take it easy on this poor dude."

Ramona didn't like guys who took liberties with her posterior but she could never really get annoyed with Johnny; his playful spirit was contagious. He always could get away with the mildly outrageous, tempering it with a mask of boyish innocence.

Cellulite, Johnny thought to himself as he headed for the parking lot. *All the broads get it sooner or later, but it's fatal for a hooker.*

Johnny fumbled for the keys to the '71 Dodge he had purchased from a dealer only that afternoon. He gave it the once-over with his practiced eye, noting the dangling exhaust pipe and the pockets of rust around the bumper. *The rotten thing's got cancer,* he thought, *I'll be lucky to get $200 for it at the auction tomorrow.* He climbed behind the wheel and turned the engine over but hesitated a moment before putting it in gear. *Why did Ted have to tell me that Scooter's in town? Who gives a damn? Ted was falling all over himself about it.*

The shoemaker had said he was going to church to hear "Scooter" Evans, a first for the huge bear of a man. He had never been inside a Protestant church. Ted went to Mass every morning like all the rest of the devout Catholics. But to hear Scooter was different. Ted would break his private tradition and risk the wrath of Monsignor Manyak to go to the Presbyterian church.

Johnny hadn't been in that church for years, not since he was married there. Richard Evans had been his best man. He owed it to him to go for his triumphant homecoming. But there would be other people there Johnny did not want to see. It could be messy.

It was already ten after eight so Johnny pushed the accelerator, speeding along the strip district of Millport Boulevard. It was seven more miles to Briarwood, seven miles of fast-food joints, used-car lots, drive-in movies, and retail stores. For Sale signs and Business Space to Rent clapboards already dotted the storefronts along the boulevard, mirroring the beginning of the economic recession that would soon paralyze this corner of western Pennsylvania. Some buildings were landmarks, impervious to the roulette game of the franchise system. He passed Marion's Tavern and thought it had been there forever and would still be there at the end of the world.

Johnny slowed down briefly to allow the relic he was driving to absorb the shock of the railroad tracks that marked the traditional line of demarcation between the milltown and the outer limits of the suburbs. Johnny was moving in the opposite direction from that of his childhood. His former passage was marked by carefree forays in his gleaming convertible or his Corvette from Briarwood to Millport. Now he moved from Millport to Briarwood, a living symbol of his personal demotion to the wrong side of the tracks.

The knot tightened in his stomach when he swung the car up Byrne Drive toward the illumined steeple atop the enormous Georgian edifice. The length of the street was crammed with cars, machines parked at attention, inert, waiting for their owners to return from paying homage to the hometown boy made good. Johnny found a spot near the school, up the street from the church, and parked where his car would not be noticed by his affluent contemporaries. It was eight twenty-nine and he could hear the lusty strains of congregational singing piercing the night.

Johnny knew the layout of the church well. The memories from his youth had not been erased by his self-imposed exile from the place. There was a time when he frequented the building not only on Sundays but also during the week. Tuesday afternoons were devoted to choir practice after school. Saturday mornings had robbed him of two years of weekend sports activity by required attendance at confirmation classes. Saturday nights held better memories as the church hosted summer evening "canteens," the best dances in town. He even went to Boy Scouts at the church, but only for a few weeks. Tying knots and doing exotic Indian dances in honor of the Webelos did not hold his interest. Assembling this storehouse of memories Johnny slipped in a side door and found an obscure pew in the shadows of the transept.

Richard "Scooter" Evans had already been introduced and was beginning his sermon. He looked good. his voice resonated through the sanctuary as Johnny fidgeted in the pew trying to adjust his body as well as his mind to this setting. It was difficult for him to concentrate on Scooter's words. His very presence conjured up too many images of the past. When Johnny thought about the past and about Scooter he usually envisioned Scooter in a baseball uniform. Though the Scooter in front of him was now Dr. Richard Evans, a polished preacher, Johnny could detect in his animated gestures the moves that Scooter had acquired years before.

TWO

It was the spring of 1957.

Johnny was working to get loose on the sideline, his warm-up jacket dangling from his left shoulder. It was April, and a chill hung in the air reminding him of the last game he had pitched, struggling in the midst of a swirling snowfall that deposited slush on the hard strip of rubber on the mound. The jacket kept some heat on his arm but functioned more as a religious relic, a holy shroud pitchers use to protect the delicate mechanism by which they ply their trade. Johnny's insides were grinding. This was the final game of the season, the team's last chance to avoid the ignominy of being the first winless baseball squad in Millport history.

Millport was a football town. The football players were the pampered princes of the high school, gaining exemptions from class assignments and school rules that bound lesser mortals like Johnny. The genetic code deprived Johnny of any chance for football. He was wiry, agile, and endowed with adequate talent but his five-foot-seven-inch frame was not enough to withstand the punishment meted out by the brutish sons of the steel mills.

Scooter moved beside Johnny and exchanged pre-game pleasantries. "How are you feeling?"

"I'm ready to go. Let's win this one."

Scooter had two streaks on the line. The winless streak ate at his gut, but the other streak evoked fierce pride. Coming into this game Scooter had played the entire season without an error, the longest errorless skein for a shortstop in the history of the school. If he could keep the string alive he would salvage some glory from this otherwise nightmarish season. He could live up to his nickname, borrowed from the legendary shortstop of the New York Yankees, Phil "Scooter" Rizzuto.

11

The stands were almost empty save for a handful of die-hard students, and some conspicuous older men. These were the professional scouts, grizzled veterans of the baseball world who scoured the school yards and sandlots of America looking for the next Joe DiMaggio. They sucked on foul-smelling cigars, casting a critical eye and furrowed brow in the direction of a hopeful player. They scribbled notes on dog-eared report sheets that recorded their Olympian judgments. Phrases like "weak arm," "limited range," or "lacks a potential bat" were hastily scrawled but remained indelible.

Today the scouts had prepared contracts in their pockets. The end of high school eligibility made the graduating seniors free to trade in their amateur status for cash, the latest nutrient for bonus babies.

Scooter pawed the ground with his spikes, uncovering stones and jagged pieces of iron ore that could frustrate his bid for an unblemished season. He laughed at the efforts of the grounds keepers to turn this area into a baseball field. They were feebly armed with rakes and a small, dented, lime-spreading machine. The field was made of sand and the residue of slag that came from surrounding steel mills.

Afternoon games at Millport Park were played in smog that cast an amber corona over the field. The smoke spewing from the chimneys of nearby blast furnaces was filled with polluted chemicals. Car windows were blurred from the fallout, and the boys found it impossible to keep the chrome strips on their cars from being pitted by acid corrosion. The chemical rain was tangible, leaving a sticky residue on the skin, and an odor of rotten eggs lingering in the air.

Millport's uniforms matched their field. They were moth-eaten and faded to a somber gray. The caps were limp, their resiliency long since vanished, making it impossible to block them in the current fashion. The *M* on the hat was made of cheap felt affixed with glue. Most of the *M*'s had pieces missing or corners flopping loosely against the bill, fighting for freedom from the last stubborn drop of glue. The costumes were made outlandish by the Millpost school colors, orange and black, lending the players the image of fugitives from a Halloween party.

Scooter continued his housekeeping chores at shortstop. The ritual served a competitive purpose. Like a dog spraying the bushes of his territorial domain, Scooter used his spikes to declare his unique sphere of authority. His cleat prints served as insult and challenge to his Gladwin counterpart whom Scooter knew lacked the throwing arm to match his.

The umpire stepped from behind home plate and bellowed in Johnny's direction, "Play ball." Johnny's first pitch was wide. His comrades chirped encouragement with nonsense sounds.

"Hot chalalhalachala . . . C'mon Johnny babe, bedebeep, beedebeep, beedebeep . . ."

Johnny's next pitch was hit sharply to shortstop. Scooter glided to his left, fielded it cleanly and gunned a throw to first. The first baseman pulled his foot off the bag to catch the throw. Scooter knew instantly that the score book would record; "E-6." With that cryptic cipher Scooter's skein was dead.

"Sorry, Bill, my fault."

Scooter kicked an imaginary pebble as he walked back to his position, privately boiling. *Stupid jerk,* he thought, *why can't he stretch without pulling his foot off the bag?*

The next batter hit a high bouncer right at Scooter with "double play" written all over it. Breaking the cardinal rule of infielders, Scooter took his eye off the ball to sneak a peek at the runner heading for second. The ball slid off his glove into short centerfield. Two batters, two errors.

Johnny called "time" and walked over to Scooter.

"Forget it, Scoot. Never mind the streak. Let's settle down and win the game."

At the mound Johnny stooped and picked up the resin bag, squeezed it gently and let it slip between his fingers to the ground, thinking, *If Scooter falls apart we don't have a Chinaman's chance in hell.*

When the game was over, Scooter's total of errors had reached five, threatening a record in the other direction. Once again Millport found a way to lose. Scooter picked up his gear and headed for the parking lot.

On the way he bumped into his coach.

"Tough luck, Scooter. We were all pulling for you to keep your streak alive. Don't sweat it, kid. You still had a great year at short. Listen, I've got good news for you."

The coach pulled a letter from his pocket and handed it solemnly to Scooter.

"This is your ticket to glory, Scooter. It's from the Pirates.

They want you to go down to Forbes Field Saturday for a tryout."

Scooter thanked the coach and stuffed the letter in the hip pocket of his uniform, too depressed from the game to open it. Johnny was already standing by his gleaming red and white '55 Chevy convertible. He was putting the top down, defying the April weather, and was snapping the boot in place.

"Why so glum, chum?" Johnny quipped, flashing his contagious smile. Scooter grinned in spite of himself, unable to parry Johnny's good mood. Both boys had infectious smiles. Scooter's was spontaneous, while Johnny's was perpetual, as if painted on his face by a mischievous leprechaun. Of the two, Scooter was the pensive one, at times bordering on melancholia. Johnny was fun-loving, finding a laugh in the heaviest moments of the hour. The game was over and Johnny had already bounced back from the loss. Scooter would take it home with him.

Millport High had recently put on their senior class play, a musical version of Mark Twain's *Tom Sawyer*. It had been a foregone conclusion that Johnny would play the lead. Marlon Brando had brought method acting into vogue with *On the Waterfront*. Johnny's method was to be himself. No makeup was necessary to transform Johnny Kramer into the incarnation of Twain's fictional adolescent hero. Sawyer came alive in Johnny. His unruly sandy hair betrayed the fact that when Johnny was a child it must have been pumpkin orange and was only recently inching toward blond. The freckles were fading but they were still evident under close scrutiny, making him the target of the fatuous query, "Hey Johnny, were you born back of a cow?"

Every policeman in Briarwood knew Johnny. They had a fond affection for him though they fought to conceal it behind officious scowls and sober-sounding reprimands. If a cantankerous old lady found a bag of fresh dog dirt in her mailbox, the police knew where to look for the culprit. Routinely they would stop Johnny in his familiar Chevy and say, "Hey Johnny, be careful with the dog dirt. You have old lady Williamson beside herself."

Johnny would utter a solemn oath with a sober face that was in danger of surrendering to the twitches at the corners of his mouth. His face always hinted at some delectable secret he was relishing in his mind, lending suspicion to the idea that he was out at night burying a dead cat to get rid of his warts.

Scooter got in the passenger side of the convertible. Judy Harvester was already nestled by Johnny's side, oozing warmth and a budding sensuality. Scooter felt the vibes. The close quarters made it impossible for him to escape the fragrance of Judy's perfume. Her neck was lightly splashed with White Shoulders. Judy's raven hair cascaded down to her shoulders, giving her a look of severe beauty. If considered by each distinctive part the facets of her face were awkwardly composed, violating several points of classic statuary. Her lips were too thick, her forehead too high, her chin a bit squat and her eyes set just a millimeter too far apart. In their assembly the parts meshed into a strange kind of symmetry that was enchanting to the masculine eye. Perhaps it was the pronounced high cheek bones setting off her flashing eyes that gave the illusion of an Indian princess. Judy boasted that she was in fact one-eighth Cherokee, according to her family tree.

Scooter absently rested his arm on the seat-back behind Judy and delicately played with a wisp of her hair, rubbing it gently between his fingers. Johnny either didn't notice or didn't mind. Judy was acutely aware of it, feeling the magnetic draw that was always there with Scooter. She could dismiss but never forget that Scooter had been her first love. He was the one to break off when he fell madly in love with a wispy blond from West Virginia. But that was eons ago and Scooter was now a loner, studiously avoiding romantic entanglements. His social life was limited to being a third wheel with Judy and Johnny, enjoying his romantic life vicariously. Judy and Johnny knew not to discuss the subject with Scooter since such forays in the past had set him to sullen brooding.

Johnny fired up his duals and left the park. They drove the seven miles to Briarwood, their spirits lifting with each mile the dismal mill town was left behind. Three years of commuting to school had not erased the trauma of the cultural collision they experienced in Millport. The daily trip was an expedition between two worlds, a transport between the promising and the grim, the affluent and the bleak.

Briarwood was a small bedroom community stolen from the steel mill and coal mining regions of the outskirts of Pittsburgh. It was an oasis in the midst of a desert of soot. Originally the tract of land was called simply #5, indicating the land mass above the #5 deep mine owned and operated by Consolidated Coal. Above the ground the scene was bucolic with cows grazing on the sloping meadows. In 1939 the first bulldozers appeared, forcing the cows elsewhere to seek their forage, and #5 was molded into a commuter's haven, a suburban ghetto for managers who made the daily trek to downtown Pittsburgh, only eight miles distant. Briarwood was lily white and prosperous, but too small to boast its own high school. There were no Blacks, few Slovaks, no mill workers living in Briarwood. Only a handful of Catholics settled there and, for the most part, they resided on the "other side of the highway" which provided the man-made barrier of ethnic and religious classes.

Johnny drove the Chevy to the "wrong" side of the highway and let Scooter off in front of a sterile apartment building. Scooter gave Judy a peck on the cheek and jumped out of the car. He climbed the steps to the modest two-bedroom apartment he shared with his mother. His sister, Roberta, was away at school.

Mrs. Evans wouldn't be getting home from work for another hour. Scooter took his time preparing for his shower. He shed the scratchy wool Millport shirt and dropped it on the floor. He slipped off the sweatshirt he wore underneath his uniform and stripped to the waist. He was in no hurry to remove his uniform pants. Taking them off involved a minor ordeal. He popped a "Lucky" out of the cellophane covered pack with the red circle logo, tapped it tight, and lit up. He exhaled the first drag with a weary sigh trying to ignore the throbbling in his right thigh. Glancing at his leg he noticed the telltale dark brown stain on his uniform pants. Nothing serious. Blood was seeping from a "strawberry" abrasion made chronic by a long baseball season. As soon as a healing scab appeared on the surface Scooter would tear it open again sliding on the rough surface of Millport Park.

Scooter unbuckled his pants and slipped them down to the thigh. As he pried at the sticky pant leg he tore bits of fresh flesh from the wound until the uniform came free. He saw tiny woolen strands still slinging to the wound along with dirt that was caked on like crust. Gingerly he picked a wet gauze patch from the middle of the oozing wound. He knew he should do it with one sudden motion like tearing a Band-Aid from a sore, but at the moment he lacked the courage. What bothered Scooter more than the wound was the knowledge that the strawberry abrasion was in the wrong place. If he were sliding correctly the abrasion would be more to the back than this. The strawberry betrayed the fact that Scooter was turning on his side while sliding. *All that practice,* he thought, *and I'm still sliding like a sissy.* He stepped out of the pants and pulled off his sweaty socks.

Stripped almost naked Scooter caught a glimpse of himself in the full-length mirror on the bathroom door. The image reflected something no one on the team knew about. Both legs were tightly wrapped at the knee with wide Ace bandages. His body looked solid in the mirror, featuring hard muscles earned by strenuous sports activity, not the kind artificially induced by gimmicks offered in mail-order ads that promised to turn ninety-eight-pound weaklings into Atlas-like brutes and end forever the sand-in-the-face humiliation imposed by beach bullies. His taut sinewy body made it possible for him to move with graceful fluidity. His legs responded immediately to whatever his brain demanded of them. He floated on high school dance floors.

But something was wrong with Scooter's legs. The athlete's most vulnerable spot is not the heel as Homer supposed, but the knee. Scooter's knees had already absorbed a savage beating in his young life. He never talked about it but he was constantly aware of it. The knees did not plague him with sharp shooting pains that would inhibit his performance; rather they were given to a dull, steady ache, much like a nagging toothache. He identified with the publicized daily agony that would shorten Mickey Mantle's spectacular career.

Scooter had gone to Pittsburgh to visit an orthopedic surgeon. The examination revealed torn cartilage and stretched ligaments in both knees, coupled with the formation of cysts beneath the kneecaps, incipient arthritis, and bone spurs. Scooter was eighteen years old but his knees were fifty. Weekly visits at $25 a treatment were devoted to attempts to dissolve the cysts by injections of a medicated liquid—almost a pint of the chalky substance at a time inserted into each knee with a horrifying ten-inch needle. After each treatment Scooter rode the bus home with the liquid sloshing in his knees. The other passengers assumed he merely had an odd squeak in his shoes.

Surgery was ruled out. The best the surgeon could promise was a 50/50 chance that Scooter would not be left with a permanent limp. When the injections proved ineffective Scooter settled for less expensive visits to his family doctor to have the excess fluid drained from his knees. Here the procedure was reversed. Instead of having liquid injected into the knees he had it extracted. The doctor joked that Scooter was making him rich by supplying him with a lucrative quantity of Pennsylvania crude oil. The doctor called it "Pennzoil." The joke diverted Scooter's mind from the needle. He hated needles.

Wincing at the memory, Scooter began the ritual of removing his leg wraps. He pried the metal clasps from their cloth moorings and tore off the adhesive tape that was there for reinforcement. Slowly he unwound the bandages and rolled them up. When they were free of the bandages his legs felt a sudden relief from pressure. He rubbed his legs to stimulate circulation, snuffed out his cigarette and stepped into the shower.

The shower was Scooter's place of refuge, his private retreat for meditation. He loved to stand under the invigorating hot spray for half an hour. He savored the warmth of the pulsating water on his aching legs. The jets of water pounding his back stimulated his mind to reflection. He thought about the letter from the Pirates. He had already spoken with scouts from the Red Sox and the Cubs. He knew that the Pirates would tell him the same thing, he was too short to be a major league shortstop but had potential as a second baseman. They encouraged him to start out in the class C league. Scooter had visions of the land of Faulkner, and of Caldwell's *Tobacco Road*. There was no glamour in the C leagues, riding back and forth in pre-World War II buses, as dilapidated as the locker rooms with their sweating water pipes and moldy benches. The scouts were not waving big bonus money in front of him. He knew they considered him a longshot.

Part of Scooter's mind told him he could make it. He knew that his intelligence would give him an advantage. His brain often served as the razor's edge between success and failure in athletic competition. He was also aggressive, a quality that made coaches salivate. He had a fierce desire to be a ballplayer, a total dedication that was born in his breast as a small boy when he huddled close to the Philco cabinet model radio that provided that ticker-tape play-by-play heroics of the Pittsburgh Pirates.

Two negative factors weighed heavily on him. The first was all the talk about being a second baseman. Scooter was a shortstop. He studied the position, he felt at home there. Whatever sport Scooter played he was the field general. In football he played quarterback, and in basketball he was the middle guard, the "playmaker." He relished the role of leader and such status was not accorded second basemen.

More importantly Scooter had to consider his legs. High school games were only seven innings with two or three games scheduled in a week. If the score was tied and the game went to extra innings, as intensely competitive as he was, Scooter found himself hoping that the other team would score and end the game, putting a stop to the agony he was feeling in his knees. Unless he could find a miracle cure for the throbbing ache he knew he could never endure a schedule of 154 games.

The full reality of Scooter's condition hit him in the shower. He knew his lifelong fantasy of becoming a major league ball player was a child's delusion, a vacant dream. It was a lousy day.

Scooter quit the shower and was dressed in time to see his mother walk in the door. Smartly attired and showing signs of fading beauty, she looked haggard when she paused in the door-way gasping for breath. A congenital defect, a hole in her heart, made the two-story climb painful. He took a bottle of bourbon from the cupboard, filled a "triple" measure in a glass and waved it once quickly under the cold water tap. The spot of water soothed Mrs. Evans's conscience so she could delude herself into thinking that she wasn't drinking it straight.

THREE

Johnny and Judy drove through the grand stone pillars which rose pretentiously from the earth like great obelisks to announce the entrance to Briarwood. They drove past the merchant zone and up the artery that flowed into the heart of the community. The verdant lawns were taking on a new lush shade of springtime that was set off by the yellow hues of exploding forsythia and the reds and pinks of azaleas. The trees were announcing their vernal rebirth, bursting their dormant red buds with sprigs of green, a signal for the real estate brokers to hike their appraisals another notch.

The Tara-View section was a suburb within a suburb, a mecca cut out of the woods for multi-acred lots, the province of upper management. Johnny drove past the expensive homes on Tara Drive to the far end of the street. His house looked like a transplanted antebellum plantation, complete with towering white pillars in front.

There was enough room in the driveway to park several cars, including Mr. Kramer's Fleetwood and Mrs. Kramer's Buick Roadmaster. As they entered the kitchen Ruby was just leaving. Ruby had served as maid and nanny to the Kramer boys for fifteen years. She was picked up at the end of the driveway by a black man in a beat-up jalopy. He was making the rounds as a shuttle service to take the maids who worked the Tara-View section of Briarwood back to their apartments in the slum area of Millport.

Mrs. Kramer was standing at the counter in the kitchen looking more like a maid than Ruby. Her hair was up in curlers exposing yellowing roots that needed a new rinse job. It was hard to believe this rough looking woman was the matriarch of such a fine house. She wore no makeup and had all the outward signs of a chronic alcoholic. In spite of her brusque manner and habitual grousing, the teenagers all loved her. She was their supreme den mother, supplying them with potato chips, sandwiches, and unlimited rounds of soda pop. It was gauche to refer to her as "Mrs. Kramer"; she was "Charlie," the nickname bestowed upon her by her husband. Charlie enjoyed alternately shocking and amusing the kids with risque vulgarities.

She was drinking a Budweiser straight from the bottle. Johnny went to the refrigerator and helped himself to a Bud. Charlie asked, "Well, did you hitless wonders win one today, or was Sydney Profater there again?"

No one knew the true identity of Sydney Profater or if he even existed. Johnny's grandmother had started the legend years before. She never asked if the boys won or lost a sports contest, but only if the mythical Sydney was there. Grandma explained that the query originated when Johnny's uncle came home crying from a baseball game in 1918 saying, between sobs, "Sydney Profater was there." Sydney was now ubiquitous, appearing everywhere to spoil countless games for the boys.

"No, we blew it again. But we almost won. It went down to the last out. Scooter had a bad day. We lost on errors."

Charlie replied, "You know what they say in hard labor: *'tough rocks'.*"

"C'mon, Mom, it was really close."

"Go tell your troubles to a policeman. You'll get no sympathy from me."

Johnny laughed and sent Judy down to the game room while he went to shower and change. A few minutes later he appeared dressed in chino khakis and a cotton shirt, his hair still dripping from the hasty shower. His eyes curled into a flirting grin as he moved to the walnut record cabinet to select a Nat King Cole album. He flipped a record on the player and started to dance with Judy, a slow swaying, rocking motion known in Millport as the "cat dance."

Judy rested her head on Johnny's shoulder, dropping her arms around his back as the slow dance left them barely moving, locked in a swaying embrace.

"Johnny, what's wrong with Scooter? He's not like he used to be. I'm worried about him. He never dates, he skips all the dances. He's just dropped out of circulation."

"Well, you know, Judy, his dad just died and he's still hung up on Patricia," Johnny offered.

"That's the part I can't figure out. I can understand him being upset about his dad, but he knew that was coming for a long time. It's the Patricia part that puzzles me. Scooter used to be the biggest girl chaser in town. He was so fickle. To go steady with him for three months was to make the record books. Then all of a sudden he just quit. It doesn't make sense."

"How many times did you go steady with him, Judy?" Johnny asked.

"At least three. But practically every girl in our class and half the girls in the class ahead of us could say the same thing."

"Right. Every one of them at one time or another was 'Scooter's girl.' Now nobody's dancing with Scooter."

"That's weird. But you know why, don't you, Johnny? You're closer to him than anybody."

"Yeah, I think I know why. But what difference does it make? That's his business."

Judy abruptly broke the embrace and backed off from Johnny, fire gleaming in her eyes.

"Don't play games, Johnny. I want to know. Scooter's my friend too."

"Oh, oh, oh—you're still soft on him, aren't you?" Johnny shot back.

"Cut it out, Johnny. He's my friend, that's all. He's our friend, both of us. He's with us all the time. He's not acting natural. Not like he used to. Now, what gives?"

"Well, he flipped over Patricia the first time he met her. In fact, I met her before he did. I'll never forget it. It was at the ball field in the summer. Let me think . . . the summer of '50. Heck, Scooter was only thirteen. We were playing a pick-up game. Scooter was in the field and my team at bat. I was sittin' on the bench and I saw this girl walkin' up toward the backstop. She was little knockout. I went over to her and introduced myself. She said her name was Patricia, not Pat or Patty, but Patricia. She was very insistent about it. She told me she had just moved into Briarwood the day before.

"We weren't talking two minutes when she said, 'Who's that boy?' pointing out Scooter.

"Scooter was wearing that crazy rolled-up sailor hat he used to wear with his jeans and white T-shirt. I told Patricia his name, and that's about all. Our team made the third out and I had to go back to the mound. By the time I finished my warm-up throws Scooter was already hustling her."

"OK, Johnny. Now I know how they met—but that still doesn't explain why he's so gone on her."

"Well, that night Scooter showed up at the canteen with her and didn't dance with anybody else. He walked her home—you know, down Constitution Drive in the moonlight and all that stuff. For the next three weeks they were a hot item. Then, wham—it was all over. Patricia shot him down."

"Why? What did he do?"

"I don't know. But I have a hunch about it. From day one all the girls were warning her about Scooter's fickleness. She was coy. She knew just how to play him, like he was a hooked fish. She'd reel him in and then let him run and do it over and over until she caught him. He must have gone with her ten times before she moved to Florida. It was always the same scene. Scooter would initiate it; they'd go together for a month or so and she'd break up with him for a couple of months and date someone else. She drove him nuts. I'm sure that if Scooter knew he could have her, he wouldn't want her anymore. She knew that. That's what the other girls never figured out. Now, Scooter's diseased with her. It's getting out of hand. And speaking of hands, let's forget about Scooter and Patricia . . ."

Johnny started to run his hands over Judy's hips, giving them a playful squeeze. Judy had a build that was out of proportion. She was not fat, but was small-busted and had a large derriere.

Judy gave Johnny a playful smack. "Cool it with the hands, Romeo; let's have a Coke."

Johnny went behind the high bar at the end of the knotty pine paneled room to set up the Cokes. The bar took up one end of the room and was stocked with glasses bearing off-color sayings and pictures of semi-nude women. By the first bar stool was a rug bearing six sets of imitation foam rubber breasts. Each set was given a name of a fruit, depending on their size. They ranged from "cherries" to "watermelons." Other bits of erotica were displayed brazenly around the bar. They gave notice that the Kramers were the avant-garde of the upper-middle class liberal spirit.

The rest of the room was a sports trophy display. The walls were covered with photographs of Johnny's father standing beside or playing golf with sports-world celebrities. Stan Musial had been in the Kramer household, as he often stopped on the way to his family home in Donora when the Cardinals were in town. The senior Kramer was the president of a large insurance agency. On the side, Jack Kramer had become America's most distinguished collegiate football referee. He handled big games—Army-Navy, Notre Dame-Pitt and was annually selected to referee a major bowl game. He hobnobbed with the sporting world's elite and the photographic gallery made it impossible to miss that point.

As a father, Jack Kramer was *sui generis,* a breed apart, a pure iconoclast of the upper-middle class mold. He was unimpressed by the legacy of Queen Victoria, flagrantly breaking the taboos of the era. He allowed the boys to drink his liquor; he gave coaching lessons in the art of seduction; and winked at their carefully planned acts of high school truancy. He was a co-conspirator, a living bridge across the generation gap.

In Johnny's eyes, Jack Kramer was king. He was the supreme man, a successful business executive, athletic hero, community leader, hard-driving disciplinarian, yet earthy enough to give Johnny a long leash in his teenage years. Jack was tough and tender—at times demanding, at times indulgent. One thing was certain; he was approachable. He leaked a mellow warmth through the pores of his steel-like exterior.

Jack was everything Johnny yearned to be, the ideal role pattern of masculinity. Johnny had two brothers, but he was the eldest, the firstborn heir apparent, the prince in waiting.

The freedom and worldly wisdom provided by Jack's tutoring made Johnny something of a hero with the boys. One day, at age thirteen, Johnny opened his wallet in the school lavatory and produced a condom. The other guys stared in awe as he casually unwrapped the mystical sign of manhood as though he knew what to do with it. In this single solemn act Johnny established himself as the undisputed authority of all things sexual. No one doubted his veracity when he declared that the condom was given to him by his father with the paternal advice to keep himself protected. Equipped with this awesome symbol, rolled up again like a signet ring, Johnny bore proof positive that he had stepped over the line, had passed muster, run the gauntlet, and joined the ranks of those who were no longer cherry. The other boys, Scooter included, could not fathom the power contained in such a sheath of smooth rubber. Their only knowledge of such things was gleaned by surreptitious searches of their father's dresser drawers where they looked at, but dared not touch, the mysterious tokens of manhood.

The first time Scooter touched a condom was in Miami, Florida, in December of 1956, just before the New Year and the Orange Bowl game. The event transpired when Johnny took him aside and, after taking out his wallet, whispered in conspiratorial tones, "Here, take this, you'll probably need it tonight."

Scooter accepted the tightly wrapped "ring" into his hand and carefully slipped it between the folds of his own wallet. He wondered if this was the same condom Johnny had brandished in the lavatory four years previously. No, he knew better. By now Johnny had gone through a gross of Trojans if truth was in any way related to reputation.

Scooter pushed the wallet deep into his hip pocket. It seemed to weigh more than usual. His stomach felt queasy, as if a trembling nerve moved directly to it from his pocket that concealed the nefarious contraband. He feared what Patricia would think if she knew he was carrying this covert sign of his passionate desires.

The night air of Miami induced a feeling of destiny, a fate riding on tropical winds. The romance of a thirteen-hundred mile, non-stop drive to see a football game had the boys acting giddy. They were hugged by the carnival spirit that hung over the city. Motel rooms were bursting, and boisterous fans were snake-dancing in the streets, already celebrating the certain victory of their college team on the morrow.

The game meant nothing to Scooter. He was obsessed with his desire to see Patricia, who had been living in Fort Lauderdale since she moved from Briarwood in her junior year of high school. Scooter had tried to keep the romance alive by long-distance phone calls and feverish love letters mailed to the exotic address 338 Camelia Drive, Lauderdale-by-the-Sea. He had never been south of the Mason-Dixon line and the address conjured up images of an army of blond-haired Adonises pursuing Patricia, armed with sleek surfboards and driving M.G.s or Porsches. Patricia hurled daggers at his heart by dropping faceless names of her suitors in responses to his letters. "Jimmy took me to a beach party last week . . ." "I went deep-sea fishing with Bruce . . ."

The airmail romance was brief. Patricia's letters were sporadic, arriving with less and less frequency until they stopped altogether. She was suddenly "out" when Scooter phoned. Her last letter had been dismally clear.

Dear Scooter,

It has been great fun getting your letters and your calls. I really am very fond of you but we have to be realistic. You're in Pennsylvania and I'm in Florida. You know me. I'm not one to miss out on anything. I've told you a million times that love is for the movies. I don't want to be trapped in a sob-story romance. I'm going to have a ball, find a nice rich sugar daddy, and get married. You are too serious Scooter. You need to loosen up a bit and have some fun.

Luv ya,
Patricia

The missive only served to increase the tempo of Scooter's letters as they took on an air of frantic desperation. He wrote lengthy epistles every night alternately demanding and begging an answer. None came.

On week nights Scooter worked after school until 10:00, except on days his baseball games were played. Usually the boss left early, telling Scooter to lock up the cash register and close the shop. On the way home Scooter's mind fixed on one thing, the mail. He calculated the time it would take for his letter to reach Patricia and for a reply to travel back to him.

Elizabeth Evans sorted the mail each day and left Scooter's allotment on the mahogany drum table by the living room window. Scooter rushed home but slowed his pace for the final steps to the apartment as if he were sneaking up on his quarry, a skitterish bird that might fly away in fright if he moved toward the drum table too abruptly.

If the drum table was empty, barren of any cargo, Scooter would ask his mother the routine question, trying to keep his voice casual, "Any mail for me today, Mom?"

Elizabeth hated the question. She easily penetrated the gossamer veil of her son's nonchalance, reading the anxiety in his eyes.

She tried to keep her own voice light and encouraging, "Nothing today, son."

The mailbox yielded nothing for the drum table for days and weeks. The message was clear. Patricia would not bend to his frantic letters. She shut them out. Scooter felt helpless. He could not compete with unseen ghosts, with enemies having a thirteen-hundred mile advantage over him. He couldn't win the game from the bench. He wasn't even that close to the action. He was so far away that he couldn't pick up the game on the radio. He wondered if she even opened his letters or if they were consigned to some dead-letter slot in her garbage can.

Scooter threw in the towel. No more letters, no more calls. Frustration had passed into humiliation. An emotional cycle set in that oscillated between hurt and anger spinning out a growing depression. Scooter withdrew into himself and dropped out of Briarwood social life. He discussed his feelings with no one, turning instead to music as an escape valve for the steam that was boiling in his viscera.

He sought solace in the ebony baby grand piano that filled one side of the Evans's living room. The poignant strains of Chopin fit his mood but lacked the more primitive link to his feelings which popular music offered. He selected the sheet music bearing the smiling image of Perry Como. It was Como's rendition of the torch ballad "Patricia." He played the music over and over again, embellishing it with dissonant chords to add a morose hint to its lyrics. The words were simple:

> Oh, Patricia, my darling
> Patricia . . . you can
> make all my dreaming come true.
> My heart is just drooling, Patricia,
> No fooling, I've fallen in love with you.

He derived a kind of catharsis, a momentary release from torment, by letting his melancholia flow out of his fingertips and into the keyboard.

Mrs. Evans heard the legato cry. She was alarmed by her son's brooding over the girl, inwardly enraged that the wispish golddigger could inflict such torture on her boy. She trusted that he was smitten by puppy love, a disease not fatal but temporarily debilitating.

The trip to Miami was a windfall for Scooter, the result of Jack Kramer's assignment to head the officiating crew for the Orange Bowl game. Jack provided free tickets for Johnny and four of his friends. Scooter was sprawled on his couch when Johnny bounded in the door two days after Christmas waving the ducats like a flag.

"It's time to start packing, Scoot. You and I are going south. It's moon over Miami for us. These sweet little tickets are for seats right on the fifty-yard line at the Orange Bowl. Dad made reservations for both of us at a motel."

Scooter jumped from the couch and examined the tickets to make sure they were real.

"How are we going? Are we flying?" Scooter asked.

"Yeah. We're flying. We have first-class reservations in the Chevy. I'm the pilot and you're the co-pilot. We take off tomorrow afternoon as soon as I have the car greased and oiled."

The convertible would be perfect in Florida. It was a summer car. But the boys were leaving in the frigid northern air of the end of December. There were mountains to cross and snow plows to follow before they could reach the balmy air of Florida. As they roared down the Pennsylvania Turnpike toward Breezewood the wind forced its way into the car fluting in the crevices between the metal snaps that tried to secure the white canvas top to the car frame. The side vents were flapping and the flimsy roof was bulging upward. Johnny had the heat on full blast but it was fighting a losing battle with the raw icy wind. The boys' heads were roasting and their feet freezing, subjecting their bodies to thermal extremes.

At least the road was clear of snow, though the mountains still bore their ivory coating, and overpasses shone with slick patches of ice. When they turned toward the Mason-Dixon line passing the myriad motels at Breezewood, Scooter's heart was racing as fast as the engine. They stopped for gas in Maryland. Scooter exchanged dollar bills for a handful of quarters and fed them to a hungry antiquated wall phone in the station. He was calling long distance—to Florida. Patricia's mother answered the phone.

"Hello, Mrs. Gregg? It's Scooter Evans calling."

"Scooter! How are you, darling?"

"I'm fine. I'm on my way to Miami. Jack Kramer is refereeing the Orange Bowl game and he got tickets for Johnny and me

and some of the guys. Do you think there is any chance Patricia
would see me?"

"I'm still her mother. I'll make sure she'll see you. Don't you
worry now. Do you know where you'll be staying?"

Scooter fumbled in his pocket for the slip of paper which had
the name of the motel.

"It's the Green Derby on Biscayne Avenue."

"Look, Scooter, I'll take care of it. Where are you now?"

"We've just crossed the border into Maryland. We plan to
drive straight through. It should take us about another twenty
hours."

"Can you call back in the morning, dear? In the meantime
I'll see what I can do."

"Thanks a million, Mrs. Gregg. I'll call in the morning."
Scooter jumped back in the car with his face beaming. Bill Mat-
thews asked, "What was all that about?"

Johnny supplied the answer, "You called Patricia didn't
you?"

Scooter just grinned and said, "Yep."

"Well, tell us about it. What did she say?"

"I didn't talk to her. I talked to her mother."

"You idiot. You spent all that money just to talk with her
mother? What about Patricia? Are you going to see her?"

"Looks like it. Mrs. Gregg's getting in the game on my
team."

They beheld the sunrise in the Shenandoah Valley. Scooter
imagined the gray-vested ghost of Stonewall Jackson riding his
steed from ridge to valley, creating havoc for the Union forces with
rapid hit-and-run tactics, his blue-gray eyes mocking his pur-
suers. But that was almost a century before. The Shenandoah
was now at peace, the rebels long since subdued. All that was left
were somber plaques along the road marking historic battle sites.
As they passed through the Carolinas they saw a thousand con-
federate flags, and a hundred signs advertising cut-rate bargains
on cigarettes and bath towels. The roadside was cluttered with
billboards announcing fireworks for sale at outlets named with a
strange kind of red-neck humor. "Loco Lois," "Crazy Bertha's,"
"Pig-Head George's." The enticement was too much for the
boys. They stopped at "Maniac Mike's" and purchased a horde

of cherry bombs and sky rockets, concealing the illegal cargo under a blanket in the trunk.

The road to Florida went on forever. Another stop for gas in the Georgia morning light sent Scooter to the pay phone again. He could hardly get the coins in the slots. His fingers were trembling. He gave the number to the operator and heard the phone ringing on the other end. His heart sank when Mr. Gregg answered with a gruff voice, "Gregg residence."

Mr. Gregg, a burly ex-Marine, sent shivers of terror up Scooter's spine. He fought the impulse to hang up, a panic response he had made on numerous occasions in the past when Mr. Gregg answered the phone.

"Hello, is Mrs. Gregg there?"

"Yeah, Scooter?"

"Yes, sir."

"Okay, boy, I'll put her on." He could hear him shout in the background. "Mary, it's Scooter Evans again."

Scooter's heart was telltale thumping against his chest, beating an accelerated rhythm while he waited for Mrs. Gregg to get to the phone. After a long silence he heard her soothing voice.

"Hello, Scooter. Where are you now?"

"We're almost to the Florida line. We should be in Miami about 3:30 this afternoon."

"It's all set. Patricia is at the hairdresser's. She'll be on the bus that arrives at the Greyhound station in Miami at 5:07. I've booked a room for her at the same motel you're in. You look after her now, hear? I'm counting on you two to behave yourselves."

"Don't worry, Mrs. Gregg. I'll take good care of her."

"OK, dear. I'm tickled that you two will be together again. I love you, Scooter."

"Yeah, Mrs. Gregg. I love you too. Bye."

It was like a B movie. Mrs. Gregg's last words echoed in his ears. "I love you, Scooter." She sounded like she meant it in more than a maternal way. Sometimes Scooter himself got a little confused about his warm feelings for Patricia's mother.

The trek down the length of Florida was sheer agony made bearable by the crescendo of excitement that arose when palm trees became more numerous and the landscape more sandy. The boys found the parking lot of the Green Derby at 3:23. By 3:45

Scooter had showered and shaved and was clutching Johnny's car keys tightly in his hand as he inquired of the motel manager for directions to the Greyhound terminal.

Scooter walked into the dismal bus depot and glanced at the clock on the wall. The time registered 4:00. Patricia was probably not even on the bus yet and the minutes were already dragging as if the second hand of the clock were coated with lead. He exchanged a dollar bill for a roll of nickles and headed for the pinball machines. He stared at the reflection of his face in the glass top of the machine while he pumped nickle after nickle into the game's greedy changebox. The depot was crowded with vacation travelers and a stale odor hung in the room. Scooter added to the bluish cast of the room by chain-smoking in his pinball playing vigil.

The P.A. blared the announcement, "The bus from Fort Lauderdale and Hollywood now arriving at ramp 37." Scooter jerked the machine rudely, forcing the tilt light to flash, and headed for the ramp. Patricia was one of the first persons off the bus. Scooter hesitated where he stood. He had forgotten how exquisite she was. She was dressed in a navy pleated skirt, a white blouse and a cardigan sweater. Blond hair framed her delicate face; her flawless complexion set off her ice green eyes. She reminded Scooter of a petite blonde of Grace Kelly and Kim Novak. It was her cat-like eyes and feline moves that suggested Novak and her hair and face that hinted of Princess Grace. For over an hour, with metal balls hitting rubber bumpers and registering points on the pinballmachine, Scooter had rehearsed his opening lines. He forgot them and simply said, "Did you have a nice trip?"

"Yes, how about you? Did you drive all night?"

"Yes, but I'm really not tired."

Scooter retrieved Patricia's suitcase and led her by the hand to the parking lot. "We'll go to the motel and get you checked in and then we'll go out for dinner."

A delicious grin crossed Patricia's face as she demurely acquiesced to the evening plan.

Seated at a corner table in the restaurant, Scooter savored the atmosphere that enhanced the rendezvous. The decor was unusual for Miami. Absent were the rattan chairs and garish greens and yellows that the resort establishments favored. Here in downtown Miami he had found a continental restaurant decorated in a federal motif with wedgewood blue wainscoting, Queen Anne chairs and portraits of Minutemen adorning the walls. It was a piece of transplanted Boston with gilded eagles perched atop oval mirrors. The brass wall sconces held neatly trimmed candles whose tiny fire dances flashed shadows on Particia's porcelain-like face.

No telephone wires separated them; no agony of one-way conversation was imposed by the cruel limits of letter writing. This setting promised an opportunity for him to be in control. But his feelings were swollen to the bursting point, fighting to erupt, to break out of the inner prison where he had sentenced them to silence. He was a living vial of nitroglycerin—unstable, volatile, in danger of being jarred into explosion.

Midway through the meal Scooter reached across the linen tablecloth and grasped her hand. "You know I love you. I've never stopped. We can make it. Forget about the distance. If you'll just wait for me I'll be the sugar daddy you've always talked about."

"Scooter, I get all mixed up when I'm with you. You make me nervous. Remember when you danced with me that night at the church canteen? I was trembling so badly I was shaking and you kept asking me what was the matter. I was fighting you inside. You overpower me when we're together. I can't stand it. You scare me," Patricia said.

"What is there to be scared of ? You know I would never do anything to hurt you. I would never hit a girl. That's unthinkable."

"I know that. I'm not talking about your temper. There are other ways to hurt people, you know. You try to dominate me. You dominate everyone and everything you're around. Sometimes I feel like you suffocate me. It's like you're trying to get me to surrender to you. I can't do that."

"I want you, Patricia. That's all. Can you blame a guy for that? Are you afraid to have someone really love you? Do you think I'm like your father? Give me a chance."

The mention of her father touched off a glint of fear in her eyes. "Why did you bring up Daddy? He has nothing to do with this."

"He has everything to do with it. Your father is crazy about you. You just refuse to see that and egg him on all the time. No matter what he does you interpret it in the worst possible way. You pick fights with him. He loves you and what's more you love him. The sooner you admit that to yourself the better it will be."

"Cut it out, Scooter. I don't need a sermon about Daddy. Let's just forget about it, OK?"

The raw nerve of "Daddy" chilled the conversation. Scooter regretted mentioning him. Patricia's strong but ambivalent feelings toward her father colored every relationship she had with men.

Scooter paid the check and escorted Patricia out of the restaurant, wondering what the rest of the evening would bring.

"You must be tired, Scooter. Why don't we go on back to the motel and you can get some sleep. We have all day tomorrow to talk."

He balked at the peremptoy dismissal and replied, "Let's have a little more time together tonight before we go to bed. I mean . . . you know what I mean."

Patricia grinned. "OK, but only a half hour or so." Scooter couldn't figure out what happened to the clock. All morning and afternoon the clock moved like a pregnant turtle and now it was racing like an ocelot.

The Chevy rumbled along the streets of Miami, the duals firing and spitting all the way to the Green Derby. Patricia whispered to him, "Give me a few minutes to freshen up and you can come to my room to talk. Be a sweetie now, and I'll see you in ten minutes." She accented the temporary dismissal by gently touching the tip of Scooter's nose with her index finger. He sauntered back to his room and was met by Johnny's incredulous stare.

"What are you doing back so early?"

"She's getting cleaned up. I'm going to see her in a few minutes."

Johnny splashed a knowing smile, "Got ya covered. Have a good time. Don't worry about us poor suckers back here all alone."

Scooter listened to the banter for a few minutes and then walked back to Patricia's room and knocked on the door. He could hear her moving toward the door and her soft query, "Is that you, Scooter?"

Patricia cracked the door open and whispered for him to come in. Scooter felt sure that every eye in the parking lot was riveted on his back and that the motel manager was monitoring his every step. He was certain that any second a policeman would jump out of the bushes and arrest him for pandering. He moved quickly, sliding sideways through the partially opened doorway with his back to the interior of the room. He snapped the door shut, put the chain lock in place, and turned around.

Patricia was standing in front of the dresser, wearing diaphanous shorty pajamas. Scooter stared at her as if he were beholding an opulent treasure in an ancient Egyptian tomb that to gaze upon was to risk some malevolent curse. "Patricia . . . you look beautiful." He crossed the room and took her in his arms, showering her lips and neck with kisses. He cupped her head in his hands and pulled her to his chest. This was the moment of ecstasy he had daydreamed about a thousand times. She began heaving with sobs. "Oh, Scooter, I knew this would happen. See what you do to me."

"Listen, Patricia. Forget about your thirty-minute curfew. I'm staying in this room every minute that you are here. I've waited too long for this."

"Scooter, we can't. You promised my mother and it wouldn't be right."

"I'm not talking about *that*. I won't let anything spoil this time. I just want to stay with you, to hold you, to sleep in the same bed with you. I won't let anything happen."

Scooter pulled down the covers of the bed and tucked Patricia in. He turned off the lights, pulled off his shoes and pants, and climbed under the covers beside her. He nestled her to his chest and intertwined his legs with hers, positioning himself at the proper angle to avoid a dangerous point of bodily contact. He ran his fingers through her hair in silence until they both drifted off to sleep.

Scooter was lying on his back when the fog of early morning wakefulness hit him. It took a few moments for his head to clear and to remember where he was. He reached to the side of the bed for Patricia. The space was empty. A rush of raw fear made him spring upright and canvass the room. It was vacant. He leaped from the bed in a staccato burst of panic that dissolved when Patricia stepped out of the bathroom clad in white bermuda shorts and an aqua sleeveless blouse.

"Good morning, sleepy head. It's about time you woke up."

Patricia had an amused look on her face. He glanced momentarily downward, becoming acutely aware of his partially clad condition and immodest state. He grabbed the cover from the bed and draped it around himself while Patricia leaned forward and gave him a playful kiss on the cheek.

"Get dressed, silly. I'm nearly starved."

Scooter grabbed his clothes, which were bunched up by the side of the bed, and went into the bathroom. He finished dressing and splashed cold water on his face. He dampened his hair and ran a brush through it to get his crew cut to stand with perfect symmetry, its tapered length trained by years of practiced brushing. No Brylcreem, no sticky pomade for him.

Patricia held the door open, allowing the fragrance of morning flowers to filter into the room. They walked across the crunchy bermuda grass to the boys' room. Johnny answered the knock at the door; water dripping from his hair and a bath towel wrapped around his waist, he was impervious to Patricia's presence.

"C'mon in you two. We're just getting ready to go to breakfast."

Scooter protested that Patricia should wait outside until the boys finished dressing, but she stepped across the threshhold with no signs of timidity. She was casual yet poised. The threatening look in Scooter's eyes was a signal to the boys to stop their leering glances. They scurried to finish dressing, obedient to Scooter's silent command.

On the way to the restaurant Scooter fell back to walk with Johnny while the other boys swarmed around Patricia. Scooter reached for his wallet and made a furtive transfer to Johnny, returning the borrowed gift. Johnny's eyebrows shot up.

"Are you telling me you didn't use this? Are you nuts? You want to get her pregnant?"

"I didn't have any occasion to use it. We didn't do anything."

"Sure, sure, and you're Robin Hood and I'm the Sheriff of Nottingham."

"And you're going to be *little* John if you don't watch your mouth."

Johnny saw the fire boiling in Scooter and eased off.

"Geez, Scooter, did you really spend the night with her and nothing happened?"

"That's right and you'd better make that clear to the rest of those yo-yos."

"You're serious. I can't believe you; you're out of your tree."

Scooter stepped up his pace to recapture Patricia's arm as they entered the restaurant.

That day in Miami was spent sitting in a swing on the grounds of the motel. The time passed with the gentle gliding action of the swing setting the tempo for prolonged intimate conversation. By the end of their tryst Patricia renounced her plans for a sugar daddy and made a solemn promise to wait for Scooter.

The Chevy pointed north again and at each gas stop on the road Scooter phoned Patricia to reaffirm his love.

The record ended and Johnny moved to replace the scratching disc. That was enough of the mood music with Nat King Cole and Joni James. Johnny put some "jump" records on the player since Judy liked the faster beat. While he was preparing a batch of 45s, Judy examined the framed photos on Jack Kramer's trophy wall. She noticed one that featured him attired in a zebra shirt standing next to the boys who had made the trek to the Orange Bowl.

"Johnny, why isn't Scooter in this picture? Wasn't he with you at the game?"

"Yeah, but that picture was taken before the game and Scooter and Patricia got there late. They came in a cab. Dad had to hustle to come up with an extra ticket for her."

Judy's face clouded with a frown. "I could kill her. She hasn't written to Scooter for two months. Do you think she ever will?"

"You should have seen her in Miami. She had nothing but goo-goo eyes for Scoot and then she dropped him again like a hot potato. Out of sight, out of mind, I guess. She won't write now unless whoever she's dating shoots her out of the saddle. I wish Scooter would forget about her; she's strictly poison."

FOUR

S cooter slept his way through high school; not in the sense of double entendre, but literally. He mastered the art of sleeping in the back of the classroom with a book propped up in front of him and his eyes closed. Large study halls held in the school auditorium were even better. There he could rest his elbows on the arm of the chair, cradle his head in his hand, and doze for the entire period. This was his way of making atonement to his body for averaging only four hours of sleep at night.

His daily routine followed a monotonous pattern. The alarm rang every morning at precisely 6:00. He dressed, ate breakfast, and was out of the apartment by 7:00. Classes started early at Millport High, arranged to accommodate parents' working shifts at the mill. The late bell rang at 7:50. Every other day Scooter drove his car to school, picking up Judy and Johnny on the way. Johnny drove on the alternate days.

School was dismissed at 3:00 P.M. Swarms of students rushed from the exits toward the long yellow line of school buses. Scooter, Johnny, and Judy walked briskly in the other direction to get in the car and move away from the congested area before the lumbering buses pulled from the curb to begin their snail-like pace toward Briarwood, stopping with red lights flashing to discharge their cargo, hesitating at railroad crossings, and pulling off the road at unexpected junctures for the bus-driving impresarios to turn around and deliver impromptu lectures on the proper deportment required if the bus was going to continue its journey. To fall behind the yellow fleet on Millport Boulevard was like being in a speed boat on a river blocked by cumbersome coal barges.

The final destination of the buses was the Briarwood drugstore, a large emporium outfitted with a soda counter and several leather covered booths. By 3:30 in the afternoon it was standing

room only in the drugstore. Evening meals were destroyed and
weekly allowances squandered on the purchase of banana splits,
hot fudge sundaes, hamburgers, french fries and milk shakes.
Everybody, every single student, save one, filed out of the buses
and into the store for the happy hour after school. Here gossip was
traded, dates were arranged, and lovers broke up.

Only Scooter passed up the daily ritual at the drugstore. Instead he went across the street to the Briarwood Appliance Store
to report for work. Since his father's decimating illness three years
earlier he had been required to take a job after school. Many of
the Millport sons and daughters held after-school jobs but Scooter
was the only one from Briarwood. The Briarwood students were
destined for college or nurses training and it was tacitly assumed
as part of the social code that the expenses of a college education
would be met by their parents.

In the fall of Scooter's senior year his father died, leaving Elizabeth Evans to complete the task of seeing their two children
through college. She was glad that her son was working, putting
all but two dollars from his weekly paycheck into the bank for
college.

While his friends were sipping chocolate milk shakes across
the street, Scooter was stationed in a small cubicle at the rear of
the appliance store checking vacuum tubes on the television tube-
tester as he played amateur TV repairman. He did it so often the
townspeople came to him for cheap troubleshooting advice.

"My picture's rolling, Scooter, what should I do?"

"Pull the 6SN7 tube and bring it in and I'll check it."

"The power's on but no picture."

"Try the 5U4."

"I'm having trouble with the sound."

"Bring in the four 6AU6s."

The miracle of the transistor and solid state television ruined
Scooter's little specialty.

He worked the night of the senior prom, plugging his ears to
his mother's urgent pleas to find a date and break his social fast.
He was back in the appliance store the next morning in time to
see Johnny and Judy walk into the shop. Johnny was attired in a
rented tux, sans tie, and Judy's bleary eyes were matched by her
wilting corsage. They had just come from breakfast after the all-
night prom party.

"How was it?" Scooter asked.

"It was great. The Twin Coaches Inn was decorated in a Cinderella theme. Judy didn't turn into a pumpkin at midnight—she became a banshee."

Judy scowled at Johnny and poked him in the ribs.

"The music was groovy. Much better than last year. Benny Benack was there with his black trumpet and they brought in the Smoothtones for a special appearance. We missed you, Scoot."

Scooter joined the solemn march to the strains of "Pomp and Circumstance" the following week. He skipped the graduation party, electing instead to take in a movie alone. He sat in the empty theatre munching popcorn and watched "Wild Bill" Haley in "Rock Around the Clock."

He enjoyed a few days respite between jobs. The minimum wage of seventy-five cents an hour was fine for after-school jobs, but he needed to make more money for college in the fall. Jack Kramer used his influence with the vice-president of the Continental Can Company of America to secure summer employment on the assembly line for Johnny and Scooter. The wages there went over $2.50 an hour.

The first day on the job was a baptism for them. The can factory was not the genteel work place of the suburban shop. Competition for bonus money and seniority made it a battleground. The shrieking din of the machines and a million cans clanging along the metal rollers of the assembly lines deafened their ears. It was their first exposure to hardened women, women with hair tied up in handkerchiefs and babushkas, women shouting dark blue obscenities at the men and mocking the young boys with salacious invitations to after-hour meetings. They peppered their overtures with obscene gestures and graphic descriptions of sexual acts Scooter had never heard of.

The boys were switched from job to job, filling in for vacationing regulars. They inspected the seams of Welch's Grape Juice cans, used mallets to pound caps on Delco Battery Fluid cans, pushed cork inserts into the tops of bottle caps, and built houses on wooden skids out of boxes of beer cans. They looked with envy at the forklift operators who enjoyed the luxury of riding on a machine at work.

By mid-summer the boys had adjusted to the noise, the tedium, and the strange hours required by working shifts. Scooter's savings account began to grow and, after he paid his initiation dues to the union, the harassment from the women stopped. They turned their mocking seductions on newer personnel. The factory was spread over scores of acres, earning its nickname as the largest whorehouse in Pennsylvania.

Johnny and Scooter were accepted at a Presbyterian church-related college in northwestern Pennsylvania. The school was named after John Witherspoon, a distinguished clergyman who was a vital force in the founding of the American republic. The college was founded in the middle of the nineteenth century and was noted for its outstanding athletic program. Scooter was going on a combined football and baseball scholarship and Johnny was accepted because he was the son of one of the school's most distinguished alumni. Jack Kramer had influence, hardball clout, at Witherspoon. He was still remembered by the college's ancient athletic director whose leathery face was known to three generations of athletes. The A.D. was a fixture on campus, having spent forty years there. Jack Kramer was the last Witherspoon graduate to be a bona fide four-letter man. He had earned varsity letters in baseball, football, basketball, and boxing. A brief note was all it took for Jack to wrangle it with the director of admissions to get Johnny and Scooter assigned as roommates.

Scooter left for college two weeks ahead of Johnny to report for football camp. Because he was needed frequently at home, he was able to gain an exemption from the rule prohibiting freshmen from having cars on campus. He arrived at the almost deserted campus in the midst of an August heat wave. He was given his room assignment and checked in, leaving half of the room space for Johnny's arrival.

Before he went to the field house to turn in his medical report and collect his football equipment he went out to the parking lot to buff his car free of road dust with a chamois. Scooter's car was the only status symbol he had left from his exile from the residential section of Briarwood. The car had been his since his sister got married and the family was reduced to Scooter and his mother, who didn't know how to drive. It was a 1957 Ford Fairlane 500 hardtop convertible with two four-barrel carburetors, twin chrome fender mounted mirrors, chrome dual exhaust extensions, and custom fender skirts. It was black and red with red leather upholstery and could do 0-60 in under ten seconds. The crucial point was that Scooter's car was two years newer than Johnny's. It was the only edge he had on his friend in affluence.

Scooter entered the swinging inner doors of the field house and went to a long table with a sign over it A-L. He filled out a few forms, handed in his medical resume and was directed to see the equipment manager in the locker room. As a freshman, Scooter was consigned to last pick of practice uniforms and had to settle for shoulder pads a size too large and practice pants a bit too baggy for an aspiring quarterback eager to impress coaches with smooth and dexterous ball-handling. He had been a first-year player before and knew how to make up for the liability by binding tight strips of adhesive tape around his thighs to correct the clown-suit look of the baggy pants. He was optimistic about his future since Witherspoon had just graduated a horde of lettermen and was in a rebuilding phase.

The first week of practice went well. His crisp passes caught the eye of the coach and he moved rapidly up the depth charts. By the end of the week he was ensconced as second-string quarterback playing behind the senior starter. This promised three years of a starting berth if he continued to play well. Monday's two-a-day practices ended with a live scrimmage. Scooter sparkled. He was feeling heady in the shower afterwards and had a swagger in his step as he walked up the hill to the dinning hall where a sumptuous spread of food awaited the football players.

He was moving through the cafeteria line when it happened. He slid his salad plate too quickly toward his tray, defying the law of inertia. The plate stopped, but a tomato which was perched precariously atop the salad stayed in motion, flying off the tray and onto the floor. Scooter stopped in midstride in a futile attempt to recover the fumbled tomato. With the sudden stop, he felt a searing pain rip through his knee and his leg gave way under him bringing the tray and the salad crashing with him to the floor. Two burly linemen grabbed for Scooter to pull him to his feet. As he came upright he balanced himself on one leg realizing to his horror that he could not straighten his right leg. His knee was frozen, completely locked in a bent position. He tried to force it to unbend but it wouldn't budge. The trainer noticed his plight and ordered him to stop the manipulations.

"Quit fooling with it Scooter. Let me look at it."

"Well, do something. It hurts like blazes."

The trainer ran his hands around the knee, applying pressure at various points. Scooter gritted his teeth but the trainer's efforts failed to move the leg.

"I can't do it. We're going to have to get you to the hospital and see if a doctor can get it unlocked."

Scooter sat in an awkward position during the car ride to the hospital. He was admitted to the emergency room and left to sit on an antiseptic stainless steel table waiting for the doctor to appear. He took solace in the knowledge that the team physician was also an orthopedic surgeon.

"Let's see what we have here, son." The surgeon probed and pried around the knee and finally looked up and said, "You have this thing locked up tight. You've broken a piece of cartilage and it's wedged in the joint like a wooden shiv in a doorframe. I might be able to get it loose manually, but if I can't we'll have to cut it."

For an hour the surgeon wiggled and pried and pulled at Scooter's leg putting him through agony. At last the knee popped free and Scooter was able to straighten his leg.

"There's a big buildup of fluid there now. We're going to have to tap it."

Scooter closed his eyes to avoid seeing the dreaded needle pierce the joint to extract the fluid. While the precedure was going on the doctor asked, "How did you do this? Were you blindsided by a clip or what?"

"You'll never believe it. It happened when I fumbled a tomato."

"You fumbled a tomato? Who was she?"

"No, no. A real tomato. I dropped a tomato off my plate in the food line and this happened when I tried to catch it."

"How in the devil are you going to write that on the insurance form?"

The surgeon produced two wooden crutches, silent harbingers of a dismal future. "I'm going to wrap the knee for you and you'll have to stay on the crutches. This knee will require surgery soon."

"What about football?"

"That's out for this year, son. In fact, if I were you I'd forget about it altogether. You'll need an operation by next summer and

in the shape that knee is in I doubt if you'll be able to recover full
mobility."

Scooter hobbled around on the crutches for the rest of the
week sporadically visiting the sidelines of the practice field until
the torture of his envy made him stop. He felt utterly useless. It
was little consolation that the school had a policy to allow injured
athletes to retain their scholarship aid.

Johnny arrived on Saturday. Scooter saw the Kramers drive
up as he sat by the window in his first-floor room. He hoisted
himself on his crutches and moved out to the parking lot to greet
them. They brought a surprise visitor. Scooter's mother stepped
out of the car, her voice tight with maternal anxiety.

"What happened? Did you break your leg?"

"No, Mom, I just had a little trouble with my knee. I'll be
fine, but it's over with football. Come on in and see our room."

Johnny's smile was absent. For once in his life he was deadly
sober as he read behind the casual words Scooter spoke. He could
tell this was no minor setback but a final chapter to his friend's
life.

The visit was brief. Scooter kissed his mother good-bye and
promised to come home as many weekends as possible when he
was able to drive again. When the Cadillac pulled out of the lot,
Scooter and Johnny were left to start a new life.

Time is the most elusive of all mysteries. We measure it but
never capture it; we contemplate it but never understand it; it
remains shrouded in some Stygian darkness. Our lives are lived
within its brackets while we move inexorably to some unknown
point of destiny. Some see its movements as chaotic, a whirling
cycle of Dionysian madness, beginning at no fixed reference
point and endlessly returning to the same vacuous point of departure. Others describe it in linear fashion speaking of a real beginning and a divinely appointed consummation.

Time has three faces—like those mirrored in the secret mystery of the Holy Eucharist. The past evokes remembrance, the
future is nourished by hope, the present is anchored in communion. For mortals, every moment has three dimensions.

For us men time stands as a sentinel, guarding the portals of
eternity like the angel posted at the gates of Paradise with flaming

sword forbidding access to the garden, keeping us exiled east of
Eden. Eternity is shut up to us now, yet we know it is there, for
time is unintelligible without it. There can be no temporal without the eternal, no contingent without the necessary, no finite
without the infinite. But the gate of heaven is marked with an
indelible sign above its entrance—*finitum non capax infinitum* (the
finite cannot contain the infinite).

Every moment in life is a suspension of the boundary between
time and eternity. The moment is incapable of fixed definition,
like the mathematical point that takes up space but has no definite
extension, so the moment takes up time but has no definite duration. Yet it is the moment that creates the crucial difference between the historical and the historic. History flows along a steady
stream of chronology, measured by hands sweeping around a dial
or tiny grains of sand slipping through a glass. The minute and
the hour may be timed by a delicate meshing of gears made by
Swiss craftsmen or by pulsations from quartz crystals. But no
gear has been invented nor crystalline substance discovered that
can measure the historic.

The historic happens in time and is conditioned by time. It is
not outside or beyond it in some super-temporal twilight zone. It
is part of history. The historic is that pregnant moment in time
made possible by the maelstrom of past moments intersecting at a
crucial point in which an event transpires that measures and conditions every subsequent interval of time. It is a moment of decisive importance by which history is made; it is the turning point.

For Richard "Scooter" Evans the parenthesis of time com-
prising the last week of August and the first week of September in
the year of our Lord 1957 were the historic moments, the transcendent turning point of his life.

Johnny was bored with the tedious proceedings of orientation
week. The battery of tests seemed endless as he sat on the wooden
funeral-parlor chairs set up at long tables in the field house. He
waded through reading comprehension tests, aptitude tests, and
English placement exams, then the droning speeches by the dean
of students communicating student conduct policies, housing
rules, and the like.

Johnny relished the freedom of being on his own, being
bound by no house "hours." He missed his car, but most of all he

missed Judy. Every evening he poured out his passions through his pen with maudlin letters of romance to her.

Scooter was not so bored. He actually enjoyed taking tests; they represented a kind of game for him. The tests they were taking this week had no bearing on his course grades. They didn't really count, and Scooter approached them with the same cavalier attitude he had carried into exhibition games on the baseball field.

Friday afternoon brought the end of the tests and the vapid speeches. The freshmen were given printed copies of the school's alma mater, which they were instructed to memorize immediately, since they would soon face the incoming upper classmen whose prerogative it was to command any freshman to sing the song on demand. Little blue beanies embellished with a white Gothic *W* on the front were issued to each member of the freshman class. The sober requirement was given in severe terms that the "dinks" must be worn in public at all times. Any infraction of the dink code brought penalties to the culprit rivaling those of Dante's hell.

After dinner, with the evening free from scheduled meetings, Johnny was itchy for some action. "Let's hit the town, Scoot, I'm going stir crazy."

"I don't know how hard I can hit it on these crutches, but I'm up for it if you are," he answered.

Scooter tossed Johnny his car keys and the boys donned their orange and black varsity jackets boasting the block *M* of Millport and headed for the door. The coats were unnecessary since the September evening was warm and the weather mild, but with the wearing of the colors their status was enhanced and their confidence buoyed for going on reconnaissance. They were careful to put the long, narrow pointed collars up in "cat" style to enhance the coolness of the image. The Halloween colors clashed comically with their royal blue dinks but they didn't seem to notice.

Johnny held the glass exit door open for Scooter. As Scooter was halfway out the door he halted and said, "Wait a minute, Johnny, I'm out of cigarettes. Let me go downstairs and get a pack."

"Forget the smokes; we can get some in town."

"It'll just take a minute, you can wait here."

Johnny relented but wouldn't let Scooter negotiate the staircase alone on crutches. The cigarette machine was just around

the corner at the bottom of the steps in the foyer of the freshman
lounge. Scooter leaned on the crutches and fished in his pocket for
a quarter. He inserted the coin and pulled the squeaky metal level
under the Lucky Strike slot. The fresh pack of Luckies dropped
into the receiving bin and Scooter picked it up. As he turned
around to go back up the stairs he saw Eddie Harper seated with
another upperclassman. Eddie was easy to recognize. He was the
star and team captain of the Witherspoon football team.

"How ya doin', Eddie?"

"The question is, Scooter, how are you doing? Where are you
guys headed?"

"We're just going to buzz the town and see what's happening."

"There's nothing shaking in this town. If you want to do anything you'll have to go over the border to Youngstown. Why don't
you sit down for a minute and meet Barry Singleton."

Scooter and Johnny were a bit awestruck, titillated by joining
the campus elite. After they were introduced to Barry, Eddie inquired about Scooter's injury. "How's the leg coming? Will you
be able to play anymore this year?"

"No, the knee's shot. The doctor says I'm through with football."

"Ouch, that hurts. I know what you're feeling. I started college at Michigan State and separated my shoulder the first season. I dropped out of school for a year and then transferred here. I
thought it wouldn't be so tough on my body. The guys at State
were monsters. I guess there's nothing you can really do about it.
It's like the preacher says, 'A tree falls in the forest and it lies
there.' "

"What preacher? I never heard any preacher say that,"
Scooter said.

"You know, the big preacher, Solomon, in Ecclesiastes."

"Solomon who? What's an ecclesiastes?"

Eddie went on to explain the story of the wisdom of Solomon
and gave a summary of the book of Ecclesiastes. Scooter was
transfixed by the narration. He knew nothing about the Bible and
King Solomon was merely an exotic figure Scooter remembered
from a Hollywood movie about fabulous wealth and diamond
mines or something. Eddie was talking about him as if he were a
bosom friend. He punctuated his narrative by saying, "That's

what I'm hungry for. Wisdom. Real wisdom, the kind you can count on."

Eddie sprinkled his conversation with references to God and dropped Jesus' name a few times as if he were on a first name basis with Him.

Scooter became taciturn. The discussion was foreign to him. He had scrupulously obeyed the mandate of his culture and never discussed religion or politics. He had never spoken with anyone who talked like this. Johnny jumped headlong into the conversation covering Scooter's silence, pumping Eddie with a battery of questions. Eddie unraveled a capsule summary of his life, topping it off with a reference to a conversion experience he had at Michigan State. "I became a Christian," he announced.

The words annoyed Scooter and he broke the silence with an acerbic question. "Weren't you born a Christian?"

To Scooter the definition of a Christian was a person who was civilized. For him the only non-Christians were cannibals and aboriginal savages.

"No, I was born a pagan and grew up a pagan. My family didn't go to church and I had no time for religion. I thought it was for pansies or little old ladies who couldn't cope with menopause. But I'm not talking about religion, I'm talking about a person, a real person who turned my life upside down."

Scooter turned to Barry for support. "Is he nuts or something? A holy roller?"

Barry was amused. "No, just change a few dates and a few names and Eddie's story is my story too."

Again Scooter retreated into silence and let Johnny continue the parrying. Scooter studied Eddie's eyes. They were haunting. There was something spooky about them. When he spoke of Jesus an almost imperceptible light ignited in them. A cloak of soberness fell upon Scooter, not unlike the dreadful cloud of depression that often befell him. He was tight-lipped for the rest of the conversation. He kept a frigid silence while Johnny ran at the mouth. The evening was consumed by the dialogue and any chance of hitting the town was lost. Scooter pushed himself up from the table and said, "C'mon, Johnny, it's late. Let's get to bed." Johnny was reluctant to quit the conversation but yielded to Scooter's insistence and helped him back upstairs.

Scooter felt a surge of relief when he reached the safety of their room. He shed his clothes and crawled into bed. Johnny was hunched over his desk scribbling a letter to Judy.

"Can't you kill that light? You can write to Judy in the morning."

"Not this time, Scoot. I have to tell Judy the big news."

"What big news?"

"Don't laugh at me. This is the biggest night of my life. Tonight I met God. I became a Christian down there listening to those guys. Tomorrow I turn over a new leaf and I know Judy'll want to know."

Scooter rolled over and faced the wall, burying his head in the pillow. He muttered an inaudible obscenity.

It was 10:00 when the morning sun shone so brightly through the window that Scooter could no longer stay asleep. Johnny was shielded from the rays and managed to continue his slumber till almost noon. Scooter showered, dressed, and went down to the lounge to watch the morning Ping-Pong action. A dark cloud of depression hovered over him conjured up by the fear that adding to his loss of Patricia was a new loss: he was losing Johnny to religion.

FIVE

The dining room door swung open announcing the start of lunch at the same moment Johnny bounced around the corner with his familiar grin fixed in place. The hour of food was more effective than an alarm clock in rousing him from bed.

"Let's eat, Scoot. I'm starved."

Johnny jumped ahead of Scooter in the food line, running interference for him past the soup dishes, moving toward paydirt, the goal-line of Saturday afternoon delight, hamburgers. Dormitory food was prepared under the diabolical dictates of the twin enemies of culinary pleasure, budget and nutrition. Saturdays the devils slept and the hamburger was king. Johnny scooped up their quota plus one extra for Scooter, a dispensation granted the warrior on crutches.

No references were made to the night before. Johnny seemed the same. The old glint was in his eyes, no veneer of nascent piety was shining. He was acting like his old self, like nothing had happened. *Let sleeping dogs lie,* Scooter thought, skirting any mention of the previous night.

The abortive mission to Youngstown was rescheduled for that evening. After dinner Johnny announced, "Let's roll. And stay away from the cigarette machine."

Johnny slid behind the wheel of the Fairlane 500 and aimed the hood ornament toward the Ohio border. This time there were no detours, no religious posses hiding in the bushes to waylay them. The city limits of Youngstown had the milieu of familiar territory, a mini Pittsburgh with grime-caked mills bearing the logo of United States Steel. A plethora of seedy pawn shops dotted the street that traversed the strip district. Scooter meticulously

counted twenty-three shops marked by the symbol of three brass
balls hanging over the doors.

"Hey, Johnny. Look! There's a pawnshop on the corner . . .
They ought to move that beauty to Pittsburgh."

Johnny laughed. "Yeah. Guy Mitchell must have been drunk
and got off the train at the wrong station. There sure aren't any
pawnshops on the corner in Pittsburgh."

They cruised past the pawnshops and Johnny pulled over
when he spied the Blue Angel Lounge, the kind of place that
looked like they might get served without anyone asking to see a
draft card for legal proof of their ages. They found a table in a
back corner decorated with a wine bottle covered with multihued
candle wax, and Johnny went to work charming the waitress. She
was an ally, a veteran of college boys' Saturday night binges, dis-
crete enough to ignore the messy subject of draft cards. She
brought them their first round of Screwdrivers. Johnny put a
nickle in the juke box and waited for the Wurlitzer to raise its
magic arm and select a disc from the stack inside the glass.
The song was by a dreamy-eyed truck driver from Memphis
who had recently made it big on the Ed Sullivan Show. The
record dropped on the turntable and a plaintive ballad sent soft
tremolos into the air. "Love me tender, love me true . . . ."

Johnny cleared his throat and leaned in Scooter's face. *Who
says you can't smell vodka,* Scooter thought.

"Scoot, about last night. Ah . . . you won't tell anybody
about it will you? I just got carried away. I really feel silly about
it."

"Hell, no. Don't worry about it. What do you think? I'm
going to write a book about it? Relax, I won't tell a soul. I'm just
glad to have you back in the land of the living."

The boys nursed their drinks, limiting themselves to three
rounds apiece. They were still intimidated by the dean's warning
that one violation of the no-drinking rule meant automatic expulsion. They had heard war stories from upper classmen about second semester seniors being bounced for one beer.

The threat of discovery made the drive back to campus a
cloak and dagger adventure. They took pains to drive around the
town and come in the back entrance to escape the vigil kept on the
front entrance by the dean. They had already been briefed by
veteran boozers of the upper class on how to avoid detection.

Chewing on Clorets, they furtively slipped in the entrance of the dorm and crept safely back to their room.

Monday was devoted to registration with classes scheduled to begin on Tuesday. Johnny and Scooter were caught in the frenzy of the mad dash between sign-up tables trying to get the course offerings they desired and, most importantly, at the preferred time slots. Both ended up stuck with Saturday morning classes, Scooter consigned to that fate by just missing the closeout time of his desired section in fine arts because he was stopped by a sophomore lunatic and ordered to stand on his crutches by Old Main Tower and sing the alma mater. The veins were pulsing in his neck as he struggled against his mercurial impulse to punch the nuisance in the mouth.

When the scramble for class assignments ended, the boys went to the bookstore to purchase their required textbooks. Johnny and Scooter were probably the only two boys in the freshman class who found it necessary to buy Bibles, required reading for the mandatory course in Introduction to the Old Testament. Everyone else had brought Bibles from home, some carrying exotic Morocco-bound volumes with indexed onion skin pages, and their names embossed on the covers. Scooter opted for a simple cardboard bound version that sold for two dollars.

Loaded down with books and syllabi, the boys stopped at the "Sub," the Student Union Building, to compare notes over Cokes and chocolate sundaes. Johnny had registered as a business major. His schedule was filled with courses like Introduction to Accounting, Business Math, and Introduction to Management Principles, in addition to other courses required in the general liberal arts curriculum. Since Scooter declared a history major the boys only managed to have one class period in common, Freshman Speech. Their attempt to get the same class in English Composition was thwarted by Scooter's high score in the placement exam that thrust him into an advanced section.

Schedule conflicts made it impossible for them to get into the same Bible class, which was the only other course they had in common. The wheel of fortune stopped on red for Scooter; he was assigned to an Old Testament section taught by the chairman of the philosophy department, an anomaly made necessary by a bulging freshman class. This single section of the Old Testament was the only venture out of the realm of philosophy made by the

bespectacled intellectual leader of the faculty. This same professor, Dr. Charles Hepplewhyte, was assigned by a fateful lottery to
be Scooter's faculty advisor, a fortuitous fact that would have a
profound effect on his life.

"How did you make out, Johnny?"

"I got all the courses I wanted but not all the times I was
trying for. I got stuck with "Wild Bill" for Bible. I hear he's a
bear. At least I got Sam as my faculty advisor."

Sam Slocum was the head of the economics department. No
one called him Dr. Slocum. It was always "Sam," the name used
by faculty, students, administrators, even by the grounds crew.
The congenial professor was a legend on campus. Well over six
feet and with massive girth, Sam looked like he had just escaped,
barely intact, from a barroom brawl. Tradition had it that he
owned only one suit and the last time it was pressed was sometime
during the Berlin Blockade. The gravel-voiced professor who
sounded like a cross between Everett Dirksen and Cardinal
Cushing had only one message for his students, a tune he played
well, if only on one string. At least six times a semester Sam
climbed onto his desk, his bulk threatening to make the thing
collapse, and, punctuating the air with his index finger, he delivered his one-point sermon, "Ya gotta worrk!" His only other
memorable dictum, which was branded in the minds of all his
graduates, was the quintessential axiom of the classical econo-
mist, "If you ain't got geld, yer a schmuck." Sam would take a
fond liking to Johnny and save him from more than one scrape.

"We need to hustle, Johnny. Let's get over to the doctor's office. I'm ready to get rid of these stupid crutches."

The late afternoon appointment brought good news. The surgeon said that the knee was coming along nicely and Scooter
could trade in the crutches for a cane, bringing him back to earth
again, with a three-point landing.

"I want to see you in a month. Keep the knee wrapped and
spend a half hour every day in the whirlpool. The trainer will set
up a schedule for you. You ought to be able to hold up until summer, but the cartilage has to come out. In the meantime, no strenuous activity, no gym classes. If that locks up again I might not be
able to work it free."

Johnny still handled the driving but Scooter felt a new lease on life to be rid of the awkward and uncomfortable stilts he had come to loathe.

Scooter stayed in his room that night while Johnny went to the Sub with some fraternity guys who were starting the moves of freshman "rush." Scooter spent the evening arranging books in his bookcase and writing out a weekly class schedule. He blocked out space for the whirlpool treatments and meal hours. While he was contemplating his chart, Eddie Harper stuck his head in the doorway and hollered a greeting.

"Hi neighbor. How's the leg?"

"It's coming along fine, Eddie. I got rid of the crutches today."

Scooter brandished his cane and playfully swished it in the air at Eddie like a sword.

"I feel more like Zorro now than Quasimodo."

Eddie laughed and said, "That's great. Well, neighbor, you take care of yourself."

Eddie called everyone "neighbor." This was before Fred Rogers made it a household word for millions of little children entering the make-believe realm of placid kindness in "Mr. Roger's Neighborhood." When Scooter heard Eddie call him "neighbor" it grated on his spine, sounding artificial and contrived, a saccharine facade of bubbly religion.

The interruption stirred negative feelings about the Friday night encounter with Eddie and Barry, and about Johnny's twelve-hour "conversion." It was in Scooter's craw. Feeling agitated by Eddie's momentary presence he tried to get his mind off of it by going to his dresser and arranging his toilet articles in systematic order. He placed a fresh white towel over the top of the dresser and set up his after-shave lotion, deodorant, talcum powder, shaving kit—complete with the new-fangled shaving cream that came magically forth from an aerosol can, and his soap, all in punctillious order, like tin soldiers standing in phalanxes.

When Scooter was bored or had work to do which he didn't relish he would find a kind of diversion like this to give the outward appearance of busyness. He was being active, if not productive, and his orderly bureau gave the semblance of dicipline. He dreaded the thought of studying, an art he religiously avoided in high school. Inwardly he harbored fears that he wouldn't make it in college. His teachers had always chided him for not working to his capacity, for not living up to his damnable "potential," a word that followed him like a curse. The fact was he didn't know how to study. It had never been necessary for him to learn how.

Now that the dresser was suitably arranged and the schedule chart completed, Scooter looked around for something to read. The formidable text on the *History of Western Civilization* was too intimidating and the anthology of literary masterpieces required for humanities appeared boring. His eyes were drawn to the cheap edition titled simply *Holy Bible*. He felt a mystical compulsion to reach for it. The book on the shelf evoked a powerful sense of ambivalence within him, a strange mixture of revulsion and fascination. It was as though the thing were alive, beckoning to him.

I've been watching too many movies, Scooter mused. *I'm acting like a vampire before a silver crucifix.* He thought of Richard Burton in his role as Marcellus, the Roman tribune, in the Lloyd C. Douglas classic, *The Robe.* Marcellus had stood firm in the presence of the histrionics of the demented Emperor Caligula but quaked in terror at the slightest thought of the haunted garment of Christ.

Scooter opened the book and slowly turned the pages backward until he found the starting point. He began to read, "In the beginning God created the heavens and the earth. And the earth was without form and void; and darkness was on the face of the deep . . ."

The opening lines hit him rudely. Words like "waste" and "void" had a menacing ring to them. He could almost feel the shadows hanging on the darkness of the face of the deep, the primordial sea that threatened the yet unordered universe with permanent chaos. He tried to imagine the Spirit of God brooding over the water, sending arrows of light into the inky blackness. He felt an affinity in his own spirit with the foreboding scene of the genesis of the earth.

It was near midnight when he saw the headlights of the Ford approaching the parking lot. He marked his place somewhere in the midst of the narrative of Moses and the exodus of Hebrew slaves from Egypt and slid the book back into its slot in the bookcase. He pulled a copy of *Sport* magazine out of his drawer and opened it on the desk in front of him lest Johnny ask any embarrassing questions.

The next two weeks brought spiritual warfare, a fortnight of agony provoked by a private and lonely battle with the Most High God. In fourteen days Scooter read the entire Bible, from Genesis through the apocalypse of Revelation. He was surreptitious in his reading, concealing it from Johnny. Parts of the book completely mystified him. He waded through the esoteric imagery of Daniel and Ezekiel, the complex poetic sections of the major prophets, and the tedious sections of the Levitical law and ceremonial rites of the ancient Jews. The overall impact of the Old Testament was exhilarating. The bloodthirsty episodes of combat, the wrenching passion of adulterous kings, the pathos of persecuted prophets banished by their countrymen, heroes fighting to cling to faith by their fingernails in the vacuum of solitude, all stirred Scooter's soul as he read on. Towering over every page of the historical recital of human sin and ecstasy was the awesome portrait of Yahweh, the Old Testament deity before whom prophets wept and kings trembled.

Scooter wasn't sure whether this God was more worthy of hatred or of honor as His judgments fell from heaven with ruthless finality and violent curses. At times He seemed tender. He was touched by the groans of His people in bondage and demanded of the unscrupulous Pharaoh, "Let my people go." He condescended to care for the body of Moses, and pardoned the conscience of the stricken David. At other times He appeared brutal and even capricious. He ordered the patriarch Abraham to sacrifice his son, his only son, his beloved Isaac on a stone altar at Mount Moriah. Could this be the same God who hovered over the primeval waters and said, "Let there be light"? The indelible impression Scooter gained from his virgin reading of the older testament was that if such a deity existed he was a Being not to be taken lightly, a God of fierce holiness who required, nay, commanded absolute loyalty.

The New Testament did not match the Old for vivid and dramatic narrative. Save for the Gospels and Acts, it was devoted mostly to the doctrinal teaching of the Epistles. At this point doctrine was the furthest thing from Scooter's mind. He saw little use for it. It was not dogma that enticed him to this marathon reading of the book. He was absorbed by the life of Jesus. In his quick reading of the whole Scripture, Scooter failed to notice any disparity between the thundering God of Old Testament Sinai and the figure of the New Testament Christ, a disjunction many lament as if the testaments reveal two disparate Gods.

Jesus seemed, to Scooter's neophyte theological mind, to be a blend of David, Moses, Amos, and Jeremiah rolled into one. Jesus breathed the vapors of the Jewish heritage and related to Yahweh in a fashion similar to that of the ancient giants. Scooter found himself rooting for Jesus in His scuffles with the odious Scribes and Pharisees and found in Him the crystallized substance of the heroic. The magnitude of Jesus' masculinity jumped off the pages, shattering with the iconoclast's hammer the fragile, fetid images of the Sunday School Jesus. *If He isn't God,* Scooter thought, *He is one incredible man.*

The days passed with the monomaniacal pursuit of finishing the book. His nights were marked by insomnia. His mind fixed on passages that had struck him like piercing arrows during the day, and sleep eluded him. At two or three in the morning he would slip from his bed and pace the hall of the dorm, his bare feet impervious to the chill of the tiled floors. He was stalked and hunted like a wounded rabbit by an amorphous, faceless hound of heaven. He was aware that the stakes were high and that this was no religious game to be played out in the carnival tent of an itinerant evangelist. Scooter was wrestling for his life like some modern Jacob striving with a mysterious visitor, a nocturnal interloper with the might and power of a troll. The limp in his step drew the bond with Jacob closer as Scooter was feeling maimed, crippled by his celestial antagonist. On the fourteenth night the battle ceased. The hound prevailed and Scooter had no alternative. This was not a religious decision; it was unconditional surrender, a docile submission to the holy rape of the soul. He moved deliberately back to his room and knelt silently on the throw rug next to his bed and whispered into the night, above the sound of Johnny's rhythmic breathing, "Forgive me. Please forgive me for my sins. I worship you and adore you. I am yours."

The tempestuous flame of Scooter's inner anger was instantly extinguished as he felt a release both *of* something and *from* something nameless. A wave of quietness flooded his being and he experienced a powerful sense of divine presence in the room. He heard no audible voice but the message penetrated his brain with no less clarity. *Fear not. I am with you.* The moment was mystical, shooting alternating currents of horrible fear and soothing peace.

It was as if the perfect priest had appeared in his room and placed his hands upon Scooter's head and uttered an infallible oath of pardon and benediction, saying with consummate authority, *"Te absolvo."*

Scooter rose from his knees, his stomach settled for the first time in weeks. As he rested his head on the pillow his final waking thought was, *It's done. This is for keeps.*

SIX

The alarm sent its unwelcome blast through the room at 6:45 A.M. eliciting obscenities from Johnny and a languid movement out of bed from Scooter. When he made it to the bathroom he inspected himself in the mirror thinking, *I look the same. I still need to shave and brush my teeth.* But there was something within that was different. A new attitude, a new perspective, something that could not this morning or any other morning erase what had happened in the night.

Fortune smiled again that afternoon when Scooter went for his first meeting with his faculty advisor, Dr. Hepplewhyte. Hepplewhyte went over Scooter's schedule and inquired about his adjustment to college life. Scooter debated about telling his professor what had happened. He felt shy about it, reticent to reveal himself to this relative stranger. Yet Hepplewhyte did teach the Old Testament and his calm manner had a tranquilizing effect on Scooter.

"Dr. Hepplewhyte, there is something I'd like to—uh—tell you about. I hope you won't think I'm nuts, but something has happened to me which I don't fully understand and I thought maybe you could—uh—maybe you could sort of—help me."

Hepplewhyte's eyebrows arched slightly and he responded in a sanguine manner, "Tell me about it Richard. What happened?"

Hepplewhyte sat quietly as Scooter related all that had transpired. The professor nodded gently in the course of the narrative, indicating with the movement of his head a quiet understanding of what Scooter was saying. Scooter ended the rehearsal with a question.

"Well, that's pretty much it. What do you think?"

Hepplewhyte remained silent for a few moments as though

caught in his own private reverie. Finally he answered in quiet
terms, a trait that made his lectures somewhat difficult to follow,
being barely audible.

"It sounds to me like you have experienced regeneration."

"Regeneration?" asked Scooter. "What's that?"

"Regeneration is the quickening of the human spirit by the
Holy Spirit of God. When a pregnant woman feels the movement
of the fetus it is called quickening. It means coming alive. The
Bible says we are fallen, that we are alienated from God. Sometimes the metaphor 'dead' is used to describe our spiritual condition. Of course we're not biologically dead. We're alive and
functioning as human beings but some aspects of life we ignore or
miss completely. For example, have you had a keen interest in
things of God for a long time?"

"Heck, no. I always figured there had to be some kind of
higher power, a supreme being or something, but it wasn't the
kind of thing that dominated my interest. I prayed once. I mean
prayed really hard when my sister was bleeding to death at the
hospital. I was sure she was going to die and I sat downstairs in
the middle of the night in the visitors lounge and prayed my head
off. I was scared out of my wits."

"What happened to your sister?"

"Oh, she came through fine. I was really relieved."

"And did you pray again and thank God for her recovery?"

A sheepish look appeared on Scooter's face that answered the
question for him.

Dr. Hepplewhyte continued his explanation. "What you've
just told me is what I was talking about. Usually people have little
or no deep interest in God, except in times of crisis. You've heard
of 'fox-hole' religion that lasts only as long as the bombs are dropping. We try to erect barriers that will keep us at a safe distance
from God. When He intrudes into a man's life He tends to make
things more complicated."

"You aren't whistling Dixie," Scooter blurted out in interruption. "I'm feeling that already."

"To get back to where I was, you're probably sensing a new
awareness about spiritual things. God is suddenly personal and a
different set of values comes into play. You're still the same person
of course; your basic personality is intact, but your life is taking
on such a new direction that it is like being born a second time."

"Wait a minute. I read about that in the New Testament where a man came secretly to talk with Jesus and Jesus told him that he had to be born again. Is that what He was talking about?"

"Precisely, Richard. But there is something I must caution you about. People get converted in different ways. For some it is sudden and dramatic, while for others it is gradual and almost imperceptible. History is full of stories of men with dramatic conversion experiences. But those, precisely because of their drama, are the ones we tend to emphasize and ignore the multitudes who come to faith in less spectacular ways. You've had a dramatic experience. You are, if you will excuse the expression, 'lucky.' But there is a danger. It is easy for people who have this experience to become arrogant and suspicious of others who haven't had the same type of conversion. That yours has been so dramatic should be humbling to you, to think that it took that much for God to bring you around."

Despite the mild chastening, Scooter wanted to run out of the office and throw his dink wildly in the air. He was jubilant to have his experience verified and authenticated by an expert. He knew that the past fourteen days had not been a bout of indigestion but it was reassuring to know that in his crisis he had not lost his sanity.

He thanked the professor profusely and returned to his dorm oblivious that not everyone would be so receptive and understanding toward his nascent faith.

Scooter looked forward to the following weekend, his first visit home since he left for football camp. The daily whirlpool treatments had soothed his knee and he was able to resume driving. In the days that passed he mentioned nothing of his new life to Johnny. Johnny chalked up Scooter's pensive attitude to a periodic mood change probably rooted in recurring thoughts about Patricia. Johnny hadn't noticed the external changes that were taking place. Scooter's vocabulary had undergone a metamorphosis, not by a willful act of discipline but by a new sense of what was appropriate. He had declined invitations for further visits to Youngstown, begging off by pleading study time as an excuse. Otherwise Scooter appeared much the same.

Johnny and Scooter left campus after their Saturday morning classes and traveled State Route 19 south to Pittsburgh.

Johnny was rambunctious, fired up to see Judy again. All the way home he talked about her. Scooter was usually spared this kind of monologue but today Johnny's tongue went over the edge like a canoe over Niagara Falls.

It felt good to drive between the stone pillars marking the entrance to Briarwood. The boys felt like soldiers home on furlough. They both wore white wind-breakers with blue lettering spelling out Witherspoon College. The Millport varsity jackets had been packed away as soon as the boys discovered that it was considered tawdry, strictly déclassé for college men to parade around wearing symbols of high school triumphs. The dinks were thrown in the back seat. It was one thing to come home like soldiers, quite another to appear as raw recruits with shaven heads.

Scooter pulled into the Kramer driveway. Johnny's younger brother, Frankie, was washing the Chevy convertible. He was not allowed to drive it but was accorded the privilege of administering its weekly bath. Johnny's return promised at least a ride round the block with the top down for Frankie, a reward for the wash job.

"C'mon in for a minute, Scooter. Charlie will really be mad if you don't say hello."

Johnny gathered his duffle bag crammed with dirty clothes and the boys went into the house. Charlie was sitting at the kitchen table scowling at them over a half empty bottle of beer. She glanced at Scooter's cane and said, "So, you traded in your crutches for a cane, huh, Scooter? Anything cooking yet in your love life? Meet any cute dollies up there?"

Scooter leaned over and kissed Charlie on the cheek.

"Don't start all that huggy bear kissy face stuff with me, Scooter, or you'll find your *a* double *s* out on Tara Drive."

"You're my only love, Charlie. I wouldn't cheat on you with the coeds," he teased. "Well, the Scooter has to scoot, my mother's waiting for me."

Charlie patted Scooter's crewcut with her bony fingers and gave a light kick at his cane saying, "You look almost debonair with that thing, a regular Fred Astaire."

He responded on cue; he bounced the cane off its rubber tip, caught it in midair, and moving his left hand to his head he doffed an imaginary top hat. With an awkward limp he did a soft shoe saying, "No, it's Ted Lewis," and went out the door singing, "Just me—and—my—shad—dow."

Scooter made it across the highway to his apartment in six minutes. He pushed the buzzer on the mailbox in the landing to alert his mother to his arrival. When he reached the second-story hall he saw her standing in the doorway with a huge smile on her face and eyes moist with tears. When Scooter hugged her hello, Elizabeth Evans held on tightly, clutching Scooter a second too long betraying an inner urgency. Scooter understood the signal, a flash revelation of the pain of loneliness endured by a widow whose only son had left the roost.

She straightened up and assumed a posture of confident independence that fooled everyone except her son. "You look better, dear. I'm glad to see you don't have those awful crutches. Here, let me have your duffle bag, I'll put a load of clothes in the washer right now."

"Don't take that, Mom. It's too heavy. I'll take the stuff to the laundry room, I know where it is."

Even on Saturday when most women were in jeans or sports clothes Elizabeth Evans looked like she was ready to leave for the office. Her makeup was fresh and not a hair was out of place on her elegantly coiffed head. Scooter took the soiled clothes to the laundry room and his mother followed behind him. "I want to hear all about school and what you've been up to. We need to do some shopping and I thought you might like to go out for dinner. After dinner maybe we can have someone in to play bridge and have some snacks—"

"Wait a minute, wait a second, Mom. You have me out of breath already. We'll do whatever you like. We have lots of time. By the way, did I get any mail while I was gone?"

"There's a letter from Rich Gilson from someplace overseas. There's also a postcard for both of us from your sister." She knew what letter Scooter was hoping for. It hurt her to be the bearer of bad tidings.

While Mrs. Evans was putting the first load in the washer Scooter went back to the apartment and sat down at the piano, one of the few treasures salvaged from their house on Woodcrest Drive. This time he didn't play "Patricia." He knew it would not only stir up feelings in him but would also put a damper on his mother's exuberance at having him home again.

The rest of the afternoon was spent at the supermarket filling

carts with food to replenish the barren cupboards that had been
depleted during Scooter's absence. While his mother was at the
bakery, Scooter carried a checklist into the liquor store. The gray
brick building was emblazoned with a black ornamental keystone
that heralded the entrance to the State Store. The shelves were
lined with bottles of distilled whiskey and exotic decanters of
wine, each treasure marked by a plastic card bearing its price.
He went to the bourbon section and filled his minishopping cart.
The clerk ignored Scooter's age as he tallied the bill. He knew
who the liquor was for.

They took the groceries home and filled the cupboards. After
a few more errands they went to the Sangria Lounge for dinner.
The waitresses fussed over Scooter's cane and proclaimed their
heartaches at missing him. Scooter and his mother had been fix-
tures at the place, appearing every Friday night for dinner in the
past ten months since Mr. Evans died. Without being told, the
waitress came and placed a dry Manhattan in front of Mrs.
Evans. She immediately rekindled the custom of taking the
bourbon-soaked maraschino cherry by the stem and tenderly
placing it between Scooter's lips.

During dinner Scooter decided to broach the subject of his
conversion. He was on the brink of delving into it when George
Marston, his dentist, spotted him from the bar. George was a
fixture in the lounge, particularly on weekends. He spent his time
at the bar alternately drowning his dental practice anxieties and
phoning his bookie about the latest Vegas line on the football
games. He had already heard of Scooter's injury and came over to
the table to express his condolences. The drink in his hand was
obviously not his first of the evening. He spoke with the maudlin
air of one whose sentiments ooze too easily with inhibitions oiled
away.

"Who do you like in the Ram-Lions game tomorrow,
Scooter?"

"Go with the Lions, George. They'll cover the spread.
Layne's hot as a firecracker right now."

"OK, pal, I'll put it down. You get a bonus if I hit big."

George part walked, part staggered back to the bar day-
dreaming of another jackpot that, if he hit it, would slither
through his fingers like quicksilver. Scooter spoke in sober terms
to his mother.

"Mom, something happened to me at school I need to tell you about."

Alarm spread within Mrs. Evans, roused by the serious tone in Scooter's voice. She was afraid he was going to tell her he had lost his scholarship or had provoked an incident by taking a swing at someone. She fought to keep her own voice free of any tightness. She dared to hope for a second that Scooter's somber tone was a preface to news of a blossoming romance.

"What is it, son? What happened?

"I became a Christian."

A quizzical look blanketed her face. "What do you mean you *became* a Christian? You've always been a Christian. Your father and I raised you as a Christian."

The defensive tone of her voice made Scooter regret that he had stated it that way. He had her feeling like he repudiated the values of his parents and by implication was repudiating them. His mother was feeling a sting of rejection.

"I guess I didn't quite say it right, Mom. What I mean is that I have a new understanding of what it means to be a Christian. You know we have to study the Bible in class and I'm learning a lot about it I didn't know before. What I'm trying to say is that I'm taking it more seriously now." Scooter backed off from rehearsal of the details of his spiritual crisis and kept the converation at a safe level of ambiguities.

His mother warmed to this different tack and a kind of pride started to show in her demeanor. "Are you telling me that you are going into the ministry?"

Mrs. Evans nurtured a secret desire that her son would choose a profession that would catapult him into a position of public leadership and community status. She had that hungry look, the look of the proverbial Jewish matriarch who can hardly wait to say, "My son the doctor," or "My son the rabbi."

"No, Mom. I haven't made it that far. But it is a possibility. I've been thinking about it a little bit."

"I think you'd make a fine minister. Oh, I'm so proud of you son." It was as though the decision was already made and the ordination service was scheduled for next week.

"Your father would be so thrilled. He was a deeply religious man you know."

Scooter remembered his father as a moral person, a man with

scrupulous business ethics and a penchant for all-American homespun philosophy, but hardly a zealot in religious matters. To be sure he was faithful in church attendance and served on the board of trustees of the community church. But trustee was not a particularly "spiritual" office as it had more to do with financial expertise than with biblical knowledge. It was the domain concerned with what his father always called "Caesar's business."

Conversations at the dinner tale never focused on religion but centered on political matters. The senior Evans was one of those who liked "Ike" even though he campaigned vigorously for Robert Taft in the '52 primaries. A dyed-in-the-wool Republican, Mr. Evans frequently groused about the residual effects of the New Deal that were dooming the nation to a ruined economy. His favorite trick was to ask the question, "Would you like to see a picture of an American destroyer?" Whoever bit on the question, knowing Evans's war record, expected to see him produce a photo of a battle-ready naval vessel. Instead Evans would pull out a dime from his pocket, displaying the image of Franklin Delano Roosevelt and say, "This is an American destroyer."

Scooter did recall that in the final three years of his life, his father was given to daily study of the Bible. By then he was a shell of a man, his body wasted by the devastating effects of three strokes, leaving him severely paralyzed and confined to an over-stuffed chair in the den. He lived out his days watching television with one eye grotesquely staring off at an angle while the lid drooped in flaccid uselessness. His mouth was twisted into a distorted smile, almost a sneer as the muscles there reacted to the hemorrhage on the brain. Interspersed with television watching Mr. Evans read his Bible with the aid of a Holmes-like magnifying glass. He never spoke to Scooter about what he was reading because speech of any kind became a slurred Herculean task. Perhaps Scooter's mother knew something more of Mr. Evans's religious affections that he confided to her in the intimacy of their bedroom.

Scooter abruptly changed the subject. They finished their meal and returned to the apartment to enjoy a bridge game with two of Mrs. Evans's widow friends.

Judy stepped out of the shower, her ebony hair made straight by the water. She swathed herself in a large towel and stood before the steamy mirror. She wrapped a second towel around her head like a turban, thinking, *Johnny's going to want to wrap me in a shroud when he finds out I've been dating.*

Judy enjoyed the breathing space the university nursing school provided. She was the type of girl who attracted male attention quickly. The atmosphere of her surroundings was more serious than Millport High, more mature, more carnal.

She was embarking on a profession that would mean facing human struggles of life and death daily, making the senior prom seem trivial by comparison. Johnny's letters were starting to sound juvenile to her. He had called and asked her to go to the drive-in, the "passion pit," as he referred to it. The night before, Judy had been wined and dined at the Royal Windsor by a sophisticated intern from Philadelphia's main line, a strikingly handsome man with swarthy features whom the girls on the next floor described with the sobriquet "dreamboat." He was obviously experienced, but not gropingly fast, behaving like a gentleman. She had already agreed to another date with him for the following Friday evening.

Judy was fond of Johnny, a term she recently began using in her mind to ease her conscious for breaking the rules invisibly inscribed on Johnny's class ring. The ring was now wrapped in tissue paper in her desk drawer, not even making it to a place of prominence in her velveteen jewel box. Johnny was cute, a lot of laughs, but she knew nothing permanent could come of their relationship despite the wild moments of adolescent passion they had shared together.

When the mirror cleared of the misty fog, Judy's thoughts sharpened along with it. For a brief instant she realized with clarity that she really didn't want to go out with Johnny tonight; in fact she didn't even want to see him, not now. She didn't want to hurt him, nor did she want to string him along. She called upon her mind to conjure up a scenario in which she could let him down gently but firmly.

She selected a casual skirt and blouse, sure that Johnny would appear in a sweater and chinos, certainly not a suit and a tie. After applying the finishing touches to her makeup and blotting her lips on a Kleenex, she removed the ring from the drawer and unwrapped the tissue paper. She methodically removed the string wrapping by chipping away the hardened lacquer that kept it from unraveling. When the ring was free of its inner bindings she polished it briefly and slipped it into her purse. Moments later her intercom buzzed and she heard the matronly voice of the resident director say between the static, "Judy, Mr. Kramer is here to see you."

When Judy appeared in the entrance lounge she smiled more to herself than to Johnny. His appearance confirmed her prediction. He was standing there, fidgety, wearing a V-neck sweater with a Witherspoon windbreaker, looking like the prototype Joe College. He seemed so slight, so young, so lacking in substance. At the moment Judy was feeling instincts more maternal than romantic.

"Hi, doll." Johnny quipped, assuming a carefree nonchalance.

Judy smiled sweetly, "Hi, Johnny."

He took her by the arm and escorted her out of the building, feeling awkward in this foreign territory, a no-man's land for him, a place where he was a total unknown to all save Judy. The stiffness of their meeting nagged at him but he chalked it up to the strangeness of the foreign turf.

When he opened the door for Judy, he saw something that made him feel like he had just caught a bullet in his chest. Judy's finger was bare, no ring, nothing—just a vague outline of whiteness whose borders were edged by a fading summer tan. It was a hurried glance but his mind was working in slow-motion and his eyes were operating like they had a wide-angle lens attached to them. That one finger stood out, ballooning above the rest like a great piece of sausage naked under the solitary bulb above a butcher's block. He felt a mad impulse to hack it off with one hard swing from a meat cleaver. He said nothing but walked silently around the car to the driver's side, his intestines writhing and tiny beads of sweat appearing on his forehead.

An optimistic thought struck him: *Maybe she's just embarrassed to wear a high school ring at the nurses hall*. The feeling was like the hollow moment of relief experienced by Poe's mourning hero at the insistent rapping of the Raven at his chamber window— "'Tis some visitor," he muttered, "only this and nothing more"—a facile explanation for his own private horror tale, *only this and nothing more*.

On the road to the drive-in, Johnny's "raven" came through

the window and aimed his cruel beak at his heart. His worst fears were being confirmed. Judy was sitting on her side of the car, her head bolt upright, and her hand resting on the door handle. She was not in her familiar position curled up at his side, snuggled there in a warm mass of flesh, teasing the back of his neck with her fingers.

Johnny pulled off Route 51 and moved up the macadam drive to the entrance booth. He switched off his head lamps and moved slowly along the rows of gray metallic speaker boxes, his way illumined by the dim corona emanating from his parking lights. He pulled into a slot near the outer edge of the bowl-like coliseum, removed from the crowd of cars that were bunched near the middle. He turned off the engine, switched off the parking lights, and opened the window.

"Blasted!" he muttered.

"What's the matter?" Judy asked.

"I always park too far from the speaker box. I'm too far away to reach it out the window and too close to it to open the door without banging into it."

Johnny had the window completely rolled down. He hunched his knees up on the front seat and stuck his torso through the open window, grasping for the metal speaker. He pulled himself back through the window, holding the box in the air until he could roll up the window far enough to latch the box on the window pane. Finally he got the window rolled up tightly, pressing the infernal box against the top of the door frame. He fiddled with the loose volume dial until it reached a satisfactory level. Turning to Judy he said, "OK, let's have it. What's going on."

"What do you mean, Johnny? There's nothing going on."

"Come off it. You're not wearing my ring and you've been as cold as a frozen fudgesicle since you got in the car. It's another guy isn't it? Isn't it?" His voice was rising in crescendo of accusation.

"No, Johnny. It's not another guy. Things are different, that's all."

"What do you mean 'different'? How are they different? We're still the same people."

"I know, but you're in college and I'm in nursing school. We're in different worlds now. I'm experiencing new things, new people, new everything."

"So what? So am I—but I still know what I want and it's you."

"That's what's different for me, Johnny. I'm not sure anymore what I want. I need time to think about things. I need space and I can't stand being crowded."

"So you just take my ring off your finger, and 'poof' you've got space, huh?"

Judy didn't answer. She fished in her purse and pulled out the ring.

"Here, Johnny. I'm sorry. I can't wear it anymore. It would be pretending and I know you wouldn't want that."

Johnny jerked his hand away from the ring as if the thing were alive and hostile. He did not want to touch it for fear of completing a transaction that would be final. His fury evaporated and he dissolved into tears. Between sobs he begged her to give him a chance to make things better.

Judy's feelings were confused. She was feeling part guilt, part pity, with a large dose of revulsion. She could accept tears, but not the display of weakness in his mendicant pleas.

Johnny forced his head on Judy's shoulder and she lightly cradled it, relenting enough to give a small measure of comfort. He fumbled for the buttons on her blouse and she pulled away sharply. He looked at her like a grief-stricken puppy and whined, "Please, Judy . . . for old times sake?"

"No, Johnny. It's over."

Johnny's mood changed abruptly, registering fury. He cranked the window down violently and half threw the speaker box back on its mooring and started the car. The wheels spit cinders behind them as he lurched the car out into the aisle and headed for the exit with head lamps on high, ignoring the angry honking of car horns. He drove all the way to Pittsburgh without saying a word, the back of his neck glowing vermillion under the street lights. For Judy the anger was much easier to bear than the whining. It salvaged a bit of respect for him. She was relieved when the silent trip ended at the front entrance of the nurses home. Johnny left the engine idling, walked briskly to Judy's side, and opened the door. He made a sweeping gesture of bowing, bending at the waist with arm thrown to the side and said, a la Rhett Butler, "Well, my sweet princess. It has been real."

Judy stepped out and walked to the door, never looking back. As it closed behind her and she heard the Chevy roar away she fell back against the door and let out a long sigh. It was an emotional ordeal, but now, for the first time in almost two years, she felt free.

SEVEN

T he person Scooter most wanted to tell about his conversion was his hometown minister. The Briarwood Community Church was the only church of significant size in the suburban area. There was Saint Catherine's, of course, but it was on the other side of the highway. Briarwood was too new for many churches to have sprung up and the founders of the community church had been clever in disguising any denominational affiliation in the name of the church. It was in fact a Presbyterian church with a formal connection to the presbytery of Pittsburgh.

The pastor, the Reverend Doctor Lindsley Oliver Franklin, Jr., had started the church as a mission venture during World War II and presided over its mushroom growth to its present membership of almost three thousand people. A few other denominations tried to plant churches in the suburb, but none got off the ground. The community church catered to Methodists, Lutherans, Episcopalians, Baptists, and anyone else who moved to town. It was a "company-store" type church, from which no management person in Briarwood could afford to be truant. Some referred to it in derisive tones as the Briarwood Country Club.

Dr. Franklin was a powerful orator, uncommonly handsome with jet black hair combed straight back, defying the strength of the receding hairline to subvert his good looks. He had a classical Roman nose and gleaming white teeth, expensively capped and giving a hint of Burt Lancaster when he smiled. His eyes seemed as black as his hair, gleaming in a fearsome way when he swept his arms in demonstrative gestures to make a sermonic point, "Barrymore . . ." the old timers said, "the man has the skill of Barrymore." The cliche that was spoken by at least one parishioner after every Sunday service was the remark, "He missed his calling. He should have been an actor."

Franklin was a total autocrat, ruling the church with an iron hand. It was whispered by a few disgruntled session members, who wouldn't dare to speak such treason aloud, that Franklin "held his board meetings in the shower." He was not the type of minister one loved with a warmhearted affection for a kindly grandfather. He was a man to be respected and admired yet also to be feared. Scooter had not met any human who intimidated him like Lindsley Oliver Franklin, Jr. He was a Presbyterian minister but, if dressed in a cassock edged in purple, he would have easily passed for a cardinal, an imperious prince of the church.

Franklin was a showman favoring creative pageantry and high liturgy. The Briarwood Community Church was the only Presbyterian church in Pittsburgh that had an altar instead of a communion table. It was possibly the only Presbyterian church in the world with an altar, as such Romanish concepts were repugnant to the sons and daughters of the Protestant Reformation. It had acolytes as well, young cherubic school boys adorned in black cassocks and angelic white surplices who lighted the candles on the altar in somber ceremony between the organ prelude and the processional hymn. At least the Episcopalian contingent of the heterogenous group was made to feel at home.

There was something for everyone. Above the chancel steps, hanging by a shining brass chain from the vaulted ceiling, was an opulent, intricately designed fellowship lamp behind whose scarlet tinted glass burned the "candle of friendship." Though cylindrical in shape the lamp was adorned on its "sides" with four great symbols of the world's religions including a cross, a star of David, an Islamic crescent, and an esoteric figure of Gautama Buddha. The walls were adorned with futuristic figures of Franklin's religious heroes, painted almost surrealistically with elongated slender bodies and oversized faces bearing the likenesses of men like Mahatma Gandhi, Toyohiko Kagawa, Albert Schweitzer, and Louis Pasteur. Relegated to smaller niches were grotesque portraits of Calvin, Luther, and John Knox, representing Franklin's tip of the hat to the fathers of the Reformation. Franklin was a modern Christian, a devotee of liberal theology and of Harry Emerson Fosdick.

More important to Franklin's flair for the dramatic than the architecture or liturgical accouterments was his passion for pageantry. The processional hymn that began each Sunday morning service was an event choreographed to such precision as to elicit envy from the likes of Hermes Pan, the genius who masterminded the Fred Astaire dance routines in Hollywood movies. The choristers practiced marching down the aisle in synchronized tempo, studying the steps of those ahead lest they commit the one unpardonable sin of this church, parading before God out of step. Even the carrying of the hymnal at just the proper angle was rehearsed weekly. The entrance of the choir was followed immediately by the elders, all wearing severe dark suits with shoes polished like Marine Corps officers. Scooter thought they must have tap dancers' cleats nailed to their shoes as they sounded like Prussian soldiers in hobnail boots marching down the aisle. Behind the elders, who came two by two, marched the solitary figure of the elaborately gowned Dr. Franklin with chin tilted upward like Henry VIII on the way to his throne.

On special occasions the processional was dressed up even more. Halloween week was given to a ceremony to honor the efforts of UNICEF to feed the hungry of the world. Their work was made famous by the humanitarian charitable labor of Danny Kaye. Thanksgiving Day became a time to honor the formation of the United Nations. Each choir member was given a colorful flag to be held aloft on large wooden poles. The "March of the Nations" began in the narthex, and when the choir members reached the chancel steps, instead of moving directly to the choir loft, they peeled off to each side of the church as if some invisible drill instructor had shouted, "To the wings—march!" The choir surrounded the sanctuary placing the flag poles in carefully constructed holders at the end of each pew. Finally the choir moved to the loft, but not until the sanctuary was bathed in the resplendent color of a sea of flags.

But Scooter's favorite was the feast of Epiphany following right after Christmas. Sunday afternoon was a literal warm-up for the evening affair as hundreds of people lugged or stuffed into the trunks of their cars their brownish dried out Christmas trees to be stacked in a huge pile in the middle of the schoolyard baseball field. With the pump truck of the volunteer fire department standing by, Dr. Franklin stood on the frozen turf bedecked in a strange black cape that reminded Scooter of the picture on the sheet music cover of "The Old Lamplighter."

Dr. Franklin read a litany devised for the occasion. At a dramatic moment he took the candle he was using to illumine his script and walked to the edge of the monstrous pile of trees and inserted the candle in a hollow place of dried branches. The needles began to crackle and in seconds the night was brightened by a blazing pyre that shot its flames skyward, giving off the scent of a fiery pine forest. The spectacle was over in minutes as the flames consumed the trees like a tinderbox. Most of the ashes and debris were swept away by firemen the next day, but it was not uncommon for Scooter to find charred remains of fir twigs when he dug up the dirt at shortstop in the heat of the summer.

The tree burning was followed at the church by a procession of Epiphany. Reenacting a festival popular in the medieval church the choir marched this night in costumes rented from a theatrical agency in Pittsburgh.. There were lords and ladies, minstrels and pages, plumed knights, and even knaves. The climax of the processional was heralded by trumpeters playing a fanfare, followed by the carrying of the flaming pudding, the spiced cake, the great wassail bowl and the *piece de résistance,* the stuffed pig. Johnny was usually given the honor of carrying the wassail bowl, with Scooter marching behind him proudly holding high the platter carrying the stuffed pig with an apple stuck beneath its pink leathery snout. Johnny and Scooter wore violet nylon leotards, velvet tights, and velvet brocade coats topped with velvet hats with large peacock feathers reaching out in the air. It was like playing Robin Hood or King Arthur's court. No one would have been shocked if Dr. Franklin had ridden in on a horse and was dressed in a suit of armor, brandishing a lance or reciting a litany out of the vizor of a steel helmet.

The spiced cake had twelve gold crosses baked within it. After the service the enormous cake was cut into tiny pieces so that each member of the congregation could have a taste. If one bit into gold that meant the lucky person could possess the cross for one year until it was returned to the church and baked once more into the Epiphany cake.

It was the man who orchestrated all this that Scooter went to visit on Sunday afternoon to receive spiritual counsel. He was always apprehensive in Dr. Franklin's presence, but this day his anxiety level was extra high. Scooter assumed that the minister would be pleased to hear of his new-found faith, bringing to fruition the goals and efforts of Franklin's own ministry. Surely the man would be delighted that this volatile boy, who had more than once stained the floor of the fellowship hall with blood dripping from the nose of some unfortunate lad who provoked him, had finally settled down to a spiritually oriented life. Still, Scooter could not instantly overcome years of intimidation and feel comfortable with the man.

"Well, Scooter, what brings you here today? I thought you would be at the football game this afternoon."

"No, sir. I wanted to talk with you about what happened to me at college."

Franklin was not only an extraordinary preacher and ecclesiastical entrepreneur, he was also the kind of pastor who kept close tabs on his flock, not missing a hospital call or shut-in visit. He possessed a magic system of grapevine knowledge, knowing what was going on behind bedroom doors and in secret trysting places. He emanated an aura of omniscience and now presumed he was about to hear a sob story from a young man who suffered the bitter ending of a promising athletic career. Instead, he heard Scooter's conversion story. Somehow it made him feel soiled, violated by a foreign type of religion.

Franklin prided himself that none of his congregation ever attended Billy Graham crusades or other types of fervent meetings that could breed virulent forms of emotionalism. It was difficult for him to contain his rage as he waited for Scooter to finish. Scooter saw no sign of the fury boiling inside Franklin save for two vertical creases on his forehead bridging the gap between his bushy eyebrows. His eyes darkened menacingly but Scooter read that merely as an indication of concentrated interest. When Scooter finished he looked at Dr. Franklin for a response. Trying to control his anger Franklin shrugged his shoulders and said, "Don't take it too seriously, Scooter. You'll get over it."

"What do you mean?" Scooter said, feeling stripped of his dignity, recoiling from the deflating words.

"I mean, young man, that I've heard these emotional stories

before, particularly from college students who get carried away with fanaticism. But they always grow up and simmer down. I'm sure you will too and become your old self again."

"But that's just it. I don't want to be my old self again. My old self was in big trouble and headed for worse."

Franklin's mood shifted from anger to tolerant amusement. "Don't be melodramatic, Scooter. It wasn't like you were on the road to the penitentiary. You sound like an Oriental mystic. It's OK, but don't get carried away with it."

"You keep talking about being carried away. You act like I'm nuts or something. I'm talking about something real, the most important thing that has ever happened to me and you want me to dismiss it, is that it?"

"No, no, Scooter. Take it easy. You've been under a lot of strain this past year. Listen, I remember last fall when I buried your father. I know that hurt you deeply. I know you idolized him. It's perfectly natural for a young impressionable boy who has just lost his father to yearn for something to fill the aching void that is left. We all do that, seek substitute father figures to take the place of our missing parent. I did it when my father died, but in a different sort of way."

"But I encountered Christ, Dr. Franklin, the real, personal, resurrected Christ."

Franklin's mood changed abruptly as if Scooter's words set off a land mine within him. He twisted his words and spat them out at Scooter, words that fell on Scooter's ears like sledgehammers. "Listen, Scooter, if you believe in the resurrection of Christ you're a damn fool!"

Scooter was stunned, frozen in incredulity. He asked weakly, "Don't you believe in the resurrection of Christ? You're a minister. You preach about it all the time. You talked about it at my father's funeral."

"The resurrection is a symbol, Scooter. It means that we are to face every day of our lives with courage. Nobody takes it literally in this day and age except illiterate fundamentalists, and you're far too intelligent for that."

"Dr. Franklin, I don't know what a fundamentalist is, but I guess I'm not very intelligent, because I do believe in a real resurrection. What good is your symbol if there is no reality behind it? What good is your symbol when you're standing beside a grave?"

The conversation was getting bitter and Franklin was wise
enough to terminate it before it got out of hand. Scooter was obviously upset and needed a respite to cool off.

"Look, Scooter, theology is not all that simple. Don't get upset. You have lots of time to sort these things out. I just want you to
keep an open mind. We can talk about it again the next time
you're home." Dr. Franklin rose from his desk which was a sign of
dismissal. He walked Scooter to his study door, a paternal arm
draped around his shoulder.

Scooter walked to his car with his head spinning. He tasted
the salty taste of the tear that fell off his cheek onto his lip.
Never—never had he ever felt so utterly and completely betrayed
by a human being. In his mind Dr. Franklin's face turned into a
diabolical mask like the hideous face on the Epiphany boar.

EIGHT

Back at Witherspoon, Johnny went into a two-week tailspin over Judy. He kept Scooter up late into the night nursing a broken heart and incessantly asking Scooter for advice.

"What should I do, Scoot? She won't accept my calls." The questions were fired across the darkness between their beds just when Scooter was almost asleep.

"What do you think I am, an expert? If I knew what to do I'd do it with Patricia."

The midnight interrogation sessions lasted for two weeks. Scooter was still paralyzed over Patricia but Johnny was back in action hustling the girls in a matter of fourteen days. He still pampered a sore spot for Judy but it didn't cramp his style. He soon began enjoying his new social freedom, dating two or three different girls a week.

The semester passed with a wedge beginning to build between the boys. Many of Scooter's old routines were jettisoned as he immersed himself more deeply in his faith. With the accelerated tempo of rushing, Johnny was spending more time with the guys he met at the fraternity smokers. Instead of their freshman speech class becoming an adhesive to bind them together, it merely served to widen the growing breach between them. Scooter, of part Irish descent, was rumored to have kissed the Blarney Stone. Even in grade school when a pupil was chosen to give a speech it was the silver-tongued Scooter who got the nod.

Johnny lived at the opposite end of the spectrum. He was fearless in sports, high-speed driving, or instigating capers that frequently ended with calls to the police. He was known to run through the backyards of Briarwood, making bedroom lights pop on in a string of houses, while burly cops panted breathlessly behind him in a wildcap midnight chase. In these things he was fearless, but about speaking in front of a class, no matter how small, how friendly, he was incurably phobic. It was an anomaly, a strange personal quirk that Johnny could perform on stage in a class play but was paralyzed in a classroom. Here were no floor lights to blind him to the gazing eyes of the audience; here he had to play himself, a role he couldn't master. It was a Chinese torture for him to be called upon to move to the front of the room for a two-minute recitation even if armed with a script or extended outline.

Scooter was the darling of the speech professor, an elderly spinster named Dr. Underwood. She selected Scooter for the freshman speech award in spite of the fact that he earned a *D* for her course. The grading system for speeches was complex, involving number scores of one to ten in six different categories including such considerations as content, delivery, outline, continuity with outline, and other factors based on preparations. Scooter routinely scored tens on content and delivery but his net score was usually six after the other categories had been factored in. He was utterly derelict about preparations. His failure to turn in the required outlines earned him a zero for the category as well as for following the outline. It was impossible for Dr. Underwood to monitor an outline that didn't exist. But Scooter could speak— there was no doubt about that. He would have his comrades in class alternately holding their sides in raucous laughter and fighting to stifle the tears he jerked from their eyes with the turn of a phrase. Scooter's ecstasy was Johnny's agony, the Waterloo that shattered his fragile self-confidence.

The nadir of Johnny's speech class miseries came when it was his turn to give his first speech without script or notes. It was a two-minute exercise, a hundred and twenty seconds of sustained anguish. He committed his speech to memory, reciting the words in front of a mirror in his room. Scooter coached and encouraged him in the rehearsal exercises, but to no avail. A spasm of raw fear had Johnny on the rim of panic.

"I have the solution, Johnny. I know how you can make it through this," Scooter suggested.

"Yeah, we murder Dr. Underwood, hack up her body in thirty-seven pieces and send them parcel post to California."

Scooter assumed the air of the Flemish detective, Hercule

Poirot, and said, "No, monsieur. It is time for the case of the mysterious resurrection of the Millport varsity jacket."

"The varsity jacket? What good will that do? We're not going to a Halloween party."

"Ah, you underestimate the clever machinations of Monsieur Poirot. Perhaps you have overlooked the salient fact, my good fellow, that Dr. Underwood always sits in the back row, the better to grade your voice projection with. I, your faithful companion, will be sitting in the front row gaily bedecked in my varsity jacket with the text of your speech taped in big letters to the lining and held open at such an acute angle that you and you alone will be able to perceive it."

"Now you're talking, Scooter. Let's get to work."

The boys prepared the script using large block letters and taped them to the lining of the coat giving Johnny at least an even chance of sleeping that night.

The speech class was at 8:00 A.M. Scooter positioned himself perfectly in the front row grabbing extra space by extending both legs to one side and slouching back where he could let his coat fall open to its fullest width and still conceal the inner lining from everyone's view to the side or behind him. When Dr. Underwood called on him, Johnny rose from his seat and shuffled to the front of the room, standing directly in front of Scooter, with his hands jammed nervously in his hip pockets.

Shifting his weight from one leg to the other he tried to adjust his gaze in such a way as to be looking both at Dr. Underwood in the back of the room and at Scooter's coat just below and in front of him, a feat impossible for a creature endowed with binocular vision. His eyes skittered back and forth between the professor and the coat like a nervous mosquito on a lily pad. His mouth opened, but no words came out. He stood there frozen like a statue. The only visible sign of life in his stiffened form was the quivering of his lower lip. Scooter had his arms spread open desperately trying to get Johnny to look full at him, coaxing furiously with silent expressions. Nothing worked. Dr. Underwood spoke reassuring words from the back of the room trying to calm Johnny.

"Relax, Mr. Kramer. You can do it."

Johnny flashed an embarrassed grin and tried to begin. "Ah,

my talk is entitled—ah—ah—" The title was written clearly on
Scooter's coat. He wanted to take it off and wave it at Johnny like
a matador waving his cape at a frightened bull.

The words simply refused to come. Waves of humiliation engulfed Johnny and a scarlet tint flushed at the base of his neck
rising upward like a thermometer casting a crimson hue to his
sandy hair. Locked in frustration he endured the freeze as long as
he could and finally blurted out. "I just can't . . ." and scrambled
for his chair. Mercifully, Dr. Underwood spoke, "That's quite all
right, Mr. Kramer, it happens to all of us," and called on the next
student quickly, to divert the class's attention from Johnny. He
slouched in his chair, mortified.

Despite the fact that Scooter tried to help him through the
ordeal, Johnny harbored a tinge of resentment born part of jealousy and part of the hangover of humiliation that clung to him.
Scooter had labored to help him avoid the disgrace, but he was
too intimately involved with it to avoid the fallout of resentment
that spilled from its cloud.

Scooter dodged the partying that accompanied the fraternity
sales pitches, the almost hysterical pursuit by upperclassmen to
win the allegiance of the plebian class to their august orders. They
pandered, wooed, indulged, did everything to make the target
frosh feel important and wanted so that on bid day the boy would
make his solemn pledge to Sigma Nu or Sigma Phi Epsilon, becoming a blood brother for life to the elite group of his choice, the
pan-hellenic counsel of men. Scooter got bids to three frats but
accepted none, choosing instead to remain an "independent,"
linking him automatically to the brotherhood of the shunned,
those miserable few whom, despite fierce competition for members, no fraternity thought worthy enough to grant an invitation.

Johnny received four bids, but was spared the anguish of decision that was wracking other freshman who held multiple bid
cards in their hands. From 9:00 to 6:00 P.M. on Pledge Day the
rule of silence was in force, an ironclad mandate forbidding any
upperclass fraternity member from speaking to a freshman.
Last-minute harangues and high-pressure proselytizing were
outlawed. The "actives" were forced to sweat it out as they waited
for the novitiates to turn in their secret cards.

At the base of the huge stone tower in the rotunda of Old Main was a large box with a slot in the top and a sign marked PLEDGE CARDS. The box sat on a riser in the center of the rotunda with refracted rays of sunlight from the high tower windows lending it an eerie countenance, almost a translucent transfiguration. The box suggested the mystery of a Druid ceremony, a high altar of sacrifice where the cards would be offered as sacred oblations.

The pledge box was guarded by a coterie of officers from the executive council of the sororities; co-eds were posted to insure no fraternity active broke the silence code. A similar scenario was played in reverse across the quadrangle where fraternity officers stood guard over the sorority pledge box. Outside the tower, things were different. At the entrance way marked by granite arches the girl friends of the actives were posted as surrogate persuaders for their pinmates, instructed to keep watch for the most sought-after pledge candidates. They were bound by no oath and could apply their wiles to help wavering pledges make the right choice at the altar of selection.

Johnny had no qualms of indecision. He was sure of his choice. He winked at the flaming redhead wearing the white Chi Omega blazer; she knew there was no doubt which way Johnny Kramer was going. Entering the rotunda he saw the pledge box elevated on its hallowed pedestal and grinned to himself. It sparked memories of an annual ritual they had in Briarwood Elementary School. Every year during the second week of February each homeroom had its specially decorated box with a slot in the top waiting to receive the secret missives exchanged in the room on Valentine's Day. All week the receptacle was filled with entries as the children waited to see who would send them cryptic messages of love; and to see which boy and which girl would receive the unofficial tally of the most valentines. The exchange took place within the homeroom, but in the morning before the bell rang, students were allowed to visit other classrooms to deposit their clandestine votives. This was another age, another box, but the game was the same.

Johnny signed his name to the card bearing the logo of Sigma Phi Epsilon and dropped it in the box, casting his lot with the "Epps," or "apes," more commonly called simply the "animals."

These were the rowdy ones, the kinds recreated in the fantasies of John Belushi. Johnny was one of them. He had been since the day he was born. Today he was merely making it official.

Once Johnny pledged the fraternity his drinking forays to Youngstown became more frequent. Instead of limiting them to weekends he began going out with the brothers during the week and sneaking into the dorm quite drunk. One night he staggered in with Art Tanzy, who was singing loudly, sure to waken the resident director, spelling certain explusion. Scooter was still up and heard the ruckus on the first-floor landing. He ran to the front door and pulled Johnny away from Tanzy, who was hugging him like a girl and singing a maudlin love song loud and off-key.

"Hey, man, whatja think you're doing. Let my pal alone," Tanzy slurred at Scooter.

Scooter ducked as the drunk swung a wild roundhouse at him. He repressed the impulse to put him on the floor with two quick shots to the head. He was more interested in getting Johnny out of there fast. He half dragged Johnny back to the room, and once safely in, shut the door, turned out the lights, and covered Johnny's mouth with his hand. Johnny was moaning and trying to yell through Scooter's hand which muffled the sound like a muted trumpet. Scooter wrestled him to the bed, all the while keeping his hand firmly over his mouth. Johnny struggled for a minute and finally went limp, passing out cold.

Commotion was still going on in the hall. Art Tanzy had a mean drunk on and was standing in the landing waving his fists in the air in belligerence. He was defiant. Bellicose. Scooter changed quickly into his pajamas and went out, feigning a yawn as if he had just been roused from his sleep by the racket. When he arrived at the scene, Mr. Reddington, the dorm director, was already there taking command of the situation. His fiery presence had half sobered Johnny's unfortunate barstool partner. Tanzy was caught *in flagrant delecti* and though he wasn't aware of it yet, it was clear to everyone else. Scooter crossed his fingers as Mr. Reddington marched Art to his room, hoping that in his drunken stupor he wouldn't mutter anything about Johnny.

In the morning Johnny summed up the outing between throbs of a pounding headache. "I had sixteen drinks, Scooter."

"Sixteen drinks! How in the world did you guys get back here? There was no way either of you could drive."

"Tony DiMarco drove. He was with us all night and never had a drop. The whole outing was his idea. He wanted to see how well we could hold our liquor. He agitated a contest between me and Art to see who could drink the other one under the table." DiMarco was a senior and held the position of pledge master for Sig Eps, a role not unlike that of a Parris Island drill instructor.

"Don't tell me you lost. No way Art could have taken more than sixteen drinks."

"Naw, I drank him under the table. He went down after ten."

"Well, he's in big trouble, Johnny. I snuck you in the room but Art was carrying on like a lunatic right in front of Reddington."

Johnny groaned, "Geez, Scoot, they'll can him for that and probably me too."

Johnny sweated it out all morning. Art Tanzy's hearing with the dean was at 10:00 A.M. He said nothing to implicate the other boys who were with him, taking his medicine like a true "Epp." By 4:00 that afternoon Tanzy's room had been cleaned of his gear and he was riding down the Pennsylvania Turnpike with his furious father.

The incident made Johnny more cautious, but he was by no means cured. He found other guys to share the bar stools, and Scooter had to put him to bed more than once.

The semester ended with an envelope containing small white slips of paper, each posting the final grades for the boys' courses. They scrambled for the mailbox and checked off the grades, translating each one into the numerical quality points they were worth, and divided the total by the number of credit hours they were taking. Scooter's grades showed an *A* in Old Testament and all the rest *D*'s except for another one credit hour of *A* for Physical Education. Injured players who made the varsity football team were granted an automatic exemption from gym class coupled with the grade of *A* for the course. This gesture pushed Scooter's grade point average to 1.78 (on a four-point system) just slightly over the 1.75 mark that was the cutoff line for academic probation. Scooter had another semester to get his cumulative all-college average to the 2-point level to avoid future probation.

Johnny did not fare as well. He also made an *A* in gym, earning it the hard way; but it was not enough to offset the *F* in Business Math and the rest *D*'s. He was placed on academic probation for one semester with flunking out staring him in the eye as a clear and present danger. With the probation came the prohibition from going active in the fraternity, the most severe blow of all.

During the first week of the second semester Scooter found a note in his mailbox summoning him to a meeting with Dr. Lenhart, the president of Witherspoon College. He asked around but no one could guess what provoked the "invitation." It was not unusual for a student to be called into the dean of men's office, which spelled a student conduct problem, or to be called before the academic dean if grades were a problem; but to be directed to report to the president's office was a harbinger of some grave urgency. Dr. Lenhart was rarely seen on campus save for an occasional appearance in chapel. Much of his time was spent on the road at alumni banquets and visiting foundations to solicit funds for Witherspoon's building program.

Scooter remembered the address Lenhart made to the incoming students during Freshman Orientation Week when he intoned a warning that 50 percent of incoming students would not complete the four-year course to graduation. Some would leave by expulsion, a few by transferring, most by flunking out. He said in almost mystical terms of reverence: "Look closely at the person sitting on your left . . . now look at the person sitting on your right. The chances are that one of those persons will not be here on graduation day"—the ominous warning sent a shiver up Scooter's back.

Scooter went to the president's office at the appointed time, filled with apprehension. He had a strange visceral feeling of guilt but wasn't at all sure why. He tried to guess the reason for the summons. *Maybe they found out about the night I covered for Johnny. No, that can't be it; that would be handled by the dean of students. Are they angry with me for not joining a fraternity? Surely the president wouldn't be concerned about that?*

He approached the president's secretary in the waiting room outside the executive office and announced his presence with a lump in his throat. "I'm Richard Evans. I have a note that says I'm supposed to have a meeting with Dr. Lenhart."

Scooter looked at the woman's eyes for a clue to the purpose of the meeting. She gave none. Retaining an officious posture she pleasantly replied, "Yes, Mr. Evans, please, take a seat. The president will see you shortly."

Scooter's anxiety level increased as he sat down. He nervously rooted through some magazines on the coffee table in front of him. His hands were clammy and he had a hollow point in the pit of his stomach much like he felt in the waiting room of the dentist's office. He studied the room, noting that the secretary didn't look up at him from her work. He saw an ebony captain's chair with the Witherspoon College seal on the back. He thought of sitting in it at a court martial presided over by Captain Queeg. The paintings on the wall were of sailing vessels, adding to the maritime delusion that was playing havoc with his imagination. He was snapped mercifully from his reverie by the sound of the secretary's voice: "Dr. Lenhart will see you now, Mr. Evans."

She rose from behind her desk and escorted Scooter to the heavy oak door that guarded the inner sanctum of the president's office. She ushered Scooter into the spacious chamber. Dr. Lenhart remained seated behind a massive desk with his imposing bulk framed against the black leather chair that supported him. He made no effort to rise or extend a hand of greeting. He said imperiously, "Sit down, Mr. Evans," indicating a chair placed at the front of the desk, the traditional spot for the subordinate who came to this place of power for an interview.

Scooter felt as if he was in a chancellery of a king. The room had a medieval feel to it. It was graced with two large oriel windows encased with stained glass panes. The ceiling was vaulted and the bookcase was gothic in style with slender vertical piers and buttresses. Opulent Oriental rugs with golden fringes graced the parquet floor. Scooter realized he was in the presence of the second man who had ever intimidated him.

Dr. Lenhart approached the reason for the summons indirectly. With eyes on the edge of blazing he abruptly picked up a volume from the edge of his desk and handed it over to Scooter. "Look at this book, Richard, and mark it well."

The book was a special leather-bound edition of *The Masters of Deceit* written by J. Edgar Hoover, the reigning plenipotentiary of the Federal Bureau of Investigation. "Open it up," Lenhart commanded.

Scooter fingered the pages of the book until his eyes fell on the dedication. There in heavy scrawl was an inscription, "To my dear friend George Lenhart, With warm personal regards, Hoover."

Scooter's fear turned to intrigue as he wondered how this book could have any possible bearing on why he was sitting in the president's office. *Surely he doesn't think I'm involved in some sinister communist cell group on campus,* he mused.

"Do you know what that book is about young man?"

"'I've never read it, sir, but I guess it's about communism isn't it?"

"It certainly is. It exposes a movement that is going on right now in this country, a movement that is a cancer eating away at the very heart of the society. A cancer of the heart. Did you ever hear of that kind of cancer boy?" The president's voice had assumed a pitch of frenzy and there was a wild, nearly hysterical gleam in his eye.

"No, sir. I've never heard of cancer of the heart but I think I see what you mean."

Lenhart interrupted Scooter sharply. "You have no idea what I mean. You're too young. I'm talking about waste. A damn pitiable waste of this country's great resources. This country was built by work. Hard, clean, backbreaking work by men and women who paid a heavy price for their liberty. The people who built this country weren't lazy. They didn't sit on their hands waiting for someone to hand them everything on a silver platter. If they had they wouldn't have survived, they'd have starved to death. They didn't have any pork barrels to put their hands in."

Scooter grew more mystified by the second, wondering how this speech about free enterprise, pioneers, and pork barrels had anything to do with him.

"The Soviets have a masterplan for undermining our nation, Richard. It goes beyond the obvious efforts to infiltrate labor unions and strategic government posts. One of their prime targets has been the leftist-controlled entertainment industry and the mass media. I'm talking about Hollywood and New York and CBS and Scripps-Howard. They're everywhere plying their subtle arts of subliminal seduction. They've even penetrated the church. They seduce the minds of young people, making fun of the classical virtues of industry and pride and duty, the virtues that made this country."

Lenhart noticed the bewildered look in Scooter's eyes and finally drew the strands of his rambling soliloquy to their predetermined point. "It all adds up to waste, Richard. That's the one thing I can't abide, and you represent the supreme example of waste in this freshman class."

With this dramatic climax, Dr. Lenhart paused to let the punch line sink in. He disturbed the pause by shuffling some papers and producing a file folder whose contents were hidden from Scooter's view.

"Richard, this file contains the test scores of every freshman, coupled with their record of academic achievement for the first semester. You are here today because of a singular achievement, or shall I say, lack of it. Your test scores show that you have the highest I.Q. of all the entering freshman, a class, by the way, which includes no less than seventeen high school valedictorians. In fact Mr. Evans, you have an I.Q. which is one of the highest in the history of this institution. Yet you failed to attain even a *C* average your first semester. That, young man, is a *waste,* and I would like an explanation."

The reason for the meeting was now perfectly clear to Scooter. He had squirmed in meetings like this before with his high school principal and with his teachers. They all went over the same ground and beat the same drum—"Scooter, why aren't you working up to your potential?" He loathed the word "potential" and seemed doomed to spending the rest of his life with a scarlet *P* taped to his chest.

"I'm not sure what the problem is, sir," Scooter began. "I did well in grade school and junior high but my main interest was always sports. I've never been much of a bookworm. I worked after school in high school and never took a book home." Scooter thought that fact might show that at least he wasn't a pork-barrel addict. "I guess I depended on my natural ability to get me through, I sure didn't study. I was scared all summer about coming to college because I felt like I sort of skipped high school and I didn't know if I'd be able to make it here. I don't have any idea how to study."

Dr. Lenhart broke in, "If you don't know how to study how did you make an *A* in Bible?"

"Well, sir, I never read the Bible before I came here and at the beginning of the semester I had a religious experience, a conversion to Christianity. Since then I've had a passion to learn about the Bible. I guess you could say I had a special motivation in that course. And . . . that course is different from the others. We don't

have essay exams, they're all objective tests, fill in the blanks, that
sort of thing. I play little quiz games with myself about all the
facts in the Bible: who was Moses' mother and that kind of stuff. I
determined that the professor would never be able to ask me a
detail about the Bible which I didn't know. I used to be the same
way about baseball statistics and trivia."

"I see. Why aren't you motivated by your other courses?"

"A couple of reasons, I think. First off, ever since I had my
conversion I've run into all kinds of skepticism in the classroom
about Christianity. I figured if that's what education gets you,
who needs it." He thought of Eddie and said, "I want wisdom,
not knowledge. There is a saying by Thomas Hobbes on a stained
glass window in the library that says 'Knowledge is power.' I
don't like that. I don't want any part of that. It sounds arrogant to
me."

Dr. Lenhart grabbed another book from the side of his desk.
"I read the Bible too, Richard. Do you know what it says in here
about knowledge?"

"No, sir. I'm not sure what you mean."

"In Proverbs it says that the fear of the Lord is the *beginning* of
wisdom. Apparently you have that. But that's only the beginning.
The Bible says that wisdom is better than knowledge but you've
made a serious mistake."

"What's that?" Scooter asked, impressed that Lenhart's tone
had changed. He was now speaking to him in a fatherly, pastoral
way.

"The Bible says, 'Get knowledge, but more so get wisdom.'
What that means, Richard, is that it is possible to have knowledge
without ever attaining wisdom. You can be an educated fool; the
world is full of them. But, you cannot have wisdom without
knowledge. Knowledge is an indispensable step to getting the
wisdom you're searching for."

"I think I understand that, sir. That's why I'm studying the
Bible so hard, to gain a knowledge of it."

"But that's not the only book God has written, Richard. It is
surely the most important and I don't for a minute want to dis-
courage your studying it. I'm a Christian too, and I know how
important the Bible is. But even that book speaks of another
book, the book of nature. Do you think that God speaks the truth
in the Bible?"

"I sure do," Scooter answered.

"So do I. But He also speaks the truth in the other book as well. What I'm saying Richard is not of my invention. It was spoken by both Saint Augustine and Saint Thomas Aquinas— 'All truth is God's truth.' All truth meets at the top. What is true in biology comes from God, what is true in sociology is of God. I'm not saying that everything you learn in biology or sociology is true. God forbid! But what is true there comes from the Source of all truth. You need to read all the books of nature if you want a full picture of God. Maybe I don't mean it or believe it the way Hobbes did, but knowledge *is* power if it is true knowledge, because there is no greater power than truth."

"I guess it is, if you look at it that way. We read about Plato's cave in Humanities and he talked about human opinions being like shadows on the wall, but I'm not interested in shadows."

"That's right. But even Plato said that shadows are better than darkness, and ignorance is darkness. You say you want the light but you're choosing the darkness to get out of the shadows. I think you need to start moving toward the sunlight. Your Bible study is good but you've consigned everything else to the darkness which will cast a horrible shadow over whatever light you find. Now that you know the source of the light you shouldn't be afraid of the light wherever you find it shining. Get my point?"

"Yes, sir. I see what you mean. I'll try to do better this term."

"You're fortunate, Richard. You have the intellectual tools. What's been blocking you is the wrong attitude. Don't be afraid of your professors. If you are wise you will know that you can learn something valuable from every person you meet. You can learn something from the devil himself, if only what craftiness is. Now get out of here and get to work. I'll be checking your progress at the end of the term."

When Scooter left he wasn't sure whether to feel chastened or complimented. The revelation of his high I.Q. boosted his confidence, and that the president cared enough to call him in made him feel important.

He knew that Dr. Lenhart was right; he was wasting his mind, letting it become lethargic like some deadened muscle that had surrendered to atrophy. But he was afraid. Afraid to try to learn and of failing in the process. I.Q. tests were so sterile. They measured a damnable potential, but offered no grades for actual performance. To perform meant to compete, to risk losing, and its inevitable escort, humiliation. It meant disciplined work, something he loved in sports but feared in the classroom.

Lenhart's rebuke sparked a spiritual struggle with Scooter. His heart was palpitating with a zealot's love for Jesus, but it was a sensuous love, a love of feelings and emotion. His was a fragmented devotion, a partial fulfillment of the Great Commandment. His soul was aflame but he was not loving God with his mind. Could religious affection be intellectual, or would the mind douse the flames of his ardor with cold and stifling concepts? He had to know if the heart could survive an inquiring mind.

His first test came the next morning when he went to his introductory course in Philosophy. The professor began his lecture by saying, "Today we will consider Saint Augustine's view of the origin of the cosmos." Scooter's ears perked up at the name "Saint Augustine"; it was a name that some benign providence kept dropping in his lap. All Scooter knew about Saint Augustine was that it was an old city on the east coast of Florida and boasted a mission made famous by Tin Pan Alley.

The professor was Dr. Hepplewhyte, Scooter's faculty advisor. He was erudite, no doubt, but his lectures were usually dry as dust. Today, however, the content was so absorbing that it seemed to explode through the dust and bombard Scooter's ears. Hepplewhyte gave the lecture as he did all his others, in quiet tones, but the softness of his voice seemed only to accent the theme of this recitation.

"St. Augustine taught the concept of creation *ex nihilo,* creation out of nothing. Remember, class, that the category of 'nothingness' in its absolute sense is unthinkable. When Augustine taught that the world was created out of nothing he did not mean that once there was nothing and *poof,* suddenly there was something. For something to come literally from nothing is absurd. It would have to create itself; it would have to be before it was. It would have to be and not be at the same time and the same way, which is something even Hamlet knew was not possible. No, when Augustine spoke of *ex nihilo* creation he was not saying, as some modern thinkers foolishly suppose, that the universe popped into being by chance. Chance can no nothing; for it is nothing. It has no power because it has no being. Augustine was saying that there was no *matter* out of which God shaped the world, that matter itself had a beginning, that it was dependent on God for its existence. But God was there eternally, having the power of being within Himself."

Scooter's head was swimming but he was enjoying the exhilaration of this dip in the metaphysical pond. For the first time in any class except Bible, Scooter raised his hand.

"Yes, Richard," Dr. Hepplewhyte called.

"Who or what created God, professor?"

"God is not created, Richard. He is eternal."

"But doesn't that mean the same thing as saying that God created Himself?"

"No, Richard. God could no more bring Himself into being from nothing than you could, or the chair you're sitting in could. Think of it. If God were created, if He had a beginning in time, and everything else had a beginning in time then that would mean that once there was nothing. Absolute pure nothingness. Now, Richard, if that were so what would there be now?"

"Well," Richard thought pensively, "I guess there would be nothing."

"Precisely, Richard. If once there was nothing at all and then there was something, that would be magic, not science—in fact such a thing would make science altogether impossible. Science depends on reason, or rational laws, for its very possibility. To assert a totally contradictory and irrational beginning to reality would make rationality suspect at every subsequent point. No scientific law would be any more credible than its opposite. That's why it is a law of science as well as philosophy that, write this down class, *ex nihilo nihil fit*, 'out of nothing, nothing comes.' The simplest way to state it is this, if something is, then something somewhere must have the power of being. If nothing had the power of being then nothing would be because nothing could be—it is as simple as that, yet a point missed by some of the most brilliant of thinkers."

Again Scooter's hand shot into the air.

"But Dr. Hepplewhyte, it can't be all that easy. Surely there must be something that has the power of being, but why does it have to be God? Why can't it be the universe or some obscure part of the universe?"

"Well, Richard. Let's see. First, do you think that it is you?"

The class giggled at the suggestion that perhaps Scooter was the one who possessed the power of being upon which the whole universe depended.

"No, sir, I know it isn't me."

"If it is the universe as a whole or some hidden part, then that part or that whole would in fact be God. But if a part of the universe lacks power of being then it must be distinguished from the "whole" which has it, and now the whole is greater than the sum of its parts. Or if some part of the universe has the power of being then it must be distinguished from those parts which do not—this one special part would be 'transcendent' to the universe."

Hepplewhyte was moving quickly and Scooter wasn't the only one to fear he was being the victim of a word game. Hepplewhyte was into it now and there was no stopping him until he made his final point.

"We usually think of 'transcendent' as meaning 'higher' in the sense of 'up there,' like it means God resides some place above the clouds. But transcendence is not a spatial term or a referent to geography. It is an ontological term—it refers to *being*. If something has the power of being in itself, that gives it the supreme kind of transcendence we are talking about when we are talking about God. Now I don't know *where* the power of being is but I know *that* it is and that without it we could not be here talking about it. You see, class, it's not just the Bible that says there is a God. All of nature screams the same message. If we had only one molecule that existed, that would be enough to demand the existence of something with the power of being, else we would be cut adrift from all knowledge, all science, all reason, from life itself."

"Whew." Scooter let out a sigh. This was just what Dr. Lenhart had been talking about the day before. He listened intently to the rest of the lecture but he was already hooked. As soon as the bell rang Scooter rushed from his chair and impulsively raced to the registrar's office to change his major. He declared breathlessly to the startled woman behind the counter that he wanted to be a philosophy major.

NINE

Scooter's change in major annoyed some of his Christian friends. He had joined his own "fraternity," meeting regularly on Wednesday nights with a small group of students for Bible study, prayer, and, what they called in their jargon, "fellowship." He surprised himself by choosing new types of friends. Heretofore, all of Scooter's friends were athletes. He held nonathletes on a level of quiet disdain as if they were slightly subhuman, failing to meet his standards of jock chauvinism. Now he was meeting regularly with boys who were music majors, some who were bona fide eggheads, and others who were clearly social misfits and outcasts, causing Scooter to wonder if they were attracted to the church because that was the only place they were acceptable. These boys had become his friends, nay, more than friends, they were comrades, brothers in a sense that Scooter thought must go beyond the brotherhood of the fraternities on campus.

These students had welcomed Scooter warmly when they heard of his conversion. Now, as he exuberantly told them of his decision to become a philosophy major, he was greeted with cold stares. Finally, one of them spoke, "Have you prayed about this?"

"No," Scooter replied, "what's to pray about?"

"Philosophy is dangerous. It's ungodly," another boy declared.

"C'mon you guys. What's the difference between studying philosophy and studying biology? Larry here is pre-med, he wants to be a medical missionary and none of you hassle him. Are you saying that you have to be a Bible major to be a Christian?"

"No," came the reply. But one of the boys opened to a passage in the New Testament and read it aloud for Scooter's benefit, "Beware of godless philosophies . . ."

Scooter retorted, "I know it says that in the Bible. But how can you *beware* of something unless you're first *aware* of it?"

Scooter was getting nervous from the mood of the interrogation. This was a new feeling. He was being attacked by his brothers and didn't know how to respond. He reached for a cigarette and lit up, trying to calm himself and assume an air of nonchalance. One of the boys began to mimic him. He took a pencil and put it between his teeth like a cigarette. He pretended to drag on it deeply and then exhaled an imaginary cloud of blue smoke saying mockingly, "Let me tell you about my experiences with the Holy Spirit."

Everyone laughed except Scooter. He slowly rose to his feet and without saying a word, left the room.

The rest of the semester marked Scooter's second conversion of that year. As he poured himself into his studies, a slow but steady metamorphosis was taking place. He was being transformed from a jock to a scholar, a change of self-identity, of the basic direction of his life. The metamorphosis did not annihilate Scooter's passion for sports any more than the body of a worm is destroyed by the emerging butterfly, but it was relegated to a lower level of importance. He finished the semester with a 3.5 making the dean's list with room to spare.

For Johnny the semester was a continuous nightmare. Not only was he forbidden to go active but intramural sports were curtailed for him as well. His social life was shot and Scooter was no fun anymore. Scooter went home every weekend which meant bumming a ride with an upper classman if Johnny wanted to get to Youngstown. Since the Art Tanzy incident he was more circumspect about his drinking escapades. A creeping paranoia was beginning to set in. He was in trouble in the classroom; he was on the dean of student's hit list; and his best friend had become a stranger to him.

He still had fraternity parties and afternoons spent in the Sub playing cards and shooting pool. At least his bank account was holding up, the ample weekly allowance his father sent him was being parlayed into a small fortune at the pool table. Johnny's specialty was 9-ball, a game where skill and cue ball control could make some fast money. The income source began to run dry, however, as the semester neared its end. Johnny's reputation as a poolshark was spreading and he was running out of suckers.

Johnny dated around, frequently borrowing Scooter's car on week nights for marathon parking sessions behind the field house. The Chi Omega's supplied a steady stream of co-eds eager for the mysteries that were lurking behind the field house.

A rumor sprang up on campus that Johnny was "pinned" to a sophomore girl named Jeanie Van Nuys from New Canaan, Connecticut. Jeanie was a petite spitfire with dark brown eyes and chestnut hair. The rumor was flamed by Johnny's boast of persuading Jeanie to accept his pledge pin according to the unwritten fraternity rules. Pledges were required to wear their inexpensive metallic pins bearing the Greek letters of their fraternity. They were mere tokens compared with the active pins that were more elaborate, usually centered with a diamond or some other precious jewel.

The rule for pledge-pinning a girl required that the pin be fastened to the inside of the girl's brassiere with the stipulation that she be wearing the bra at the moment she was pinned. This was before the decade of the sixties, before the sexual revolution and the appearance of Mario Savio on the steps of Sproul Plaza in Berkeley, a time when a girl's reputation could still be severely tarnished by such rumors.

Only three people on campus knew for sure that the rumor had no basis in fact; Johnny, Jeanie, and Scooter who saw the pin in the back of Johnny's desk drawer when he was rooting around searching for paper clips. The discovery stung Scooter. It represented one more lie he had caught Johnny in. The pattern was mushrooming in frequency, alarming Scooter by the evident troubling of Johnny's spirit that was provoking the repeated blatant falsehoods. Scooter wondered what hidden ghosts were at work in Johnny's psyche leading him not merely to the fun-and-games type of tall-tale telling but to what seemed on the surface to be the profile of an incipient psychopathic liar.

A spring day on the Witherspoon campus was not conducive to serious study. Here, in the snow-belt of northwestern Pennsylvania, spring was a late-comer, like the tardy student who slinks into his seat after the bell has rung. With promising pangs of false labor, spring had made several bogus beginnings in March with the appearances of a few avant-garde robins who were deceived by the sudden warming trend only to find their wings encrusted by a sudden snowfall of ten inches. The March snows melted as rapidly as they appeared bringing the more reliable promises of April. The towering sugar maples on campus had bulging scarlet buds, clusters of them at the tip of each branch. The forsythia had already spread their hue of golden butter to the borders of the fields of grass that linked the redstone Georgian buildings. The fragrance of hyacinths was in the air. Jeanie Van Nuys saw Johnny walking across the quadrangle toward the Sub. She smiled sweetly to Johnny and purred, "Going to buy me a Coke?"

"Sure, babe, why not?" Johnny rose to the bait like a mouse to the enticements of a cunning she-cat. The cat was not interested in killing the mouse, just in capturing it and batting it back and forth between her paws.

Johnny found a table at the Sub for her and went to the counter for Cokes. Jeanie maintained her congenial manner using coquettish charm as a facade to conceal the vindictive rage simmering inside. Johnny appeared back at the table with two large glasses shaped like the bosom of an opera singer. Tiny crystals floated like a thinly connected ice-floe on top of the world's most popular soft drink. Johnny hoisted his glass to his lips and said, "Here's to you, Jeanie." Jeanie extended her glass and clinked it lightly on Johnny's, completing the ritual, "And to you, Johnny."

Jeanie's smile was composed as she kept the conversation flowing in a pleasant tone. Casually she mentioned the pin, "Where's your pledge pin, Johnny?" The question was asked matter-of-factly as if she were genuinely puzzled by its absence.

"Oh, I guess I left it in the room, why?"

"Aren't you supposed to be wearing it at all times, in plain view?"

"Yeah, but nobody's going to get uptight if I forget it once."

"Well I heard that you got pinned, Johnny, and that some sweet co-ed was walking around with it pinned inside her bra giving her a chafed breast."

Johnny suppressed a gulp and his face blushed beet red, "No, I didn't get pinned. Where did you hear a silly thing like that?" he bluffed.

The pleasant tone vanished from Jeanie's voice. Her words now were hard and cutting.

"It's all over the campus, Jerko. I heard from three different people who told me that you said you pinned me."

"Jeanie. Honest. I didn't tell anyone that."

Jeanie just stared at Johnny in disgust, fighting the urge to hurl a glassful of Coke in his face, thinking for a moment of how he would look with the reddish-brown liquid dripping off his chin leaving eddies of fizz bubbling in a trail. She thought how the sticky syrup would feel and of the residue that would entice spring honeybees to draw nectar from his face—and then sting the creep. Instead she snatched up her purse and bolted from the Sub leaving Johnny with a smitten look on his face.

Final exam week was a time of horror for Johnny, the moment when all the bets were collected and he was coming up short. He didn't wait around for the posting of grades but cleaned out his room and headed for Briarwood with Scooter after his last exam. The following Friday the bad news was handed to Charlie Kramer by the neighborhood postman. Enclosed with the individual class slips indicating the final course grades was a letter informing Johnny that his presence on campus would not be required in the fall semester. The academic dean's form letter cordially explained that Johnny would be eligible to apply to Witherspoon for re-admission after a "sabbatical" of at least one semester. Remedial and tutorial work were advised to make the second chance more fruitful than the first.

Charlie was unruffled by the notification. She had seen Johnny's midterm grades and knew that her son was not a miracle worker. Johnny was out in the driveway waxing the Chevy when she walked outside to bear the tidings to him. Johnny saw her coming from the house, gingerly holding the letter in her fingers like it was the body of a mouse about to be disposed of in the garbage can.

He put down the cheesecloth that was oozing paste wax through its pores and greeted his mother, "What's up?"

"This is up, Johnny," she said brandishing the letter. "And you're down. The college wants you to take a little vacation, lover boy."

Johnny's eyes moved to the ground as he stood looking like a contrite Tom Sawyer in front of Aunt Polly. He muttered, "What do I do now, Mom?"

"How should I know? Do I look like a guidance counselor? You've played the tune, now you have to dance to the music. Talk to your father about it." Charlie turned on her heels signaling that the matter was between Johnny and his father. She would have nothing more to do with it.

Johnny pressed hard with the smooth cotton cloth to remove the last section of wax that by now had turned powder white. The surface powder came off effortlessly leaving a soft luster but not the real shine. That required hard buffing with a strain that soaked his armpits. He knew there was no such thing as an easy-on-easy-off wax. Not for the kind of shine that bounced the image of his face back to him as he looked at the hood.

With the waxing finished he reached for a different rag and a can of chrome polish. He applied the liquid to the bumpers, the grill, and the chrome extensions on the exhaust pipes, waiting for it to set up. The final gesture was the application of the chrome polish to the back of the outside mirror. He noted with a mild sense of alarm that the mirror was beginning to pit and that part of it had taken on a dull gray sheen, yielding to the passing years and the ravages of salt used to melt Pittsburgh's roads. At least they were just tiny pit marks like blemishes of adolescent acne, not pot holes. The final buffing of the chrome was easy and one of the most rewarding parts of the ritual. The gleaming chrome, firing echoes of light off its prismatic surface, is what made the sheen come alive.

He screwed the cap on the chrome polish bottle, pressed the lid tightly on the wax can, and replaced them in the special wooden box in the garage reserved for these utensils, sheltered like some consecrated host in a golden tabernacle. Now that the car was immaculate it was time for Johnny to perform a cleansing rite on himself. He went upstairs to take a shower.

When he finished dressing, Johnny bounded down the stairs, passed through the kitchen and gave his mother a playful peck on the cheek. "Where are you going, Romeo?"

"I'm going to Pittsburgh. Scooter's in the hospital. I'm sure he's ready for visitors."

"Tell him that if he said his prayers like a good little preacher-boy he wouldn't be in the hospital in the first place." She muttered when Johnny was already through the door, "I still can't picture Scooter with his collar on backwards."

Finding a place to park at Saint Francis Hospital required the powers of Saint Francis himself. Johnny wished for a moment that he had a printed plastic card that said CLERGY that he could post on his windshield. He found a parking place two blocks from the hospital and made the rest of the trek on foot. He felt a kind of spiritual claustrophobia creep over him as he entered the hospital. The place was surrounded by nuns in severe black and white habits with starched bonnets pressed tightly on their heads. He strained his eyes to see if he could discern the slightest whisper of hair at the point where the bonnet met the top of the brow. He heard rumors that nuns kept their heads shaved and he wondered if it were true.

He passed a group of Franciscan monks walking around like a band of Friar Tucks with brown cowls and white braided ropes around their waists. Unconsciously Johnny pressed his hand into his back pocket to feel if his wallet was still in place. He caught himself doing it, and a sly, secretive smile crept across his face. He thought of the private joke he had with his dad dating back to the first time his father took him to see the Pirates play at Forbes Field. Just as they passed through the turnstile Jack Kramer had said to son in mock urgency, "There's a priest, son. Hold on to your wallet." Johnny clutched his wallet for all he was worth, squeezing it tightly until they were well inside the ballpark. Jack roared when he noticed Johnny still grasping his wallet with both hands. "You can stop now, Johnny. It's OK. The priest is gone."

"Is the priest bad, Daddy?" the boy asked, still confused by his father's change in mood from urgency to laughter. "No, son. I was just kidding. Priests and nuns are always asking for money and I was just trying to teach you a lesson. You've got to keep your wallet closed when they come around."

Johnny went to the information desk and got Scooter's room number from a stern-looking nun. He rode the elevator to the third floor of the south wing and went to the room marked by the gilded numerals 37 on the door. He knocked lightly and heard Scooter's voice, "C'mon in."

Johnny entered and saw Scooter lying on his back with his leg elevated and a metal trapeze apparatus dangling over the bed.

Scooter grabbed the trapeze bar with both hands and pulled himself up. He slid one hand to the center of the bar to maintain his support and extended his other hand to Johnny. Johnny took Scooter's hand in both of his and squeezed it warmly.

Scooter broke the emotional silence. "Gee it's great to see you, buddy. I was hoping you would come."

"Hey, Scoot, you don't think I'd leave you here to be molested by all these women running around looking like Zorro, do you?" Johnny made a pretend moustache by placing the index finger of his left hand horizontally between his nose and upper lip and swishing an imaginary sword, singing, "Out of the night when the pale moon is bright . . . comes the sounds of the hoofbeats of Zorro." He got the song messed up but Scooter's sides were starting to hurt from laughing.

"What's that, Scooter, your own private throne?" Johnny teased, pointing to the stainless steel bedpan.

Scooter rejoined, "If Mohammed can't go to the mountain the mountain must go to Mohammed."

Turning suddenly serious Johnny said, "Today, good buddy, the 'postman cometh.' He cameth with the word from the dean. I washed out, roomie. The terrible twosome is breaking up."

The news was not a surprise to Scooter yet the full reality of the expected hit him harder than he thought it would. "Oh, no, Johnny. What'd they say? Can you come back after one semester?"

"Yeah. But that depends on what the old man says. He doesn't know yet. I'm going to talk to him tonight and it's going to hit the fan."

Scooter was enveloped by a wave of guilt as he thought of ways he could have been more helpful to Johnny with his course work. His self-recriminations were interrupted by Johnny's continuing report.

"I don't know what Dad wants me to do now. I'm sure he'll have some plan cooked up; he always does. This stuff of following in your father's footsteps is a crock." Johnny had recently become deferential to Scooter's religious bent by deleting the expletives from his conversation. Though they were omitted directly, somehow they were always there, hanging in hints like some scatological dangling participles.

"When are you getting out of here?" Johnny turned the attention to Scooter.

"They're getting me out of bed tomorrow to start moving with crutches. I'll be able to get rid of this throne and the worst part of all—the blasted catheter. Then, if things go well, I can go home in three or four days."

"Why do you have to have a catheter?"

"They put it in the day they cut my knee. With the effects of the anesthesia and lying flat on my back nothing was happening in the plumbing department. You know the law, pal. Water runs downhill. I don't get much gravity flow on my back."

"Geez, Scoot, what a pain in the—."

"Groin." Scooter finished it for him.

"Yeah, groin. That's exactly what I was thinking."

Just then a nurse walked in with a thermometer and a chart and whisked past Johnny like he was a mannequin.

"That's my cue, Scoot. I'll be talking to you in the next couple of days. You get better now and we'll have some fun this summer."

"Thanks, Johnny." Scooter's eyes were filling as the post-surgery feeling brought his emotions very close to the surface.

As Scooter heard Johnny's footfall fade down the hall, an awful feeling of loss gripped his chest. They had drifted apart a bit this past year, yet there was some cohesive force that bound them soul to soul, and Scooter could not bear to think of that being ruptured altogether. It was natural for Johnny to show up here at the hospital. They always stuck together in the tight spots. Now the decree of the academic system, like some blind Olympian thunder god had forced them onto separate paths, at least for the immediate future.

TEN

The summer of 1958 was as far distant from the turbulent decade of the sixties as one could imagine. Storm clouds were gathering on the horizon but were almost unnoticed. A black preacher was getting local press notices in Atlanta for stirring his people to acts of non-violent resistance over issues of civil rights, and Nikita Khrushchev was rattling the Russian saber for the world to hear. A bearded, baseball-playing guerrilla dressed in combat fatigues was wreaking havoc for Cuba's Batista, and the tempo of modern music was beating faster than even Bill Haley anticipated. Yet all was well with the world. Ike was in the middle of his second term and the country was enjoying the *pax Americana,* a brief interlude of peace between the cessation of the United Nation's police action in Korea and the escalation of American involvement in Viet Nam.

There was turbulence in the Kramer household. The U.S. was at peace but Jack Kramer was at war, furious at his son for flunking out of school.

"What were you doing up there, partying all the time? You spent a year wasting time and a considerable sum of money. Do you think money grows on trees? Do you think I have a money press in the basement? When are you going to grow up?"

The questions came at Johnny like staccato bursts from a machine gun—there was no time to answer them. They were, after all, rhetorical and didn't require answers; Jack Kramer already had the answers to them in his own mind.

"Well, boy, you've made your bed, now you have to sleep in it. What does this mean for your draft deferment? Are you prepared to spend two years dragging your butt through some swamp in Mississippi with a rifle slung over your shoulder for the glory of Uncle Sam? You want to go back to the can company and punch out beer cans on an assembly line for the rest of your life?''

Johnny tried to speak. He had to speak before his father's attack reduced him to ashes.

"Dad, I want to go back to school. I guess I wasn't ready this time around, but maybe if I change my major I can make it the next time. About the draft. They have a new deal. I can sign up right now for a tour of six months active duty and then I'm out, except for two weeks every summer in summer camp and some reserve meetings. If I did that I could go back to school as soon as I finished my six months. I talked to the Army recruiter and if I sign up right away I can be out in time for the spring semester. I hear the school likes that, too, 'cause the guys come out more serious about their education.''

Jack warmed to the idea. Just having a short-range workable game plan in front of him did a lot to soothe his anger, an anger that was merely a ventilation for his frustration at his son's failure. Failure was a word Jack Kramer despised and in a twisted way he read his son's failure as his own, a gruesome blight on his personal track record.

Johnny drove to Pittsburgh the next day and worked out the arrangements with the Army recruiter. He would leave for boot camp the following week. After signing the forms he drove out Bigelow Boulevard and swung over the Bloomfield Bridge and went on a search mission for a parking space near Saint Francis Hospital.

When he went to the nurses station on the south wing's third floor he was informed that Scooter was downstairs in physical therapy exercising his leg and getting crutches. The nurse was cheerful and told Johnny that if he would like to wait, Scooter would be back in his room in a few minutes. Johnny picked up a magazine and savored a leisurely cigarette.

He saw an orderly pushing Scooter down the hall in a wheelchair. Two crutches were standing upright at the back of the carriage like goal posts for midgets. Johnny moved toward the door and reached Scooter just as the orderly was making the turn into his room. Scooter managed a weak smile in recognition but Johnny could not stifle a startled look as he gazed at Scooter. His face was chalk-white, ashen, like a pallid mask of death. His hospital gown was drenched with perspiration and he was sure the simple matter of transferring Scooter from the wheelchair to the bed would push him over the precipice into unconsciousness. Scooter groaned as his leg made contact with the bed and he let his back flop down on the mattress, his eyes hovering between wakefulness and semi-sleep. He instinctively reached his hand out for Johnny to hold.

"It was a killer," Scooter gasped, breathing heavily. "Whew, Johnny, it was a beast."

The heavy breathing slowly diminished and Scooter settled into a more relaxed state.

"What happened, Scoot? What'd they do to you?"

"Had to get up . . . try walk with the parallel bars . . . forced knee lifts . . . steps on crutches . . . It was a bear, Johnny . . . I wanted to cry . . . like a thousand razor blades slicing my knee joint . . ." Scooter's breath was coming in gasps.

"Holy . . . on a stick, Scoot, what kind of creeps are they?"

"Had to . . . , Johnny. Can't let the joint freeze . . . got to avoid atrophy . . . it's better this way."

Johnny unashamedly held Scooter's hand and let him drift off to sleep. He sat there in a vigil of loyalty for almost an hour until Scooter stirred into consciousness again. When he opened his eyes his face was once more full of color and he looked like a new person. This time there was strength in his voice.

"Did I doze off, Johnny?"

"Yeah, you sent up a few *Z*s. Feeling better now?"

"Yeah. Wow, man, that was a bull." (Scooter was running short of animals whose names began with a *B* in his menagerie of metaphors for his ordeal in physical therapy.)

"You looked white as a sheet when they wheeled you in here."

"I know." Scooter agreed. "I was afraid I was going to spill my cookies. It was a regular bitch." (Scooter found another *B*, borrowed from the jargon of the canine world.)

"What happened last night? What did your dad say?"

"He said I should go to camp this summer and get my head together."

"You're kidding! That's what I'm doing this summer too."

"Whaddya mean—you can't go to camp, Scooter—you can't even walk yet. What is it, a CCC Camp, Camp for Convalescing Cripples?"

"You nut. No. Scotty McTavish got me a job working as a counselor at a Jewish boy's camp in Ohio. I start July first and it runs till the end of August. He put me down to run the craft shop. I'll be able to manage on crutches."

"Aha. So you will be a crafty cripple? A counselor on crutches? Summer camp's answer to Tiny Tim." (At least Johnny's alliteration had moved from *C*s to *T*s giving Scooter's ears a sonorous break.)

"What camp are you going to, Johnny?" Scooter asked.

"Boot camp. I'm going to be a 180-day wonder, six months of service to my country; six months of unswerving dedication to mother love, apple pie and, you guessed it, Chev-ro-let. I've signed up for the quickie six-month deal of active service and the reserves forever. I'll be back at school for the spring term. Save me a bed, roomie."

"That's fantastic Johnny. That's a great idea. I will, I promise."

Johnny glanced at his watch and stood up. "I gotta shove, partner. Hang tough now."

"I will, Johnny, and—Johnny, please write. OK? I want to hear all about boot camp."

"Sure will, Scoot, I'll give you a full report. Just think of all those chicks who go bonkers over a guy in uniform. No dogs. No woofies. Just the kind that stand there with their long black hair blowing in the breeze, and they're too lazy to chase after it."

Scooter laughed as Johnny left the room. He began humming to himself, "When Johnny comes marching home again, hoorah, hoorah . . ."

Scotty McTavish pulled up in front of Scooter's apartment on the morning of July 1, and beeped the horn. Scooter was already on the first-floor landing was his suitcase and dufflebag ready to go. Mr. McTavish was double-parked and had his trunk open. He left the engine running and came over to help Scooter with his gear.

"Like old times, eh, coach? Remember when you used to come around at 6:00 A.M. and pick us up in the 'Green Hornet' and later the 'Gray Ghost' to shoot foul shots?"

"We did all right, didn't we, Scooter?" Scotty replied.

Thomas McTavish was the ninth-grade history teacher and basketball coach at Briarwood Junior High. All the kids at school called him Scotty behind his back but the basketball players were allowed to use the term of endearment to his face, enjoying the exemptions of the varsity elite. No one else dared violate the sacrosanct mandate of protocol that required the formal address, "Mr." McTavish, with the accent on the mister. No one was permitted to answer his questions with a slovenly "Yeah"—it was "Yes, sir" or his piercing black eyes would melt a hole through the culprit's head. The "sir" part was as mandatory as the formal "yes" or "no."

Scotty was in his mid-thirties and on this unseasonably cool first day of July he was wearing a varsity baseball jacket from Kitanning High School, a trophy Scooter figured must have been won sometime during the war in a baseball conference that included teams from Titusville, Oil City, and Punxsutawney.

Scotty joined the navy out of high school, seeing action in the South Pacific on a destroyer in the final months before Hiroshima and Nagasaki. He went to college on the G.I. Bill and his first teaching assignment was in the Briarwood school system.

When Scooter was ten years old his cousin Bob came to live with the Evans family while he completed his education at the University of Pittsburgh Medical School. Bob Evans, after getting his M.D., was called into the service in Korea where he was severely wounded during a helicopter rescue mission at Inchon, his back and legs shredded by the exploding fragments of a mortar shell. Before he shipped out he broke his engagement with a voluptuous Briarwood girl named Alice Forrester. Alice had always been fond of "little Scooter Evans" and frequently stopped him on the street, in the weeks following Bob's departure, pumping him for information about his cousin.

By a strange twist of fate, Alice met and married the new teacher in town, Scotty McTavish. Scooter's cousin had been his childhood hero, and when Alice married Scotty, Scotty became a more than adequate replacement. Scooter's prior acquaintance with Alice gave him an "in" with Scotty that none of the rest of the guys enjoyed.

In the intervening years Scotty graduated to a heavier heroic role in Scooter's life, being in succession his teacher, his coach, his adult confidant, and finally, in the years of the senior Evans's lingering illness, his substitute father. Everything about Scotty was angular, from his personality to his physical appearance. His face was angular with high granite cheekbones, sharp chin, and eyes deeply recessed in bony sockets. His Adam's apple jutted out of his throat at an acute angle. His hair was red, not the carrot color associated with the Campbell Soup boy, but the more mature type, splashed with a sandy tint. When he was angry his hair borrowed a hue radiating from his face making it appear as if flames were bursting from the crown of his head. When his temper flared, he became a fiery Scot erupting in paroxysms of fury. He was, in a word, mercurial, with the warmth of his kindness as passionate as the heat of his anger.

Few coaches could persuade their players to rise from their beds at 5:00 A.M. to arrive at school while it was still dark outside to turn on the lights in the gymnasium and shoot foul shots for an hour and a half every morning. The boys felt privileged to do it for Scotty. The starting five were driven personally to school each morning by *the man*. To them he was Claire Bee, Bobby Knight, Red Auerbach, and Bear Bryant all rolled into one.

He taught them the old fashioned way of foul-shooting, the "sissy style" of using both hands on the ball swinging it up underhand toward the basket. The shot followed a regimented procedure of a mechanical two bounces, the placing of the feet perpendicular to the foul line, eyeing the front of the rim, taking a deep breath, bending the knees with back held straight and executing the shot while exhaling, with both hands following through and finishing high. This choreographed method produced two-hand control and, most importantly, a soft shot, the kind that forgives a slightly errant throw and lazily hangs on the rim before dropping through. It was repeatable and able to withstand the pressure of the loneliness of the foul line in a close game when adrenaline sought to coerce the body into overshooting. Scotty told the boys about once witnessing a seventy-year-old man, seated in a wooden folding chair at a foul line, sink a hundred foul shots in a row using this method. It worked. Briarwood had a championship season with several games decided by the slender margin of advantage won at the foul line.

That year was one of the happiest of Scooter's life. Basketball and Scotty McTavish were at the center of it. Scooter was elected president of the student body, captain of the basketball team, made almost straight *A*'s and was madly in love with Patricia Gregg. It was the most miserable year of Scotty McTavish's life.

Midway through basketball season, during one of Mr. Mc-

Tavish's free periods, Scooter was summoned to the principal's office and given a note instructing him to go the coach's office. A strange summons. Scotty was never there except before and after gym classes and for basketball practice. Curiosity quickened his pace as he hurried to the blond swinging doors that led into the new olympic-sized gymnasium with its bright tiled walls and glass backboards suspended by supports hanging from the cavernous ceiling. His feet felt funny as he walked the length of the hardwood court in his street shoes. Scooter was feeling a twinge of guilt, like a pedestrian crossing the street against the light. The lights in the locker room were off and Scooter could see a single light burning through the glass partition framing the coach's office. There were no windows in the locker room so that, even though outside the sun was high in the sky, there was a foreboding darkness in the room. The quietness of it was eerie. The sound of basketballs thumping against the floor and the jocular banter of nervous boys before the start of a game were absent.

Scotty McTavish was slumped forward with his head in his hands and obviously did not hear Scooter approaching. Scooter tapped on the door and McTavish slowly raised his head and motioned for him to enter. In the light Scooter could see that Scotty's cheeks were streaked and his eyes were puffy and bloodshot.

"What's the matter, coach?" Scooter asked nervously.

"Scooter. I'm sorry for you to have to see me like this." McTavish's lips were trembling and he struggled to hold back sobs that threatened to burst out of control.

"I can't make practice tonight. I want you to take charge. You know all the drills. Tell the boys I'm sick or something. I just can't make it."

"What's wrong, Scotty?" The familiar form of address sprung out of Scooter's mouth.

McTavish made a valiant effort to pull himself together. Drawing in a deep breath he tried to affect a quick recovery and mask his dissolving spirit.

"Nothing serious, Scooter. Really I just got upset about something I heard today and I guess I got carried away. You know I get a bit emotional at times."

Scotty feigned a smile but it was too late. A line had been crossed between a man and a boy; a line that is never to be crossed but undeniably and irretrievably was crossed. Scooter would not buy the recovery act.

"Don't tell me that, coach. What did you hear today?"

McTavish knew that it was futile to try to con Scooter at this point.

A sallow look clouded Scotty's face, a greenish yellow hue cast by the single bulb illumining the room. The words spilled out of his mouth in gushes.

"It's Alice . . . our baby . . ." His chest drew in a convulsive gasp that was released with a racking sob.

"She gone. She took off with her lover—and the baby." The last words were shrieked in maniacal tones.

Scotty let his head fall into his hands, surrendering to the full force of his agony. He sobbed and sobbed as Scooter sat feeling helpless. Scotty fought again for control but his words were interrupted by involuntary spasms of gasps, the kind of choking breaths children make after they cry. "Please, Scooter. Promise me you'll tell no one about this." The entreaty was forced out of McTavish's mouth between spasms.

Scooter touched his coach lightly on the shoulder as if it were a fragile piece of china. "Don't worry, Scotty. I'll never breathe it to a soul."

Scooter pulled off the charade at after-school practice. No one challenged his announcement that Scotty was sick and that he was in charge. Scooter himself practiced as one obsessed, pouring out his feelings in wild drives for the basket and fierce grappling for rebounds.

It was about a month later that the rumor broke loose and swept through the school. The McTavishes were getting a divorce. The students were stunned by the news. Scotty and Alice often chaperoned dances and when they moved onto the floor the students quit dancing and formed a circle around them just to watch. Scotty moved with the grace of a cat leading his alluring wife across the floor. It was Ginger Rogers and Fred Astaire, Gene Kelly and Cyd Charisse. They were the supreme model of marital bliss. Hearing the news of divorce was like seeing a bespectacled antiquarian interviewed on the evening news announcing that he had uncovered a dust-covered, unknown fragment of Shakespeare's work, revealing that Romeo and Juliet had really ended in divorce.

Scooter listened intently to the scuttlebutt but heard no mention of infidelity. The accepted story was simply that "it didn't work out." Scotty never mentioned it again to Scooter but the quiet understanding deepened the bond between them. They became co-conspirators in a pact of silence.

The students' shock passed in a short time, yielding to the incurable fickleness of youth. By the end of the school year new rumors buzzed through the school that Mr. McTavish had started dating the girls' gym instructor. The rumor was confirmed when McTavish and Miss Edwards were married near the end of the summer. A more unlikely union could not be imagined. Helen Edwards was the polar opposite of Alice, more fitting the image of the prototype librarian than that of a girls' gym teacher. She was matronly in appearance, her hair pulled back in a severe bun topping off a dress style that was perpetually gray. She was older than Scotty and it had been a foregone conclusion among the students that she was firmly fixed on the pathway to spinsterhood. A practicing psychologist would have viewed Scotty's hasty remarriage with a jaundiced eye, it was for better or for worse, sickness and in health . . . for as long as they both shall live. They were married, privately and quietly with no prior formal announcement.

Now, half a decade later, Scooter was riding with Scotty McTavish to Ohio, wondering why the second Mrs. McTavish was not with them in the car.

"Well, Scooter. Tell me all about your first year in college."

Scooter was grateful for the invitation as he was bursting to tell McTavish about his life-changing conversion. He poured out the story with unbridled enthusiasm. He held back nothing. He felt safe with Scotty, able to express the full measure of his feelings. He was the one adult Scooter was sure he could tell anything without fear of rejection of recrimination.

Scotty's reaction was remote. Not hostile, not warm, just perplexing blankness. His distant mein made Scooter uncomfortable.

"Do you believe in Christ, coach?" Scooter pressed for a reaction.

"Yes, Scooter. I go to church but I'm not really what you would call religious. You should be talking to Helen. She really takes it seriously, too damn seriously by half, if you ask me. It has become a sore spot with us. She's forever going to prayer meetings and quoting Bible verses at me. She voices constant disapproval of everything I do. Just don't get pushy, Scooter, I get enough of that at home."

Scotty dropped hints, big hints that things were not going well in the second marriage, a marriage that had already borne the fruit of three children. McTavish also made it clear that religion had become a divisive point in the marriage, making its strongest impact in the bed chamber. It was apparent that Helen McTavish unleashed a strident moralistic spirit, a critical and negative attitude that was chafing the nerves of her husband. It was a conflict between two traditions, one from the soil of pietism and the other from the heather covered ground of Scottish Presbyterianism. It was like a Southern Baptist fundamentalist living in the same house and sharing the bed with the son of a Boston Unitarian.

The conversation ended in an awkward truce. McTavish looked at Scooter in a funny way, as if he were seeing someone else. They turned off the highway and drove along a red-dog road winding through woods for a few miles until they moved into a clearing. A man-made lake was visible as they entered the grounds of Camp Neacondi. The lake formed a basin surrounded by forest rising steeply in the background. It was serene, a seraphic sense of peace was in the air. Scooter could almost see a solitary Indian leisurely paddling a canoe across the water in this unspoiled secluded spot. Scotty helped Scooter check his gear and get settled in the rustic cabin that would be his domain for eight weeks and a day. The cabin bore the number 2 tacked under the peak of the sharply rising roof. There were nine cabins in all, numbered from zero to eight, that on the morrow would spring to life with the animated activity of twelve boys per cabin.

ELEVEN

The campers arrived the next day appearing in cars with license plates from all over the nation, most of them bearing the markings of Cleveland and New York. Eleven of the twelve campers in Scooter's cabin arrived in Cadillacs. The other came in a chauffeur-driven Rolls-Royce. The camp reeked of *nouveau riche* exclusivity. Scooter was dumbfounded by the sophisticated and expensive gear the kids had with them. Their idea of roughing it for the summer was living in a penthouse suite in the Waldorf-Astoria. Nine- and ten-year-olds carried fishing equipment from Abercrombie and Fitch. Their outfits made it seem as if the L. L. Bean catalogue had come to life. Many of the parents spoke loudly about their own summer plans for the Catskills or Nice or Cannes. Scooter was jarred by the leave-taking ceremonies. No tearful hugs, no good-bye kisses. Merely an outstretched arm and a handshake terminating with, "Be a good boy, Benji." More than one father pressed a $10 bill into Scooter's palm whispering, "Take good care of my son, now, you hear?" making him feel more like a bellhop in an affluent hotel than a counselor in a boys' camp.

Scooter's group looked like a small army of midget soldiers committed to an armed revolution, determined to establish the first state in history of pure anarchy. Their obvious leader was the son of a famous Hollywood film producer who listed the Gary Cooper triumph *High Noon* among his credits. Scooter wondered if his eight-week encounter with this overindulged crew would end in a twelve o'clock showdown with them.

Crucial to the *esprit de camp* was the creation of an ongoing sense of competition among cabins and larger units. The whole camp, including counselors and cooks, even the family members of the owner, was divided between two great Indian tribes, the

Chickasaws and the Choctaws, shortened to "Chics" and
"Chocs." For eight weeks a scoreboard was kept monitoring every
conceivable kind of competition between tribes involving softball
games, boat races, craft-shop awards, archery, riflery—
everything down to the dishwasher who finished his daily chores
the fastest. If a Chic camper caught a fish during his free time,
points were awarded to his tribe for the feat. The competition
ended on the final Saturday of camp with an all-day Olympiad
culminating with a capture-the-flag game to end all capture-the-
flag games.

The daily competition centered on the morning inspection
contest. A half hour after breakfast was allotted for bed-making,
cabin cleanup and straightening. The nine cabins were divided
into threes, according to age groups. Each cabin had to stand
inspection and a banner was awarded to the winner of each
group. This was presented to the kids at lunch time by the chief
inspector, Scotty McTavish. Bragging rights for the day were
symbolized by the banner proudly displayed, hanging from a
hook on the door of the cabin. The competition was fierce, but
again, over the course of the summer, the daily victories tended to
be balanced out. All except for cabin 2.

The first week passed with the banner awarded four times to
cabin 0 and three times to cabin 1. The boys in cabin 2 were
agitated. On the night of the seventh day they held a council of
war. They were united in defeat, tired of losing and determined to
turn the tide.

"All right, guys, here's the plan," Scooter spoke as the boys
huddled around.

"No fun and games tonight. We're going to make this place
gleam like the Oval Office at the White House. Every shelf is
going to be unpacked, dusted, and repacked. Every bed is going
to be moved into the center aisle and we are going to eliminate
every cobweb in every nook and cranny of this room. When we're
finished you will be able to eat off the floor. Every pane of glass on
every window will sparkle without a streak. Then, tomorrow
morning we'll get up an hour before reveille and make the beds
over and over until there is not a wrinkle on any of them. tomorrow, the banner is ours."

They screamed their approval and went to work like Snow
White and the Seven Dwarfs. Counselors and campers walking

down the line thought the kids in cabin 2 had gone crazy. They were singing and laughing while they attacked the room with brooms, dust rags, and aerosol cans of Windex. In the morning, while the sun was casting a shadow of red on the eastern horizon, the boys were already out of bed putting Army folds on their sheets and blankets. When the breakfast bell rang, Scooter made an inspection, examining each bed for wrinkles or dust balls on the floor underneath. At the breakfast table the boys ate with enthusiasm, smug looks of satisfaction on their faces. Today was their day. There was no way they could lose.

In the half hour allotted after breakfast Scooter checked and rechecked the room. Finally Mr. McTavish appeared in the door holding a clipboard in his hand. He walked slowly through the cabin glancing at shelves and under beds and at the windows. He said nothing. Scooter followed him out the door and when they were out of earshot of the boys Scooter asked, "What do you think, coach?"

Scotty turned, and with eyes flashing, snarled at Scooter, "The place looks like a pigpen."

An equally fierce lightning blazed in Scooter's eyes and between clenched teeth, while leaning heavily on his crutches, he snapped back,

"OK, Scotty, if that's the way you want it." He pivoted on the crutches and headed back to the cabin. At noon the banner was awarded to cabin 1. The boys tramped back to their cabin in a daze. When they got inside two of them burst into tears.

"What happened, Scooter? What did we do wrong? What did he find?"

"Nothing." Scooter answered soberly. "I don't know what's wrong guys, but I know it isn't your fault. It's me. For some reason, Mr. McTavish is hot at me and you guys are getting the dirty end of the stick."

That night sleep eluded Scooter as he tossed fitfully on his bunk. He was feeling worse than if he had just been jilted by a fiance. *Why, God?* he thought. *Don't take Scotty away from me. Please. I need him.* Scooter was too old to cry, but he did it anyway, staining his pillow with silent tears. He felt utterly alone, forsaken and rejected by the dearest man in his life.

The next morning the boys went through cleanup like zombies, their spirit quenched for the competition. As a fiendish sort of insult, cabin 2 got the banner that day which only infuriated them.

Scotty avoided Scooter all summer, leaving him to guess the reason for the cold shoulder. Scooter was the darling of the owner of the camp and she invited him to "preach" the weekly Friday evening vesper services. Scooter regaled the boys with adventure stories from the Old Testament. They especially liked the gory battle stories of the book of Judges: stories of the feats of Samson slaying a thousand Philistines armed only with the jawbone of an ass; of Jael killing Sisera by driving a tent peg through his head, nailing him to the floor; and of the left-handed Ehud plunging his knife into the stomach of the obese King Eglon until his hand was engulfed in folds and layers of fat. Occasionally Scooter quoted Jesus referring to Him indirectly using the circumlocution, "A famous man once said . . ." Mr. McTavish, the director of the camp, was noticeably absent from vespers, leaving Scooter with a nagging ache in his chest.

Saturday was Scooter's day off. He got a ride to Pittsburgh every Saturday for the first month. Still hampered by crutches he spent his evenings lounging around at the soda fountain at the Briarwood drugstore, exchanging notes with other lads home for the summer from college.

The second Saturday night home he was approached by George Larkin, an awkward behemoth of a boy who was unpopular among his peers. He appeared in the drugstore carrying a plastic black and pink Motorola portable radio, snapping his fingers to himself trying a bit too hard to look cool. His dark hair was slicked back with more than a dab of Brylcreem and he combed it incessantly as a nervous gesture, drawing a long black plastic comb from his hip pocket. George was having problems with his girl friend and poured out his troubles to Scooter. He showed up again for a repeat performance the next Saturday night and the one after that.

During the first week of August, another counselor, having an important family event scheduled on Saturday, arranged to trade his day off with Scooter. Scooter had finally been able to quit his crutches and resume driving. He left the camp at 6:00 A.M. on Sunday morning taking advantage of the two-hour grace rule that permitted counselors to depart at six in the morning of their off day while being required to be back on duty the following morning at eight.

It was a two-hour drive to Pittsburgh. Scooter broke the journey in half by stopping at a roadside restaurant for breakfast at 7:00 A.M. He pulled in the gravel lot and stopped to buy a paper at the coin operated stand outside the door. He folded the paper, the *Pittsburgh Post Gazette* early edition, and carried it under his arm into the diner. While waiting for his order to be filled he spread the paper open on the table in front of him. His eyes skimmed the headlines and the feature stories on the front page. He suddenly froze. At the bottom right hand corner of the page was a brief notice: BRIARWOOD YOUTH TAKES OWN LIFE. Scooter read the terse report in disbelief. It announced that George Larkin, despondent over breaking up with his girl friend, had taken his own life by shooting himself with a light caliber rifle.

Scooter could barely eat his breakfast. His stomach recoiled at the ingestion of food. This simply couldn't be . . . it was Scooter's first exposure to teenage suicide, a matter too macabre to fathom.

The Briarwood drugstore was open on Sunday afternoon, immune to Pennsylvania's Sunday blue laws. Scooter went there after church and sat down on a red leather swivel stool at the counter.

"Scooter. Did you hear about George Larkin?" The voice belonged to Jamey Marsh who was working behind the counter of the soda fountain.

"Yeah. I read it in the paper this morning on the way in from Ohio."

"I thought Saturday was your day off. Where were you last night?"

"I switched my day off with another guy. Did George come in here last night?" Scooter asked hoping for a negative response.

"He sure did, and he was looking for you. He was being real loud and arguing with some guys. He kept asking if you were coming in. He told the guys that his girl friend broke up with him. He was really down. The guys laughed at him about being shot out of the saddle. About 10:00 he said, very calmly, 'Well, I think I'll go home and shoot myself.' And, Scooter"—her voice began to crack and she started to cry, "that's just what he did. I can't believe it."

Scooter found out later that George went home, loaded a .22 caliber rifle, put it in his mouth, and pulled the trigger. He was found about 11:00 by his parents when they came home from a movie.

Scooter played the scenario over and over again in his mind, alternately blaming himself and the cruel twist of fate for not being there the night before. The trouble was that he didn't believe in fate anymore, yet he could not conceive of a loving God allowing this to happen. He knew such tragedies were reported in newspapers every day, and that suicide was a leading cause of death in teenage fatalities but this one was different. He knew the boy.

That evening the community church had a special meeting scheduled for college students home for the summer. It was great to see his friends again, many of whom he had not seen since graduation day at Millport. Mingling with them made it possible to get his mind off the death of George Larkin. He was not prepared for the second shock of the day presented to him by Carole Keener, home for the summer from Ohio Wesleyan.

"Hi, Scooter. Did you hear the news about what happened today?"

"Yes, I read it in the paper."

"What paper? They wouldn't have it in the paper would they?" Carole asked.

"You're talking about George Larkin aren't you, Carole?"

"Oh, no, Scooter. I'm sorry. I was talking about Patricia."

Scooter's face tightened. "What about Patricia, what happened to her?" His teeth were grinding, and his jaw was locked in suspense.

"Nothing *happened* to her, silly. She was married this afternoon in Pompano Beach."

The pain registered visibly on Scooter's face. Carole picked up on it instantly.

"What's the matter, Scooter? You're not still carrying a torch for her, are you?"

"Well, I'm not exactly the Statue of Liberty but it does come as a surprise to me. She just finished her freshman year of college. Who'd she marry?"

"Are you ready for this? It seems your friend and mine, Patricia Ann Gregg, has up and married Robert McClellan Lindsey IV. She's joined the ranks of the Gold Coast's roman numeraled set. It seems that Mr. Lindsey the fourth is the only child and principal heir of the real estate baron, the condominium captain, the magnate of Miami, Robert M. Lindsey III, whose net worth is estimated by *Forbes* magazine as being in the very exclusive neighborhood of eighty-seven million dollars."

Scooter let out a soft whistle and muttered, "Sugar daddy."

"What's that, Scooter? What did you say?" Carole probed.

"Nothing. Just a private thought . . . It must have been some wedding."

"Like royalty, I heard," Carole added.

Scooter's alarm clock sent its impertinent shrill into his room at 5:15 A.M. He stumbled out of bed making for the bathroom. At that hour his eyes were more thirsty than his mouth. He turned the cold water faucet on almost full to provide an ample source of liquid to splash on his face. He quickly washed the sleepers out of the corners of his eyes and forced his body to wakefulness. Rising before seven left him with a burning sensation in his eyes and a nagging headache. The next item that required attention was his stomach. A hollow feeling brought to the point of irritation by the assault on his stomach lining by too many cigarettes the night before would not be quieted without food. There would be no time to stop for breakfast on the road so he popped a single slice of bread in the toaster and poured himself a glass of iced tea. The cold tea felt soothing on his throat, silencing the nagging of the dry tissues in his mouth. One piece of toast with butter and jelly was enough to get him ready for the return drive to Ohio.

Scooter moved quietly, tiptoeing past his mother's door. He glanced at the clock and saw that it had moved to 5:45 and obviously had no intentions of slowing down. He had his headlights on and his car moving toward the highway by 5:50. The extra ten minutes came in handy as the return to Ohio was slowed this morning by stubborn patches of low-hanging fog.

The rest of the camp season passed with the daily routine of chores accorded to each counselor. Scotty remained aloof. Scooter thought several times of going to him and getting the matter out on the table but thought better of it, knowing that Mr. McTavish had an extra measure of the stubborn genes allegedly distributed to clan members of Scotland. He knew such a gesture would not only be futile but would only serve to increase Scotty's nameless hostility.

The middle of August brought a letter from Johnny in the morning mail call. Scooter brightened when he saw Johnny's name scrawled on the upper left hand corner of the envelope. He opened the letter and read each line carefully to himself:

Dear Scoot,

I thought it was time I kept my promise and let you know how things are going here. I have been pleasantly surprised by the whole experience. I guess I had seen too many movies about drill sergeants kicking the bejabbers out of us raw recruits. It seems like my platoon sergeant has actually taken a likening to me and has put me in several leadership roles. I don't care much for the rack time we get as they roust our butts out of bed while the roosters are still sleeping. I kind of enjoy the march drills as they bring back memories of some of McTavish's games of "Simon Says."

You should see some of the guys in my outfit. They are so out of shape it's a crime. For those poor slobs this camp is a killer. They make me look good by comparison. Dear old Jack went on a fishing expedition in Washington and it seems that he caught himself a junior congressman who slipped the hook by setting up a deal for me to go to OCS. I'll go straight there after this is finished which will get me a commission in the reserves. Save a place for me at Witherspoon cause ole Johnny is going to come marching home again.

Send up a prayer for me. I'll probably need some influence in circles higher than Washington.

Your milk-stool buddy,
Johnny

Scooter saved Johnny's letter, stashing it carefully with his private gear in the shelf over his bed. The letter quieted his fears that Johnny would have a rough time at boot camp. Johnny's attitudes sounded good and his eternal optimism was intact.

During the final week of camp Scooter was awakened in the middle of the night by an attack of nausea that came on so swiftly he barely made it to the bathroom. His head was swimming, spinning toward a faint. He emptied his stomach by harsh retching, feeling a dampness about his chest. His vision blurred, made shadowy by bobbing specks of light that danced like paramecia under a microscope. A dull pain centered in his head and radiated into his limbs. He splashed water on his face and pressed a towel to it trying to clear his senses. He stripped off his pajama bottoms, pulled on his pants and left the cabin.

He walked down the cabin line, the towel draped over his head and his pajamas clutched under his arm, weaving along the path to the white frame building that served as Camp Neacondi's infirmary. He pushed the night buzzer and waited for the shifting of footsteps inside. The camp nurse appeared at the door in a terry cloth bathrobe with the silk lace of her nighty peeking out at the bottom. She led him to a side room, turned down the covers of an army cot and left while he changed back into his pajamas. When she returned she was all business, sticking a glass thermometer into his mouth and wrapping a gray cloth pad around his arm. She squeezed the black ball attached to the pad and recorded his blood pressure.

The nausea passed but the dizziness remained and Scooter was attacked alternately by chills and hot flashes that left him soaked with perspiration. He slept most of the day, being barely coherent in his moments of wakefulness. The second day showed no improvement and Scooter was visited by a doctor summoned from the nearby town.

The doctor stood at the foot of the bed asking him questions. Scooter was alarmed by the fact that, though he could hear the doctor clearly, in the swimming daze of his brain he could barely see the man standing no more than six feet away. His features were blurred, encompassed in a swirling fog. The doctor's prognosis was an educated guess, that Scooter was having a severe allergic reaction to something unidentified. He prescribed some medicine and ordered further rest in the infirmary coupled with close observation.

Two more days passed and camp was rapidly drawing to a close. Everyone's mind was on the coming Olympic games and the grand finale of the capture-the-flag war. Scooter was sleeping less and the chills had disappeared but the dizziness and lethargy hung to him. He received an afternoon visit in the person of Mr. McTavish. When Scooter saw McTavish enter the room he entertained hope that his illness had melted the fiery Scot's heart and that he had come to the infirmary to patch things up. The hope was short-lived.

"How are you feeling today, Scooter?" The tone was civil but not warm.

"I'm feeling much better, coach, just weak and kind of wiped out."

"Do you think you are able to drive?" Scotty asked.

"I suppose I could. What do you have in mind?"

"I've been thinking about it, and with the pressure of the Olympics coming, I don't think you'll be up to that. You'd probably be in the way and you should be convalescing at home. I told your junior counselor to pack your things and they are all in your car. If you can drive I think you should head on out today."

Scooter felt like Scotty kicked him in the stomach with a lead boot. He was stunned by the cold dismissal and was hardly aware of Scotty handing him his paycheck. McTavish turned on his heels and without saying good-bye, left the room. The infirmary nurse had witnessed the exchange and felt waves of compassion for Scooter. She spoke with a contrasting tenderness trying to undo the obvious devastation Scooter was feeling.

"He's right, Scooter. You need to be home. He really is trying to care for you in his own way." The nurse went to the closest and retrieved Scooter's clothes, laying them out on the chair beside the bed.

Scooter dressed quickly and went to his car, thanking the nurse but not searching out anyone else for good-byes. He wanted to sneak out of camp, concealing his total humiliation. He drove out of the gate with a bitter taste of bile in his mouth. *I was just fired,* he thought. *That's what it was, pure and simple, I was fired. Scotty fired me.* The man who would never reject Scooter had just written him off. Scooter felt like an orphan. He did not see Scotty McTavish again for over twenty years, two decades of exile, two decades of feeling the anguish of his rejection.

TWELVE

It was 1965. Seven years had passed since Scotty McTavish banished Scooter from the gates of Camp Neacondi. Like Ishmael, Scooter was a castaway, dismissed to an emotional desert on the wrong side of the Jordan. The *Pax Americana* had ended, not abruptly but gradually, with an undeclared war that accelerated so slowly that its shift in gears was almost imperceptible, being carried forward like an old Buick touring car with Dynaflow transmission. The foment of the new decade made the fifties, in retrospect, seem like an idyllic dream, a parenthesis of naivete in the republic's history. In those seven years Grandfather Ike had lied to his people about the U-2 incident and Camelot had come and gone, shattered in the streets of Dallas across from a decrepit depot for children's school books. The Beatles had made their American debut, Castro had prevailed over Batista, the twenty-seven-year ban for obscenity had been lifted from Henry Miller's *Tropic of Cancer,* and the nation was divided, not between Chics and Chocs but between "doves" and "hawks."

Scooter Evans and Johnny Kramer were both residing at addresses outside the United States. Scooter was on the continent of Europe; Johnny was on the continent of Asia. Scooter was still in the classroom; Johnny was fighting for his life in a rice paddy.

On August 4, 1964, the *Maddox* and the *C. Turner Joy,* two U.S. naval destroyers were attacked by North Vietnamese patrol boats in the waters of the Gulf of Tonkin. President Lyndon B. Johnson dispatched an order, as commander-in-chief of the United States armed forces, for a retaliatory bombing strike on coastal installations of North Viet Nam. *Escalation.* On August 7 the U.S. Senate, by an 88—2 margin passed a resolution authorizing the longest and most controverted foreign war in American history. The mini-involvement of military advisors under the

Kennedy administration turned into a humiliating blood bath for
thousands of confused and bewildered American boys. Johnny
Kramer was one of them. He had been moved from the military
reserves to active duty.

The tiny nation of Viet Nam forms a slender ribbon of real
estate stretching from China to the Gulf of Siam, its serpentine
shores lining the South China Sea. Since the tenth century Viet
Nam had been under the colonial control of the French. A nation-
alist guerrilla movement to drive out the French was carried on by
the Vietminh. Their tactics to stop the Japanese juggernaut in
World War II made them popular heroes. Their leader was an
aged, goateed, frail figure named Ho Chi Minh who dreamed
of a unified, independent Marxist state. An international crisis
evolved in 1954 when a bloody siege of the key fortress of the
French at Dien Bien Phu ended in victory for the determined
Vietminh.

Dien Bien Phu provoked a peace conference in Geneva,
Switzerland that produced a "temporary" division of Viet Nam
into two sectors buffered by a demilitarized zone along the 17th
parallel. Some ninety thousand Vietminh troops, many southern-
ers by birth, were relocated in the north, while others returned to
their village in the south. International elections were to be held
in 1956, which the Vietminh were certain would reunite the
country under their control. They did not foresee the court intrigue or consolidated power that would thwart their plans with
the rise of Ngo Dinh Diem.

Diem gained the support of the Eisenhower administration
and in October of 1955 named himself president of the Republic
of Viet Nam, quickly moving to cancel the scheduled elections.
Diem instituted a purge of Vietminh members, seeking to root
them out of the south, driving them into the jungles and swamps,
which only served to turn them into a strong cohesive counter-
revolutionary force. They organized secret committees until, finally, in 1960 they formed the National Liberation Front whose
military wing became known as the Vietcong, an indigenous
force controlled neither by the Saigon government in the south
nor the Vietminh government in the north. Their numbers grew
as did their threat to the dictatorial leader, Diem. Diem's urgent
requests to Kennedy brought nine hundred U.S. military advi-

sors to Viet Nam, authorized by a president fearful of the impact of a communist victory.

When the populace of South Viet Nam could no longer stomach Diem's ruthless policies of repression, they rose in protest dramatized by the self-immolation of Buddhist monks. The coup that finished Diem was not opposed by the United States. What followed was a merry-go-round of coups and counter-coups leading to a protracted period of political instability in the south.

The Gulf of Tonkin resolution sent thirty-five hundred U.S. Marines to Da Nang, ostensibly to guard the American air base there. *Escalation*. Raids by the Vietcong alarmed the U.S. military command, so more troop deployments were ordered. In August of 1965 there were 90 thousand U.S. troops in Viet Nam; by the end of the year the number climbed to 184 thousand; by 1968 the number reached 540 thousand. *Escalation*.

Johnny Kramer stepped on the escalator early. He was shipped to Viet Nam two and a half years before the Tet offensive that was launched by the Vietcong on January 30, 1968, the date of the lunar New Year.

Johnny's first glimpse of Da Nang was from the air. He saw a long stretch of white sand beach set off in stark contrast by mountain ridges that followed the sides of the bay. From the ground the city looked like New Orleans overrun by primitive orientals. The French influence was still apparent with French colonial buildings lining the streets and black wrought iron balconies jutting over the sidewalks. Johnny expected to see a swinging black Dixieland funeral procession snaking through the marketplace at any moment. Instead he saw peasants, laden down with their wares stuffed in baskets balanced on their shoulders by bamboo sticks, a basket on each end like a comic set of barbells.

He saw sampan villages crammed along the river that flowed through the city, and peasant shanties, hovels built from scraps "borrowed" from the military. There were two wars going on here—one with the Vietcong, the other with the mosquitoes.

Johnny Kramer was now First Lieutenant Kramer, leading a small squad of soldiers on regular search missions into the swamps and jungles near Da Nang. Their unit was constantly harassed by the Vietcong who were masters of hit-and-run forays. It seemed to Johnny and his men that they were making war on

ghosts, vaporous apparitions who had the uncanny knack of appearing and disappearing at will.

At this stage of the war the casualties were still considered
light, nothing compared with the gruesome total that would bur-
geon to over fifty-five thousand American deaths by the morning
of April 30, 1975 when President Duong Van Minh announced
the Saigon government's unconditional surrender.

Despite government euphemisms, the casualties in Johnny's
outfit were as real as they were "light." What the men feared most
were the hidden booby traps, concealed along jungle trails or the
banks and pathways bordering the rice paddies. The custom of
the Cong was to disguise themselves as rice farmers stooped over
their primitive tools, ankles covered with water, and their heads
shielded from the sun by wide-brimmed hats. The sudden trans-
formation of innocent rice-farmers into savage guerrillas—
spraying machine gun fire—had been witnessed often enough for
Johnny to be nervous when patrolling the rice paddies.

He was on patrol on a September morning when he passed
along a rice paddy with his men. Today his patrol moved without
the benefit of a Hoi Chanh, a local scout who guided Americans
through booby-trapped areas. The group of night-shirted peasants with colie hats ignored the passing of the American soldiers.
The silent ignoring should have been a tip-off but Johnny missed
it, warily leading his men across a pathway at the top of the bank.
Johnny felt more secure and less guarded with each step they
made in single-file procession. Johnny reacted to the sudden motion by the rice farmers. Out of nowhere machine guns started
bursting, splashing water and dirt on the bank where Johnny was
walking. The Americans dove headlong over the side of the bank
to escape the ambush. One GI fell on the path almost severed in
half by the machine-gun shells. Johnny made it to safety but not
before feeling a searing flash of heat tearing at his leg. His comrades were returning the fire, dispersing the Vietcong who vanished from sight in moments, content with the limited success of
the ambush.

Johnny bit his lip as he extended his left leg. It was oozing
blood through the jagged tear in his pants. He grabbed at his
wound frantically trying to stem the flow of blood with his hand,
like the Dutch boy holding back the sea with his finger in the
dike. Johnny's comrades scrambled to his side taking over from

his self-ministrations. They applied a firm tourniquet and made a human litter with their arms carrying him back along the pathway to their outpost. Medics transported Johnny by helicopter to the main base in Da Nang. Surgery was performed that evening. Johnny was transferred to a hospital in Saigon and from there to Tokyo for further convalescence.

As the wound was healing, Johnny faced the rigors of rehabilitation made necessary by the shattering of part of his tibia. He thought about Scooter when his nurse posted his physical therapy schedule. The regimen called for two workouts a day designed to strengthen the muscles in his leg to add support to the weakened appendage. The routine required six weeks of treatment after which he would be shipped back to the United States. His was a million dollar wound earning him a Purple Heart and an honorable exemption from further combat. *Maybe,* he thought to himself, *they'll change the words of the song to "When Johnny comes limping home again."*

The therapist assigned to Johnny was a petite woman in her mid-twenties from Chicago named Leah Sabans. Leah was soft and her gentle features fit her Florence Nightingale role in Johnny's life. She sparkled with a kind of sterling silver midwestern brightness, modest in her hairstyle and makeup.

"Hi, soldier," Leah beamed at Johnny. "Are you ready for the fun part?"

"Hey, anything is the fun part compared to Nam. Are you going to make it so I can walk without a limp?"

"That's the goal. But the hard work is up to you. I'm just here as sort of a cheerleader."

"If you're the cheerleader then I'm going to be sure I make the team."

Johnny was partial to brunettes and he found himself feeling a growing affection born partly from his appreciation for her daily words of encouragement and partly from the chemical reactions that were set in motion by the catalyst of daily contact. Leah was unlike the other girls Johnny had dated. She was the kind of girl a young man could introduce to his parents without causing raised eyebrows. Part of Leah seemed to go beyond innocence to naiveté, a throwback to a virginal madonna out of step with the fast-moving pace of her generation. Yet she was a woman, a woman of wide horizons who had crossed halfway around the world to taste different cultures, acquiring a veteran sense of the ravages of war. Naiveté did not last long in a military hospital, yet the feel of it hung on her. There was something inside Leah that could not be spoiled or easily tarnished by the environment in which she worked.

"What do you do in your free time?" Johnny asked during a morning session.

"Oh, I do some sightseeing and stuff. You know, take the tour of Tokyo and visit the Shinto temples and the cultured pearl works. Mostly I just sit at home and read."

"What kinds of stuff do you read?"

"I like the serious type of literature—Arthur Miller, Samuel Beckett, Golding, Ionesco, Camus, Kerouak . . . I look at them as my friends. They are in touch with how people are feeling these days."

The only name Johnny recognized in the list was that of Arthur Miller, not because Miller was famous for his association with Willy Lowman, but because of his association with Marilyn Monroe.

"Do you like to read, Johnny?" Leah asked.

"Sure. The sports page, the market reports and sometimes some real heavy stuff like Mickey Spillane." He reached out and teased Leah's hand. "An intellectual I am not. Hey, the doctor said I could go for walks on the grounds as soon as I'm sure I can navigate safely. He said I'd need an escort to make sure I don't fall on my dupah. I sure don't want that battle-ax on my ward to go along. What do you say, Leah, will you take me for an afternoon stroll on the lawn?"

"I'd love to, Johnny. How about if I sign you out at two o'clock?"

"If you sign me out they might never get me to sign back in."

The afternoon strolls became a regular event and soon graduated to longer hours. On Leah's days off Johnny wrangled full-day passes from his doctor. They spent most of the day on foot, therapy for Johnny who limped along on a cane. They avoided taxis as much as possible, partly because of language difficulties and partly out of respect for the legend that Tokyo's cab drivers were all ex-Kamikaze pilots. The streets were safer than the train and subway stations where the huge crowds were not conducive for mingling with a cane.

They shopped in the Ginza district, browsing in antique and curio shops. Leah had a glint in her eye when she asked Johnny, "Would you like to eat some takos?"

"Tacos? This doesn't look like Mexico to me. I love tacos. Let's go."

Leah walked to a *yatai,* a street stall where vendors sold an oriental type of pancake. She bought *tako yaki* and brought it to Johnny. "Here, Japanese takos."

Johnny tasted it. "It tastes great, but it doesn't taste like a taco. What's in it?"

"Chopped octopus feet," Leah giggled.

"Octopus feet! You said it was a taco!"

"*T-a-k-o.* That means octopus. They chop up the feet and bake them in batter. Now you must try the *yaki imo,* you'll love them. They're roasted sweet potatoes."

Leah introduced Johnny to Tokyo's night life with visits to the Kabuki theater, the Shimbashi Embujo, and to the symphony at the Bunka Hall. Johnny wanted to visit the Nichigeki Music Hall to sample eastern burlesque but Leah vetoed the idea.

Their time together was rapidly running out. Johnny was smitten with Leah. "What am I going to do after I ship out? We both know this is no mild patient-therapist interlude. I'll go nuts without you, Leah."

"It will only be for a month, Johnny. My orders send me back to the States soon. We can see each other at home."

THIRTEEN

S cooter walked with his mother through the long canopied tunnel that connected the wharf and the gangplank of the S.S. *Statendam,* an oceanliner belonging to the fleet of the Holland-America line. The steward showed them to the C-deck stateroom that would serve as Scooter's quarters for the eight-day voyage across the Atlantic. The deskette in the room boasted a large basket of fruit wrapped with a red satin bow. Beside it was a split of champagne with a bon voyage note from his mother. Elizabeth Evans was fighting back tears as she made her last-minute farewell. She had a premonition that this was the last time she would see her son alive but shielded her anxiety from Scooter.

"I want you to call me transatlantic as soon as you arrive, son. Indulge your mother's fretfulness. I'll pay for the call."

"I'll call as soon as I get in my apartment. Don't worry. I'm a big boy, and it's not like I was shipping out to Viet Nam or something."

The cabin steward called through the hall for all visitors to disembark. The *Statendam* was ready to sail. Mrs. Evans made a hasty retreat, forswearing a teary farewell that Scooter fully expected and had braced himself for. He turned around and she as gone. He moved quickly out the cabin door trying to wedge himself between the people who were moving to the gangplank. He hurried upstairs but saw no sign of her. He went to a higher deck on the ship until he reached the side rail overlooking the pier. He saw his mother standing below smiling and waving her goodbyes.

The blast of the whistle signaled the removal of the gangway and the ship began to move, inching away from the dock. It was a gala but emotional moment as passengers hugged the rail throwing kisses and waving tearfully to those left behind. Within min-

utes the figures on the wharf had shrunk to pin-size specks in the
distance. Passengers settled into deck chairs not willing to return
to their cabins until after the ritual of passing the Statue of Liberty. The silhouette of the huge upraised torch was visible on the
horizon topping the massive greenish-tinged gift from France
commemorating America's joint commitment to *liberté, egalité,*
and *fraternité.* Scooter thought of the statue in quasi-religious
terms as "Our Lady of the Harbor," a sobriquet suggested by a
love song crooned by Frank Sinatra. His thoughts were cynical as
the ship neared the towering figure, *Don't shed any tears for me
woman, I don't care if I ever see you again.*

Scooter was eager to get to Europe, far away from the bitter
experience of the three miserable years he had just completed at
seminary. He longed for an environment where the classical
things of beauty that inspired his soul might be appreciated, a
place far removed from the plastic covered pragmatism of the
United States.

Scooter's mind honed in on his future expectations of Europe,
wondering if the same fate of unrealized hope would befall him
that befell Melville's fictional hero, Redburn. Redburn sailed for
England armed with a faded map of the streets of Liverpool given
to him by his father. He was crestfallen to discover upon his arrival in the British port that the city had changed, old landmarks
had crumbled into ruins and modern changes made the map ob-
solete and useless. Maybe the same fate would befall Scooter and
he would rue these moments of cynicism at the feet of the world's
tallest day.

He thought of another character created by Melville; Ishmael,
the lone survivor of the ill-fated *Pequod.* He recalled the immortal
opening line; "Call me Ishmael . . ." Ishmael was the incurable
wanderlust, the young man who grew excited at the smallest rivu-
let, the slightest tributary, knowing that ultimately these trickles
would spill into creeks, and creeks into rivers and river inevitably,
inexorably into the sea. He was a man drawn, nay compelled
when the smell of salt air hit his nostrils, to sign on for a voyage.
The sea owned him, claiming a mastery over his soul. Scooter
reclined in a deck chair on the leeward side and indulged his fantasy of re-creation, his romantic chimera of recapitulation. His
was a Nietzschean myth of return, of eternal return.

Scooter was not a native of New Bedford nor of Martha's

Vineyard. His rearing ground was nearly five hundred miles inland. But the romantic spirit of the seafarer was his, a dream
kindled in his heart by the antics of Errol Flynn and Tyrone
Power. As a boy he depleted the town library of sea stories, pensively digesting everything from *The Cruel Sea* to the *Wake of the Red
Witch*. Now for the first time in his life he would leave the shelter
of the harbor and cast out into the mystery of the deep, perhaps to
do battle with the primordial mythical sea monster, Tiamat.
Never mind that the voyage was neither on schooner nor frigate,
or that there was no mainsail or jib; the plush accouterments of
this floating hotel could not obscure the fact that beneath his feet
was the sea, fathom after fathom of brooding water that no man
could fully or finally tame.

The S.S. *Statendam* glided smoothly past the Statue of Liberty
heading for the mouth of the harbor and the black sheen of open
sea. Scooter rose from his deck chair drawn by some arcane mag-
netism and stood at the rail of the fantail. New York was fading in
the background with the silhouette of its skyline now barely visible against the horizon. He stared dirt at the vanishing shore and
then directly toward, mesmerized by the swirling eddies agitated
by the ship's propeller. The wake of the *Statendam* turned the trail-
ing sea into a cauldron, its foam hugging the crest of the undulat-
ing waves. He could see small whirlpools sucking the water into
funnels of bottomless darkness. They reminded him of the fascination he knew as a child when he helped with the family dishes,
watching the dishwater disappear down the drain and wondering
why it didn't simply drop straight down instead of funneling. He
thought of the commercial ditty branded on his brain by the ad-
vertisers' art of countless repetition, "Ajax, *boom, boom,* the foam-
ing cleanser, *boom, boom, boom,* floats the first right down the
drain, *boom, boom, boom, boom.*"

"Down the drain." For Scooter it was a morbid thought, one
he could not tolerate. Like Dr. Lenhart, Scooter hated waste. His
mind was strafed by the nagging thought that the past three years
of his life had been precisely that, a waste, a three-year flirtation
with a garbage dump. They were years he had looked forward to
with joyous hopes that had been sliced to raw shreds. Scars had
not yet formed. As ugly as a scar may appear, it is at least a sign of
healing. There are no scars in death, only the cosmetic art of the
mortician. Scooter's wounds were still bleeding, oozing and fes-

tering inside. Perhaps this journey would be the balm he needed
to close the gash and renew his hope for the future.

He was encouraged by the cyclical character of his life so far, a
series of ups and downs that moved from zenith to nadir and back
again. He loved junior high, and hated high school; he loved college, and hated seminary. Now it was time for an upswing as he
set out for graduate school on the continent of Europe. The
thought of successive downs, of freezing the cycle at the nadir,
terrified him. He was fiercely determined that it would not happen. Yet he realized that to resist the omnipotent force of providence would be like pitiful Hungarian youths throwing stones
at the Russian tanks. But the God who had hid His face from
Scooter in seminary, the place he most expected to find Him,
would surely understand. He would not sentence him to the un-
remitting torture of a perpetual dark night of the soul. Surely
God understood that much more disappointment would put him
down the drain.

Scooter had finished college with a flair. His years at Witherspoon were idealized in his memory, positive feelings treasured
by the remembrance of every tree of the campus. That was his
Peniel, the place where he wrestled his own private angel. That
was his Bethel, where he had his own midnight glimpse of the
ladder that closed the gap between earth and heaven.

That was the place where his theological understanding of the
world, of things holy and profane, took its embryonic form. He
studied Greek and relished the pregnant moment when the
strange configurations of the ancient script took meaningful shape
for him. He began to decipher it, turning cryptic lines into letters,
and letters into words until he could look at the Greek text of the
New Testament and read it. To read the original was like taking a
peek behind the veil that concealed the vague outline of God.

He studied philosophy, going through stages and fads of pre-
occupation with the philosophers who captured his thoughts for a
season. Scooter was philosophically impetuous, plunging madly
into the works of those who caught his fancy. He had a Plato stage,
captured by the other-worldly aura of the Ideal. He had his Descartes stage where the premium of reason honed his mind to a
sharp edge of rationality. Descartes fed his mind but was unable
to charge his emotions. It was Kierkegaard, a man of passion,

whose intoxicating writings inflamed Scooter. He found in Kierkegaard a kindred spirit. He read quickly through both volumes of *Either/Or,* then on to *Sickness Unto Death* and *Fear and Trembling,* and finally to the heavier works. But on every page of Kierkegaard he could feel the Dane's pain seeping from his pen. Scooter knew. Regina was everywhere in Kierkegaard's thoughts, the lost love, the tragic broken engagement, the poetic trauma from which Kierkegaard never recovered. Scooter knew. Kierkegaard's Regina was Scooter's Patricia.

Scooter fought a war with his own personality. His character was shaped in tension with a struggle for supremacy between two aspects of his being: his mind and his heart. Scooter's mind was inclined toward reason; but reason alone was cold, lifeless, barren of nourishment for his heart. His heart was stirred by emotions. His mind recoiled from irrationality, despising contradiction; antinomies were repugnant to him. Yet he loathed a sterile logic, a frigid syllogism. He demanded from Truth a reasoned passion and a passionate reason. Heart and mind had to be reconciled or Scooter would surrender to intellectual schizophrenia.

He found two men who satisfied him, the titans of the sixteenth-century Protestant Reformation, Martin Luther and John Calvin. But even in these two giants Scooter required a synthesis. Luther was a man of incendiary passion coupled with intellectual brilliance that towered over the ages. But the brilliance of Luther was not systematic. He was the type of genius, a counterpart of the modern Sartre, who had flashes of insight, lucid vignettes of perception that made Scooter stand in awe. Yet the big picture somehow eluded the German reformer. His style was not macrocosmic. That was the great strength of Calvin. Calvin had the orderly mind of the systematic philosopher coupled with the warmth of a heart beating for God. The prayers of Calvin stirred Scooter's heart as much as his learned doctrines satisfied his mind. His brain leaned more to Calvin while his heart tugged him toward Luther.

Much of the attraction Luther held for Scooter was his legendary earthiness. Though Luther had a heart for God he never got lost in the ethereal planes of the divine. He was to the end, a man. He enjoyed a mug of beer with his colleague Philip Melanchthon at the local tavern after giving lectures on the fine points of theology. He was more comfortable with coalminers like his father, Hans Luther, than with the princes of the church. Most of all, Scooter was captured by the romance of Luther. His love for his bride, the ex-nun Catherine Von Bora, rivaled that of Tristan and Isolde and Abelard and Heloise. Calvin's marriage to Idelette was also moving, but it lacked the verve that attended the Luther-Von Bora *affaire de coeur*.

The ache of the loss of Patricia could not be left behind. It would travel with Scooter across the sea and follow him wherever he journeyed. Farewells like he experienced this day at the dock in New York provoked the melancholy memory of his last and final farewell from Patricia. It had happened four years earlier. After the shocking news of Patricia's marriage Scooter heard nothing more from her or about her for two years. His final thoughts at night when he rested his head on his pillow were fantasies of the magic return of Patricia. He would drift off into sleep while his imagination created dramatic scenes of Patricia appearing and announcing that she was divorced, wanting Scooter after all. His mind composed a novelette worthy of a Harlequin romance with a whirlwind courtship and exotic cruise to a Caribbean Island where the two could find the Shangri La they were destined for. Scooter had the kind of fixation for Patricia that makes a man see a woman's face on a stranger walking down a busy street, or in a crowd attending a basketball game. Scooter scanned the faces of all the blonde-haired strangers he encountered looking for the tell-tale cat eyes of Patricia. He saw them more than once, only to be jolted back to reality by the sound of a stranger's voice.

Then the dream came true. At least in part.

FOURTEEN

I t was the day after Labor Day, 1960. The public school children made their annual return to the classroom on this day, leaving country clubs without caddies and swimming pools with no alternative but to close for the winter. The humid days of summer would linger a few more weeks before the sugar maples of western Pennsylvania would vie with the dogwoods for the annual award of most spectacular foliage. The fiery hues of red from their changing leaves would stand in bold relief on the sylvan borders of the fields dotting the countryside of the forests of William Penn.

The day after Labor Day was a day of transition. It marked the real end of summer and the signal for fall preparations for winter. For the people of Briarwood it meant checking the leaf rake in the garage to make sure its teeth had not been extracted during the summer and that it was strong enough for another season of Saturday afternoon raking. It meant that soon a Saturday would have to be given over to trips to the attic. Storm windows needed to be brought down and washed before sealing up the apertures that in summer were adorned by screens allowing fresh breezes in the room. The ritual of taking down screens and putting up storm windows was like entering an annual kind of imprisonment. The house would be shut off from the music of children playing on the lawn and laughter drifting in from the neighbor's barbecue patio. It was as if the neighborhood went into hibernation for the winter until the April thaw came and people would see each other again in the outside world.

This September, the September of 1960, would create a strange statistic in the Pittsburgh area. It would break all monthly records of pharmaceutical merchants for the sale of digitalis. This would be the stretch drive, the drive for the pennant by the Pittsburgh Pirates marked by late-inning heroics, nail-biting thrillers, and heart-stopping pitches by the world's tallest little man, relief pitcher Elroy Face. Cardiac patients had the dosage instructions for their little pill bottles of digitalis changed from "Take one every four hours" to "Take one every four innings."

Scooter's summer job had ended on the last day of August and this day was spent packing and making final preparations to return to Witherspoon for his senior year. He was scheduled to leave in two more days. Shortly after dinner the phone rang. Scooter answered it, recognizing the voice of one of the boys who had made the winter trip to the Orange Bowl, nearly four years earlier.

"Hi, Scooter, this is Bill. Doing anything special tonight?"

"No, Bill. I'm just getting things ready to go back to school. Why? What's up?"

Bill ignored the question and pressed on with another of his own. "Is your mother home?"

"No, she's out playing bridge for the evening. Why?" Again the question was sidestepped.

"I was just curious. Well, have a good year at school. Bye." The line went dead in Scooter's hand. He held the phone out in front of his eyes and stared at it. *He must be looped or something. That was a weird conversation,* Scooter mused.

Within minutes the strange phone call receded from his mind and Scooter's thoughts were lost on other matters. He sat down at the piano and began playing nostalgic ballads. His playing was interrupted by the sharp sound of the apartment buzzer. He terminated the piece with a hurried arpeggio and stood up from the piano. He casually turned the brass doorknob and swung open the door. The muscles in his arms tensed and his eyes froze, fixed on the apparition in front of him. Standing in the doorway with a teasing smile, was a woman. She was alluring in a black sheath that revealed deeply tanned shoulders.

"Well, Scooter, aren't you going to ask me in? I've come a long way to see you."

Scooter felt a tangible flow of adrenaline beginning to pump through his veins. He was suddenly disoriented, stupefied by the figure speaking to him. He could not distinguish for a moment between reality and hallucination. He backed awkwardly into the room and spoke in stumbled words, "Yes—of course—come in."

Patricia walked into the room, an air of maturity and sophisti-
cation about her that necessitated an adjustment of Scooter's
image of her. He forgot to ask her to sit down, his throat still
partially paralyzed. He had rehearsed this scene a thousand times
with his head resting comfortably on a pillow, but now no glamorous words popped into his mind. His speech was inane.

"How are you?" he stammered.

"I'm just fine." Patricia's smile broadened, betraying her en-
joyment of Scooter's obvious discomfort.

Scooter tried again. "What are you doing here?"

"I drove up here to see you."

"But why? You're still married, aren't you?"

Patricia's face clouded and her lower jaw started to tremble.

"It's not working. It's no good, Scooter. Nothing turned out
like I planned." Her voice gave way to sobs.

It was awkward for Scooter. He wanted to put his arms around
her, to draw her to himself and comfort her. But he could not
move. He stood fixed to the spot, afraid to reach out. She was still
married. Untouchable. A priceless artifact that would be blemished if he put his hands on her.

Patricia struggled for control. She looked at him and spoke
words that could never be erased from his mind.

"I want you, Scooter. I want to go away with you. Just you
and me. No more sugar daddies. I want you and that's what I've
always wanted. Now I'm old enough to do something about it."

The scenario was going like Scooter's favorite dream. She was
here, and now she was his. His heart was pounding inside as if he
had just witnessed a miracle, as if a statue of Aphrodite stirred,
grew warm, and delicately stepped from a pedestal into life.

"The marriage is over. I left him. I just wrote him a note, left
it on the dining room table, got in the car and drove here. The
marriage is finished. Let him get a divorce, I want to be with
you."

Scooter groaned. The impact of her explanation tore at him.
Reality was rushing in, forcing the miracle dream into oblivion.
She was still married. If a divorce ensued it would be his fault; he
would be the correspondent, a breach of ethics he could not allow.
He suddenly felt as if he were thrust into a naked desert ruled by a
diabolical overlord pressing him to the supreme test of his faith.
He was offered the one prize he valued on a parity with the worth

of his own soul. His thoughts were inchoate, jumbled by the feast of his eyes. He was numb, incapable of decisive action. He knew he should run and tie himself to the mast like a modern Ulysses. He must plug his ears to the enticing power of the sirens screaming to him from the shore. This was the battle Saint Paul called the war between the spirit and the flesh.

The spirit won the first round. "That's out of the question, Patricia. You're a married woman. Things have changed. I'm different now and so are you. You belong to another man, and whatever we had before is over. I'm sorry you had to drive all the way from Florida for nothing."

"No one changes that much, Scooter. What are you telling me? Don't you love me anymore? Look me straight in the eye and say that and I'll leave."

"You know better than that. That's not what I said. The point is, Patricia, you're married. I can't get involved with a married woman."

"But I told you, my marriage is finished. It's a washout. What does that have to do with us?"

Scooter's frustration mounted, climbing to a rigid point of tension. "This conversation is getting us nowhere. Where are you staying?"

"My suitcase is at Carole Kenner's. Why?"

"I think you'd better go back there. Call your husband and let him know where you are and make arrangements as soon as possible to get back to him."

"You're serious aren't you? What happened to all that talk about love forever and waiting for me all your life? You waited and here I am. Now you tell me to get lost. Is it revenge you want, Scooter? Are you trying to get even?"

Scooter walked to the door and opened it, a nonnegotiable sign of dismissal. Patricia jerked to her feet, her jaw iron-tight. "All right, Scooter. I'll leave. But you'll regret this. You'll be sorry. I won't make a fool of myself twice."

She descended the stairs in a simmering rage. Scooter backed into the apartment and went quickly to the window overlooking the street. He stood off to the side, shielded from view by the curtain. His covert standpoint was unnecessary. Patricia never glanced back in the direction of the apartment. She walked directly to a late model Jaguar XKE and stepped in. In seconds the engine roared to life and the car screeched from the curb, the exhaust pipe exuding the fury of the driver.

Inner voices of recrimination began to assail Scooter. *You stupid idiot. You stupid proud idiot. How can you let her go like this? She said her marriage was finished. Whatever ruined the marriage had nothing to do with you. You're not the correspondent. You acted like a sanctimonious jerk. She was right. It was an act of revenge. You were getting even for rejection and you cloaked it in some moronic act of piety.*

The internal battle was short-lived. Within minutes Scooter was pierced with grief for dispatching Patricia as if she were a streetwalker soliciting him for the evening. He knew exactly what he had to do. Further debate was both useless and tortuous. He picked up the phone and dialed the Keener residence. At the end of the second ring Scooter heard Carole's voice on the line. "Hello."

"Hello, Carole. Scooter. Did Patricia come back?"

Carole's voice turned to ice. "Yes, she's back. What do *you* want? Don't you think you've done enough damage for one evening?"

"Put her on." Scooter's voice was terse, laced with a tone of command that preempted argument.

Scooter winced as he heard the phone rudely placed on the table. He listened to the garbled, muffled sounds of background noise filling the interlude. A new voice spoke, noticeably changed from the one he had heard earlier. Now it was husky, rasping with the hoarse tones of someone who had been crying.

"Patricia? I'll be there in five minutes."

Scooter didn't wait for a reply. He dropped the receiver into its cradle and scribbled a hasty note to his mother telling her not to wait up for him. He took the steps two at a time and was in the Ford in seconds. In less than five minutes he tramped on the brake in front of Carole's house. He moved toward the house with strident steps and pressed the bell. Patricia answered the door. She looked as if she had just been in a brawl and lost. Scooter grabbed her hand and said, "Let's go."

He led her to the passenger side of the Ford and helped her in. She slid onto the front seat like a wounded bird, all the fury from her earlier tirade dissipated. She was broken and pliable, her puffy eyes heaping pangs of guilt on Scooter. Again he thought, *You stupid idiot.*

Scooter eased himself behind the wheel and turned over the ignition. The fan belt let out a screeching protest at the rough start. He reached over wordlessly with his right arm and pulled Patricia to him. She nestled like a rag doll against his shoulder. They rode in silence, leaving the stone pillars of Briarwood to vanish in the rear view mirror. Scooter drove the Hollow Road, past the immaculately manicured Briarwood Memorial Gardens with its statuary masking the truth hidden beneath its turf.

He broke the silence. "We have to talk. I meant what I said before. I can't be involved with you as long as you are married. But I have to see you while you're here."

"You're not making sense, Scooter. You say you can't be involved with me, yet you want to see me. What are you saying?"

"I'm saying that I can't stand having you this close without at least talking with you. I leave for school in two days. I want to talk. But no more. That's how it has to be."

He was reciting these platonic rules to Patricia while his arm was around her and her cheek was resting against his. Patricia listened silently to Scooter's noble oration. The rules prohibited romance. This was to be merely an encounter between two old friends, one of whom was married. Patricia nodded her assent to his litany of laws, knowing full well that they would not be enforced for long. Scooter seemed blind to the fact that while he was talking like this he was heading the car toward the China Wall, Pittsburgh's most famous hideaway for young lovers.

China Wall was so named for the waist-high stone barrier that guarded the edge of the highest hill in South Park, overlooking a breathtaking vista of the picnic groves and woods that comprised this idyllic sanctuary. From the vantage point of the Wall one could see the county fairgrounds below, the site of an annual extravaganza featuring livestock shows and farmers' competition. The "Oval" was also in view, marked by a cavernous amphitheater that hosted colorful harness races with standard-bred horses pulling two-wheeled sulkies around the track. The Wall extended for almost a quarter mile, ostensibly a simple roadside rest stop for people who wanted to pull off the main drive to enjoy the panoramic view. Its real function, however, was to serve as a designated lover's lane, designed for that purpose by the county commissioners who had the foresight to anticipate that the curling country roads of the park would be a strong temptation for the area youth. The side roads could be dangerous and the Wall was more efficient as a safe place to neck without fear of being mugged or harassed by fiendish bushwackers.

The Wall was patrolled regularly, at fifteen minute intervals, by park police who cruised slowly down the lane, equipped with a large spotlight that probed the night for offenders to the code of the Wall. The rules were simple: anyone could park there without fear of police disturbance as long as their heads were above the seat. If the police cruised by and saw no heads, or only one head, the unfortunate occupants of the car were treated to the full measure of the giant spotlight shining through the window like a prison yard beacon, flooding the interior of the car with light. The only other rule was a strict midnight curfew. No one was allowed to be parked at the Wall after twelve o'clock.

When Scooter pulled off the main drive and edged toward the Wall he noticed eight or nine other cars already hugging the macadam parking strip bordering the parapet. Scooter turned off the key and reached down for the lever that freed the front seat to slide back. Patricia laughed and said, "I wonder how many married women come to the Wall like this? I feel like a high school sophomore again."

Scooter cringed at the comment, trying to suppress the stab he felt at the mention of a "married woman." Patricia's eyes were languid, yielding a hint of weariness that went beyond the fatigue of travel. She was silently pleading with Scooter to forget, for the moment, abstract discussions about duty and responsibility. Right now she didn't care about such things.

Scooter was equally weary of the moral struggle that was draining his resolve. He cradled his right hand on the back of Patricia's head and eased her toward him until they were face to face, the tips of their noses brushing slightly. He felt her breath on his face. Both of them had their eyes wide open, Scooter with a strange stare in his gaze, and Patricia with eyes still pleading and watching intently for a momentary flicker that would signal the surrender of Scooter's head to his heart. Scooter dropped his eyelids closed like a knight in defeat dropping his sword to a cold stone floor. Patricia got the message instantly. She closed her eyes to enjoy the euphoric touch of Scooter's lips on hers. Their lips were barely touching; Scooter was fighting his conscience to the final gasp. His kiss became urgent, the floodgates of his feelings released. He kissed frantically, moving to her ears, her neck and her throat, deluging her with the pent-up love he had nurtured for so long.

He moaned the triad of words over and over, "I love you . . . I love you . . ." Patricia responded with a female urgency that matched his. Their frenzy abated for a moment and he held her quietly, stroking her hair. They sat for a while in silence, content to communicate without words.

Patricia seemed to feel safe here, as if she were sharing a private existence, cut off from the rest of the universe. She was being held by a man who was neither rich nor titled, but who had what she needed at this moment—the virtues of strength and tenderness. She dropped her head to his chest and listened to the metronomic rhythm of his heartbeat. The flicker of headlamps in his rear view mirror warned Scooter to boost Patricia's head above the level of the backseat. "Remember the rules, Patricia. We have to keep our heads above the seat or the gendarmes will be here with their sound and light show."

"Oh, those rules. I thought for a second you were talking about some other rules I heard about long ago and far away."

At 11:59 Scooter revved up the engine and joined the train of cars that were leaving the oriental haven for another night. "Two days, Patricia. That's all we have. I want to spend every minute of them with you."

It was 12:30 when Scooter dropped Patricia off at Carole's house with the promise of a 7:00 A.M. rendezvous.

When Elizabeth Evans returned to the apartment she was surprised to see Scooter's note. She picked it up and studied it for a moment before pouring herself a nightcap, one final bourbon and water before retiring. She pondered the meaning of the note, indulging the hope that it was prompted by a girl. Her alarm over her son's disinterest in dating had swollen to the fear that Scooter had made some holy vow of perpetual celibacy that would cheat her of a grandson. The Evans family name would perish with Scooter, printed for the last time on his tombstone. Elizabeth sipped her drink, trying to force the morbid thought to flee.

For the next two days Elizabeth barely saw her son, a fact she interpreted as solid confirmation of her maternal hope. She felt a slight twinge of jealousy, but the thought that he was finally emerging from his cocoon more than compensated.

The forty-eight hours sprinted around the clock for Scooter. They were spent for the most part at the Wall, provoking the police's curiosity at the red and black Ford parked there all day in broad daylight, save for respites during meal hours. They were curious and amused, but gallantly abided by the code and left the amorous couple undisturbed as their heads were always properly visible when they patrolled the area.

The interlude ended on Carole Keener's porch with a lingering kiss long after the bedroom lights of Briarwood were quenched for the night. Scooter was spent, his emotions raw and battered. The time had passed in a kaleidoscope of sensations. Convictions, dogmas, and desire were colliding in his conscience. At the very moment he wanted God to be remote fro his God intruded, making His presence felt, putting restraints on Scooter's passion. In heated moments Scooter willed the absence of God but the Deity refused to abscond. It was Patricia who must leave, Scooter understood that, but he hated it. He cursed the Bard of Avon for describing parting as a sweet sorrow. Not now. Not here. There was no sweetness to it.

Scooter's parting words were insipid. "Let me know how you're doing. Don't contact me directly but stay in touch with Carole. She'll keep me posted. Remember that I love you."

Scooter was dressed and on the highway by 7:00 A.M. heading north to Witherspoon. He visualized the silver XKE headed in the opposite direction. Patricia had kept her end of the two-day bargain by calling her husband and telling him that her flight had been impulsive. She assured him that she was safe and would return as soon as she rested and visited briefly with her girl friend. Her husband was not happy with the delay but his relief outweighed his anger and he was willing to accept her terms.

At noon Scooter finished registering for his senior courses and went to the bookstore to procure his texts for the coming semester. He spied Johnny sitting in the Sub, laughing it up with some of his fraternity brothers. Now that he was an active he was almost a permanent fixture at the frat house. His brothers had pressed him to move into the house but Johnny elected to continue room-

ing with Scooter until Scooter graduated. Johnny seemed certain
to graduate, though with his absence to the military and a few *F*s
on his early grade sheet he was more than an academic year behind Scooter.

"Scooter. What have you been up to? You look like the cat
that swallowed the canary."

"You would never believe it, roomie. Maybe some day I'll tell
you, but not now. One thing, though, it was a whole lot better
than a canary."

"Hey, what's this? Since when do we have deep dark secrets
between us? C'mon, what did you do, or better yet, what's her
name?"

"No names, Johnny. This one stays a secret."

"Don't tease, Scooter. C'mon baby, this is hot stuff, this is
news. Sterling-silver Evans, the campus monk has been seeing a
dolly. Out with it. What's her name?"

"A hint, Johnny. That's all you get. If you can figure this one
out you're a genius. Are you ready, chief inspector?"

"Spit it out, Scoot. If it's a real hint I'll nail it down sooner or
later."

"You'll probably need a pencil. Here's the hint:
One evening long ago a big ship was leaving,
One evening long ago two lovers were grieving,
The crimson sun went down,
The lights began to glow.
One evening long ago . . ."

"I don't know where that's from or what it is, but I sure know
who it is. It can only be one person. Where is she?"

"That's it, pal. No more questions." Scooter got up from the
table and left the Sub. He walked to the door humming softly the
theme from *Harbor Lights*. It had been his and Patricia's song since
high school.

Walking out of the Sub, Scooter encountered Phoebe Johnson, a friend from his biology lab. "Scooter, there is a lady trying
to find you. She's up at the rotunda in Old Main."

"A lady? Who?"

"I didn't get her name but she looks very official, she's wearing a business suit."

"Thanks, Phoebe, I'll hustle over there and see who it is."

Scooter nervously touched his back pocket to confirm that his wallet was in place, suspecting that the official Phoebe mentioned must want additional information for registration: social security data, selective service information, or something he forgot earlier that morning. The bureaucratic gods had to be appeased, so he moved toward Old Main to finish the rites.

She was standing in the rotunda where the refracted rays of sun struck her hair, casting an effulgence to it as if she were somehow translucent, a touch of Venus. Phoebe's term "woman" coupled with "official" had set his mind on the wrong track. The thought of Patricia appearing here had simply not occurred to him. But here she was, her hair bathed in light, framed by rays so distinct that he could see tiny particles of dust swimming in their bands. She was indeed dressed in a stylish tweed business suit setting her apart from the girls on campus.

"Patricia!" Scooter called.

Her response was an easy grin, the kind she used to tease. The grin was followed by a provocative gesture she adored using on him. She showed her teeth, gently biting down on her lower lip like a German shepherd showing his fangs or an angry cat spitting through its teeth. She knew what the gesture did to him. For her it was not a sign of anger but of overt feminine aggression.

"What are you doing here? I thought you were going home."

"I started to leave, Scooter. I got as far as McKeesport to get on the turnpike, but after I went through the toll booth I took the ramp that headed northwest instead of the one going southeast. I had to see you again. I wanted to see the college man in his natural habitat."

Scooter was suddenly frightened. He had made peace with his conscience for the two-day interlude. He justified his compromise by assuring himself that, after all, he had persuaded Patricia to return to her husband, and though he had not entirely kept the law of God at least he had kept the code of the Wall, keeping his passion in check within those limits. But now he was on holy ground. To see Patricia here was like profaning a temple, like mocking God at the spot where His hand had first beckoned him. It was one thing for a priest to talk with a woman friend on his day off, it was another to bring her brazenly into the cloister itself. He had one consuming thought: get her off the campus. They had to get out of sight before any of Scooter's friends saw them together. Panic was shaking his voice, "Patricia, where's your car? We have to get out of here."

Patricia's car was parked just outside the entrance to Old Main. Scooter hurried her to the Jaguar and opened the passenger door for her. As he walked around the car to the driver's side he saw Nancy Lincoln waving to him. Nancy was a senior Christian education major, a girl of unusual spiritual ardor and in integral member of Scooter's Christian Fellowship group. Scooter returned a perfunctory wave and ducked into the safety of the car, hoping that Nancy would not detect his scarlet face. He wanted to peel out of the parking lot as fast as possible but he sat paralyzed in front of the wheel, baffled by the instrument panel of the XKE. "How do I start this thing?" he grumbled in frustration.

Patricia nearly climbed into his lap as she playfully explained the exotic mechanisms of the Jag. Scooter was certain that every passerby was observing their intimate contact in the conspicuous car. He finally got the car started and lurched it forward, shocked by the surge of power from the engine. He sped out of town, moving away from the campus, away from the temple and into the world.

He found a secluded spot in the countryside on a side lane off a rural road. He parked the car by a grove of trees bordering a broad expanse of farmland that provided a vantage point to see cars coming from a distance in either direction. Here there was no wall, no code.

They stayed until darkness crept from the woods and covered the fields. Foregoing dinner, they lingered in love. Scooter had not yet told Patricia of his religious conversion, though he had mentioned to her that he planned to enter the ministry, an announcement she heard with equanimity. He was no longer the frenzied new convert with an impulse to tell everyone he knew about his meeting with Christ. He had become guarded, wary of the vicious responses he had experienced too many times. He talked freely about theology to people but not of the intimacy of his personal experience with God. Too many people had tramped on his soul. He couldn't bear to have Patricia's spiked heels add to the footprints.

Now, however, he had to tell her. The secret was swelling into a monstrous millstone around his neck. It was like a supernatural burden of guilt he could not carry for another minute. He withdrew from an embrace and leaned back against the door saying, "Patricia, there is something I have to tell you."

He poured it out to her in detail. The night with Eddie and Barry. The midnight struggle in the corridor of the freshman dorm. The intensity of his reading of the Scripture. His prayer by the edge of his bed. He spoke of the subsequent firming of his resolve to live for God, of his pilgrimage of faith that was heightened by his search of Christian philosophy. Patricia listened in silence, no hint of hostility or attempts to make light of what he was saying. When he finished his story she spoke softly, "Scooter, darling, I don't fully understand what you are saying. I've never had an experience like that. But I don't question for a minute that you did. I'm glad you told me; it explains a lot about these past few days. I always knew you had something special inside you. I think you were destined to the ministry before any of this ever happened. I always felt something from you that was spiritual."

Scooter was soothed by the warmth of her understanding but frustrated by her allusions to his earlier "spiritual" inclinations. At that point he wanted to shake her and say, "No, no, Patricia. I may have appeared spiritual before but I wasn't really at all. That's the whole point. I didn't care at all about spiritual things in the past. Yes, I thought about life and about God and tossed in my bed at night, disgusted with the things I did during the day. A thousand times I promised myself, with my head on the pillow, that tomorrow I would turn over a new leaf, but tomorrow was always the same. Yes, I felt soiled when I adjusted my ethics downward from my childhood idealism to accommodate where I really was with my life. I did all those things and I did not know God. I didn't know Him at all. Yes, I knew He existed and all that, but I didn't know Him like I do now. I was not spiritual. I'm still not spiritual but God knows I want to be."

Scooter said none of those things. He accepted Patricia's facile explanation and let it go. That she did not react in hostility was enough.

"Do you see now why I can't run off with you? Do you understand why I have to plead with you to go back to your husband?"

"Oh, Scooter, you make me feel evil, like a scarlet woman who has despoiled a priest. Why didn't you tell me earlier?"

"Don't feel like that, Patricia. It's not your fault. You're not a scarlet woman. If we've done anything wrong it's my fault. But it has to stop, right now, right here. I don't have to stop loving you but I have to stop seeing you. One more day like this and we'll be in so deep that there will be no way out for either of us."

Patricia started to cry, first softly then heaving with sobs. "Oh Scooter," she blurted. "How can I go back to Florida and pretend that I'm a loving wife when all I want is to be with you? Isn't there some way we can stay together? God is surely a merciful God. How could He object to this?"

"But He does, Patricia, and we both know it. You may not take your marriage vows seriously, but God does. There is no way. Right now we're on a fantasy trip, we're kidding ourselves and trying to find a way to justify what we want. If I've learned anything so far it is that a man can't beat God. I tried it, Patricia, and I lost."

Rehearsing the events of his conversion reawakened Scooter to the reality of his duty. He could not indulge himself with a married woman for another moment. He pressed the engine to life and drove back to the college. He pulled into the driveway of the Victorian frame house where he and Johnny had rented a room from a matronly spinster who supplemented her pension by taking in students as borders. He got out of the car and held the door open while he reached in to help Patricia across the front seat to the driver's side. She adjusted her skirt and slid the seat closer so that her feet could reach the pedals. She straightened her hair, preening as she pulled herself together to leave. Scooter shut the heavy door slowly, but firmly and looked at Patricia through the open window. Rivulets of tears were streaming down her cheeks, ravaging what was left of her makeup. He leaned over and stuck his head through the open window. "Remember that I love you."

He kissed her for the last time and withdrew his head from the window. Patricia forced a smile as she roared the car into gear. She backed out of the driveway and moved away into the darkness. Scooter stood at the edge of the driveway and watched the tail lights fade into the night. He had a nostalgic thought of a little boy watching his hero ride into the sunset while he screamed after him, "Shane! Shane! Come back, Shane."

But this was not a movie, and Patricia was not Alan Ladd. When the house lights came up she was gone. Scooter fled into the house, went straight to the bathroom and threw up, retching with racks of dry vomiting, his stomach protesting the lack of food it was denied this day.

In the months that followed, Scooter heard nothing from Patricia. His midnight fantasies increased and he fostered a hope that Patricia's husband would not be forgiving, that he would force a divorce leaving them free to be married. Instead he heard nothing until a year later when Carole announced to him that Patricia had given birth to a baby girl. The news was like a final curtain dropping on his life, consigning him to the final fate of Kierkegaard.

Scooter's senior year was spent with an intensified pursuit of academic matters. He threw himself into his studies finding fuel for his melancholy in the sonorous poems of Edgar Allen Poe and the mystical themes of his hero, Herman Melville. He wrote his senior research paper on a philosophical analysis of Melville's greatest work. It was titled, "The Existential Implications of Melville's Moby Dick."

In Melville, as with Kierkegaard, Scooter found a kindred spirit. Here was a man who was tortured by some nameless wound inflicted by the Almighty. Melville's monumental work chronicled the ambivalence of the author to a great and mighty God who wore the opaque mask of whiteness, a symbol both of purity and of horror. The albino whale was Melville's symbol of God, a ghostly monster shrouded in the whiteness of ambiguity, the one who bore the absence of color, from whose bosom men shrank in terror. At times he felt the deep loathing of the monomaniacal captain of the *Pequod*. At other times he felt the awe of the sailors in the presence of the indestructible force who sounded the depths when harpooners drew too close and breeched the waves in fury at their impertinence. Melville had penned a personal note to Nathaniel Hawthorne, "I have written a wicked book."

Scooter identified with the ambivalence of Melville, feeling at times befuddled by God like the irrational cabin boy, Pip, and wounded by his Maker like the crippled Ahab. Yet he was drawn as inexorably to the hunt as Captain Ahab was to his watery grave. Scooter had to see beyond the mask of the pallid cloak of whiteness that hid the furrowed brow of the face of God.

FIFTEEN

The skyline of Manhattan faded in the distance, disappearing beyond the curvature of the earth that ancient mariners could not envision. Scooter left the rail of the fantail and made himself comfortable in a deck chair. The deck steward passed and Scooter stopped him with a question, "Sir, do you ever see whales on voyages like this?"

"Oh, indeed we do, sir. Quite frequently in fact. Mostly we notice them playing in the water at a great distance. Their spouts are usually the first thing we see. Some folks still shout, 'Thar she blows' when we come upon them."

Out of sight of land Scooter had a gripping feeling of anxiety, as the reality of his departure from home began to sink into his mind. He had burned his bridges; he sold his car, his stereo, and everything of value he possessed to purchase his one-way ticket to Europe. The thought of graduate school both excited and intimidated him, especially since he had no training in the Dutch language. The last few weeks had been spent in intensive listening to Linguaphone records to secure a modicum of knowledge of the language. The next several weeks would be devoted to even more strenuous study of the soft and lilting cognate of German.

Holland was his destination, a tiny piece of real estate reclaimed from the sea by courageous men and women, fiercely working in the muck, attired in funny wooden shoes, *klampen,* one of the few words Scooter had already learned. He was glad to pay the price of foreign language study necessary to attend a university where classical Christianity was still pursued with intellectual vigor. He expected a dramatic contrast from the three years of skepticism he endured from his professors in the American seminary from which he had graduated only a few days before sailing. That place had been a monument of unbelief, a citadel of doubt

where biblical faith was openly assailed by those who held high
positions in theological education and in the ecclesiastical hierarchy.

Scooter whispered a silent prayer, "Please God, don't let this
experience in school be as shattering as the one in Pittsburgh."

Scooter stood at the entrance gate of the Pittsburgh Presbyterian Divinity School. The building was gray. A drab gray born of
too many decades of incinerated ashes raining from the sky, too
many years of smoke particles peppering the pores of the original
brownstone edifice. Now only the pneumatic force of a sandblast-
ing machine attacking the cold stone could restore the halcyon
lustre of its pristine beauty. But that was too expensive. And futile. To restore this grime-covered building to its Victorian splendor would be like giving a face lift to a cadaver. Long ago the
building had uttered its final sigh of resignation, bowing to the
encrustations of time. Other circles could restore the faded beauty
of their antique buildings, but not Pittsburgh. No magic of urban
renewal had yet been found to make this section of town anything
but dreary. To make the attempt was to flirt with the deluded
mind of the medieval alchemist.

The seminary was located on the edge of the combat zone of
Pittsburgh's Northside, directly across the street from the city's
most notorious red-light district, a row of houses cloaked with
garrish curtains that allowed the eerie glow from Tiffany lamps to
seep onto the dark sidewalks at night. The streets had lampposts,
but they were mute, darkened sentinels, their globes smashed and
bulbs shattered so often by vandals that the city abandoned hope
of keeping them in repair.

Once this had been a fashionable district; not as splendid,
however, as the east side that was distinguished by the row of
patrician mansions along the tree-lined avenues of Shadyside
where the Mellons, Carnegies, Fricks, and the Hillmans built
their ornate palaces during the gilded age of marble pillars and
stone gargoyles. This was the Northside, populated chiefly by immigrants from Poland, Germany, Croatia, Czechoslovakia, and
other eastern European nations. The immigrants fled from poverty, famine, and oppression in the old country, coming by boat to
New York and then on to Pittsburgh by trains drawn by steam-
puffing locomotives, seeking their fortunes on the banks of the

Monongahela and the Ohio where the titans of steel used the miracle of the Bessemer process to create a new world.

Scooter stood before the building like a spiritual immigrant. He was Redburn at the wharf in Liverpool; Luther at the steps of the Scala Sancta in Rome; Jacob by the ford of the river Jabbok. He was dazed in awe, at once frightened and exhilarated by the sight of this holy institution. The school was surrounded by a huge wrought iron picket fence, its edges raised by rust bubbles covered over with globs of black paint. From the street it looked more like an archaic prison, a detention center, than a sanctuary of learning for students preparing to enter the sacred guild of the cloth.

Scooter entered the building. It's interior was as somber as its facade. He walked through the dimly lit hall and stepped to the registrar's desk to enroll his name on the roster that dated back to the middle of the nineteenth century. The office walls were adorned by portraits of bearded scholars of Calvinistic heritage who once graced the lecterns of this institution, some of whom went on to teach at the grand Presbyterian Seminary at Princeton.

Now a bona fide divinity student, Scooter was given a room assignment on an upper floor. He got a private room, a cubicle with high ceilings, walls covered with yellowing wallpaper, and a single window made almost opaque from grime. The window "looked out" on a rusty fire escape and on the blackened red brick of the building next door. The room contained a metal bed, an old oak desk and a cheaply finished stand-up closet covered with a thin mahogany veneer. This would be his home for three years, a sentence that Providence would refuse to commute.

The first day was given to class registration followed by an assembly for the entering class to hear an orientation speech by the dean. Scooter looked forward to hearing the address. He had heard Dean Alexander Jefferson speak when he had visited Witherspoon College as a vespers speaker. Scooter had been assigned as the dean's campus escort on that occasion and had arranged dinner and housing accommodations for him. It was the dean's sanguine manner and personal vitality on that visit that had convinced Scooter to enroll in the Pittsburgh Presbyterian Divinity School.

Dean Alexander rose to speak:

"Gentlemen, we welcome you to this institution. We are called a divinity school. Some refer to us as a theological seminary. Those words are accurate to a degree, but they fail to capture the spirit of this place and this faculty. Our goal is to be a theological university where the highest level of scholarship is performed, the most rigorous academic curriculum. Your class will be the first to follow it. The curriculum will be exacting, innovative, and I trust, exciting. You will be challenged. The assumptions you brought with you will be tested.

"We have assembled a faculty that we believe is one of the finest in America. We do not speak a party line. We are not monolithically committed to one theology. We are diverse. We are critical in the academic sense. You will certainly not be sheltered. We want you to be exposed to a broad spectrum of theological viewpoints. 'Iron sharpens iron,' gentlemen. We will have spirited debate, open dialogue, and candid criticism.

"This is not a 'safe school.' We put the accent on risk, on challenge. There will be times when you will struggle. You will be confused, frustrated, and sometimes downright angry. But those are the price tags for any man's honest pursuit of truth.

"The door to my office is always open to you. I want your time here to be rewarding. Let us make the pilgrimage together."

Scooter was moved by Dean Jefferson's speech. The ringing challenging was taken by the new students as a compliment, a transparent assertion that they had the maturity to handle difficult issues and critical analyses of their faith without lapsing into sheltered retreat. Scooter was confident that subjecting his faith to rigorous intellectual scrutiny would only serve to strengthen it.

His confidence was shaken on the third day of classes. Two events converged to kick the props out from him, leaving him flailing in the air for something to grab on to. In theology class he was exposed to a German scholar who added academic prestige to the institution. Both his personal bloodline and academic credentials were impeccable. Dr. Hans Mannheim was noted for his brilliance as well as for being a nephew of one of Germany's most famous theologians. Mannheim's bohemian style, punctuated by a heavy accent, gave him an added measure of charisma.

In his first lecture Mannheim declared with Teutonic bombast, "Gentlemen, the truth of God can never be contained in the earthly vessel of human logic. For ultimate truth we must go the way of the paradox. Reason is a whore. She will seduce you and leave you spent but unsatisfied. We must defy logic, say, 'To the gallows' with reason. We must walk to the edge of irrationality and peer into its pit. And then jump. Jump with reckless abandon. We must go over the brink and into the abyss. That is where authentic faith is found. It is Abraham hearing the summons of God to kill his own son, what Kierkegaard called the 'temporary suspension of the ethical.' It is believing against reason that makes us Christians. Put your logic away; nail it to the cross. We must destroy reason to make room for faith."

The class exploded in spontaneous applause. They were thrilled in their souls by Mannheim's eloquence, by his passion; and most of all by his words of liberation. Scooter didn't clap. He sat there confused. What the professor said had moved him too. He responded to the dynamism of the lecture with an inner excitement, but his mind was baffled.

Another student asked the question aloud that was squeezing Scooter's brain: "Dr. Mannheim. Can you give us an example of how theology goes beyond logic?"

"Yes." Dr. Mannheim responded. Consider the nature of God. The classical textbooks declare that God is immutable. He never changes. Yet if God were absolutely immutable, incapable of any change, He would be inert—static—a frozen being locked in eternal permanence who could not act. Such a torpid God would differ not at all from a dead God. Yet the fathers were right: God is absolutely immutable in His essence. We must hold to that at all costs. We dare not abandon that truth lest we worship a God who is ephemeral, who changes His character whimsically like a will-o'-the-wisp.

"But—at the same time we must declare that God is mutable. He does change. He is alive, dynamic, perhaps even a part of the cosmic process scientists are only now beginning to probe. So with our ancient confession we must also boldly declare that God is absolutely mutable in His being."

Now it was becoming clear to Scooter. The veil was starting to lift. He raised his hand and was acknowledged by the professor. "Dr. Mannheim, do you mean that there is paradox in God, an apparent contradiction that can be resolved by closer scrutiny? That looking at God from one perspective shows a kind of immutability, but from another perspective a kind of mutability?"

"No, no, young man. That is precisely what I do not mean. You are still trying to force God to be logical. Did you hear my words? I said that 'God is *absolutely* immutable in His being and *absolutely* mutable in His being.' Absolute and altogether both! At the same time! In the same relationship! From the same perspective! Not merely paradox, boy, contradiction pure and simple. That is the scandal of Christianity. Contradiction. You must be mature enough to accept it and rest in it. Think about it. Deeply. It will force you to faith."

When the class ended, Scooter walked to the student lounge in a daze. His classmates were buzzing excitedly around him outdoing each other with glowing epithets of praise for their professor. Scooter was hardly listening. Key words from their dialogue hit his ears like poisoned darts: "deep," "profound," "genius," "scintillating"—Scooter remained silent. He was obviously dejected. One of the students prodded him, "Wasn't that fantastic, Evans? Mannheim is incredible. Best lecture I ever heard."

"Was it?" Scooter asked coldly, his shock giving rise to anger.

"What's the matter with you, Evans? Didn't you like what Mannheim said?"

"What did he say?" Scooter asked.

"You know what he said. You were there."

"Yeah, I was there. I heard it. I know what he said. Maybe I should have asked, What did he mean?"

"You asked that in class. He told you what he meant. He meant what he said, 'God is absolutely immutable and absolutely mutable.' He's both. At the same time. In the same way. Don't you get it, Evans?"

"No, I'm sorry. I don't get it."

"Why not?"

"Because it's nonsense, that's why. The only absolute about it is its absolute nonsense."

"But that's the whole point. You're all hung up on logic. You have to get past that. Go beyond it, man. That's what Mannheim was saying."

"Yeah, I know. That's what bothers me."

"Why? Surely you believe God is greater than logic?"

"Yes. But is He less? He may be above reason but not against it."

"Do you think you can know all about God just by reason? That stuff went out in the seventeenth century, Evans."

"Of course we can't know all about God by reason. I told you I believe God is beyond reason. There are lots of things I can't fathom. That's one of the reasons I'm here. There's a whole lot of mystery in my faith. Mystery I can live with. But contradictions? Never."

"Sounds to me like you're really a rationalist. Where's your faith? Or don't you have any?"

"Maybe I don't," Scooter said. "Maybe I don't."

Scooter felt lousy. He went back to his room thinking, *What is this place? A seminary or a madhouse?*

Later that afternoon Scooter had his second shock of the day. This time it was a New Testament professor who delivered the jolt. Dr. Nelson Tweedy, American by birth but educated in Marburg, German, was giving an exposition of the theology of Rudolf Bultmann.

"It is Professor Bultmann's thesis that the Bible is a mixture of history and mythology. There is an historical core to the myths that sprung up about Jesus, but it is like a small kernel encrusted in a husk of mythology. It is the job of the serious student to cut through the husk and get to the kernel. We must use the method of demythologizing the Bible. The Bible was written by ancient men in a primitive and prescientific environment. No one can live in our modern age, making use of radio, television, atomic energy and microbiology, and still believe in the miracles of Jesus. The New Testament stories of virgin birth, resurrection, atonement are all mythological embellishments added to the historical Jesus."

Scooter was not disturbed by the exposition. He was aware of such theories emanating from the continent, especially from Germany. He was aware that nineteenth-century critics had argued that the resurrection was at worst a hoax and at best a parable of sorts. He patiently waited for Dr. Tweedy's critique of Bultmann. None came. The lecture continued sounding not so much as an exposition of Bultmann but as a declaration of the professor's own beliefs.

Larry Knapp, a student rooming on the same floor as Scooter, engaged the professor in debate.

"But, professor, if we discount the resurrection of Jesus what happens to Christianity?"

Dr. Tweedy replied, "There is much more to Christianity than stories about dying and rising gods. There is an existential spirit in Jesus that we need to grasp to be authentic men. That's what we must look for."

"But what about Christ's deity?" Larry complained.

"Maybe we need to redefine what we mean by *deity* to be modern Christians." Dr. Tweedy was alert to the rising sense of consternation in the room. He spoke in pastoral terms, gently, to assuage the anxiety of the students. "I'm afraid that some of you have come here with too many assumptions. Relax. This is the place to test your assumptions. Those that are sound should be able to survive intact. Those that won't stand up to criticism will have to be discarded."

Tweedy's words echoed in Scooter's ears after class, almost making him forget Dr. Mannheim's morning lecture. *Some of you have come here with too many assumptions. The deity of Christ an assumption? Wow! I guess I'm one of the culprits. I've come here with two assumptions: that truth is rational, and Christ is divine. Already I'm 0 for 2. Maybe I don't belong in the ministry.*

Scooter resolved to keep his mouth shut in class and to avoid unsavory arguments. He told himself that the professors' private beliefs didn't matter. He was here for education, not inspiration. He combed his textbooks carefully, screening what he judged to be true and discarding whatever he thought was false. *I can learn something from anyone,* he thought. *I'll never find a person with whom I'll be in agreement about everything. No matter, I can still learn.*

His heart was saying something different. He was feeling the excruciating pain of disillusionment. The hurt was fomenting within, threatening him with bitterness. Part of him was hurt, part of him was angry and he feared a growing paranoia. *Why am I so upset? The other students are taking it in stride. Don't they understand? Don't they care?*

Scooter held his silence in class until the end of the first semester when he listened to another New Testament professor lecture on the meaning of the Sermon on the Mount. When he came to the Lord's Prayer he said to the class, "Gentlemen, the point of this model prayer is found in its lesson in brevity. The entire prayer takes approximately eighteen seconds to recite. The lesson for us is that we ought not to waste our time in pious outpourings of lengthy prayers as the hypocrites do, but we ought to be men of action, not slowed down or retarded by so-called spiritual exercises. Jesus is saying here to never pray for more than twenty seconds. Any more is a waste of time."

Scooter raised his hand, a gesture met by a synchronized response of the professor's raised eyebrows. "What is it, Mr. Evans?"

"Sir, it seems strange to me that Jesus Himself never made such an inference about the time duration of prayer. If He were implying such a rule here, why didn't He obey it Himself ? The Gospels record several occasions when Jesus spent protracted periods in prayer. Luke says Jesus prayed all night before He selected His disciples, and in His agony in Gethsemane He rebuked His disciples for not persevering in prayer as He did."

An electric sense sparked the air as Scooter opened his mouth uttering a direct challenge to the renowned scholar. A sardonic grin curled the corners of the professor's mouth and he said in imperious tones, "You . . . Mr. Evans . . . are not Jesus!"

The class exploded in laughter and Scooter slouched in his seat, crimson-faced in humiliation.

When the class was dismissed Scooter was consoled by a small cadre of friends who shared his faith in historic Christianity and felt the pangs of his shame in the class with him. The five of them met weekly in Scooter's room for a time of prayer that always exceeded the new orthodoxy of eighteen seconds. They gathered that week in Scooter's cubicle to join together in adoration and intercession. In the quietness of their prayer vigil they were startled by the acrid smell of smoke and jolted to their feet by the sudden flash of flames shooting like orange hands from the edge of the door. The flash fire subsided as quickly as it had ignited. Scooter leaped to the door to investigate the source, his heart pounding with fear that the building was on fire. He broke all rules of safety by flinging open the door. His friends were already at work prying open the crusty window in the event they would have to flee by the fire escape.

Scooter stood frozen at the open door instantly realizing that he was the butt of the amusement of some twelve to fifteen students who were roaring in laughter, two of them physically rolling on the corridor floor holding their sides in convulsive mockery.

The leader stood there with the explanation of the flash fire visible in his hand. He was holding a can of lighter fluid that he had just emptied on the veneer of the door before striking a match to it. He said with a sneer, "Well, Evans, that ought to teach you and your Christian buddies. The God Squad got bombed tonight."

Scooter trembled in rage, his right hand clenching and un-clenching a fist. His tormentor started to speak again but Scooter cut him off. "That's enough. Don't say another word or you'll be saying your own prayers in a hurry."

The gangling antagonist was livid, not about to be put down in front of his friends. "What's the matter, Evans, are you forget-ting to turn the other cheek?"

Scooter threw. No hesitation. His right hand flew out so fast the ringleader never saw it coming. Scooter felt the nasal cartilage snap as his fist smashed the student in the center of his face. The impact of the blow knocked the student into the wall and blood oozed from his nostrils. The rest of the students froze, flabber-gasted in numb disbelief. Scooter stared at them, and said, "You'd better take care of your buddy. He's going to need a re-pair job on his nose."

The group dispersed. Scooter stepped slowly into his room and shut the door that was now stained by a thin layer of soot like a glass lamp chimney. He turned the lock and leaned his back against the door heaving a sigh.

"I'm sorry, guys. I thought my fighting days were over. I haven't thrown a punch at anyone since high school. I don't know. I can't figure it out . . . When he started in after I warned him not to say another word, it was like a steel trap went off inside me. A fine minister I'll make."

"Stop it, Richard. It was sheer grace that kept you from bust-ing him as long as you did."

"Yeah," one of the others chimed in. "I'm glad you did it. I would have myself but I didn't have the guts. They could have burned this whole building down with their nonsense."

"You guys are a lot of help. I can hear it tomorrow. 'Quick trigger' Evans breaks senior's nose in divinity school brawl. I'll put it in my dossier when I'm searching for a parish. 'One-Punch' Evans, the 'ministerial mauler,' or call me 'killer-clergyman' for short."

"Seriously, Richard, what's the matter with those guys?

They're so hostile to prayer and the Bible, what in the world are they doing in seminary?"

Another friend gave answer. "Don't you guys know that seminary students get a beautiful deferment from Uncle Sam's military lottery? We are classified with the certified insane. Women and children have to go in the army before we do."

"I know," Scooter said. "But there are lots of other reasons too. Some guys go into the ministry because the church offers them a great platform for community leadership."

"But what are these guys going to do to the church? I mean what's the point of having a church if you think God is dead? The church will be a mausoleum."

Again Scooter demurred. "You watch these guys. I'll bet at least half of them will either never finish seminary or will quit the ministry within ten years. This stuff may be stimulating in divinity school but it won't wash in the local congregation. You don't tell people God is dead or that Jesus was resurrected when you're standing by a casket in the funeral parlor. But who am I to talk. I'm standing here with blood on my knuckles."

Scooter tossed in fitful insomnia that night. He tried various methods of self-hypnosis including counting backwards from one hundred and counting the intervals in seconds between the sounds of wailing sirens that were a nightly cacophony, with ambulances racing through the streets of the combat zone, rushing to the illumined parking lot and entrance ramp of the emergency room of the Allegheny General Hospital. He thought about quitting, or at least transferring to another school. All in one day he had been humiliated by challenging a professor in class and had blown his cool with a tempestuous act of violence. He was sure that two and a half more years would not be enough time to live down a reputation that would be in cement throughout the student body by noon of the next day.

The last time he glanced at the greenish luminous dial of the alarm clock on his desk it was approaching 3:00 A.M. He mocked himself thinking, *It's a quarter to three. There's no one in this place except you and me. So set 'em up Joe . . ."*

Sleep finally came when Scooter rekindled his favorite nocturnal fantasy. He saw Patricia standing in the doorway of his mother's apartment, dressed in a black dress. He imagined her head snuggled against his shoulder as they watched the stars dancing over the South Park Oval from their vantage point at the China Wall. He revived the memory etched in his brain of her tear-stained face as she pulled out of the driveway at Witherspoon. He saw the red taillights disappear in the night. But this time the car turned around and came back. Scooter ran to the roadside and jumped in laughing like a mad man saying, "Drive, let's go . . ."

The dawn brought no peace to his turmoil. Four hours of sleep left him sluggish, irritable, and hung-over with depression. An anxiety attack swept over him and fear emerged as the dominant emotion. He had to talk to somebody. He was feeling like an orphan, exposed to a hostile world with no parental support system, no inner strength to fall back on, and the urge to pack his bags and go out the iron gate was overwhelming. His father was gone. Patricia was gone. Scotty McTavish was gone. Again he thought of Ishmael, the lone survivor of the crew of the *Pequod,* helplessly floundering in the water, thrashing through the flotsam and jetsam, grasping for the top of Queequeeg's floating coffin, his only hope of life.

Scooter's single ray of hope lay in the person of one faculty member who swam against the current of the divinity school, Dr. Edward Morrison. Dr. Morrison was an anomaly, a maverick, a misfit in this place. A Harvard Ph.D., Morrison was far and away the most erudite professor on the faculty and also the most conservative. He was shunned by the rest of the teachers, partly out of fear and partly out of contempt. They referred to him behind his back as "Medieval Morrison" the ossified anachronism who seemed to be unaware of what century he was living in. His acute logical mind and penchant for classical orthodoxy earned him the reputation of being the last of the seventeenth-century Protestant scholastics, a fossilized vestigial remnant of bygone days. Put a scraggly beard on his ruggedly handsome face and his portrait would blend in perfectly on the walls of the registrar's office. Dr. Morrison was the Pittsburgh Presbyterian School of Divinity's token conservative.

In the late fifties, the largest Presbyterian body in America, the Presbyterian Church in the U.S.A., merged with a tiny denomination called the United Presbyterian Church. It was an unusual alliance as the larger body, the so-called "U.S.A."

Presbyterians, were clearly the most liberal of the American Presbyterian Churches. The "U.P.s", the United Presbyterian were
one of the smallest of the Presbyterian bodies and also one of the
most conservative. It was not really a merger but an absorption,
with the U.P.s being rapidly swallowed by the power structures in
the new, liberally dominated organization that called itself the
United Presbyterian Church in the U.S.A. One of the terms in
the final negotiations for merger set forth by the minority group
was that their champion, Dr. Edward Morrison, be appointed to
the faculty of the Pittsburgh Divinity School with the rank of Full
Professor of Systematic Theology, and be granted automatic and
immediate tenure. The condition was nonnegotiable so the bone
was thrown to the minority to insure the union.

Morrison assumed his post working like a Daniel in a den full
of lions. He was fearless in debate, quite able to stand alone as a
thorn in the side of his colleagues. His scholarship was impeccable
and, though the faculty despised him, none could assail his academic credentials, which made him all the more loathsome to
them. He was the theologians' William F. Buckley, a man liberals
love to hate but none wants to face one-on-one in public debate.
Morrison was encyclopedic in his knowledge, mastering the latest
German theology before his comrades, to their constant chagrin.

Scooter's problem was that Dr. Morrison frightened him as
much as he intimidated the faculty. His courses were so demanding that it was said he would flunk his grandmother if she couldn't
spell "Schleiermacher." Morrison's class syllabus declared that
students were welcome to make appointments for private inter-
views with him, but Scooter was not aware of anyone who had the
nerve to visit the "awesome one" in his private chambers. But if
anyone could understand Scooter's problem it was Morrison, and
his fear of the professor was now slight in comparison to the anxiety he was feeling about staying in school.

Dr. Morrison's secretary was ebullient, pleasantly chatting
with Scooter while she penciled in a 4:00 P.M. appointment on
Morrison's schedule book. He was granted an audience of fifteen
minutes, hardly time enough to resolve his difficulties, but at least
it was something to look forward to to keep his mind occupied
during the day. Scooter could feel the furtive glances of the students as he walked the halls between classes. Maybe his imagina-

tion was working overtime, fueled by guilt feelings, but it seemed
as if the men were giving him a wide swath in the corridors like he
was a madman about to explode and lash out at anyone treading
too near. *Paranoid,* he thought, *I'm getting stinking paranoid.*

The 4:00 meeting was a pleasant surprise. Morrison was
warm and compassionate, ignoring the clock as he listened to
Scooter rehearse his problems of the previous day and confess
his thougths about quitting. He saw another side of Morrison, a
gracious wit that sparkled in his repartee. "Aha. We have a Presbyterian pugilist in our midst, a Calvinistic Cassius Clay, our
theological answer to the Loquacious Lip of Louisville."

Scooter was shocked that Morrison, with his head usually
buried in tomes in the library would be remotely aware of the
young boxer who profoundly proclaimed to the world that he was
the "greatest" while composing awful poems predicting the exact
round of his next opponent's demise. This was before Clay's conversion to Islam, his name-change to Mohammed Ali, and the
"Thrilla in Manila."

That Morrison could jest about Scooter's "pugilistic procliv-
ity" without coming down hard on him for losing his temper put
a warm blanket of peace on his soul. He listened with growing
hope as Morrison encouraged him to stay, to put his misconduct
behind him and stick it out at the seminary. "Richard, if you stay
here and master the material I give you, which I can supplement
beyond your course requirements, plus master what the liberals
are teaching you, you will gain the benefit of the equivalent of two
educations. You'll know both sides, learning them from advocates
of each."

Scooter gave Dr. Morrison his solemn assurance that he
would follow his counsel, jubilant inside that he had discovered
another coach, an ersatz father who would believe in Scooter
when he didn't believe in himself. He stood up to leave, filled
with a rekindled optimism.

"One more thing to remember, Richard. Never argue with
the man who's holding the microphone."

"What do you mean?" Scooter asked.

"What I'm saying is, keep your ears open and your mouth
shut in class. Don't try to argue with your professors. It's like
debating with a talk-show host on television. They control the

game. Their finger is on the microphone switch. They can shut you off any time they feel like it. Only a fool plays against a stacked deck."

"Yes sir. I'll remember that."

For the rest of his seminary career Scooter functioned like the prototype of the wise monkeys with hands covering their ears, their eyes, and their mouths. "Hear no evil, see no evil, speak no evil" became his academic code. No more debates with professors were waged, no more fists were thrown in frustration. Scooter applied himself to master both poles of the theological spectrum.

His opportunity to speak out came in the fall of his senior year when his homiletics professor selected him to preach in chapel at an annual event when student body, faculty, and over two hundred clergy of the presbytery assembled for a special convocation.

He began his sermon by saying, "As a seminarian I have learned some new things about the nature of evil, of what it means to sin. I've learned that 'sin' is a 'necessary condition of finitude,' or that it is a 'psychological problem of neurosis,' or that it is a failure to achieve 'existential authentic existence.'"

Scooter exaggerated the buzz words common to contemporary theological views of sin. He went on:

"Fathers and brothers, I ask you. Who would question that we are indeed finite, or that our lives are plagued by neurosis, or even that it seems at times we are bent on destroying whatever authenticity there may be to our existence? But, gentlemen, these are euphemisms, circumlocutory devices that tone down what the Bible calls sin. Our forefathers preferred a more honest definition. The catechism asks 'What is sin?' You've all memorized the answer: 'Sin is any want of conformity to or transgression of the law of God.' That is the problem, gentlemen. We are lawbreakers. We have violated the commands of a just and holy God. None of us can stand before Him pleading the feeble excuse of finitude or of our nervous insecurities or our existential pathos. We are guilty, and we hate that. Under divine conviction of sin, sometimes we cry out in horror as Luther did, 'You ask me if I love God. Love God! Sometimes I hate Him . . .'"

Scooter paused, letting Luther's excruciating cry sink in.

"What can we do about it? It is futile to seek the empty solace of euphemisms. Utterly foolish. We need grace . . . the redeeming grace that saved the sanity of Luther and rescued the integrity of Augustine . . ."

Scooter went on, graphically describing episodes of biblical heroes, their faces in the dust before God in sorrowful repentance.

He declared that apart from the reality of the cross, mankind was without hope, having no exit, no comfort from the hounding pangs of a guilty conscience that all men share and none can escape.

The climax of the sermon came when Scooter quoted the words from the old-time hymn by Augustus Toplady, "Rock of Ages."

Nothing in my hand I bring,
simply to the cross I cling.

Scooter shouted the word "Nothing . . ." and stretched his arm over the edge of the pulpit, brandishing a tightly clenched fist. Then he modulated his voice almost whispering the word again, "Nothing . . ." At the precise moment of drama Scooter released the fist, slowly opening his fingers to reveal that they were empty. Then he finished the sentence, ". . . in my hand I bring, simply to the cross, I cling." The outstretched hand closed again in a gesture of tenacious grasping. He held the pose for a moment, then bowed his head for the closing prayer.

The organ postlude signaled the end of the convocation. Scooter stepped down the chancel steps to fall in behind the crowd heading for the exits in the rear of the chapel. But nobody was leaving. The students were milling around the chapel steps with outstretched hands, showering him with compliments and patting him on the shoulder. The most radical of the leftist students were greeting him with laudatory comments. He felt as he used to feel after a winning basketball game when the fans would swarm all over him as he made his way to the locker room.

The congratulations finally ceased and Scooter followed the last of the crowd toward the exit. In the foyer he was met by three angry professors, including the academic dean. The dean was boiling, on the edge of apoplexy. He gritted his teeth at Scooter and loudly rebuked him. "What do you think you're doing, bringing the sawdust trail in here? This is no cheap evangelist's tent. You distorted Presbyterian theology with that diatribe on sin."

The dean was poking his finger in Scooter's chest. Scooter tried to back away, to find some avenue of escape. His way was blocked by the other two professors who were glaring at him like wolves. The dean made his final point by physically shoving Scooter against the wall so that the back of his head came in rude contact with the plastered surface. Abruptly the dean and his cohorts turned around and stomped away, leaving Scooter dazed, his head throbbing. The sharp pain from crashing into the wall brought involuntary tears to his eyes. Through blurred vision he could see a remnant of students who had witnessed the encounter, standing with horror on their faces, shocked by the dean's display.

Scooter went immediately to Dr. Morrison's office, fighting waves of nausea. He ignored the protocol of an appointment and knocked directly on the door. Scooter heard words of invitation to enter and walked in breathing heavily, his face white from the trauma.

"What's the matter, Richard?" Dr. Morrison rose from his chair and came around his desk to help Scooter be seated. Scooter breathed rapidly relating what had just happened in the chapel foyer. "You were there, professor. Was I arrogant? Did I distort Presbyterian theology?"

Scooter had never heard Dr. Morrison speak in derogatory personal terms of his colleagues on the faculty. He criticized their views but never their persons. This time he let drop a thinly veiled personal attack. "It's like Luther used to say, 'You preached the truth and the dogs are starting to bark.' No, Richard, you were anything but arrogant. You pointed us all to our need for grace. Your sermon was masterful without the slightest nuance of theological distortion. That's what made them so angry. I am sure that every saint in heaven from Saint Paul to B. B. Warfield threw his celestial hat in the air. The angels are having a party this very minute, celebrating your sermon. There hasn't been a sermon like that heard in this chapel for decades."

Again Scooter left Dr. Morrison's office with his head held high. The Student Executive Committee filed a formal protest that afternoon against the dean, demanding that he apologize in writing to Scooter. The carefully worded apology appeared in his student mailbox the next day.

Mr. Evans,

I want to apologize for my actions against you yesterday. It was inexcusable for a man in my position to lose my temper as I did, and personally attack a student. I hope you will forgive the offense and that we might enjoy once more a cordial relationship. You know the regard I have for you. I think you have one of the most scintillating intellects of any student we have ever had here. That, Richard, is why I got so upset, to see someone of your great talent get caught in seventeenth-century orthodoxy . . .

The note went on to repeat all the charges he had made the day before, effectively rescinding the apology he made under duress. Scooter made a gracious written reply and the incident was quickly forgotten. Scooter continued to behave as a gentleman in the dean's classroom, not rising to challenge him, even when the dean presented his theory that Jesus was guilty of an illicit clandestine love affair with Mary Magdalene.

SIXTEEN

Scooter's senior year of seminary marked the beginning of his ministry. His preaching skill made him an easy winner in the competition for the few student pastorates that were available in the area. While the men who had graduated and were ordained were scrambling up the ecclesiastical ladder vying for the "plum" churches, the seminarians were competing for the "crumb" churches. Plums and crumbs, cathedrals and storefronts, these were the horizons of men and boys. Small parishes, ravaged by the moribund slump of dying towns that no longer could afford the required minimum salary of an ordained minister, plundered the ranks of the seminary for cheap labor as they struggled to keep their church doors open and their minicongregations intact.

Most of these churches were in rural communities east of Pittsburgh with charters dating back well over a century. They were hampered from further growth by the flight of young people from the barnyards. The modern lure of the city made it almost impossible to keep them down on the farm. These congregations watched their numbers dwindle down to thirty or twenty members, with the old-timers hanging on, refusing to transfer to more active congregations. They still came out each week for "Sunday-go-to-meeting" services marked by wizened old men singing gospel quartet music and a farmer's wife forcing groans out of an antiquated organ as the congregation sang a shrill, off-key version of "Bringing in the Sheaves."

There were scores of such churches in the mountain areas east of the city, most too impoverished to support even a part-time student minister or too far distant from the Northside for a young man to commute daily to school. Such parishes had to settle for the preaching ministry of the Student Preaching Association.

The preaching association drew weekly lots, the lucky winner gaining the privilege of an early morning drive to preach at two, sometimes three of these parishes, earning for his services a paycheck of $25 ($5 of which went back to the association) and a Sunday noon dinner of chicken and dumplings.

Scooter worked the weekend lottery for over a year, driving his now cancer-stricken Ford over the mountains to "break the Bread of Life" for these forgotten people of another world. Now, he hit the big time, getting the plum of the crumbs, an assignment as full-time student pastor at a church with 110 members on the roll and about 35 of them actually in church on Sunday. This one was west and north of Pittsburgh, far from the seminary and even further from the rural country churches. He landed a job in Lynnfield, a tiny borough across the tracks from Armco Steel in the county seat of Butler. Lynnfield was almost forty miles from the divinity school, a factor that provided Scooter with early release from the cubicle atop the Northside fortress. The job paid $40 a week and provided the free use of a manse. It was a handsome package for a senior seminary student.

Lynnfield was an ethnic ghetto, almost exclusively eastern European with Poles, Russians, Slovaks, Hungarians living in the shadow of the mill and of the wheelworks that ground out huge steel wheels for train cars and engines. The main town of Butler was large enough to have once supported their own minor league baseball team, a class *C* farm team that was the property of the New York Yankees. It was here that the millworkers once cheered the pitching magic of the shy, freckle-faced, tow-head youth named "Whitey" Ford.

The census map of Lynnfield showed a population of 98 percent Catholics and 2 percent Protestants. The Lynnfield Presbyterian Church was the only Protestant church in the borough. Its membership for the most part was made up of fall-away Catholics, those who had left the church to marry Protestants or those disenfranchised due to divorce. Lynnfield had a Russian Catholic, Greek Catholic, Serbian Catholic, Ukrainian Catholic, Polish Catholic, and a few other ethnic Catholic churches, varieties Scooter had never heard of. The town was made up of bars, poolhalls, ethnic clubs, and union halls.

Scooter's arrival in Lynnfield was met with enthusiasm by the congregation. It had been years since they had a full-time pastor. In the United States there were 112 Presbyterian churches with membership rolls numbering between 100 and 115 members. The Lynnfield Church ranked 111 in terms of their annual budget. His first Sunday on duty was a gala affair with a banquet scheduled in the church basement following the morning worship service. This congregation, predominantely Hungarian, with first and second generation Hungarians clustered together, knew how to put on a feast. The table was spread with platters of roast beef, heaping dishes of mashed potatoes, freshly baked pies, and side orders of what the president of the women's club told Scooter were the delicacies of pirogi, halupki, piroshki, and garaghski. Scooter recognized the pastry ingredients of most of them but was stumped by the last in the series. "What's a garaghski?" he asked.

"Oh," the heavily-accented women replied with great amusement, "that's a little metal thing we use to unlock the garage door."

Scooter joined in the good-natured laughter. He fell for the Hungarian's favorite joke. Laughing with the people snapped him back to his childhood. Pirogi was a delicacy his aunt used to serve him when he was a small boy. Scooter's mother was of Serbian descent. Her father and mother emigrated to America from Yugoslavia. Scooter's mother and aunt were reared on the Northside a few blocks from the Presbyterian Divinity School. Her name had been Elizabeth Yarnic.

Elizabeth Yarnic and her older sister Anna worked, as young girls, in a large factory situated at the foot of Troy Hill, a section of the Northside boasted by Germans and Slavic people. Shops in the Northside boasted large wooden barrels filled with briny water and large pickles that were sold first for a penny and later for a nickle. School children dipped their hands in the barrel fishing for a choice pickle before handing their pennies over to the shopkeeper. The pickles were made in the big factory where the Yarnic girls worked, a huge plant owned by H. J. Heinz who gained fame not only for the production of pickles but for fifty-six other varieties of food stuffs.

Anna quit high school to marry a tough German mechanic and motorcycle racer and moved with him to Troy Hill. Elizabeth finished a commercial course in the high school where she excelled in typing and shorthand. The girls' father died while they were in school, succumbing to pneumonia made virulent in a body weakened by chronic alcoholism. Shortly after the death of Jozef Yarnic, the girls' mother entered Mayview, Pittsburgh's most infamous institution for the hopelessly insane. Scooter grew up thinking his maternal grandmother was dead. It was not until he was in college that he learned that she was still alive, but not well. The family story was that she had fallen from a porch, impaling her head on an iron fence spike that took her mind but not her life. Scooter saw her once when he was twenty years old. Her hair was snow white and wild, her eyes filled with dark hatred. She babbled at him in a foreign language shrieking hysterically. She lived in Mayview for forty years, spending her days in babbling idiocy, convinced that family visitor's were demons in disguise. She spat at them through rotted teeth cursing them in her native tongue.

Elizabeth had two brothers. The elder, Scooter saw only twice in his life. He was a recluse, poverty-stricken and bitter due to a childhood accident. Mike Yarnic was going to downtown Pittsburgh one Saturday morning. He stole a ride on a streetcar by chasing after it and jumping on the rear step, hanging on to a side railing. At an abrupt turn Mike lost his grip and fell off and under the streetcar. The steel wheel of the car sliced his leg off above the knee. It was a clean slice, leaving him unconscious and bleeding profusely. He never accepted his wooden leg, hating it and himself the rest of his bitter life.

The younger brother, Joseph, was the baby of the family, cared for in his youth by Elizabeth and Anna. Together they reared him, becoming mothers as well as older sisters to him. They doted on Joe, caring for him through his childhood illnesses and demanding strict discipline in his schoolwork. They made certain that little Joe was going to be somebody.

When Elizabeth Yarnic graduated with honors from the old Allegheny High School, she crossed the river bridge and found a job as a secretary in a large accounting firm that specialized in corporate bankruptcy cases. Its owner and chief executive officer came to the office from the opposite side of town, from the elegant section of Mount Washington, overlooking the Golden Triangle of

Pittsburgh. Mount Washington rose sharply from the bottoms of the Southside to lofty heights settled by the Scotch-Irish wasps who dominated Pittsburgh's management class.

Elizabeth started in the secretary pool of the firm. She rose through the secretarial ranks to become executive secretary to the president. Her corporate rise reached its zenith when she married the boss, Charles Evans. The marriage was storybook, a modern version of Cinderella or the Prince and the Pauperess. Her joyous marriage to Charles Evans was her ticket out of the squalor of the Northside. She became for Charles his real-life Pygmalion.

Scooter's childhood was a recapitulation of a tale of two cities. He alternated weekend visits to Troy Hill to visit his maternal relatives with visits to Mount Washington, to the Victorian home of his paternal grandparents. Scooter was an ethnic and socio-economic half-breed, the fruit of the conjugal union of labor and management.

The family history mirrored the irony of nineteenth century life in Pittsburgh. His paternal great-grandfather had come to this country from Donegal, Ireland where he had lived in a thatched-roof hut with a mud floor. He was a peasant. Scooter's maternal great-grandfather was numbered among the landed gentry of Yugoslavia, a blue-blooded aristocrat of the princes of Serbia. In one generation the fortunes of the two bloodlines were reversed. The Serbian line became laborers, as princes who could not speak English were handed coal shovels to keep the blast furnaces burning. Those who could speak English, like Scooter's paternal grandfather, rose quickly to the level of management and professional jobs.

Scooter always claimed the Irish part of his heritage but felt a secret warm kinship with Slavic people. His baptism among the immigrants of Lynnfield was one he welcomed. There was an earthy honesty about these people, an inner toughness that he admired.

Each week Scooter was required to turn in a written report to the professor of Practical Theology who supervised the student enterprises. He remarked that Scooter had more bizarre experiences working among these Hungarian people than the aged clergyman had encountered in his lifetime.

The event that most horrified the venerable pastor happened

within weeks after Scooter began his work in Lynnfield. When the sacraments were administered Scooter was required to enlist the assistance of an ordained minister in the presbytery who would come to the sanctuary and perform the rite. Scooter's first service of baptism was scheduled. He met with the mother of the newborn infant and arranged the service. In the meeting it was apparent that no father was around. Scooter's discreet inquiries uncovered the fact that this child was conceived before marriage and an irate father had enforced a marriage, old-country style. The young husband, a vagabond carnival worker, a roustabout, was forced by his father-in-law to sleep in a chicken coop, an indignity he suffered for a week before he fled the coop, the town, and the marriage.

A month after the child's baptism Scooter received a frantic call from the infant's mother. The woman begged to see him about an urgent matter. When she arrived at the church study she was dabbing her eyes with a handkerchief and and handed a tear-stained letter to Scooter. He read the letter that was scrawled in sloppy handwriting and crude grammar. The letter had been written from a cell in the Allegheny County Jail. The missing husband was facing trial on charges of statutory rape. His letters were a plea for help, coupled with saccharine pledges of love and future fidelity. When Scooter finished the letter he looked at the distraught young woman and asked, "What do you want me to do?"

"Please get him out of jail. Please get him back to me. You're the only one I can turn to. If Daddy knew Paul was in jail he'd go down there and kill him."

"I'm not sure what I can do, Shirley. I've never dealt with anything like this before, but I'll try."

After classes on Tuesday Scooter drove across the bridge to downtown Pittsburgh. First he went to the district attorney's office to seek permission to visit Shirley's husband. The office of the D.A. was ratty and unkempt. The outer reception area was manned by hard-looking people, people who looked like they belonged on the other side of the law. Scooter was shuttled between junior grade clerks until he found a benevolent bureaucrat who made out a clergy visiting pass giving Scooter rights to the visitor's room of the county jail comparable to the rights of defense attorneys. He was ushered into a sterile room containing a large table with hard-backed wooden chairs.

Moments later Paul Crafton was escorted in by a deputy and seated across the table from Scooter. He was tall, lean, and blond, with his unruly hair, too long and apparently unmanageable, sticking out at wild angles like straw on a hastily constructed scarecrow. His face was heavily pockmarked, evidence of a severe bout with teenage acne. A pungent smell emanated so strongly from him that Scooter made an involuntary gasp. The acrid stench was the most offensive case of body odor Scooter had ever encountered.

"Paul, my name is Richard Evans. I'm the minister at the Lynnfield church. Shirley asked me to come and see you and find out if I can help."

Crafton's eyes brightened. "Is she willing to take me back?" he asked.

"Yes, but first we have to get you out of here. What's your present situation?"

"It's a bum rap. Statutory rape. The whole thing's crazy. My buddy and I were workin' a gig with a carnival out in Washington County. One of the local girls was hangin' around our booth all evening and made it clear she wanted some action after we closed. Me and Billy took her to a tent where she put on a helluva show for us and took us both on. Hey, man, it wasn't like we forced her or anything. She was one willin' babe. Well, while we was goin' to town, if you get my drift, Reverend, her old man comes bustin' in the tent with two cops. They grabbed me and Billy and threw us in the tank in Washington, 'cause the broad was under age. She lived across the county line so they brought us here to this tank. Hey, man. I gotta get out of here. This place is a rat hole."

"Have you contacted a lawyer, Paul?"

"Are you kiddin'? I ain't got no bread for a lawyer. They assigned us one of those public defenders, you know a 'court appointed' counselor. He tried to shake us down."

"What do you mean?" Scooter was in over his head.

"He came in once to see us. He asked me if I had any money and I told him no. Billy had $200 on him when he was arrested and the guy said for the $200 bucks he could get Billy off but unless I came up with $200 he said I'd rot in here. Our hearing is tomorrow and I hope to hell we don't pull Judge Aiken. She'll cream me."

"Doesn't your lawyer have to be there too? I mean he's legally bound to defend you even if you can't pay, right?"

"That's the way the game's supposed to be played, but that ain't how it works."

"Look, Paul. I'll see what time you're on the docket and I'll be there. Maybe I can help."

Paul's eyes showed fear mixed with a glimmer of hope. "I sure hope so. Thanks, man."

Scooter pushed his chair away from the table and stood up, signaling the deputy that the meeting was over. He stretched out his hand to Paul who responded with an awkward handshake, his giant paw almost crushing Scooter's hand.

"See you tomorrow, Paul. Hang tough."

Scooter went directly from the jail to the posh office suite of Bernstein, Crawford, and Schwartz, on the seventh floor of the Grant Building. He was greeted there by Virginia Lincoln, the executive secretary of the firm's senior partner, Albert Bernstein. Bernstein was the dean of Pittsburgh's corporate law practitioners, a past president of the Pennsylvania Bar Association. More importantly he was chief counsel for the Evans family affairs. He had been Charles Evans's closest friend, a comrade who worked hand in hand with him on their biggest reorganization cases during the prosperous years of the senior Evans's accounting firm. The Evans office complex had been located a few doors down the street on Grant Street. The team of Bernstein and Evans had been linked together before World War II. Albert Bernstein was now a multimillionaire living in a lavish estate on Fifth Avenue on the edge of Shadyside.

"Scooter Evans! What in the world are you doing here? I haven't seen you in ages. Look at you, you're a grown-up man now." Virginia gave Scooter a motherly embrace and a kiss. Scooter blushed feeling the eyes of the cadre of stenographers looking at him. He recovered and switched on his charm button.

"Hi, Virginia. You look terrific. I'm finally old enough to ask you for a date. That's why I'm here. All these years I've been waiting to hustle you. How about it? Let's hit the town."

Virginia let out a guffaw, roundly enjoying the playful overture from a man twenty years her junior.

"You sweetheart—I'd take you up on it but Albert would have to bail me out for contributing to the delinquency of a juvenile."

"Juvenile!" Scooter recoiled in mock protest. "Oh, Virginia, I'm crushed. Here I am, asking the lady of my dreams for a date and she calls me a juvenile. Speaking of jew-veniles, is that two-bit Jewish shyster boss of yours in? I've got some heavy legal-beagle type stuff for him if the old goniff can handle it."

"What's this business about an old goniff?" The booming voice belonged to Albert Bernstein who emerged from his office with a mock scowl on his face.

"Whew, boy am I glad you're here, Albert. I was just about to call a cop. This two-timing secretary of yours was putting the make on me, trying to turn my handsome, debonair, sophisticated person into a gigolo."

Scooter cast a wink at Virginia and went into Albert Bernstein's private chambers with Albert's arm resting on his shoulder.

"What's up, Scooter? You didn't come here just to banter with Virginia."

Bernstein sat behind his desk steepling his fingers as he listened intently to Scooter's summary of the Paul Crafton case.

"Well, Scooter, I'm honored that you've come to me with this. I'm not at all involved with criminal law cases, but I'll look into it. I'll see what's going on over there and I'll be happy to attend the hearing with you. Let me check it out. Don't you worry anymore about it, OK?"

"Sure. That's great, Albert. But what about the guy trying to shake Paul down?"

"I'll look into that too. But there's not much we can do about it. In the first place all these arrested guys cry foul like that. It probably never happened, though I'll grant we have some bad apples in our ranks. If the guy did try a shakedown we'd have a rough time pinning it on him. I'll find out who it is and look into it. You just show up in court and leave the details to me."

"OK, Albert. You're the boss. I really appreciate your taking the time for all this. I know it's a nickle and dime deal, but it's important to me, you know. It's part of my job."

"Yes, yes, Scooter. I know. I still can't figure out why you're messing around in this kind of work. Your friend Crafton is going to make a habit of landing in the tank. You can bet on it. I told you a thousand times to go to law school but you're as bullheaded as your father was."

Scooter was hopeful the next morning when he entered the court at 9:45 with the hearing scheduled for 10:00. Paul and Billy were there in the custody of a deputy.

"Hi, Paul. Is your lawyer here yet?"

"Haven't seen the creep. He probably won't even show."

At five to ten Mr. Bernstein walked in, impeccably dressed in a tailored business suit, certainly from Larrimor's, the graduate level of haberdashery that reaches the ozone above Brooks Brothers. The docket was running behind schedule. At 10:25 a disheveled man in a seedy suit, looking like he slept in it, blustered in looking for Paul and Billy. He was their court-appointed lawyer, obviously drunk. Not hung-over. Drunk. Stinking drunk at 10:25 in the morning.

With slurred speech he incriminated himself in front of Scooter and Albert Bernstein by saying to Paul, "Did you come up with the bread? Two hundred clams will get you off."

Scooter was furious. He took charge of the scene to Albert Bernstein's amusement.

"Look, pal. There's no bread. You're off this case. Get out of here before I throw you out."

The lawyer started to reply in blubbery words but Scooter cut him off.

"Now, Mac. Beat it. I don't want you anywhere near the courtroom. Get out before I call the bailiff."

The drunken attorney was just lucid enough to know it was foolish to argue and made a hasty but staggering retreat.

The judge called out their case. He looked at Scooter and asked, "Are you counsel for the defense?"

"No, sir, I'm Mr. Crafton's minister."

The judge glanced at Albert Bernstein, obviously recognizing him and wondering what he was doing here for a hearing like this. Bernstein spoke. "May I approach the bench?"

The judge motioned Bernstein forward and the two exchanged a whispered dialogue that Scooter couldn't hear. Albert stepped away from the bench and the judge declared, "You men are charged with one count of statutory rape committed in the county of Washington. I sentence you both to six months in the county workhouse and a fine of $80 each. The sentence is suspended. Mr. Crafton you will pay your fine and be released in the custody of Reverend Evans. I don't ever want to see you again in my courtroom."

SEVENTEEN

S cooter cracked the window open in the car on the drive to Lynnfield seeking a breeze to relieve the malodorous stench of Paul's body odor. In the close confines of the car it was becoming unbearable. Scooter searched the recesses of his brain for a sensitive ploy to get the man in a shower with a fresh bar of soap but shied from a direct suggestion, hoping instead that Paul was human enough to crave the sanctuary of a shower stall after several days in the fetid quarters of the county jail. Scooter's foot pressed harder on the accelerator as if a taut nerve ran a direct route from his olfactory system to his right foot.

"I think it would be best for you to stay at the manse for awhile until we can smooth things out with Shirley's father. When we get to Lynnfield you can get settled in, cleaned up, and I'll contact Shirley and let her know you're out of jail and back in town." *There, I did it, a direct reference to cleaning up. Surely he'll want to shower and shave before he's reunited with his wife.*

The manse had two bedrooms but only one contained a bed; the other had been converted into Scooter's study. He offered Paul a berth on the sofa bed in the living room and showed him the downstairs bathroom for his use. "Go ahead and get cleaned up and I'll get in touch with Shirley and let her know you're here."

Scooter went to the kitchen and placed a call to the department store where Shirley was working as a salesclerk. When she came on the line he told her the good news of Paul's return. She was ecstatic and promised to come over after work to welcome her husband home. Through the doorway of the kitchen Scooter could see that Paul was changing his clothes, shedding his scuzzy army fatigue jacket but making the change without benefit of a shower. *Maybe Shirley will tell him to take a shower.*

Scooter excused himself to make some pastoral calls and

promised to look into work possibilities for Paul. He drove straight
to the personnel office of Armco Steel and asked to see a man
there who was a member of Scooter's church. The man invited
him into his office. "Reverend Evans. It's nice to see you here. Is
this a pastoral call?"

"Sort of, Bill. I need your help. I was able to get Paul Crafton
out of jail this morning. The judge released him in my custody.
You remember him, don't you? He's the guy that married Shirley
Bosich."

"Oh, that one? He's the fellow that ran out on her just before
the baby was born. I think I can guess your next question. You
want to get him a job, right?"

"You are truly amazing Bill. What foresight. No wonder they
put you in charge of hiring around here, you have such a remarkable grasp of human nature. Can you help me? Any job would
do. That's part of my responsibility since he's in my custody, to
try to get him employed. And, Bill, I have a vested interest in
this. He's living with me now in the manse and the sooner I can
get him a job, the sooner I can get him moved into an apartment
and out of my house."

Bill gave Scooter some forms to be filled out and told him to
have Paul come by the personnel office the next morning. "I think
we can find something for him, but he has to be on the ball, and
he better not cause any trouble."

"I have no idea what kind of worker he is, Bill. All I know
about him is that he has worked the carnival circuit as a roustabout. By the way, do you have any departments that are heavy
with the use of foul-smelling chemicals?"

"No, why?"

"Cause this guy reeks. I mean reeks. You can smell him from
twenty feet away and I was just thinking of the well-being of your
other employees. I thought if you had a section of foul-smelling
chemicals or something you could move him in there and nobody
would notice . . ."

"C'mon Reverend, nobody's that bad."

"Bill, I'm afraid I'll have to take back all those kind words I
said about your knowledge of human nature. You think I'm exag-
gerating, but your nose will prove I'm understating the case.
Thanks for the papers. I'll make sure I have Paul here first thing
in the morning."

Scooter got back to the manse just moments before Shirley appeared. He was in the middle of explaining the job opportunity to Paul when she came to the door. Their meeting was charged with emotion and Scooter quickly found an excuse to leave to give them time alone for their reunion. He gulped an extra dose of air as he went outside and decided to make some pastoral calls. *So this is the glamour of the ministry. Now I have to flee from my house so two lovers can have some privacy in someplace other than a chicken coop.*

The following night, while Paul and Shirley were out together, the telephone rang. Scooter answered it and heard a slurred tirade begin on the other end. It was Mrs. Bosich, obviously drunk and obviously very angry.

"Do you have that no good Paul Crafton staying there?"

"Yes, Mrs. Bosich, I have him here temporarily until he can get an apartment. The court released him in my custody."

"Is Shirley there?"

"No, m'am, she isn't."

"I told her to stay away from that no good. She's sneaking out to see him, I know it. She's not good either. She just a *h-o-r*. I want to talk to you, Mr. Preacher man, because I want him out of this town!"

"Settle down, Mrs. Bosich, I'll come right over now to see you and we can talk about this."

Scooter was laughing to himself in the car on the way to Bosich's. *H-o-r. She can't even spell it. Maybe it's her way to swear in front of the minister.*

Scooter's jocular mood changed the instant he walked into the Bosich kitchen. Mrs. Bosich was dressed in a seedy nightgown and was holding a bottle of whiskey in her right hand, drinking it straight from the bottle. Her eyes were glazed and fanatical. In her left hand she was holding a .38 revolver pointed at Scooter's chest. Mrs. Bosich was swaying in a drunken rhythm. Her voice was singsong, her words spoken in tempo with the slow rocking, "I'm going to blow your *d-a-m* brains out, preacher."

Scooter stared at the cold blue steel of the gun barrel swaying in front of him in her unsteady hand. He affected a breezy manner of nonchalance trying to joke her back to sobriety. "C'mon, Mrs. Bosich, you don't want to shoot me. We're buddies. Put that thing down and let's talk about it."

Scooter smiled his warmest smile and started to walk toward

her. She jerked the gun up, her muscles suddenly rigid. No more swaying. "*D-a-m* you, preacher. I don't swear around ministers, but *D-a-m* you."

Scooter had an insane urge to give the woman a spelling lesson but figured this was not the best time to do it. He tried a new approach. This time instead of moving toward her, he casually backed away from her and eased himself into an overstuffed chair, desperately trying to calm the electric atmosphere in the room.

"You know you want Shirley to be happy, Mrs. Bosich. You're just upset about all this jail business, and I don't blame you a bit. But we have to work together to find a way to help these kids. I'm sure you want what's best for them."

Mrs. Bosich took a seat opposite Scooter and gingerly laid the gun down on the table next to her, well beyond Scooter's reach. "I told you she's just a no good *h-o-r*. She can go to *h-e-l-l*."

At least her spelling is starting to improve, Scooter thought. This was her final protest. The wall of hostility crumbled and she gave way to weeping. Scooter moved to her side and patted her shoulder, surreptitiously picking up the gun and jamming it in his hip pocket out of sight. By now Mrs. Bosich had reverted to a docile mother, begging Scooter to help Paul get straightened out and to save her daughter's marriage.

"You go get some sleep. I got Paul a job at the mill and he plans to move into an apartment as soon as he gets his first paycheck. The kids need to be out on their own if they're going to have a chance to make it."

"OK, reverend. I'm sorry for yelling at you. Where is the gun?"

"It's in my pocket and that's where it's going to stay until this thing settles down. You know better than to be playing with guns when you're drinking. Just imagine, Mrs. Bosich, you could have blown my brains out. Think of the newspaper headlines 'Lynnfield Gun-Slinging Momma Blows Preacher to Kingdom Come.'" Mrs. Bosich said, "Oh, reverend, you know I really wouldn't shoot you."

Scooter laughed unconvincingly, "Now you tell me."

Paul's job at the mill lasted two weeks. He was fired for arguing with his foreman. The next day Scooter secured him another job, though with less pay, driving for the Butler Cab Company.

He seemed to like this work and was diligent about his hours and saving his paycheck. He stayed in the manse for six weeks without the benefit of a single shower and finally moved into an upstairs apartment over the Lynnfield Bar and Grill. Shirley refused to move in with him. She claimed she wanted to wait until they saved enough money to buy some nice furniture. Her reluctance to move in sent Paul into a wave of depression and heavy drinking. It was a week later that Scooter got a call from the desk sergeant of the Butler Police Department. The sergeant was a member of the Lynnfield church and had become a friend of Scooter's. His nickname for Scooter was "The Greatest."

"Hey, 'Greatest,' this is Eddie. I'm down at the station and we have a friend of yours in the tank. In fact he is wearing your South Hills championship baseball jacket."

"What did he do this time, Ed?"

"Well, it seems he didn't like one of the assignments the dispatcher gave him so he relieved the guy of about a pint of blood from his nose. We've got him here on assault."

"What should I do, Ed?"

"Well, buddy, we can let him out on your recognizance for fifty bucks, but he'll still have to face a hearing if the dispatcher presses charges. He was a wild man when we brought him in."

"Thanks for calling, I'll be right over."

Scooter almost had to close out his bank account to come up with the fifty dollars to spring Paul. When the deputy brought him out he was contrite and embarrassed that Scooter had to bail him out of another jam. They drove in silence back to the bar and grill. Before Paul got out of the car Scooter laid it on the line, "Look, Paul, I'm out of job leads. You're going to have to get your next job on your own."

"Yeah, I know. I really screwed up. If Shirley would just move in I know I'd be OK. I'll find something, and don't worry about the fifty bucks, I'll pay it back to you."

The next call, the following afternoon, was from Shirley. "He's gone, Reverend Evans. He just took off again. You got to find him for me."

"Are you sure you want him? You keep telling me you want the guy and then you won't move in with him."

"I know, but I really do want him. Please find him for me just once more."

In the mill area of Butler, the state of Pennsylvania was growing rich from the sale of liquor licenses. There was at least one bar
for every hundred people in the population. They were everywhere, each one more shabby than the last. Scooter assumed the
role of his radio hero in the forties, "Mr. Keen, tracer of lost
persons." He went from bar to bar flashing a photograph of Paul
to the bartenders and to the men hunched over the bar. In some
bars he was roughly dismissed, the men assuming he was a cop
looking for one of their own.

After a week of missed classes at the seminary, and pounding
his feet on the sidewalks covering the maze of bars, Scooter found
a man who had seen Paul Crafton get in a taxi on the day he had
disappeared. Scooter went to the taxi office and was greeted by a
less than cooperative dispatcher who sported an ugly scab on the
bridge of his nose. His only reason to cooperate in the search was
so that he could see Paul back in jail. A few inquiries located the
driver who had picked Paul up that day. He knew Paul from
working in the same company. He related that he had driven Paul
to Greater Pittsburgh Airport and that Paul had a ticket to Phoenix. He said he was going west to visit his mother.

He was gone. Scooter never saw his coat, his clock radio, his
fifty dollars, or Paul again. It was a hard lesson in the realities of
the ministry where not every effort of altruism yields a miracle
story of redemption.

The disappointment of the Paul Crafton episode did not spoil
Scooter's time at the little Hungarian church. He finished the
year there with a warm affection for the people and the lavish
appreciation they showed him. It was a weekly occurrence for him
to hear the doorbell ring and find no one at the door but a freshly
baked pie sitting on the stoop. He was invited three or four nights
a week into the homes of families where he was fed like a king.
When he made pastoral calls to shut-ins and the elderly, he took a
bilingual elder with him to translate the conversations in Hungarian. The old people referred to him fondly as their "new Father"
still understanding religion in terms of their old-country Roman
Catholic roots.

EIGHTEEN

The gentle rocking motion of the *Statendam* was soothing to Scooter as the ship's bow split the inky waters of the Atlantic. The stabilizers were doing their job. From the vantage point of plush chairs in the ballroom, Scooter watched the sea alternately appear and disappear as the ship rode the crest of the waves. The crossing was tranquil until the night before they reached the turbulent waters of the North Sea.

It was Talent Night on board and the recreation hostess had put together a gala show, drawing from the talent of the more than one thousand passengers on board.

The highlight of the show was the colorful folk dances put on by Dutch nationals wearing the native costumes of their home provinces. The passengers were united in a bond of friendship and awarded lusty applause to the quaint dancers. The final act, however, brought turbulence. It was a choral presentation by a tightly disciplined corps of professional German soccer players returning to Europe after an exhibition tour in the United States. The soccer players did not walk, they marched onto the stage, goose-stepping in the strident paces of a military unit. Instantly the atmosphere of the ballroom changed. Something was stirred within the audience as they listened to the well-rehearsed blend of strong teutonic voices. Their repertoire consisted of bawdy drinking songs capped off with the song banned from postwar occupied Germany, *Deutschland, Deutschland uber alles*. As they broke into the final song, fear gripped the audience and feelings of deep alienation wafted into the air. There was no applause save for the weak clapping of a handful of Americans on board who had no sense of what was going on. The gaiety of the previous acts was dispelled in an instant. It was like a frolicking clown was unmasked to reveal a sneering fiend whose grotesque face turned laughter into screams. The party was ruined.

At the breakfast table the next morning Scooter was jarred by the appearance of a Dutch-Canadian priest who sat across from him. The crossing had kindled a shipboard friendship with the sanguine cleric. Today his face was doleful, red strings marring the whites of his eyes. He was unshaven and sat limp in his chair.

"Father Van Duren, what's the matter?"

The priest was on the edge of tears. "Please forgive my appearance, Richard. I've had a dreadful night. I'm lost in horror, uncertain about my vocation. What happened last night tore me apart. I discovered something about myself I'm not very proud of . . ."

The priest's tale stabbed Scooter in a visceral way. It was a story of horror that was lived in the flesh, the narrative of an eyewitness.

"I boarded the *Statendam* in New York to go home. I've waited for this trip for twenty years. When we sailed, the prayers of two decades were answered for me. I was the happiest priest in the church. No more. Not now. Not after last night."

"But what happened last night, Father?"

"Memories, Richard. They can be like time bombs. Mine exploded in the ballroom."

Father Van Duren pressed his fingers against his temple. A single blood vessel was visibly throbbing on his forehead. The priest grabbed a handful of his own hair, squeezing it in a vicelike grip, inflicting pain on himself like some ascetic act of self-flagellation.

"When I was ordained to the priesthood my first parish assignment was in a small Dutch *dorpje,* a tiny village of a few hundred people. I loved my work. Then the Germans came. The invasion of the lowlands happened in the second year of my pastorate. Everything changed, Richard. Everything. It was a reign of terror for five years. My people were hungry. We lived for awhile by eating tulip bulbs. We never knew when our houses would be searched and our young men taken away to work in factories in Germany or shipped to the camps. The Dutch underground fought fiercely at the time. The resistance was well organized. Some of my friends died in the resistance, Richard. They were good men. Brave men.

"Our underground was invisible. It was like guerilla warfare. Sudden strikes of sabotage against the Nazis. I was involved, Richard. Even the confessional of my church was used to pass messages. We had one quite successful strike against the Wehrmacht. The next morning the Gestapo rounded up the people of my parish and made us stand in the village square. The Gestapo officer in charge was enraged. He screamed at us, threatening reprisals for the midnight strike.

I was standing next to a young woman. Lonnika was her name, Lonnika Van Der Kamp. She was holding hands with her little boy. He was only three years old. The officer walked toward us and stood right in front of us. I'll never forget his eyes. They were evil, Richard. Unspeakably evil. He opened the leather flap of his holster and drew out his Luger. He had a horrible grin on his face. He started to toy with Lonnika.

He put the tip of the gun barrel right in her face and started teasing her. He traced figures with it on her face and then ordered her to open her mouth. I could feel her fear. She was shaking and huge drops of perspiration were dripping from her forehead. I can still see the dark circle in the dust where I saw a bead of sweat splash. It's strange, I guess, the things that stick in your mind. He pushed the steel barrel in her mouth and screamed at her, 'Taste it! That's right.' I thought she was going to faint, her face was white. The Gestapo leader pulled his gun back and barked, 'There must be payment for this outrage, *nichtware, Fraulein?*' Then he turned to the little boy and teased his face the same way with the heavy Luger. The boy started to cry, 'Mama, Mama.' Suddenly the officer's face grew stern and he stiffened. He rested the barrel of the gun point-blank against the child's temple . . . and pulled the trigger."

Scooter sat in stone silence. Waves of nausea flooded his stomach. He didn't want to hear the rest but Father Van Duren went on.

"When I saw the boy slump like a rag doll at my feet I screamed at the officer. I cursed him to his face. '*Gott verdammed ye—Rotsoi!*' He laughed at me and ordered the crowd dismissed. I prayed every day for the total destruction of the Nazis. It became a black obsession for me, poisoning my soul with bitterness. After the liberation I confessed my sin to my father confessor. I told him I was no longer worthy to be a priest. A man with so much hate can never be a minister of God's love.

"I tried to resign from the priesthood. Instead my superiors ordered me to transfer my ministry to Canada, away from the scene of so much violence and hatred. They said time would heal my soul and that someday I would be free of the demons of hatred and bitterness I held for the Germans.

"As the years passed in the quiet rural parish in Canada my faith was restored. I was certain that all that hatred had been exorcized from my soul. I applied to be transferred back to Holland, assuring my superiors that I was ready for reentry. Then last night it happened. When those German soccer players started to march and sing, a feeling of bile came from my stomach and I wanted to rush onto the stage and strangle them. The hate is still there. It is still there. Don't you understand? It still burns my soul and I cannot love."

Father Van Duren began to weep. "Please excuse me," he said, getting up from the table and fleeing to his stateroom.

Scooter could not speak. He sat in silent horror, the scene of the dead boy lying at the feet of his black-booted murderer was incomprehensible. But the sight of the trembling priest made it sickeningly real.

The North Sea was not impressed by the technological wonders of modern stabilizers for ocean-going vessels. The travel agency's promises of immunity to *mal de mer* were a fraud. Scooter felt like he was on a ceaseless ride on an amusement park Tilt-a-Whirl. The North Sea was angry. When Neptune has a bad day his vengeance arises out of the foam and whitecaps of this stretch of water. When the water king explodes, a geyser shooting from his head finds its release point in the North Sea. Man cannot be assuaged by Dramamine or any other fabled remedy. He is helpless on the slippery decks of the largest ships, which are reduced to corks bobbing in these waters. By noon of the day the ship entered the North Sea, half of the passengers were missing from the dining room. By dinner the cast of hundreds was reduced to a handful of persons who were either superhuman or, more likely, subhuman. No normal creature could think about food at a time like this without adding a hue of green to his face.

When *mal de mer* hits there is no warning. It is like a troll jumping up suddenly from under a bridge or a mugger springing from behind a garbage can in a darkened alley. When it hits, all conversation ceases and philosophical reflections terminate. Nuns drop their heads in the middle of the rosary and waiters quit their trays en route to the table. It hit Scooter in the safety of his state-room. He was naive enough to assume one visit to the water closet would restore his equilibrium. Instead a silent roulette wheel op-erator spoke to his stomach, "Round and round and round she goes, where she stops nobody knows."

Fresh air was an absolute requisite. Scooter had to get on deck, far from the room where the walls were squirming their way towards him to crush him like a trash compactor. He made it to the stairwell but once on the stairs he was sure they were built on a hydraulic lift system like a fun-house trap. The stairs alternately rose toward his face and then suddenly dropped into an abyss. The up and down movements of the ship turned them into a crazy imitation of an escalator without a motor.

The fresh air on the deck brought a modicum of relief. The chairs were crowded with people huddled under deck blankets, their teeth chattering and their hands clutching small morsels of soda crackers, another old wive's tale panacea. Scooter found a vacant chair on the fantail next to a Scotchwoman who was equally miserable. Scooter was too sick to talk, thinking that if anyone were in danger of falling into the violent sea over the side rail the most heroic gesture he could offer was to whisper through chattering teeth, "Bon voyage." He stayed rooted in the spot for hours, peering into the darkness of the evening. Near midnight a grim-faced deck steward appeared with an apology.

"I'm sorry, sir, but I must collect your blanket. It is the cap-tain's rule that all blankets must be stowed by midnight."

Scooter reluctantly handed over his blanket thinking, *Is there no balm in Gilead?*

When the steward reached for the Scots lady's blanket she clutched it fiercely, tugging against the efforts of the steward. "You can't have it. I'll freeze out here without it," she said.

"But m'am, it is the captain's orders. I must take the blan-ket."

"Listen, young man, go tell the captain that I said if he wants this blanket he is going to have to come here and take it from me personally."

The steward realized he was in over his head. He turned to Scooter and tossed him a blanket, "Here, you may as well keep yours too. I'm sure the captain is no match for this lady." It felt good to laugh for the first time in hours.

At first Scooter was sure he was going to die, aborting his hegira to Europe and the promised land. Then he was afraid he would not die but be consigned to the perpetual fate of continuous life on the sea. Suddenly his childhood heroes became villains. Melville must have been insane. Anyone that could glorify this cauldron of torment in print must have been an unqualified misanthrope.

At last the ship docked at Le Havre to allow those passengers destined for France to disembark. In the quietness of the harbor King Neptune went back to sleep and as suddenly as the assault on his stomach had begun it now departed from Scooter. He feared the respite was temporary and that he would have to endure a recurring torture on the rest of the voyage.

He was pleasantly surprised by the tranquil cruise to Holland. The ship glided smoothly off the coast of the Netherlands passing down along the "Hook of Holland" and into the harbor at Rotterdam. In the early morning mist Scooter was enchanted by the sight of the Dutch tugboat captains and the quaintly dressed men in small fishing boats out for their daily catch. This was his first taste of a new world and its enchantment had already captured him.

The strength of the American dollar on the international market made the first-class compartment an inexpensive option for the train ride to Amsterdam. The immaculate window provided a clear vista of the Dutch countryside as the train streaked north. In the distance Scooter caught an occasional glimpse of the *moie molen,* the beautiful windmills, romanticized in folk ballads. Their canvas-covered arms were still, hanging limp, as most were not in use since serving as secret aerial signals for the Allies in World War II, the set of the angle of their blades hiding cryptic messages of German troop movements.

Fantasies were aroused in Scooter's mind, triggered by the sound of the railroad-crossing bells, advancing and retreating with eerie sounds of the Doppler effect. Spy movies on late-night television conjured up images of secret agents plying their clandestine arts of espionage on this European train. Sitting in the green armchair of the compartment, Scooter imagined men moving covertly, wearing black raincoats and felt fedoras, creased down to shield their faces. He envisioned one sneaking with stealth up to the conductor to slip a stiletto between his ribs.

The clock on the wall inside the cavernous *Centrale Station* of Amsterdam spoke an international language. It told Scooter that his arrival was on time, to the minute.

Free of cumbersome baggage, which he had arranged in Rotterdam to be delivered to Amsterdam by truck, Scooter strolled through the station, feasting on the sights of this strange world. The colorful kiosks of flower stalls struck his eyes. For pennies one could buy a bunch of velvet roses or other fresh flowers. He walked outside the boulevard toward the dam, the central esplanade of the city of Rembrandt. He passed a barrel organ on the way and soon learned that the *draiorgel* was a national institution, sending the sounds of a calliope into the air making the afternoon sound like a day at the circus. The oompas of the bass and tinkling sounds of the upper registers put a lilt in the steps of pedestrians and filled the air with a friendly atmosphere. At the dam he boarded a tram for the short ride to the Beethovenstraat where he had secured the temporary use of a small apartment until he could find more permanent quarters.

The city reminded Scooter of a miniature Christmas train display with its tiny cars and gingerbread buildings. The streets were jammed with thousands of bicycles that forced cars to creep through their swarms at a snail's pace. Business executives pedaled along in three-piece suits and women pedaled in shoes with spiked heels.

It was May of 1964. Amsterdam was enduring an uncommon heat wave with the thermometer pushing its red colored mercury into the eighties. Scooter rode the antiquated elevator and opened the caged door at the third floor of the apartment building. Once inside the apartment he went to the refrigerator to get some ice to fix a cold drink. There was no ice. There was no refrigerator. Ice, he soon discovered, was a luxury used only by self-indulgent Americans. It was difficult to come by, even in luxury restaurants that served it in drinks only upon request and then in miniscule portions. To relieve his consuming thirst Scooter went back outside and searched until he found a roadside kiosk that sold fresh oranges. He took them to the apartment and squeezed them pretending that the juice was in fact cold.

Finding a place of permanent residence was an exercise in

despair. In the process he learned his first phrase of Dutch idiom, a refrain that would trouble his ears again and again as he paced the sidewalks looking for a place to live. The phrase was *"Niets on te doon mijnheer."* "There's nothing we can do about it sir."

Scooter searched for the hidden spirit of men and women who had conquered the sea and spent five years of heroic resistance against Nazi occupation. He suddenly longed for Yankee ingenuity and the spirit of pragmatism that gave birth to such aphorisms as "The difficult we do immediately; the impossible takes a little longer." Instead he found a malaise of indifference, a torpid spirit of apathy spawned by an offensive and debilitating statist bureaucracy.

The housing problem was compounded by a fact Scooter was astonished to learn—that Holland is the most densely populated nation in the world, a dubious honor he had assumed belonged to India or China. But the statistics did not lie; there were more people per square mile living in Holland than in any country on earth. And, Scooter was certain, they all pedaled their bicycles on the streets of Amsterdam. Since most of the land area was reserved for farming there was precious little space for building housing units. The soggy soil placed further restrictions on the building of high-rise apartments. The average age of marriage in Holland was considerably older than in the United States because of the staggering housing situation. Amorous couples put their names on waiting lists for apartment space, often delaying their nuptials for several years.

Scooter discovered that as a visiting foreigner, a *buitenlander,* the only housing possibilities open to him were those priced above the reach of Dutch natives. The housing authority made it illegal for foreign students to secure apartments within the range of the average middle-class Dutchman. Fortunately the American dollar's buying power was so superior to the Dutch gilder that Scooter was able to find a third-floor apartment in a patrician villa in a community twenty-five miles outside of Amsterdam. For the privilege of this dwelling place he had to pay seven hundred and fifty Dutch gilders per month, which translated into slightly over two hundred American dollars. Even this would put a severe burden on the five thousand dollars Scooter had borrowed from Pittsburgh's Mellon Bank. His note was cosigned by Albert Bernstein.

The forced rental of the villa had its added benefits. It included the supreme luxury of central heating and a geyser shower that he was permitted to use at the indulgent level of three times a week. Scooter made one more concession to American creature comforts by purchasing a half-size refrigerator, which kept him supplied with necessary-for-life ice cubes.

The fact that Scooter's landlady spoke no English was a boon and a curse. It made initial forays of communication almost impossible but afforded him added incentive to master the language and ample opportunity for daily practice. He fractured the Queen's Dutch, eliciting frequent puzzled looks from the kindly *muffrow*. On one occasion Scooter tried to explain to her that he was "taking a break." By the time he rendered the American idiom into Dutch he had told her in her language that "the pope has a hernia." Her good humor eased the pain of such embarrassing moments.

Scooter secured an appointment at the university with the professor who would be supervising his work in theology. The professor scribbled out his first assignment on a sheet of paper. It was a list of twenty-seven books, all five-hundred-page tomes of technical literature in theology. The list included sixteen volumes in Dutch, four in German, four in French and three in Latin. When Scooter saw the list his face fell. He was gripped with utter panic. He read no Dutch, no German, and the only Latin he had was elementary introduction in high school. French was a complete mystery to him; he could not even decipher a menu at a French restaurant. The professor noticed his crestfallen countenance and asked in fatherly tones, "What's the matter?"

Scooter stammered an awkward reply, "I—er—I don't read French."

The professor guffawed and said brightly, "Oh, that's all right, most American students don't even read German or Latin. Many of them can handle Dutch because they're from Dutch families. Here, we'll switch the four French volumes to four more Dutch ones. Scooter wanted to tell him that his real name was Van Der Evans but he didn't think that would fly.

Scooter spent the summer months tackling his first assignment and immersing himself in language study. He became an academic hermit, a modern day ascetic, like Simeon Stylites who once perched himself atop a minaret, like an eccentric flagpole sitter, to devote himself to self-denial. Scooter's hermitage was a corner nook of his third-floor bedroom where he wedged a small desk between his bed and the sink. There he fastidiously maintained a strict regimen of study beginning promptly at 8:00 A.M. and going to midnight, with half-hour breaks for lunch and dinner. He maintained this spartan routine six days a week subsisting on peanut butter sandwiches and chicken noodle soup.

He began his intimidating reading assignment with the only means he could think of, by starting at the beginning. He opened the cover of the first Dutch tome to page one and looked at the first word of the first sentence of the first paragraph. He did not know the meaning of the word so he reached for his Dutch/English dictionary and looked it up. He wrote the Dutch word on one side of a small white card and its English meaning on the other side. He repeated the tedious process with the second word, the third, fourth, and on into the page. At midnight he stared at the stack of white cards in front of him, the single paragraph of notes he had taken from the text and he wrote the cipher $1\frac{1}{2}$ on the calendar on the wall above that day's date. He had worked fifteen hours and completed the reading of a page and a half. He estimated that at this rate of progress he would finish the first assignment in twenty-five years and complete the full program in the year 2087. Panic was already stirring acidic juices in his stomach that he sought to soothe by repeating an adage he learned as a child, a ditty to serve as solace when faced with Herculean tasks, "Inch by inch it's a cinch."

As the cards mounted the pace quickened. After six months Scooter was reading Dutch theology as rapidly as he read English. After eight months he was dreaming in Dutch and after ten months he had memorized a ream of cards totaling twenty thousand words.

Classes began the first of October. Scooter's Dutch was still marginal. He listened to his first lecture with rapt attention forcing his mind to fierce concentration. He was pleased that he could decipher enough to compile four pages of notes. The professor met him in the corridor after class and solicitously asked him how he had fared. Scooter replied, *"Ik fond het erg moelijk"* ("I found it very difficult.")

The professor smiled warmly thinking back to the subject of the lecture, the philosophy of G. F. Hegel. He nodded and said,

"Ya, Hegel—Hij is moelijke en iedere tal." ("Yes, Hegel—he is difficult in any language.")

Scooter adjusted quickly to the formal atmosphere of Dutch
higher education committing only one faux pas of academic protocol. On lecture days the students were seated in an amphitheater with rows of seats extending up and away from the bottom of
the bowl where the professor's lectern was situated. The upper
row where Scooter sat afforded him a view out of the classroom
windows. He enjoyed watching the antics of ducks paddling on
the murky water of the *gracht,* the canal that ran along the edge of
the university building.

Classes began with the pontifical grand entrance of the professor. As soon as he appeared in the door the students rose from
their seats and snapped to attention waiting for the illustrious descent to reach the lectern. The professor averted his eyes from his
postulants, walking sternly with head bowed to the podium.
Without glancing up he arranged his notes while the students remained at attention. Finally he lifted his eyes to the class and nodded, the unspoken "at ease" signal, and the class was seated. The
lecture followed without interruption. Students' comments or
questions were anathema. No hands were raised during the monologue. To interrupt the professor was a serious breach of protocol, an act of arrogance that was simply not tolerated.

During one class, Scooter was uncomfortable in the heat that
obeyed the laws of nature by rising to the top row where he was
seated. He silently slipped off his sportcoat and folded it over the
empty chair at his side. Abruptly the professor stopped in mid-
sentence and glared at the class, but mercifully not in Scooter's
direction, and said, "Will the *American* student please put his coat
back on." The professor could not have recognized Scooter from
the distance between them but he accented the word *American*
knowing that only an American could be so cavalier in such a
staid and formal place. Scooter quickly grabbed for his sportcoat,
but not fast enough to avoid the backward glances of his classmates.

The time in Holland was glorious for Scooter. No time was
wasted. There were no busy-work assignments. Every second of
research was opening Scooter's mind to the riches of solid theological content; the kind that survives the fleeting chimeras of the
fad. It was heavy theory but of the sort that carried a charge to the

inner chamber of the heart; the solid rock of truth that centuries of critical barrages could not dent; gold, not dross, with the brilliant ring of lasting truth.

The courses at the university were cosmopolitan, avoiding the stodgy parochialism some Dutch institutions are noted for. No one poured lighter fluid on Scooter's door and the cynical views so popular in Pittsburgh Divinity School were considered the nadir of theological nonsense.

Scooter lightened his regimen to take advantage of late night concerts at Amsterdam's *Concertgebow* hearing everything from Mozart concertos performed by Van Cliburn to freaked out gigs by Thelonius Monk. His favorite Saturday afternoon pastime was visiting the Rijksmuseum and, occasionally, the Stedelijk Museum. For Scooter the Rijksmuseum was holy ground, rivaling the Louvre for its artistic treasures. The majestic Goyas seemed to leap from their frames with the brilliant blacks and reds of scenes of Spanish violence. Degas, Matisse, Reubens, Vermeer, Hols, De Kooning—they were all there. But nothing compared with the vast hall, the inner sanctum of hushed mystery devoted exclusively to the master of the *Muiden Kring,* Rembrandt Von Rijn. For Scooter the Rembrandt Hall was a religious experience. His theology drew a circle around the triad of virtues including the good, the true, and the beautiful. He regarded any religion that despised art not merely as truncated, but sinister. To exclude the beautiful, the aesthetic, from the realm of God, was to crucify theology on a Philistine cross.

The canaled city of concentric circles emanating away from the "dam" like ripples on a pond, the city of diamond merchants, the Anne Frank house, the matchless window displays or etalages of the Kalverstraat, also had other tourist attractions that far outweighed the culture centers of the esplanade with the *Concertgebow* on one end and the *Rijksmuseum* on the other. In the sixties the city of Amsterdam was the unchallenged prostitution capital of western Europe. The red light district stretched from *Centrale Station* several blocks to the dam along a piece of real estate called the *oudezsijds voorburgwal.* This section boasted a population of ten thousand registered prostitutes, all police protected, all subjected to regular medical inspection; a gourmet treat for sailors on shore leave.

A novice at the theological school was quickly given a tour of the city at night by veteran graduate students. The final show-place, for which the innocents abroad were always unprepared, was the *oudezsijds voorburgwal*. Scooter's escorts were two American graduate students who paraded him down the street past ornate windows of the establishments. Picture window after picture win-dow was adorned with alluring girls dressed in taffeta gowns or silk sheathes, seated in provocative poses, smiling and beckoning at potential customers who walked the streets window-shopping. The windows were framed with luxurious curtains and illumined by Tiffany lamps. Scooter was surprised that so many of the girls were not hard looking or overpainted like American hookers, but were elegantly dressed and, some, breathtakingly beautiful. One standing at the doorway of her parlor said directly to Scooter, "Hi, sweet pickles. Want to come inside?"

Scooter flushed beet red and kept walking. His virgin reac-tion to this panoply of flesh was one of spiritual compassion. He turned to his comrades who were giddy about his embarrassment and said, "Doesn't anyone minister to these girls?"

The question was asked in naive innocence but was obviously the wrong question to ask.

"Oh?" one of them asked, "are you looking for a parish? Do you suddenly feel a calling to minister to these sweet young things? We can see it now. The invitation will read: 'Mr. Richard Evans cordially invites you to his sacred ordination service to the ministry among the prostitutes of Amsterdam. Donations for this ministry are urged to support this work as the overhead expenses are large.'"

"Cut it out you guys. I'm serious. This is all going on right in the shadow of the *Ouderkerk,* the city's most revered spiritual sanc-tuary. Doesn't the church care? Is there no mission here?"

One of the students pointed to a young woman crossing an arched bridge over the canal and said, "See that? The girl over there who looks like a pilgrim?"

Scooter followed the pointed finger and saw a girl dressed in strange garb, wearing a plain dark dress down to her ankles, black shoes, a gray bonnet, and carrying a large book, obviously a Bible. "Who or what is that?" Scooter asked.

"That my good man is a missionary to the prostitutes. She works for the *Leger Des Heils*."

"What is the *Leger Des Heils?* Wait a minute. I get it, the

'Army of Salvation.' Do you mean the Salvation Army is over here engaged in this ministry?"

"Yes, in fact, among the common people the Salvation Army is more highly respected than the institutional church. They go to places of pain where no one else dares."

NINETEEN

As the months passed in Amsterdam Scooter became increasingly edgy about his lonely bachelorhood. His soul was being nourished but his body was being starved. It began to protest its frustration by bombarding his mind with images of alluring women beckoning him. His thoughts of these girls trapped in white slavery turned from spiritual compassion to hungry lust. At times the enticement grew so overpowering that Scooter made a point of taking just enough money with him to Amsterdam to pay for his train ride back to the villa plus a dollar for a hamburger and *potat frittes* at Wimpy's on the dam. Still he would torture his libido by window-shopping on the way to *Centrale Station* feeding his lust by a compromise ethic of looking but not touching.

It was Scooter's second year at the university when he received an alarming letter from his mother.

Dear son,

I am afraid I have some bad news to report to you though it could be far worse. I've just received word from Charlie Kramer that Johnny was wounded in Viet Nam. I don't know the full extent of his injuries but, though the officials said he would survive, his wounds are severe enough that he has been hospitalized in Tokyo. . . .

The letter continued with more news from home and included Johnny's address at a military hospital in Japan. Scooter promptly composed a lengthy letter of encouragement to his friend and gave it to the *postbode* for overseas mailing the next morning.

Within the time frame of one week Scooter received three letters whose cumulative effect would rudely interrupt his graduate studies. The first was from Dr. Hepplewhyte at Witherspoon explaining that he was taking a sabbatical leave for one year and had been authorized to invite Scooter to return to America for a one-year appointment to fill the vacancy in the interim. The second letter was from Johnny. It was filled with a cheerful report of his steady recovery and paragraphs of praise for his newfound love. The capstone was the announcement of his wedding plans and a request for Scooter to fly home to be his best man in the wedding. Jack Kramer had already promised, by a transoceanic phone call to his son, to finance Scooter's trip home for the occasion.

The third letter was from a woman in a neighboring apartment to his mother's and a regular bridge partner of hers. The letter was an urgent appeal for Scooter to return for a visit. The woman gave an ominous report of Mrs. Evans's rapidly deteriorating health, evidence of which was immediately apparent in the enclosed photograph of Scooter's mother. The recent photo pictured a woman Scooter barely recognized. She was gaunt, almost to the macabre point of being skeletal and her eyes were vacant. She seemed ten years older and was the image of frailty. Nothing of health problems had ever been mentioned in her letters and monthly phone calls, but the proud woman was obviously dying.

Scooter cabled Hepplewhyte that he would accept the invitation, shot off a congratulatory letter to Johnny with the answer that he would be proud to stand as his best man, and phoned his mother with a jubilant announcement of his imminent return, giving no hint of his knowledge of her failing health.

Scooter sat impatiently waiting for his boarding call in the modern concourse of Schipol International Airport. Any homesickness he had repressed was now pushing its way to the surface. A sense of satisfaction for his outstanding performance in his oral exams was mixed with a sense of anxiety about getting the long journey home over with. He had developed a reborn loyalty to his homeland after missing the things he took for granted in earlier years. He was not disillusioned about the grandeur of Europe but, as much as he loved it, it was not home. It was strangled by a virulent strand of bureaucratic inertia, made torpid with ineffi-

ciency, and it whined with envy about ugly American imperial-
ism with the hollow gripes of the poor cousin.

The nation he left in juvenile cynicism he now defended in
heated arguments with his Dutch friends, his only allies in debate
were their aged parents who remembered the forties. Once the
plane reservation was made and the ticket was in his hand, a
floodgate of yearning for his native soil, pent up by Spartan discipline for two years, was released. He wanted to go home. He
wanted a shrimp cocktail, a barbecued steak, a standing rib
roast, a Big Boy hamburger, pizza pie and a bona fide chocolate
sundae. He wanted a dentist with a high speed drill and Novo-
cain, an eighteen-hole golf course, a department store with esca-
lators, popcorn at a movie theater, and enough ice in his Coke to
make a snowcone. He wanted to go where people stood in lines
instead of crushing each other to get on a bus, where girls shaved
their legs and their armpits, and people didn't eat raw fish with
onions for breakfast. He wanted to go home.

It was Scooter's lot to be an appendage to a group of Hungarian refugees carrying extra possessions on the plane with them in
clothes bags. He got a middle seat squashed between two matronly immigrants neither of whom spoke English or Dutch.
Scooter was forced to balance a lady's bag of goods on his knees
for the duration of the seven-hour flight. The highly skilled stewardesses, fluent in German, Dutch, French, English, and Spanish could communicate nothing to this chaotic mass of bewildered
pilgrims.

A lingual crisis hit about an hour out of New York when the
custom's immigration cards were distributed to each passenger to
be filled out before landing to expedite disembarcation. The passengers stared at them in blank incomprehension turning them
over and over searching for a third side which might have instructions they could read. A voice over the intercom pled for someone
who could translate the instructions into Hungarian. No such
person was aboard the aircraft. Scooter was growing annoyed envisioning an interminable delay at the airport while the group
found an interpreter and filled out the forms before anyone could
deplane. He silently prayed for a quick solution.

His prayer was answered when he noticed one passenger
seated on the aisle dressed in priestly garb. Scooter transferred

the cumbersome bag to his seat, stood up and squeezed past the woman next to him and into the aisle. He tapped the priest on the shoulder and began to recite the "Our Father" in Latin. Using his hands in animated gestures Scooter encouraged the priest to join it. It clicked with the priest that they shared a common language. Scooter pointed demonstratively at the green immigration card and set about the task of translating the English instructions into Latin which in turn the priest could render into Hungarian. They giggled like school boys trying to move from the holy sphere of ecclesiastical Latin to such mundane matters as the words for "address" and "birthdate." Scooter groped for a pidgen Latin to get "birthdate" choosing a mongrelized form of his limited knowledge of the language. He said, *"Natum datum," "Natum datum."* The priest's eyes brightened and he roared his approval in recognition of the litany. Scooter felt like he was back in grade school speaking pig latin, or imitating an episode of dialogue from the Lone Ranger. The words rolled off his tongue sounding like, "Me got heap big *'natum datum,'* Kemo Sabi."

The stewardesses brightened when the priest stood and spoke to the group explaining the forms in Hungarian and Scooter settled back in his seat, a hero to the cabin crew. The 707 started a gradual descent from forty thousand feet, bringing an exclamation of wonder from the group when it broke through the clouds unveiling the metropolis of Manhattan. People jumped from their seats, pressing their faces against the small windows, babbling in excitement at their virgin view of the new world. They cheered when the pilot lazily circled the harbor providing a clear view of the Statue of Liberty. Scooter said silently, "Forgive me dear lady for my crude and unchivalrous words to you the last time we met. Here in this plane are more tired and poor of the hallowed masses yearning to be free. You are a gorgeous and splendid figure and I love you." His right hand went to his forehead as he saluted the torch-bearing goddess.

Within minutes the giant tires touched down lightly, leaving a fresh streak of black on the tarmac surface of the runway. The plane taxied toward the terminal and Scooter thought about the mystical value men assigned to their native soil. He felt a kinship with every Jew who said, "Next year in Jerusalem," every Cossack who wept at the sight of Mother Russia, every Scot who sang of the Highlands and the bonnie bonnie banks of Loch Lomond. The words of the anthem by Fred Waring and the Pennsylvanians popped into his mind, "This is my country, land of my birth . . . "

After clearing customs Scooter walked through the terminal building of Kennedy International Airport and outside to the taxi stand. He was oddly frightened by the frenetic pace of New York City. After two years in Holland, stepping onto the sidewalk in New York was like being planted on a whirlwind, everything happening at double time. He hailed a cab and for the first time in twenty-four months was able to announce his destination and banter with the driver in English, if that word can be used for the speech patterns of New York cabbies.

Scooter spent the night in an airport hotel, devouring a hamburger in the coffee shop, before completing his journey home to Pittsburgh the next day.

Adrenaline was pumping through his veins on the morning flight to Pittsburgh. The mildest turbulence evoked clammy fear in Scooter. *Not now, God. Please don't be cruel. Let me get home. All the way home.* In the descent pattern Scooter recognized the Gulf Building, the Koppers Building, the Grant Building, and the familiar sights of bridges and barges. The plane banked toward the Greater Pittsburgh Airport flying over Neville Island before gliding in low over the tees and greens of Montour Country Club, Scally's Driving Range, and the Penn Lincoln Parkway where it seemed that any second the landing gear would brush the tops of cars beneath them. His heart lept with the touchdown, a bit bumpy, but safe, and Scooter was now in the Steel City. A mellow voice came over the intercom. "Welcome to Pittsburgh. The local time is 10:47. Please remain seated until we have parked at the ramp and the captain has turned off the seat belt sign. Thank you for flying T.W.A. We hope you have a pleasant stay in Pittsburgh."

Scooter got his suitcases from the baggage terminal and headed for the taxi stand. He climbed in the Yellow Cab with a Cheshire grin on his face. "Briarwood," he said to the driver and settled back for the thirty-five-minute drive home. Every building on Route 51 seemed to smile at him as he passed them, each one kindling memories of his life lived in this area. The cab pulled up in front of his apartment and Scooter hastily paid the driver, giving a generous tip to this man who was now a co-celebrant in his homecoming.

He didn't bother to ring the buzzer, fumbling for his key ring that still had the brass key that would open the door to the apartment. He knew his mother would be at work, not expecting him to return for a few more days. He inserted the key in the door and pushed it open, totally unprepared for the sight that greeted him.

Johnny was resting in a chaise lounge in the backyard of the Kramer residence, his leg propped up on a pillow. Leah was in the kitchen listening to a racy story embellished with expletives from Charlie. Charlie was teasing her to death but in a spirit that made Leah feel welcome, already accepted as part of the family.

Charlie was relentless. "You mean to tell me that of all those gorgeous soldier boys you met, you fell in love with this one? Did you think you were Becky Thatcher? You let Tom Sawyer con you, didn't you? You'll rue the day, sweetie pie. Look at him out there sitting on his duff with his leg propped up, like a king waiting for us to smother him with attention. You believe that cock-and-bull story about gettin' shot by some slant-eyed Chinaman? The little goldbricker probably shot himself so he could come back here for us to wait on him."

"Don't listen to her, Leah," Johnny shouted from the patio. "She missed my beautiful bod so much she probably hired her own private Charlie-Cong to do a job on me."

Leah was overwhelmed by the continuous lighthearted mien of the Kramer household. In serious moments Charlie had been tender, weeping privately with her when Leah had answered her questions about the painful time of therapy Johnny had undergone in Tokyo hospital. This afternoon they were going to Pittsburgh, to Kaufmann's department store for last-minute shopping. Charlie had taken charge of the wedding details, playing mother rather than mother-in-law to Leah. Because of Johnny's continued convalescence, tradition was broken and the couple was being married in the groom's home church, The Reverend Doctor Lindsley Oliver Franklin, Jr. presiding.

The wedding was only ten days away and Charlie was leading Leah on a whirlwind binge of last-minute preparations. The last fitting of the bridal gown would follow the visit to Kaufmann's.

The engraved invitations had already been sent, the cake ordered at Dutz's Bakery, the flowers from Hill's Florist sure to be delivered on time if the winged Mercury himself had to bring them. The maitre d' of South Hills Country Club had received his instructions from Jack Kramer for the lavish sit-down reception dinner to follow the wedding, and reservations were made at the Pittsburgh Athletic Club for the rehearsal dinner. Johnny had a bachelor party scheduled for two nights before the wedding at the Duquesne Club, Pittsburgh's most exclusive blue-blood, male only, social club.

Jack Kramer was busy meeting over lunch with his real estate broker going over the details of the closing on a charming three-bedroom house set on a wooded lot with a split rail fence, only two suburban streets over from the Kramer residence. Johnny and Leah knew nothing of the surprise wedding gift Jack was planning. Their questions about housing were stiff-armed by Jack who said, "Don't worry about that. There are plenty of apartments available. Let's take care of the wedding and the honeymoon before we worry about housing."

Jack was going through a maudlin period of mellowing toward his son. Johnny was the firstborn, the eldest son, the screwed-up kid who was finally a man with a Purple Heart to prove it. The shock of the message of Johnny's casualty in Viet Nam provoked sleepless nights for the weeks following the news. Jack assailed himself with recriminations, and was now given the benefit of a second chance to Johnny. His son had survived, was home in one piece and ready to embark on an adult career. Jack was determined to set Johnny up in royal style, giving him a grubstake that would insure his success. He had already made the necessary arrangements to set him up in his insurance business. He pulled all the strings to enroll Johnny in a special September seminar in management put on by the home office in New York. In the interim following the honeymoon Johnny would be his shadow at the Pittsburgh office.

When Scooter walked in the doorway of the apartment he found his mother lying on the floor on the living room rug writhing in pain. He rushed to her side shouting, "Mother, what's wrong?"

Tears of joy flooded her eyes blotting out for a moment the excruciating pain in her abdomen. She put her hand on her cheek crying, "Scooter, Scooter . . . you're home!"

"Yes, Mom, I'm home, but what's wrong?"

"I'm just having gas pains. It will be over in a minute."

"Gas pains my eye. How long has this been going on? I'm calling the doctor now!"

"Please, no, Scooter, don't . . . I'll be all right. Oh, it's so good to see you."

Scooter helped his mother onto the sofa where she sat grimacing in pain, clutching her stomach. Scooter reached for the slender metal indexed telephone guide, moved the arrow to *B* and pushed the mechanism which popped open the directory. He scanned the list of handwritten names, addresses and telephone numbers until he saw the name Bremer, Dr. Warren. He grabbed the phone and dialed Dr. Bremer's office. In urgent tones he persuaded Bremer's nurse to put him through to the doctor, stressing that it was an emergency. Dr. Bremer came on the line, "Dr. Bremer, this is Scooter Evans. I just came home and found my mother doubled over in pain on the floor. She says it's gas pains but it's surely worse than that. She can hardly talk."

"Listen, Scooter. You stay right there with her. I'll call an ambulance for her immediately. I want her in Allegheny General Hospital right away. I'll have a doctor waiting for the ambulance at the hospital."

"Yes, sir, I'll wait right here."

Scooter hung up the phone and said, "We need to pack your things, you're going to the hospital."

Mrs. Evans tried to protest but saw that it was useless. She was still doubled over and had difficulty telling him what articles to pack in her overnight case. Scooter stuffed things in the case and had just clicked it shut when the knock came at the door. Two men were there holding a collapsible stretcher. Scooter held his mother's hand as the men put her on the stretcher and carried her down the stairs to the ambulance waiting outside. The driver asked Scooter if he wanted to ride along.

"No. I'm going to need a car. I'll be there as fast as I can. You just get her to the hospital."

He kissed his mother on her perspiring forehead and promised to follow as quickly as possible. The driver flipped on his flashing red dome light, holding back the siren until he reached the highway. Scooter rushed back into the apartment, picked up the phone and dialed the Kramers. Charlie answered the phone.

"Charlie, this is Scooter—"

"Scooter! Darling, you're home, I—"

Scooter cut her off. "Yes. Listen, Charlie, I don't have time to talk. My mother just left for the hospital in an ambulance. I need a car to get there. Can you help?"

Charlie's voice became deadly serious. "Of course, I'll send Tommy over right away with the Buick."

The car rounded the corner minutes later, Johnny's younger brother Tommy at the wheel. He screeched to a stop and got out, leaving the motor running and the door open. "Here, Scooter, take the car. I can walk home."

Scooter slid behind the wheel urgently. "Thanks, Tommy, I'll get it back as soon as I can."

He drove furiously, weaving in and out of lanes dodging the traffic along Route 51. The traffic through the Liberty Tunnels and across the Liberty Bridge was light at this hour and his progress was not impeded. He beat a yellow light at Sixth and Grant and made it across town to the bridge spanning the river to the Northside. He found a parking spot along the edge of the park in front of Allegheny General Hospital. Scooter raced up the steps to the front entrance of the old brick hospital and asked at the information desk for his mother.

"Yes, Mrs. Evans was admitted through Emergency," the volunteer woman working at the counter replied. "Are you family?"

"Yes, I'm her son."

"Mrs. Evans is still in the emergency room. If you'll take a seat in the waiting lounge you'll be notified as soon as there is word."

Within the hour Scooter was paged again. This time he was met at the desk by a physician. "Mr. Evans, your mother is resting comfortably in her room. She has been sedated and given medication for her pain. Our preliminary x-rays indicate the need for a surgical procedure, which will be performed by Dr. Blair tomorrow morning at 7:45."

Scooter was unable to get any more details. The doctor expressed a preference that he not disturb his mother, and asked him to return in the morning.

At 7:00 A.M. Scooter found a seat in the lounge across from a haggard woman clutching the hand of a girl who was obviously her daughter. They were locked in their own private drama, enduring a vigil for someone else upstairs, some other poor soul held captive in the bowels of this place that had one elevator leading to the nursery where the newborn infants were spanked into life, and another elevator that went from the sixth floor to the basement, to a refrigerated room with stainless steel tables marked by drains in the center and storage lockers housing bins on slides for corpses with tags on their toes. The nursery, the autopsy room and the hospital morgue defined the parameters of this house.

He picked up a copy of the morning *Post-Gazette,* leafing through its pages, but his eyes were not able to focus on the print. The only story he cared about was the one unfolding in a brightly illumined room upstairs where masked men and women probed the internal organs of his mother's body while sophisticated machines beeped and blipped, monitoring her fragile hold on life. Scooter quit the lounge and walked to the small chapel, past the bronze plaque on the wall commemorating the generous donor who had provided this sacred alcove, perhaps out of gratitude for an answered petition of intercession.

The chapel was vacant. He went to the kneeling rail and made his prayer. He had a strong inner sense that his prayer was too late, that his mother had already been assigned by the Almighty to an angelic squadron commanded by the black angel of death.

He returned to the lounge to continue his helpless vigil, pacing the floor and filling the ashtray with cigarettes. The nervous women were called to the desk and disappeared through swinging doors for a conference with their physician. Within the hour other anxious pilgrims took their place. The vigil was broken with a call from the front desk.

"Mr. Evans. Front desk, please. Mr. Evans."

Scooter tried to control his frantic fear by walking slowly and deliberately to the counter. The kindly matron spoke to him in hushed tones. "Dr. Blair will see you now." She gave directions through the swinging doors to the surgeons' meeting room. Scooter knocked hesitantly at the door and was invited in. Dr. Blair was seated at a small wooden table drinking a cup of coffee.

His head was covered by a light green cap and his surgical mask was dangling from a cloth string around his neck.

"Sit down, Mr. Evans." His tone was gentle but serious, ominous and foreboding. "Your mother is still in the recovery room. She's stable but I'm afraid her condition is not good. We found an advanced carcinoma in her abdomen. The primary lesion was in the uterus but matastasis has occurred and the malignancy has spread through her abdomen. We could not remove it surgically. I'm afraid that she is a very sick woman."

Scooter nodded silently, knowing the implications of inoperable cancer. "What happens now doctor? What's the procedure? Cobalt or radium treatments? How much time does she have?"

"We won't be sure of a treatment procedure until we get the full results from the pathology. None of us can say how long this kind of illness will last. There are always surprises. It may be days, weeks, or even months. I can assure you that we will do everything in our power to make your mother comfortable."

"I understand, sir. Will she be told of her condition?"

"That depends on you, Mr. Evans. It is my policy that it be a family decision. I generally advise that the patient be told. I consider it a matter of their right and their dignity. I realize, however, that there are certain conditions and certain people who are better off not knowing."

"No," Scooter spoke up, "she's the kind who would want to know. You can't fool her anyway and I suspect she knows already. The big question is, who should tell her?"

"I think you should let me handle that and you be the support system. She'll be out of the recovery room in another half hour or so. You can see her for a moment in her room, then I suggest you go home and get some rest. She'll be heavily sedated and will sleep the rest of the day. If you come by in the morning, say about 11:00, I'll speak to her privately just before you arrive."

Scooter drove home with his heart encased in an iron weight. He noticed people on the sidewalks smiling and children romping in playgrounds. He listened to inane jokes by disc jockeys on the radio before he switched it off. The world outside the hospital was business as usual where human beings perfected the art of insulating themselves from misery.

Scooter went to the apartment first. The telephone suddenly became an assault weapon with fire power strong enough to pierce the insulation. The dialing of a few digits was all that it required to penetrate the private world of relatives, ruining their day with the bad tidings. The most painful call was the long distance connection to Iowa to his sister who once had cheated death in the same hospital where their mother was now confined. The last call was to the neighbor woman who had written Scooter in Holland and had enclosed the ghastly picture of his mother.

Once the phoning chore was completed he felt the walls of the apartment closing in on him. The apartment had a sense of death about it, as though black crepe should be hanging in the windows. He was surrounded by tokens of better days: photographs, knickknacks, clothing, all pulsating with vibrations of memories of Elizabeth Evans in more robust times. Scooter had to get out. He drove to the Kramer's.

From the edge of the driveway he could see Johnny reclining in a chaise lounge, nursing a cool ice-sludged rum drink in a tall glass, with Leah and Charlie seated on either side of him. Scooter broke into a grin thinking that it was only proper that their reunion should be marked by Johnny at ease, surrounded by women pampering him while Scooter marched alone. The moment of greeting was a bit awkward with no one being quite sure what spirit was appropriate—somber words of concern or ebullient outbursts of the joy of the reunion. In Johnny, as usual, the exuberance won out.

"Roomie! Get over here and let me look at you. Whadya think Charlie, does our boy look like a starched-shirt saint? Come here Scooter and give us some pious mumbo jumbo."

"I'll mumbo your jumbo so you'll need ten beautiful nurses, you reprobate! Who is this gorgeous creature with you?" Scooter turned to Leah. "You must be the nurse Jack Kramer bribed with his filthy lucre to come over here and relieve Charlie from taking care of her worthless son."

Leah smiled, enjoying the silly banter of the two friends, feeling as if she had known Scooter for years.

"I'm Leah Labans, the bride to be of this conquering hero."

Scooter feigned a swoon, slapping his forehead with his hand saying, "Call a doctor! I'm losing my mind. I thought for a second this gorgeous doll said she was Johnny's fiancée."

Johnny howled, "What did you expect, Scooter, something that growled and barked and bit the mailman on the leg?"

"Of course not, Johnny. I expected a white cane." He turned to Leah. "What's your problem, do you have a fetish for midgets or just an exaggerated compassion for sick little dogs?"

Charlie interrupted, "OK, motor mouth, can I fix you something to drink?"

"Sure, Charlie. I'd love a nice cold Coke."

"A Coke? You sure you don't want lemonade? Listen to this, sports fans, our sissy-pants scholar, our wimpy preacher boy wants a Coke. How about a little rum in it for old times' sake, Scoot?"

"'Rum and Coca-Cola' has a nice ring to it. It should be a song or something, maybe with a calypso beat. OK, Charlie but just a pinch. You don't want me to be the Reverend Mr. Lush do you?"

Scooter kissed her on the cheek and gave her a big hug which she held for a fraction too long, her face clouding with concern. "How's your mother, Scooter?"

Scooter's mood adjusted to the question, frivolity vanishing with the words. "Not good, Charlie. Cancer. It's all through her. They opened her up and explored around, then sewed her back up."

Tears flooded Charlie's eyes. "Oh, Scooter . . ." was all that she could say.

Scooter filled them in on the doctor's report, then turned the conversation to the wedding plans. At the end of the visit, Charlie told Scooter to keep the Buick as long as he needed it.

"Thanks, Charlie. I thought about seeing Frank Carter tomorrow about getting a clunker to use till fall. Once school starts I'll be a rich man, a real-life college professor with a salary."

"Big deal. With a teacher's salary all you'll be able to afford is a little red wagon. Hey, that would be neat, you can be the story of 'Scooter and the little red wagon.'"

"Save the little red wagon stuff for your midget soldier boy. I can't believe the Cong shot him. I was sure they would think he was one of them."

Johnny threw a pillow at him as Scooter got up to leave.

TWENTY

Scooter entered his mother's room at precisely 11:00 A.M. She was propped up in bed with a sly smile on her face. Scooter couldn't believe how she managed to have her hair looking perfect and her makeup impeccable. He leaned over the bed and kissed her.

"Has the doctor been in yet, Mom?"

Again she smiled. "Yes, he just left a minute ago. I told you it was just a gas pain."

"Yeah, yeah, Mom. Listen. I already had a long talk with the doctor; so I know the score."

"Well then get rid of the long face. I can handle this. Your mother is a tough bird."

"You're a bird all right, but I don't know how tough."

"Tough enough, Scooter. You can bet on one thing. I'm going to live to see you ordained." She choked on her words and said, "So you'd better do it fast."

"Does it hurt, Mom?"

"No, they have me on something that makes me feel like I've had six Manhattans and a sidecar. I'm floating. Now, what about your ordination?"

"I wrote to the presbytery from Amsterdam. The Witherspoon job is a valid 'call' to the ministry. They've scheduled my ordination trials for the first week in June. If I pass them I can get ordained immediately afterwards."

"Well, get in touch with Dr. Franklin and schedule it. You know you'll whiz through those exams."

"I won't have any trouble with the test questions but don't forget, it's a liberal presbytery and they don't have much love for conservatives."

"Well, just charm the buzzards. You know how. By the way, how did you get here?"

"Charlie Kramer loaned me her car. She sends her love."

"She really is a sweetheart under all that phony gruffness. She's been good to you, especially since your father died. But you're going to need a car. Hand me the phone."

"What for? I can take care of that, Mom. That's the last thing you need to worry about."

"You listen to me. You may be almost a doctor of theology and a minister, but you're still my son. Now hand me the phone."

Scooter picked up the phone from the nightstand and stretched out the cord so it reached the bedside. Mrs. Evans asked for information, then dialed the number of the Briarwood Ford agency.

"Hello, I would like to speak to Frank Carter . . . Frank? This is Elizabeth Evans. My son just got back from school in Europe and he needs a car. I'm calling from Allegheny General Hospital and they won't let me out of this place. What? No, it's nothing serious, just routine tests. I want to send Scooter in this afternoon. Pick out the best car you have in the showroom. It's his ordination present. Yes, he's being ordained in June. . . . Of course, I'm proud. Now you do as I say. The best, you hear? And send me the bill. . . . All right, Frank. Yes, I know. We'll discuss that later. . . . I know, dear, you'll never forget. You've made that clear. Thanks. Bye."

"What was all that 'you'll never forget' stuff about?" Scooter asked.

"Oh, your father bailed him out of a jam once. He blubbers about it every time he sees me. Now you get out of here and go straight to Frank Carter and pick out your ordination present."

"Mother, you can't do that. You know we can't afford a new car."

"Who can't afford a new car? I've been working haven't I? I have some money saved up. What do I need it for? I can't take it with me."

Scooter winced. "Don't talk like that, Mom."

"I told you to get rid of that long face. None of that around here. And stop arguing about the car. Let me have a little fun if I want to. Now scram."

"OK, Mom. I'll be back tonight."

"No, you won't. I don't want you driving in here every day fussing over me. You need to get ready for Johnny's wedding and your ordination. It's enough for me that you're home and that I can see you again."

Tears rolled down Scooter's cheeks in concert with the descent of the elevator to the hospital lobby. Again he made the journey across town and out Route 51 to Briarwood, pulling into the lot next to the showroom of the Ford agency. Frank Carter was standing in the showroom with a cigar clenched between his teeth. He was dressed in a garish suit looking like the quintessential car salesman. He spied Scooter and came over talking with his hands, using the cigar as a pointer, falling all over Scooter with flattery about his ordination and how he would make a "fine young minister."

"Your mother ordered the best in the place, Scooter. Feast your eyes on this."

A spotlight, suspended from the corner of the ceiling, was strategically aimed to produce sparkling highlights dancing from the gleaming chrome molding of a brand new white Thunderbird convertible. Scooter just laughed.

"I can't drive a car like that. Ministers can't get away with driving Thunderbirds. Besides the whole thing is crazy. I'm only home for a year and then I have to go back to Europe to finish my degree."

"Not to worry, not to worry. Why not drive a Thunderbird? Father Crowley does. And I'll buy it back at top dollar when you're ready to go back to Europe. Who knows, maybe your plans will change. Give yourself a break. Ministers have been driving black clunkers around too long anyway. Your mother said the best and this is the cream of the lot."

"Well, I'm not Father Crowley, and look at the sticker price. My mother can't afford that."

"Don't worry about the sticker. That price doesn't apply to Elizabeth Evans. Or to her son. Your father did a lot for me and I'm not the kind of guy who forgets." The last point was made with a grandiose gesture with the cigar.

Scooter was starting to salivate, staring at the leather upholstery and envisioning himself driving to classes at Witherspoon in this beauty. It made his love affair with his old '57 Fairlane 500 seem like an adolescent infatuation with a piece of junk. A week ago he was pedaling an austere black bicycle to the train station where he left it at the depot with a hundred other bikes that looked exactly the same.

"No, Mr. Carter. You better show me something else."

"Not until you take it for a test drive. You try it, and if you don't like it then I'll show you something else."

Carter opened the showroom garage door and put a temporary license tag on the T-Bird and handed Scooter the keys. The top was down and ready to go. Mr. Carter got in the passenger side and Scooter eased the white stallion out of the showroom and pointed it toward the main street of Briarwood. As they breezed past the shopping center Frank inquired about Mrs. Evans. "What's wrong with Elizabeth? Why is she in the hospital?"

"She's real sick, Mr. Carter. Cancer. That's why the rush on the ordination present. I don't think she'll leave the hospital alive."

"Oh, no. I had a bad feeling just from how she was talking on the telephone. Why does the big C always hit the best people? I hate that disease. It killed my father. That settles it. You can't go to the hospital and tell her you bought some stripped-down stick-shift standard Ford. Light up her lights with this baby. Your mother's got class kid. She'll get a kick out of this buggy."

Too many fiery darts were scoring points in Scooter's weak spot. He was already in love with the car and his mind was in high gear trying to rationalize indulgence in his fancy. He could always tell people it was a gift so no one could accuse him of an addiction to crass materialism or wasteful consumption while children were starving in Africa. He was already seduced and he knew he couldn't even look at another car. This one had his name on it. It was a gift from heaven—or from hell, but at the moment he really didn't care which.

He drove down the wooded lanes of his hometown, past the residences of his childhood friends, and made the turn onto Woodcrest Drive, approaching his childhood home like a Muslim pilgrim drawing near Mecca. He stopped in front of the house peering out over the neatly manicured hedges at the front of the house. The blue spruce in the front yard now towered over thirty feet, its branches spread so wide that it seemed to engulf the whole yard. Scooter thought, *I bet it wouldn't take me so long to mow the lawn with that tree taking up so much space.* His eyes moved left, focusing on the large addition, a den graced by a cathedral ceiling with huge natural wood rafters and cobblestone fireplace whose stonework ascended to the peak of the outer wall. It was in that room Scooter had lifted his comatose father from the bloodstained rug where he fell from the effects of his fourth and final stroke. Scooter eased his foot off the brake allowing the car to drift past this place of ghosts and memories past.

"OK, Mr. Carter. You got me. You hit me where it hurts. This is the car. Mom will love it."

They drove back to the agency and signed all the forms. Mr. Carter called in the service manager and ordered a rush, top-priority dealer preparation job on the car, assuring Scooter that he could pick it up the following afternoon.

Scooter went home and called the hospital, telling his mother he had made a deal for a car but refusing to give any details over the phone. "I pick it up tomorrow afternoon. I'll drive it to the hospital and find a place to park it where you can see it from the window of your room."

The next afternoon Scooter nursed the car daintily along Route 51, sure that some wild driver would sideswipe him or plow into his side door turning it into an accordion. He savored the aroma of the new upholstery and the enchanting new-car smell that no used car dealer could emulate with an aerosol can. He dreaded the fallout of grime that Pittsburgh's inner city would deposit on the virgin exterior sullying it like the rape of the Sabine women. He was already thinking of the car as "she," and demanded respect from others to its pristine beauty like a chivalrous knight his lady. He wondered if the Apostle Paul ever had thoughts like this while driving his chariot along the Appian Way. The Bible did make mention of the Old Testament Jehu who became the patron saint of reckless drivers. Scooter found a spot along the avenue within eyeshot of the hospital wing where Mrs. Evans was housed.

Directly across the street from the hospital was a city park, an island of grass garnished with shade trees and wooden-slotted benches supported by wrought iron legs. The park was a haven for elderly immigrants who viewed this place as a waiting room for heaven. It was as if they were staying close to Allegheny General Hospital where they could walk, rather than ride in a screaming ambulance, to their final checkout center. These people, forgotten exiles of the Northside's working class, spent their days reading the newspaper, playing checkers, and feeding pigeons. The pigeons were the most numerous social group of the Northside, the only genuine indigenous natives of the place.

The white Thunderbird looked out of place parked there, and the gray pigeons looked black next to the pure whiteness of the car. Scooter noted their waddle, a lethargic strut of imperious indifference to their loss of dove-like silver sheen. Their feathers were made leaden by soot while they pecked at the sidewalks for morsels of bread and peanuts tossed there by their comrades in gray.

Once in the hospital he helped his mother from her bed and into her slippers. She used his shoulder for support, inching her way to the window overlooking the park.

"See if you can pick it out, Mom."

Elizabeth Evans scanned the cars parked along the sidewalk below until her eyes came to the white Thunderbird. They stopped right there, her eyebrows arched in amusement. "You little devil. You devil. You incredible devil. That's it, isn't it? The white convertible. You devil."

"What do you think, Mom? Do you like it?"

"It's perfect. White as angels' wings. You little devil."

"Make up your mind, Mom. You have to get your theology straight. Am I a devil or an angel?"

"Now that's a hard one. I'm not quite sure. I can't decide if you're a devil riding in an angel's car or an angel riding in a devil's car."

"Why don't we compromise and think of it as an angel riding in an angel's car?"

"Good idea. Now get me back in bed before the nurse comes in and has a fit."

After he got her back in bed she started in with a battery of questions.

"Did you speak to Dr. Franklin?"

"Yes."

"Did you set a date for your ordination."

"Yes. It's scheduled for June 9."

"We need to order invitations. Call Clair DeWalt and have her call me. We'll work out that detail."

For the next twenty minutes Mrs. Evans dictated a list of

things to be done for the big event, including contacting her friend at Maxine's dress shop to order a special dress for the occasion. Again she insisted that she would walk out of the hospital and get to the church for the event, only five weeks away.

"Now, son, there is something else we need to discuss. You are twenty-six years old and single. It is high time you quit carrying this burned-out torch for Patricia. Don't interrupt me. I've watched you. You never give any other girl a chance. You have this fixation, this idealized, romanticized image of Patricia arrested in your brain. You're all grown by now. Look at you. You're a man, and it's time to grow up all the way and leave your teenage broken heart behind you."

"Mother, I'm perfectly happy being single. There just aren't any girls that interest me."

"Nonsense. You won't give them a chance. You don't even date. You're an incurable romantic, just like your father was, but you keep it all bottled up inside. That car out there is your girl friend. Now it's time to find the real thing. I don't want to die thinking you'll go through your life unmarried. I can't bear the thought of the Evans line ending with you. You must promise me two things. First, that you will get married, and second, that you will name your first son Richard Evans IV."

"Mom, we're not working on a dynasty. This is not exactly the House of Windsor or the Tudors. Besides, etiquette requires that the grandfather still be alive if you paste Roman numerals on a boy's birth certificate."

"I don't care what Emily Post or Amy Vanderbilt says. I want a Richard Evans IV. Now promise me."

"Whatever you say. I promise. I'll get married and produce a Richard Evans IV and make him promise to bring the V along into the world. People will tease my grandson. They'll think he is a walking whiskey bottle, Richard the 'Fifth.'"

It is not common for a Presbyterian church building to have a sacristy, but Lindsley Oliver Franklin was not one to supervise the construction of a sanctuary without one. From the first turn of the earth with a silver plated spade it was a foregone conclusion, an inviolate certainty, that a narthex, nave, transept, and altar would be part of the church. All that was missing was an aspe. For Franklin, the sanctuary was not a commonplace Protestant church building, it was a basilica. Franklin's "sacristy" was hardly a room; it was more of a cubicle with floor to ceiling cupboards painted white. The cupboards contained Franklin's magnificent vestments; three black robes with velvet doctoral chevrons, three sets of starched Geneva tabs, three multihued processional hoods, and an assortment of regalia used in his ceremonial extravaganzas. The sacristy led to a narrow passageway that went behind the altar hidden from the congregational view by a false wall.

Scooter and Johnny got last-minute detailed instructions for their entry from Dr. Franklin and walked together from his study into the passageway behind the altar and into the sacristy. Their watches were synchronized with Franklin's exquisite timepiece so that at the precise moment Franklin would enter the chancel from the congregation's left, Johnny and Scooter would enter from the right. Franklin dismissed them to the sacristy a full ten minutes before the wedding was to begin, condemning them to a nervous ritual of waiting. Johnny was visibly anxious, his forehead perspiring and his palms clammy. For him it was the final six hundred seconds of his bachelorhood. Johnny's nervousness was made acute by the ominous knowledge that the only thing that separated him from the congregation, the audience here to listen to his "speech," was the sacristy door.

"What if I forget my lines, Scooter, with all those people staring at me?" Johnny said, panic building in his voice.

"Relax, Johnny. You don't have to give a speech. Besides you'll be facing the altar, not the congregation. The only person you'll have to face is Dr. Franklin."

"I think I'd rather face the congregation."

"Well then, look at Leah and just repeat the phrases Franklin says. You don't have to have the lines memorized."

"What if I freeze? What if my mind goes blank when he tells me what to say?"

Scooter laughed. "Then I'll poke you in the ribs and wake you up."

"Let's go over it one more time, OK?"

"Sure, repeat after me, I, John Harold . . ."

"I, John Harold"

"Take thee, Leah Helene . . ."

"Take thee, Leah Helene . . ."

Scooter took him through the brief ceremony for one last trial run. The minute hand approached the half-hour.

"I'm sweating to death in this monkey suit," Johnny complained.

"You should have worn your full-dress military uniform and we could have done the crossed swords routine."

"No thanks, I've had enough of that. I'd have to use my cane for the sword salute. This collar is choking me and I'm getting a razor rash."

"You look great, Johnny, like Tom Sawyer in tuxedo. I think we look more like we're going to the races at Ascot than to a wedding."

"Yeah, I know. 'The rain in Spain falls mainly on the plain.'"

"No, Johnny. For you it's 'The rine in Spine falls minely on the pline.' Hey, we have thirty seconds, partner. Take a deep breath then open the door and break a leg."

Johnny glared over his shoulder at Scooter. "Nice talk."

At that exact second Scooter prodded Johnny and said, "Let's go. I'm right behind you."

They marched out to the center of the sanctuary, to the foot of the chancel steps as Dr. Franklin moved toward them from the opposite wing. At the center aisle they did a three-quarter turn so that by a slight swivel of the head they could gaze at the narthex to watch the bridal procession. The organ burst into strains of the "Wedding March" from Mendelssohn's *Midsummer Night's Dream* with its trills and crescendoes. Dr. Franklin prohibited the Wagnerian *Lohengrin* claiming it was too pedestrian for his tastes and smacked of militaristic overtones by its link to its composer beloved by Hitler. The ushers had already unrolled the white linen crash and the first of the bridesmaids began her slow march down the aisle, her feet a bit wobbly and her bouquet trembling in her hands. A forced smile broke into an elastic grin when Johnny winked at her as he caught her eye.

Four bridesmaids and a maid of honor made the lonely trek down the aisle. A brief interlude of hesitation brought a hush of anticipation to the congregation. Leah's aunt was seated in the front row acting as her surrogate mother. Her eyes were riveted on Dr. Franklin to catch the almost imperceptible signal from him to rise, a signal in turn for the whole congregation to stand in honor of the march of the bride.

The organist touched the stop for a full diapason and Leah took her first step, holding lightly to the arm of her father who had flown in from Chicago for the event. She was radiant, dressed in a full-skirted organza gown trimmed in chantilly lace. Her train brushed the linen cloth on the floor. She processed with regal bearing, her smile barely visible through her gossamer veil.

Johnny stepped forward into the aisle and received the bride from her father's arm. The bride and groom stood facing the unctuous Dr. Franklin. In sonorous tones he began the rite of marriage, "Dearly beloved . . ." With the urbane skill of an actor, Franklin transformed the encrusted commonplace prose of the ritual into lyric poetry. When he said, "Dearly beloved" the congregation felt as if suddenly the voice of Christ had fallen on their ears with special words of endearment.

"We are gathered here today in the presence of God and of these witnesses, to unite this man and this woman in the holy bond of matrimony . . ."

A drama was unfolding. One could sense the gazing eyes of God peering down through the roof observing every detail, hearing every syllable as He recorded the vows of *this* man and *this* woman on tablets of stone. Franklin had the ability to make each marriage ceremony sound as if it were the first solemn contract ever sealed by man and woman; a primal event of uniqueness; Eden revisited; that no mere mortal ever dare put asunder. His voice reverberated through the sanctuary with a Goliathan challenge: "If any man knows any just cause why this man and this woman may not lawfully be wed, let him speak now, or *forever* hold his peace."

The word *forever* hung over the congregation like an angelic sword of flames daring anyone to speak. Had J. Edgar Hoover himself been there with rock-hard evidence of Johnny's being already married and about to commit bigamy, the challenge of Franklin would have left him mute.

Johnny recited his vows flawlessly. No hesitation, no nervous stuttering. The eyes of Dr. Franklin drew the words from him. He could not falter. Not here. Not in the presence of this man. Had Johnny's mind gone blank Franklin would have willed the words out of him.

Scooter passed the ring to Johnny following the explicit form of exchange dictated by the minister. Johnny cupped his hand

and Scooter placed the golden circle, the symbol of endless time, precisely in the center of it, allowing no risk for the holy litany's disturbance by a clumsy exchange. From his own hand Johnny completed the transfer by tenderly pressing it into place on the third finger of Leah's left hand.

"With this ring I thee wed. In the name of the Father, the Son, and the Holy Ghost."

Johnny and Leah left their comrades in waiting and moved together to the kneeling bench before the altar, following the retreat of Dr. Franklin. There the couple knelt to receive the prayer of consecration and the benediction. Scooter felt a twinge of fear, noticing as Johnny knelt that he had neglected to fulfill a command given by Dr. Franklin at the rehearsal the night before. The groom, best man, and ushers were ordered to make sure their shoes were not only well polished but that the soles of their shoes be also covered with boot black lest their variant grains detract from the impeccable symmetry of their dress. Scooter offered a silent prayer that Dr. Franklin, standing above the couple, would not notice the offense and do something drastic like halting the wedding in mid-prayer. Scooter's petition was granted and Dr. Franklin signaled the couple to rise. Nodding to the maid of honor to step forward to assist in the lifting of the veil, he said with an obvious change in tone from the solemn to almost mischievously amused, "You may kiss the bride."

The congregation stifled nervous giggles as they beheld the mystical kiss as though they were intruding on the privacy of young lovers. Once more the voice of Dr. Franklin filled the sanctuary.

"Ladies and gentlemen, I present to you Mr. and Mrs. John Kramer."

Instantly the organ broke into Purcell's "Trumpet Voluntary," and the recessional began, the bridal party joining at mid-aisle to follow the jubilant celebrants out of the sanctuary and into the narthex. Scooter cashed his claim to be the first to kiss the bride, then hurried the couple out to the parking lot where the white Thunderbird was waiting to drive them to the reception.

Johnny helped Leah into the back seat of the car while Scooter opened the door to assist the maid of honor to her place at his side in the front. With horn blaring they drove to South Hills Country Club for the festive reception.

Jack Kramer spared no expense at the club for this occasion. He usurped the role of the father of the bride using as his excuse that Providence had failed to bless his marriage with a daughter of his own. Charlie spent the evening enticing Scooter to too many champagne toasts. She insisted that he offer a toast to the bride, and the family members and to their birthdays, to Christmas, Easter, the Fourth of July, Labor Day, Groundhog's Day, Arbor Day, Armistice Day, until her knowledge of the calendar collapsed. Had he been there that night it would have been Johnny's turn to tuck Scooter safely in bed. The party ended with Leah throwing her bridal bouquet to a group of single girls fighting each other for the glory of being the next one destined for marriage. Charlie said to Scooter, "Too bad they don't throw anything to the guys. You could use a marriage omen yourself."

TWENTY-ONE

While Johnny and Leah were cruising the Caribbean, Scooter was preparing for his ordination exams. He had a wedding of his own to enact, a binding of himself to the church, an act almost incestuous. Scooter knew the words of Saint Augustine, "He who does not have the Church for his mother, does not have God for his Father."

Holy Mother Church. She would now pass judgment on her maverick son to see if he was worthy of her cloth. In many ways Scooter felt like a bastard son to this Mother whose insouciant, Laodicean regard for orthodoxy made her appear to him at times as a scarlet woman. His feeling toward her and to his own ordination were, at best, ambivalent. To Scooter, the church was the most important institution in the world, yet also the most hideously corrupt.

Not that the church was more wicked than other institutions. For him it was a relative matter. Corruption was measured by a barometer of sanctity. The church's frailties were exaggerated in Scooter's mind by her singular call to holiness. She bore the unique institution and consecration of Christ Himself. Her vocation, her mission, alone had the divine guarantee that the gates of hell could not prevail against her. No service club, no social agency, no other human institution held such a warranty. Scooter rested his troubled spirit in the comfort that if the church was corrupt she was precisely so because she was so important.

Here was the target of every satanic attack. Here the means of grace were concentrated, the sacraments endowed, the oracles of God entrusted. No wonder every malevolent evil sought a foothold here. This bride for whom Christ waited for the final wedding feast was marred and soiled by the miasmic spirit of this world. Yet He promised one day to present her to His Father spot-

less, without blemish or wrinkle, purified not by the decrees of
men but by the same sacred blood by which He purchased her.
The church was more than synods and counsels, more than con-
fessions and canons, more than assembly pronouncements and
interdicts. In a sense it was Christ in His brokenness, in His
humiliation, in His pain, called to fill up the afflictions left over
for her mission.

For Scooter the "true" church, the church catholic, was invisible, made up of those whose hearts rejoiced in Christ. Yet he took
no refuge in a church so invisible, so ethereal, so platonic that it
had no earthly manifestation. For him the invisible church was
discovered within the visible church, the wheat among the chaff,
the truth in the midst of error, the real within the counterfeit. He
was sure no church was perfect; its holiness was extrinsic, derived, dependent, helpless without divine assistance. Otherwise
he could not join it, let alone represent it. It grieved Scooter to
know that however corrupt the church already was, and however
much he longed for its earthly purity, that he too would add blemish and wrinkle to it by his very presence within it.

Ordination trials were in three parts. The first section was a
written exam in theology, biblical exegesis, and personal Christian experience. The second phase was a rigorous oral examination before the Committee on Candidates and Credentials of the
presbytery. If the first two parts of the trial were successful the
ordinand was then presented before a plenary session of the presbytery to be examined by the whole.

Scooter had no problem with the written parts of the trial.
Fresh from doctoral exams in Europe he was ready for the committee orals as well. He waited with five other seminary graduates
who were pacing the reception area of the exam chambers for his
name to be called to go before the committee. He faced this part
of the trial carrying into it both an advantage and disadvantage.
The other five candidates had just finished their seminary training and, each possessing a "call" to a church position, were moving immediately toward ordination. Scooter had gone on to
graduate school and just completed doctoral exams in theology far
more *de rigeur* than presbytery trials. That was his advantage. His
disadvantage was that he was conservative, and some members of
the committee were openly hostile to conservatives fearing the

presence of reactionaries who might work to thwart the progress of the church.

At this moment the church was embroiled in a dispute about changing its historic creedal stance. The traditional confession, the Westminster Confession of Faith, which had served as the doctrinal base of the church since the seventeenth century, was about to be neutralized by the addition of a book of creedal statements, including one recently drafted. This move would accomplish two important goals. It would chart a new course for the church on the basis of theological pluralism, widening the limits of acceptable beliefs, and more importantly, it would legitimize the presence of members of the clergy who had committed themselves to the vows they once made to embrace, confirm, adopt, and follow a credal statement they believed was archaic. Subscription to the confession had become a *pro forma* matter, causing uneasy consciences. The church was now taking steps to alleviate the difficulty.

The United Presbyterian Church carried no brief for an infallible church and considered all her pronouncements, including her creed, open to change, reform, and reformation. For students trained in modern theology the prose of Westminster seemed arcane. But the hierarchy feared a conservative backlash to the bold move to change the church's official confessional position and was particularly guarded against the threat of conservatives with advanced academic degrees.

Scooter's fear of prejudice against him by the committee was wasted. He breezed through the oral exam as the committee, to a man, was cordial and positively sanguine. Scooter was articulate and nonbelligerent, qualities admired by members of both sides of the debate. They warmly congratulated him on his trial and promised a glowing recommendation before the whole presbytery.

The general session of presbytery met a week to the day following the committee exam. The six young ordinands were facing the last step to the qualification for entering the long procession of ordained clergymen. Today the spotlight would be on them, one at a time, as they articulated their beliefs on the floor of presbytery. Any member of the two hundred clergy could rise to challenge an ordinand. All theological questions, theoretical or practical, doctrinal or social, were fair game. A man's exam could be over in twenty minutes or it could go on for five or six hours, forcing later special called meetings of presbytery.

In the waiting room, one of the anxious ordinands whispered to Scooter, "Should I go with the resurrection of Christ or not?"

Scooter was startled by the question. "What do you mean?"

"Should I say I believe in the resurrection or not?" was the repeated entreaty.

"Do you believe it or not?" Scooter replied.

"I don't know."

"Then I think you'd better say that." Scooter was both hurt and angry that the question was posed as a matter of expediency. It was asked as a political question, not an ethical one.

His discussion with the ordinand was interrupted by the entrance of the chairman of the Candidates Committee who called the first to go before the assembly. Scooter and the others left behind offered words of encouragement to the first of their number to take the lonely walk to the chancel steps to await interrogation. Scooter asked, "Who is the examiner today?"

The chairman answered, "Rev. Tom Beardsley."

Scooter didn't know whether to laugh or cry when he heard the name. He thought, *Tom Beardsley! This is surreal. I must be dreaming. This is too ironic for words.*

Tom Beardsley had been a close friend in seminary. He started his seminary studies committed to Christian orthodoxy. His three-year exposure to radical criticism of the Bible left him shaken in his soul. Two days before his own ordination trials, Tom had called Scooter pouring out a tale of moral anguish. He was going through a crisis of faith. He confessed to Scooter that he no longer believed in the deity of Christ, in His resurrection, or His atoning death. His ordination was scheduled, pending the outcome of his examination before the presbytery. Beardsley was a scrupulous man, sensitive to moral issues. He was weeping on the phone.

Scooter urged him to tell the truth, to hold on to his integrity. He gave a ten-minute sermon to his friend about the evidence for Christ's resurrection in an eleventh hour attempt to shore up his crumbling faith. Scooter never heard back from him. All he heard was that Beardsley passed his trials with flying colors, was ordained, and took a position as assistant minister at one of the city's most prestigious churches. Scooter didn't know if Tom lied, making a fraudulent confession before the presbytery or if he had a sudden resurgence of faith before his ordination, a thing not uncommon for men leaving the skepticism of the seminary and wrestling before God hours before the moment of truth of ordination. Today Tom Beardsley was the presbytery's appointed examiner, the grand inquisitor of the hour, the church's designated watchdog of orthodoxy.

After a full hour of interrogation the first ordinand's examination was sustained and Scooter was called next. He walked down the center aisle of the sanctuary feeling the inspecting eyes of the fathers upon him. He was greeted at the chancel steps by Tom Beardsley who introduced him to the presbytery and read the glowing report from the Candidates and Credentials Committee of Scooter's exams to this point. Scooter then gave a brief statement of his personal beliefs before the assembly. The next step was the interrogation by Beardsley.

Scooter awaited the first question. He stared into the eyes of Beardsley noting the glint of fear in them. Scooter thought, *He's terrified, and I'm the one who is supposed to be scared.*

Beardsley looked like a man who had just been stripped naked before his peers. He appeared to be waiting for Scooter to do something sensational like turning the tables on him, examining the inquisitor with his own questions. As they stood facing each other, a silent dialogue was passing between them. Scooter's eyes were saying, "Get on with the interrogation, Tom. I'm not going to embarrass you with impromptu questions of my own. This is my trial, not yours. Whatever happened at your trial is between you, the presbytery, and God."

Beardsley seemed to receive the silent message and moved to the questions. Scooter answered them flawlessly and Beardsley turned to the assembly. "The floor is now open for further questions."

None came. After a decent interlude of silence the chairman of the committee rose to speak, "I move that we sustain the examination of Richard Evans and commend him for ordination." The motion was seconded and the vote to sustain was unanimous. The entire exam lasted less than fifteen minutes and Scooter was now authorized to proceed with his ordination service. He was excused from the remainder of the meeting. He would not become a member of the presbytery until he was ordained.

Scooter received the congratulations of the ordinands still waiting for their final trials and left the church. When he arrived at the apartment, a large box was leaning against the door bearing the logo of Maxines. The arrival of the package made an afternoon visit to Allegheny General Hospital mandatory.

It was pitifully obvious by now that Elizabeth Evans would not be leaving the hospital to attend the ordination. Her condition had deteriorated rapidly; the malignancy was ravaging her body. There were no drugs potent enough to enable her to make the trip to Briarwood and still be conscious. Her time was now being measured in days, if not hours. The ordination was eight days away; it seemed unlikely that she could keep her tenuous grasp on life that long. She was so heavily sedated when Scooter visited her that her lucid moments were brief.

Scooter carried the unopened package under his arm during his ascent in the elevator to Mrs. Evans's floor. When he entered the room she was asleep, semi-comatose, the private room echoing the rattling of her labored breathing. Scooter took some ice chips from the plastic pitcher on the nightstand and gently applied them to her parched and cracked lips.

"Mother, it's Scooter. I brought something for you."

Mrs. Evans's eyes opened, the pupils disappearing for a second into the upper lids until they finally centered, focusing on her son. They were vacant of anything more than vague recognition.

"Mother, look here. A package from Maxines."

Elizabeth tried to speak, her tongue thick from medication. "Open it," she rasped.

Scooter opened the cardboard clothes box and unfurled an elegant primrose dress. He held it up full length by the edge of the bed. Elizabeth placed her bony hand over Scooter's and squeezed it. "The dress. Scooter, it's lovely. I'm so happy."

Scooter felt her hand relax and she lapsed back into unconsciousness. A nurse entered the room to make a routine check on Mrs. Evans. Scooter showed her the dress. "Can we hang this up somewhere in the room where she can see it when she's awake? This dress is special to her."

"Yes, I know. It's the ordination dress isn't it? She talks about

it when she is conscious. I'll hang it up for you. It's the best medicine she has right now."

"Do you think she'll last 'til the ordination? It's still eight
days away."

"You know I can't answer that. She's very weak and I guess
there isn't much medical hope of it, but I wouldn't bet against
her. She has a fierce will to live for that day. She still talks about
going."

Scooter drove into Pittsburgh every day the next week per-
forming a death vigil. Elizabeth was unconscious most of the time
but seemed to sense Scooter's presence when he was in the room.
She simply refused to die, holding off the black angel until the
appointed time.

Scooter was ordained to the Presbyterian ministry at 3:00
Sunday afternoon, June 9. The sanctuary was crammed with
people who barely had enough time to finish their afternoon meal
following the 11:00 service and be back in their pews by 3:00.
The choir was enhanced by a special performance given by a
Metropolitan Opera star flown in from New York by Dr. Franklin
for the event. For weeks in advance Franklin announced the
scheduled ordination featuring the command performance of the
operatic tenor who would sing a selection from Mendelssohn's
Elijah. Officials from the presbytery were also present along with
Dr. Thomas Hepplewhyte who was invited to preach and Dr.
Edward Morrison whom Scooter invited to deliver the Charge to
the Ordinand. The front rows were filled by members of Scooter's
family with a seat for Elizabeth Evans conspicuously vacant.

Scooter was moved in the inner recesses of his spirit by the
ritual, the sermon, and the charge. The opera star was magnificent in his virtuoso performance, though he annoyed Scooter by
nodding into obvious slumber during the sermon. The most solemn point in the service was reached when Dr. Franklin intoned
the rite for the Laying on of Hands of the presbytery. This was the
moment of consecration, the instant that marked Scooter's passage from layman to minister, the ancient rite of sacralization that
transformed him from rank and file to the holy order of the cloth.
Every ordained Presbyterian minister in the sanctuary was invited to come forward to assist in this act of anointing to ministry.

Scooter kneeled at the chancel steps, his back ramrod straight, his head bowed. Dr. Franklin placed his hand upon Scooter's head while the other celebrants clustered around, placing their hands jointly on top of Franklin's. There was no single bishop present to perform the act. To Presbyterians the corporate body of the presbytery is the bishop. Dr. Franklin led them in prayer, asking for the unction of the Holy Spirit to fall upon the kneeling ordinand that he might be equipped to transcend the ordinary and reach beyond the commonplace. He was anointed as a servant, consecrated to the teaching ministry of the church.

With this act came the formal ecclesiastical authority to administer the sacraments, solemnize marriages, and pronounce the benediction with arms uplifted—a rite denied to student pastors who were allowed to pronounce the "closing prayers" but never benedictions.

Scooter was lost in the moment. The weight of hands touching his head was made preternaturally heavy by the duties imposed upon him by this symbolic gesture. He felt the weight descend upon him from on high, a physical sensation that charged his body. He had moved forever from the secular to the sacred, from the profane to the holy.

The Laying on of Hands was followed by the singing of the ordinand's favorite hymn. Scooter had selected a little known communion hymn, "'Tis Midnight and on Olive's Brow," a mournful song commemorating the agony of Christ in the Garden of Gethsemane. When the last stanza of the hymn was sung and its final strains hung in the sanctuary, Dr. Franklin made the final announcement, "Please stand for the benediction offered by the Reverend Mr. Richard Evans."

Scooter turned to the congregation and raised his arms for the patriarchal blessing. He performed his first act as an ordained minister.

"And now may the God of peace, that *brought again from the dead* the Lord Jesus, the great Shepherd of the sheep, through the blood of the everlasting covenant, make you perfect in every good work to do His will, working in you that which is well-pleasing in His sight, through Jesus Christ; to whom be the glory forever and ever. Amen."

Scooter was now ordained, still believing in the reality of the resurrection of Jesus and, in Dr. Franklin's eyes, still a damn fool.

The Kramers hosted an ordination reception for Scooter at their home in Taraview. Johnny and Leah were there, well-tanned from their cruise, ecstatic over the new home Jack Kramer had surprised them with upon their return. A lavish spread of hors d'oeuvres was passed about by the caterers while Scooter un-wrapped his ordination gifts from well-wishers. There were reference books, Bible commentaries, a set of Geneva tabs, a Book of Common Worship signed by his sister, an expensive clerical robe presented by the Kramers, and a home communion set, designed to take the sacraments to shut-ins, offered by a smiling Dr. Frank-lin. For all his acid cynicism in his teaching sessions, Dr. Franklin was a compassionate pastor at the bedside of the ill and the grave-side of the grieving. Scooter couldn't begin to understand the man but he was deeply touched by the gift. It was like the passing of the baton between racers. Franklin, despite his disapproval of Scooter's theology, was extending the right hand of welcome to his fraternity.

Everyone understood when Scooter excused himself early from the celebration to perform his second official act as a minis-ter of the gospel. His sister left with him as they rode together to Allegheny General Hospital. They had not seen each other since she moved to Iowa five years earlier. They caught each other up-to-date and Scooter tried to prepare her for the sight of their mother hovering near death.

Roberta recoiled when she opened the door of her mother's room. Scooter's words were totally inadequate to prepare her for the sight. Elizabeth Evans's emaciated form was barely recogniz-able, a hollow shell of her former self. Scooter walked to the bed-side and lightly stroked her forehead. She moaned inarticulately, giving no initial signs of recognition.

"Mother, it's Scooter. Roberta is here. She came to see you."

Roberta was standing by the bed with tears cascading down her cheeks. "Mother, can you hear me?"

Mrs. Evans opened her eyes and saw her daughter and son standing by the bed. Their faces were vague. Her consciousness made them seem distant like they were reaching down to her through a mist. There was no doubt that she recognized them. She spoke Roberta's childhood name, "Bobby Ann . . . I can see you darling." A feeble smile crossed her face. "And Scooter . . . "

"It's not Scooter anymore, Mom. Now it's Reverend Richard Evans."

A single tear formed on the edge of Mrs. Evans's left eye, swelling to one large drop but defying gravity in its refusal to spill out.

"I made it, Scooter. I promised I would."

"Yes, Mother. And guess what. I've come to serve you the sacrament. My first celebration."

"Good . . . good . . . ," Mrs. Evans muttered.

Scooter opened the communion kit and placed it on the nightstand. He opened the small cruet and poured a measure into each of the three glass cups and set them down, beginning the Words of the Institution:

> In the night on which our Lord was betrayed, he took
> bread. And when he had blessed it, he broke it saying,
> 'This is my body broken for you. . . .'

After the prayer of consecration, Scooter handed a small paper-thin wafer to his sister, then placed one on his mother's tongue. It dissolved there, required no chewing or difficult swallowing. Next came the cup and Scooter could barely manage to apply a few drops to his mother's lips.

> The cup of the New Covenant. The blood of Christ, shed
> for the remission of sins. Drink ye all of it.

Scooter finished with a prayer knowing his mother had already slipped back into unconsciousness. He touched her hair and prayed for the comfort of Christ to be with her.

Scooter repacked the communion kit and quietly left the room with Roberta. The hospital called at 6:45 the next morning notifying him that his mother had died. She never regained consciousness after her last Holy Communion.

Elizabeth was buried in her primrose ordination dress. Scooter's third official ministerial task was to preach the sermon at her funeral. He presided through the entire service, including the graveside commission to the eternal care of God. It was Scooter's hands that dropped the sandy granules on the coffin, his mouth that spoke the words, "Dust to dust. Ashes to ashes."

Richard "Scooter" Evans was twenty-six years old; an ordained minister, and an orphan, save for the ministrations of Holy Mother Church.

TWENTY-TWO

In the days following the funeral Roberta extended her stay to
help Scooter with the details of closing down Mrs. Evans's
apartment and disposing of her effects. This conventional rite
always borders on the macabre as each handkerchief, each knickknack, each toilet article that survives the passing of a loved one is
a grim spectre of the obscenity of death. Legal matters also required their attention; the posting of the will; the provisions with
the attorney for probate; and the redeeming of life insurance policies.

Elizabeth Evans left this world with her affairs in good order
and with some spectacular surprises. During the early weeks of
her hospitalization she had talked freely with Scooter about these
matters. During each of these visits she besieged Scooter with
questions and instructions about the apartment. "If I die in here I
don't want my friends to visit you in an untidy apartment. Did
you clean the tub? Have you waxed the kitchen floor? Did you
dust the furniture? Don't forget to clean the ivory keys on the
piano. When you play you leave smudges on the keys."

A detail of great concern to Elizabeth was the whereabouts of
the key to her safety deposit box. "When I die you be sure to get
my safety deposit box. All my valuables are in it, including my
will and my insurance policies. You'll need the insurance money
to pay for the funeral. And no elaborate casket and that nonsense.
I don't want you spending money on a fancy coffin. You know I
won't really be in it anyway, just this old worn-out body. And no
flowers. Put the notice in the paper. 'In lieu of flowers . . . and so
on.' Suggest contributions to the church or to a favorite charity."

"Yes, Mother. Please don't worry. I know how to take care of
those matters." Scooter hated these discussions.

"I'm sure you do. You've had enough practice. Now don't

forget where the safety deposit box key is. Have you checked to make sure it's still there?''

"Yes. It hasn't gone anywhere. It's in the same place you've kept it since we moved into the apartment, hidden in the Lenox china swan on the knickknack shelf over the loveseat."

"Good. Now let's go over the checklist again . . ."

Scooter followed her instructions to the letter, dusting the furniture, scouring the bathtub, waxing the floor, and keeping the ivory piano keys free of the telltale smudges. The day after the funeral he removed his shoes and stood on the loveseat to retrieve the small metal key from its hiding place in the belly of the fragile china swan.

"We need to go to the bank and get the will for Albert Bernstein. I talked to him at the cemetery and we can see him this afternoon. His secretary, Virginia, is coming out tomorrow to help us go through Mother's clothes. What are we going to do with the furniture?"

Roberta answered swiftly. "We'll divide it up, but since she gave me her ring—I know that's in the will because she told me a thousand times—you take whatever you want."

"Let's not play 'Alphonse and Gaston.' What am I going to do with the furniture? My apartment at Witherspoon is furnished and I'll only be there a year anyhow."

"I can't haul all this stuff out to Iowa. It would cost more than it's worth."

Scooter agreed. "Well, then, let's sell it."

Roberta reacted to the suggestion in mock horror. "What? Did I just hear the son of Elizabeth Evans talk about selling her furniture? She would turn over in her grave if she heard you say that."

"Careful, Roberta. Your penurious knowledge of theology is showing. Don't you know that nothing could possibly disturb the felicity she is enjoying at this very second. Let's sell it. I need the money."

"You don't need the money that badly. We'll give it away. We have cousins in Pittsburgh and they have plenty of friends here that could use these things."

"What about the baby grand?" Scooter asked.

"I have a piano. You take it. Let's keep it in the family. You can haul it to Witherspoon and then store it when you go back to Holland. Let's quit fussing and go get the safety deposit box."

Roberta was the executor of the will. She retrieved the contents of the safety deposit box including a standard form Last Will and Testament, insurance policy, and what looked to Scooter like a pile of stock certificates with a rubber band around them. They drove to downtown Pittsburgh and entered Albert Bernstein's office at the appointed time. Albert read the will aloud. It was filled with cabalistic language, the esoteric jargon of the professional lawyer. The diamond ring was specifically mentioned and the rest of the estate was divided between the two heirs, Roberta and Richard Evans. When he finished reading, Scooter asked, "OK, Albert, what does all that mumbo jumbo mean?"

"It means simply that you and your sister will divide the estate. What you don't know Scooter is that your mother was a somewhat wealthy woman and you will come into a sizeable inheritance when the estate is settled."

"What do you mean 'somewhat wealthy'? She wasn't making more than ten thousand dollars a year when she died. I know that for a fact."

Roberta laughed at Scooter's consternation. Albert spoke, "Elizabeth didn't need to work. She could have lived very comfortably without working a day. Your father left her a substantial amount of money. He was quite heavily insured and had a nice stock portfolio."

"Albert, Dad didn't work for over three years before he died."

"I am well aware of that but after the war your father's business was very prosperous. He made over $100,000 on a railroad case in 1948 alone. That was a nice piece of change in the forties. He invested wisely in stocks and bonds. He also inherited money from your grandfather. In 1956 he invested $60,000 in IBM alone not to mention the enormous profit he made in Oklahoma oil. I know because I was in that deal with him."

"Are you trying to tell me that all of a sudden I'm a millionaire? That John Bairsford Tipton or whatever his name was has just sent his messenger boy to ring my doorbell and present me with a check for $1,000,000?"

"Not quite, Scooter. But close. My preliminary estimate is

that when the estate is settled and all taxes paid, you and Roberta will receive something in the neighborhood of $750,000 each."

Scooter whistled. "Whew! That is a pretty fancy neighborhood. I can't believe this." He turned to Roberta. "You knew this all along didn't you?"

Roberta was thoroughly enjoying her brother's incredulous stupification. "I had a pretty fair idea," she allowed.

"Why didn't Mother tell me? She was always poor-mouthing about how tight things were." The question was directed to Albert.

"For several reasons. We spoke of it often, Scooter. You must remember that your mother was both proud and cautious. She was reared in poverty. She lived through the depression. She sold newspapers on the street on the Northside when she was in high school. When she married your father it was a Cinderella story for her. She never forgot where she came from and she became a very shrewd businesswoman in her own right. She wasn't just an executive secretary at the fuel corporation where she worked. She virtually managed the operation. And you're dead wrong about your 'fact' of her $10,000 earnings. That was her salary but she owned a piece of the business there."

"That still doesn't answer my question about why she never told me any of this."

"She thought you were too young when your father died to know about the money. Remember it was your dad who insisted you work after school in high school. He was afraid he would linger for years and exhaust the family income. He also wanted you to gain character. He didn't want to hand you everything on a silver platter. He was from the old school. Once you decided to go into the ministry your mother didn't want you to be distracted. Remember when I cosigned that note for you at Mellon Bank so you could borrow the money to go to Europe?"

"How could I forget it? I've been wondering for two years how I'll ever make enough money to pay it off," Scooter replied.

"The day after I signed the note your mother sent a check for the full amount to the bank. She instructed me to make sure you were covered for any financial crises you might have. She called you every month didn't she? You were covered over there every second. You just didn't know it."

"When will the estate be settled? I'm tired of living on peanut butter and chicken noodle soup."

"It should take a year to eighteen months. In the meantime you have insurance money coming which will more than tide you over."

Scooter shook hands with Albert Bernstein and walked out of the office, in a state of stunned disbelief, with Roberta. In the car he said to his still amused sister, "Pinch me. Tell me I'm not dreaming. This simply can't be happening."

"What are you going to do with the money, brother, dear?" Roberta asked.

"How should I know. Do I look like some kind of financial wizard? After I pay my dues I'll have Albert manage it for me. I don't have a clue about these things. I've never made enough money to pay income taxes and Mother balanced my checkbook for me."

"What dues?" Roberta asked.

"You know. The first $75,000 goes to the church, right off the top. You too. We can't rob God. We'll make a nice memorial gift. Maybe a new organ or something."

Roberta knew there was no arguing about this. Even before his conversion experience Scooter had been required by his father to put 10 percent of his allowance money into the plate on Sunday mornings. Tithing was a nonnegotiable law with the senior Mr. Evans. To fudge on this was to commit larceny against the Almighty.

Albert Bernstein's secretary, Virginia, appeared the next day at the Evans's apartment and spent the afternoon helping Scooter and Roberta go through Elizabeth Evans's clothes and personal effects. For her assistance, Roberta insisted that she be the beneficiary of Mrs. Evans's elegant wardrobe. Virginia wore the same dress size as Elizabeth Evans and was overwhelmed with the reward of a closet full of dresses from Maxines. The grand prize was Elizabeth's full-length beige leather coat with a mink-trimmed hood. Roberta received the jewelry including the two-caret diamond ring Cecil Evans had purchased from Roberts Jewelers as an engagement ring for Elizabeth some thirty years earlier. It was an exquisite stone, its flawless facets scintillating in the sunlight like dancing prisms. The other gems in Elizabeth Evans's jewel box, an assortment of garnet, jade, opals, heliotrope, and rubies set in earrings, bracelets, brooches, and lesser rings all paled in comparison to the engagement ring. The jewel box was a small thesaurus that housed memories of love as well as precious and semiprecious stones.

Roberta was not greedy. She demanded that Scooter take a sumptuous string of pearls and his mother's amethyst birthstone ring. An emerald pin was also exchanged with the sisterly admonition that Scooter save them for the future Mrs. Richard Evans. Scooter glared at Roberta and said, "The voice of Elizabeth Evans lives on, alive and well and incarnate in the mouth of her daughter, the corn-fed oracle of Iowa."

Roberta flew back to Iowa at the end of the week. Scooter made arrangements to distribute the furniture to relatives and have the piano, his mother's leather-topped desk, and two oriental rugs, taken to his apartment at Witherspoon. He moved at the end of June, transferring his ministerial credentials to the Northwest Pennsylvania Presbytery and went to work preparing his lectures for the fall term.

TWENTY-THREE

The autumn wind sucked the chlorophyll from the leaves of the maples bordering the Witherspoon campus, leaving them with radiant hues in their final gasp of life before fluttering to the earth to perish under a blanket of snow, rotting in decomposition, nature's way of refreshing the soil for the promised vernal rebirth. Their last stand before surrendering to the icy swords of Jack Frost was glorious, like defiant redcoats hoisting their colors before the bugle sounded the last retreat. The crisp air bit into Scooter's cheeks while he joined the milling throng walking to the stadium for the homecoming game. He walked beside Johnny and Leah, escorting them with proud ownership. This was his school, his cradle of learning where he had made the transition from the kingdom of darkness to the kingdom of light. Now he labored on the other side of the desk, on the side where one man spoke and the students wrote furiously, committing to notebooks the thoughts he uttered, the axioms he declared. His words were laden with a power designed to seduce the brain, to excite the imagination, perchance here and there to enter the bloodstream of the students' lives, shaping values that would endure to life's end. It was now his turn to apply his finger to the malleable clay, adding his creative touch to the final product that emerged.

But today was not for teaching. It was a time of annual pilgrimage to the goddess of nostalgia. It was a time for football, pom-poms, freshly cut yellow mums, fraternity house floats and reminiscences embellished with outrageous lies of madcap adventures of a faded youth. A panoply of faces crossed the quadrangle, some bearing the wrinkles of age and others crowned with freshman dinks. There was the inevitable sport from the class of '39 in his raccoon coat and porkpie hat. Individual band members slipped through the crowd, their chinstrapped hats askew, toting trombones, saxophones, tubas, clarinets, and drums, all walking toward a point of assembly near the end zone of the field. The gladiators were locked in the cement floor room in the fieldhouse, hunkered on wooded benches with their eyes fixed on the blackboard, following the fluid chalk lines the coach was drawing between x's and o's.

Johnny relished his homecoming. It was the first he had made with Leah. He was king for these hours, acting as Leah's private tour guide in the morning hours before they rendezvoused with Scooter. He pointed out trophies in the antiquated gym that stood as a museum on the edge of the campus. He walked her through the Sigma Phi Epsilon house, rehearsing war stories with his own dash of embellishment, then across the street to the venerable ivy covered stonework of Old Main. He saw Sam Slocum lumbering along the sidewalk, his heavy girth threatening to pulverize the stone beneath his feet. Johnny wondered how many desks had collapsed underneath Slocum in the intervening years. He shouted in greeting, "Hey, Sam, don't worry, I'm working!"

Sam returned with a playful sneer, "Got any geld, or are you still a schmuck?"

"Same old Sam," Johnny said before taking off on a protracted explanation of the legendary teacher for Leah's benefit. She was enthralled, having missed all this hoopla in the sterile quarters of her nursing school. It was like a miniature Mardi Gras, a carnal vale of merriment where the sober claims of daily responsibilities were shoved in the corner for a few hours of unfettered hilarity.

They walked hand-in-hand, the lustre of newlyweds still clinging to their skin, passing the new fine arts building on the way to the Sub. It was time to meet Scooter, have a hamburger and maybe a quick game of nine-ball on the faded green tables in the lounge, before making the walk to the stadium. Scooter was easy to find, sitting at a table, hands gesticulating in animated conversation, with a cluster of students peppering him with questions of urgent matters in metaphysics.

"Hello, professor. May we interrupt, or is this a meeting of Philosophy 102?"

Scooter stood and hugged Leah pretending to ignore Johnny. He said to the students, "Sorry, guys, but you'll have to excuse me. The love of my life is here and, as you can readily perceive, she is alone and unattended. If you see some skinny little guy who looks like a fugitive from a carrot factory wandering around, limping like a wounded puppy dog, tell him we're in the faculty lounge having lunch." He took Leah's arm and marched her to the faculty section of the building leaving Johnny to follow along behind.

"Hey, the inner sanctum. I never thought I'd see the inside of this room," Johnny exclaimed.

"Maybe we can change that on a more permanent basis, Johnny. The dean told me they're looking for a new faculty member for the speech department and I submitted your name. Dr. Underwood thought it was a great idea."

"Is she still here? She's older than Old Main and twice as musty," Johnny said.

"I can see it now. Professor Kramer, the extraordinary, eloquent, extemporaneous eunuch, the prince of rhetoric, the salacious speechmaker, inspiring the youth of America to forensic glory."

"That's not bad, Scoot. It's almost believable except for the eunuch bit."

After lunch they joined the crowd at the stadium, watching the fans more than the players during the game for faces they recognized from undergraduate days. The Witherspoon Blue Devils had an easy time of it, thrashing their opponents 44-7. Scooter was certain that the athletic director made it a point to schedule patsy opponents for the homecoming games to insure a pleasant day for the old grads and one more year of boasting when they returned home, making the recruiting regimen a little bit easier for next year's crop.

A month before homecoming, Scooter had made reservations for three at the Tavern, the town's revered landmark of country cuisine. Even then it was almost too late because many had booked reservations a year in advance. But the owner, Mrs. Durkin, promised Scooter she would find him a table and make sure that he and his guests would get a double portion of the cinnamon sticky buns that were the Tavern's trademark. Directly across the street from the Tavern was Scooter's apartment, a third-floor facility that once was the loft of a gristmill. The building was erected before the Civil War, though no one used the term "antebellum" in these parts. The bricks were faded and porous, having lost their shape since emerging from the kiln over a century before. They seemed to swim in the thick layers of mortar that held them together giving the clear and certain impression that the edifice was out of kilter and ready to collapse. For Scooter it only added to the charm of the hoary establishment and was fitting for the quarters of a young professor devoted to the classics.

The Widow Durkin had already claimed her dominance as Scooter's newest stepmother, sending a waiter across the street each night with leftover sticky buns and an occasional cherry pie. She greeted Scooter fondly when he entered with Leah and Johnny.

"Mrs. Durkin, this is the lovely Leah Kramer and her infamous husband, Johnny, whom you may sadly recall as my recalcitrant, reprobate roommate from college days."

"How could I forget Johnny Kramer? I'm so pleased to meet you, Leah. These two men you are with are trouble. But I'm sure you already know that. I could tell you a few stories about their escapades but I wouldn't want to spoil your dinner. I have a nice table for you. Walter will seat you right away."

At dinner Johnny asked, "What's it like, Scooter? Do you enjoy your classes?"

"Love it, Johnny. I love everything about this place. Things have changed though. I can't believe it. I'm only five years older than most of my senior students but there really is a generation gap. This is the postwar gang and their outlook is miles apart from the outlook we grew up with. They're mad about everything. Where we used to have panty raids, they have protest marches and sit-ins. The SDS is organizing here and they run around the campus like maniacs with bullhorns blaring. I had to throw one of them out of my class in Medieval Philosophy last week."

"Why, Scooter? What did he do, smoke pot during your lecture?"

"No. He walked into class with his shirt unbuttoned and hanging out of his pants."

"You mean he was 'loafing out' in class?"

"No, no, no. His shirt, dummy."

"You mean you threw him out of class because his shirttail was out?"

"Exactly. He came bopping in my room like a Neanderthal. I

called him down before he got to his seat and told him to please put his shirttail in. He got smart with me claiming an inalienable constitutional right to dress any way he pleased at school. I told him his inalienable rights only applied in a democracy and that my classroom was a monarchy and I was the king."

"I can't believe you. What happened? No, let me guess. He refused to leave so you walked back and threw his butt, out the window."

"No, I told him to leave or I was calling Sam Slocum and he jumped out the window by himself."

"Cut it out, Scooter. What did you do?"

"I just told him to tuck in his shirt or leave. He got up grumbling and walked out. No fuss. No muss. No protest demonstrations and not a peep out of the class. I get along great with the kids. I'm still under thirty so they trust me. But this SDS thing is organized insanity. I had a freshman come up to me and tell me he wanted to be a philosophy major and demanded the right to outline his own curriculum for the degree. Can you imagine that? The kid wanted to tell the professor what he needed to learn to master the field. They're doing that all over the place and some schools are so intimidated they're actually letting them do it."

"What did you say to the guy?" Leah asked.

"I told him, 'Sure, I'll let you design your own curriculum if you can answer ten questions correctly.' Then I rattled off ten questions about the history of philosophy and he couldn't answer any of them. He didn't know David Hume from Madam Butterfly. I told him to come back and see me when he knew something about the subject, and that was the end of it."

"But you like it," Leah added.

"I love it. Sometimes it's a little like a siege but basically it's a lot of fun. Hey, Johnny, you'll never guess where I'm going in January."

"Let me see. Steubenville, Ohio?"

"C'mon, get serious."

"Serious, huh? OK. I've got it, Little Rock, Arkansas. You're going to lead a freedom march."

"No, you'll never guess. I'm going to Florida. To Fort Lauderdale, Florida. I'm reading a paper at a Philosophical Theology Society meeting."

"Are you going to look her up?"

Leah's ears perked. "Look who up?" she asked.

Johnny answered the question for Scooter. "Patricia. That's where she's from." He said to Scooter, "Does she still live in Fort Lauderdale?"

"I don't know. I don't think so. I think she's living in one of the other towns nearby on the coast. Boca Raton or Deerfield Beach. I'm not sure. Carole Keener came to my ordination. She hears from Patricia. Carole said Patricia has two children now and that she moved but I forget where."

Johnny pressed the point. "You still haven't answered my question."

"What question?"

"Are you going to look her up?"

"You know I can't do that. I tried to get out of going down there but the dean insisted that I represent the school since Dr. Hepplewhyte is away. I really don't want to go. The fact is, I'm terrified. What if I run into her?"

"Fat chance of that. Fort Lauderdale is no small burg anymore. It's a large town, a city in fact. You won't bump into her unless you go out of your way to look her up."

"Well, you can rest assured I won't do that."

The Eastern Airlines jet settled down smoothly on the runway of Fort Lauderdale's International Airport. Scooter left his stomach somewhere in the clouds around seven thousand feet. His welcome to sunny Florida was marred by a tropical rainstorm that pelted the passengers leaving the terminal building. Scooter jumped in the first taxi he saw and spoke the name of the Golden Slipper Motel to the driver. He had no idea where the motel was located except the travel agent said it was near the Galt Ocean Mile Hotel where the conference was being held.

Scooter paid close attention to the street signs during the ride from the airport to the northern tip of the city. His eyes brightened when he saw a white metal signboard just north of the Galt Ocean Mile announcing the corporation limits of Lauderdale-by-the-Sea. The cab pulled into the parking lot of the Golden Slipper Motel on A-1-A, just a block or so from the wharf. Scooter paid the fare and went to the office to register in the motel. The conference began the next morning, giving him the rest of the afternoon and evening to enjoy the liquid sunshine that was now starting to let up. He switched on the TV in his room to drown out his fierce desire to reconnoiter the area, to see if by some miracle Oleander Drive was somewhere nearby. The sun broke through the clouds, shattering rays into his motel room, inviting him outdoors to explore the neighborhood. Scooter told himself that he ought to walk up the street to the wharf and look at the sea.

Instead he walked inland, crossing A-1-A to get a better look at the street sign jutting away from him at an angle. It was like the sign was alive, beckoning him, drawing him irresistably to its silent letters. He lifted his gaze to read the sign, standing there in staggering disbelief. By a coincidence impossible to believe, by the whimsical caprice of fate, not fifty yards from the Golden Slipper Motel was a sign reading "Oleander Drive." This simply could not be. There must be hundreds, perhaps thousands of streets in Fort Lauderdale and by the flick of a travel agent's guidebook he was plopped down in a motel across the street from the place where the mailman once carried a ream of unanswered letters.

He started to walk northwest following the street numbers. He was in the 2200 block and he was searching for the mystical cipher of 2364, the four-digit number engraved in his memory marking the residence he imagined in a thousand nocturnal visions. In minutes he stood before an apartment/motel complex aptly named the Castaway. Arranged in the diagonal descending a pillar of stone at the entrance was the number 2364. He followed the signs to the manager's office remembering that Patricia's parents were in the motel business. A card was taped to the office door with the words printed.

MANAGER IN APARTMENT 1-A
Mary Gregg

The familiar name released a spurt of adrenaline in Scooter's veins. His steps were measured as he ascended the stairs to the corner apartment marked 1-A. He felt like a schoolboy knocking on the door of his girl friend's house for his first date. He knocked at the door with less temerity than was his usual style. The door opened with a graying Mary Gregg gazing at him with no glint of recognition.

"May I help you?" Mrs. Gregg asked politely.

Before Scooter could reply a sudden dawn of recognition

transformed her countenance from one of cordial indifference to galvanized delight, a raptured smile sending wrinkles scurrying from the corners of her eyes.

"Scooter! Scooter Evans. Just look at you. My word. I can't believe it. Dave! Come here. It's Scooter Evans."

"Are you going to invite me in or do I stand out here waiting for another rain shower?"

"I'm just too shocked for words. Come in, dear. Let me look at you. Just look at you; you're not that little boy I remember standing on the playground nervously blowing on your hands. Sit down. Dave! Come in here, did you hear me? Scooter Evans just came in," she shouted to the other room.

Mr. Gregg walked in, black eyes shining. He was actually smiling and his hand was extended in warm welcome. It was the first time in his life that Scooter was not afraid of him.

They fired on question after another at him. "What are you doing? Are you married? Are you a minister now?" They came in rapid succession with not enough space between them for Scooter to begin to answer. He felt like he had a family again and was being welcomed home after a long absence. A color photograph displayed on an end table caught his eye. It was a recent portrait of Patricia, her eyes staring off to the side, wistful, dreamy looking. Instantly his hopes that seeing her again might throw cold water on his fantasies about her were demolished. Surely age would add blemishes, a hardening of the porcelain profile that tormented his brain like a savage covey of harpies— wrinkles, perhaps, or sagging chin line. The photograph told a different story. She was more beautiful than he remembered, the years adding a more mature facet to her loveliness. Mary caught him glancing at the picture.

"How long will you be in town?" she asked.

"Only four days. I'm involved with a conference at the Galt Ocean Mile Motel."

"That's awful. Can't you stay on a few days? Patricia will die if she misses you. She went with Robert on a Caribbean cruise. They'll be back in five days. You must stay over. I absolutely insist."

"Believe me, Mrs. Gregg, I would love to, but I can't. I have to be in class on Monday morning."

"Don't tell me you're still going to school."

"Well, yes and no. I'm still in graduate school but I took a year's leave of absence to teach. I'm teaching at Witherspoon College in Pennsylvania. It's where I went to college."

"They can get along without you for a couple of days. You just do what I say and we'll take care of everything."

"I really can't. I'm the junior faculty member. I can't take off work when I feel like it."

"Well then, while you're here you'll eat with us every night and we'll show you Fort Lauderdale. Dave will take you up in his airplane and show you the coastline, won't you, Dave?"

Dave mumbled his assent not daring to challenge his ebullient wife. Mary got up from her wicker chair and said to Scooter, "Now I'm going to give you the Cook's tour of the Castaway so that you'll think about coming down again and staying with us."

Mary's words were a ploy, obvious both to Scooter and to Dave that she wanted to whisk Scooter off for a private conversation. Dave made no protest. When they were out of earshot of the apartment Mary spoke in conspiratorial tones. "I know all about what happened when Patricia went to see you at Witherspoon College, Scooter. She told me everything. I mean everything. She always does, you know. You should never have sent her back. I like Robert. Don't misunderstand me. He's a fine young man and a good father. But he is not what Patricia wants. She still loves you, Scooter. A mother knows about things like that."

Her words hit his intestines like an ice pick. *She still loves you* were the cruelest words he had ever heard.

"You shouldn't talk that way, Mary." A transition had been made, a crossing of a threshold that could never be recalled. By one word, *Mary*, Scooter had altered a relationship from parent/child to adult/adult. He was speaking now as a pastor, not as a boy. "What's done is done. For me marriage is for keeps. Patricia is married to Robert and that's it. I can be Patricia's friend, but never her lover. In fact, I really can't even be her friend. There's just too much between us."

"That's a high and mighty speech, Scooter, but you're not married are you? I see no ring on your finger. You're still waiting for her. You may not admit it or even be aware of it, but you're still waiting, I know it. Mark my words, you two will get together yet and someday you'll be calling me 'Mama Mary.'"

Scooter flinched and muttered, "Nevermore."

"What did you say?"

"Nothing. It wasn't important."

The visit to Fort Lauderdale took an important twist for
Scooter's life, not at the Castaway but at the conference meeting.
He delivered a brilliant paper on the impact of Occam's Nomi-
nalism on the theology of Martin Luther. Listening to papers being read at a society of pedantic scholars was always a boring
affair. But not when Scooter spoke. He could read the telephone
directory and make it electrifying. He was the hit of the conference, an unknown star rising to find a place in a resplendent gal-
axy. He received a standing ovation from his learned colleagues, a
warm message of welcome into a fraternity of erudition. He was
mobbed by well-wishers after his presentation. An editor of a
well-known scholarly journal asked for the publication rights to
the paper. A distinguished British professor asked him to go to
lunch. Scooter was dazed by the attention but reveled in it. It was
like scoring thirty points in a championship basketball game.

He was awestruck, seated across the lunch table at Wolfie's
from the renowned Mr. H.L.M. Barton, former Oxford don and
now principal of Lattimer College in Bristol, England. Scooter
had read many of his books and felt as though his card catalogue
had just come to life before him. Barton was tall and gangly with
a woolly mane of snow-white hair sweeping down his cheeks into
puffy mutton chops. He looked like a cross between Ichabod
Crane and Ebenezer Scrooge. He spoke with the thickest British
accent Scooter had ever heard. He thought it must be exaggerated
for an American audience, an affectation that made it seem like he
had gone to a finishing school for English butlers. He addressed
Scooter in somber terms, sitting fully erect with his long boney
fingers steepling as he spoke.

"Ah—ah—Mr. Evans, I wish to discuss with you a modest
undertaking I am about to commence. There is a new Institute of
Classical Christian studies being organized in Philadelphia. The
board of directors has asked me to be the president. The venture
has received a three-and-one-half million dollar endowment from
a wealthy businessman. Ah—ah—that is a lot of 'clams' as I believe you Americans would put it. We have also received a magnificent mansion to serve as our lecture hall. It is positively
charming with teak-paneled walls and hardwood floors. It is quite

loaded with mosaics, and priceless antiques all—*in situ*. It is indeed, ah—ah—shall we say, palatial?"

Scooter did not dare interrupt the monologue; it would have been like sneezing in the middle of a Shakespearean soliloquy. Dr. Barton, after considerable rambling, finally got to the point.

"I am endeavoring, you see, to establish a faculty of men who are either European or educated in Great Britain or on the continent. I detected in the society bulletin that you have studied in Amsterdam. I should like to—ah—ah—add you to our team, shall we say. Would you be agreeable to accepting a position as, ah—given your youthfulness, assistant professor of Philosophical Theology?"

"But you hardly know me—I don't understand."

"Please, I have already read through no less than sixty dossiers for this position and have not discovered what I am searching for. Try not to be either impertinent or impetuous. I assure you I am in earnest. I think you would add—ah—what shall we say . . . ? You would add some—ah—pizazz to our seminary. Our constituency shall be interdenominational, a heterogenous lot of Anglicans, Presbyterians, and perhaps even some—ah— Baptists." The latter group was mentioned with obvious distaste.

"If you are agreeable I shall present the terms of the contract to you by post. We would need you to begin in the fall term."

"Sir, I would be quite honored to accept your offer. I have read about the institute and find it a quite exciting venture."

"Very well, then. I shall post the contract immediately upon my return to Philadelphia. Here is my card. Please ring me up if you have any further questions."

They shook hands and returned to the conference meeting for the afternoon session.

Scooter heard little of the droning readings of the afternoon. His mind was fixed on the noontime conversation. Not yet twenty-seven years old, he had already secured an appointment to a theological seminary faculty. Providence and coincidence were working overtime, bent on topping each successive surprise with one better. This had been a Dickensinian year, the worst of years and the best of years. Maybe not quite so noble, more like the Morton Salt slogan, "When it rains, it pours." Scooter was not yet ready to believe all that had taken place. So much was still harbored in the waters of uncertain promises. The stock market might crash and wipe out his inheritance. Barton might change his mind, perhaps more impressed with a speaker later on the program. The chickens were not yet hatched and a fox could still sneak in the henhouse.

He enjoyed the nightly meals with the Greggs and the two-hour flight in David Gregg's Comanche up the coast to West Palm Beach and back down over Miami Beach before landing again at Fort Lauderdale. Mary Gregg made no more cryptic prophecies and their time was spent catching up on news of family, jobs, and friends they knew in common. The Greggs drove Scooter to the airport on Sunday, leaving him with promises of keeping in touch. As the plane took off, banking to the east and moving out over the shoreline before turning north, Scooter heard himself humming "Harbor Lights."

No fox appeared in the henhouse. The contract from the Philadelphia Institute of Classical Theology arrived in the mail the following week. Scooter signed it without hesitation and returned it the next day. The signing of the contract was the beginning of a five-year odyssey marked by a meteoric rise to national recognition and acclaim.

TWENTY-FOUR

A troubled wind was bringing clouds rolling over the mountain ridges and settling over the house on Windy Tor Drive in Briarwood. On the outside, the Kramer house seemed tranquil and placid. Leah had brought her midwestern roots to the surface, now plainly visible in the decor of their home. The house was done in casual colonial style with wingbacked chairs and oval rugs. A folksy blend of Pennsylvania Dutch wall plaques and copper kettles on the hearth announced a cheerful ambience to the place. Johnny took to growing roses, hybrid teas and an assortment of red beauties and yellow floribundas. The rose beds were immaculately groomed, each cluster of canes surrounded by rich loam and a heavy carpet of Michigan peat. The shelves of the garage were lined with bags of rose food and nutrients, dusting powder to ward off hungry parasites that might spoil the bloom, stainless steel rubber-handled pruning scissors, spray cans, and mulch bags. Johnny spoke affectionately of his roses as his children. After five years of marriage no real infants graced the household. There was no "little Leah," no John Kramer III. Leah was barren.

Besides serving as an ammunition depot for Johnny's war against aphids and brown spot, the garage contained an economy size bag of barbeque briquets and cans of lighter fluid. There were paint cans, garbage cans, and gasoline cans all crowding the space designed to house two cars. Leah's car occupied the right stall, furthest from the entrance to the paneled basement. It was a 1971 Chevy Impala that she used to drive to work at the hospital. The left stall contained a 1970 fire-engine red Corvette, at least when Johnny was home. The stall was vacant more and more frequently.

The insurance business required Johnny to be out at night,

making house calls on prospective clients when both husband and wife were at home. At first Johnny came straight home after these contacts, arriving at the nest around ten o'clock. Then, occasionally he stopped off at the Red Fox Lounge for a drink before coming home. After five years, the layover at the Red Fox was now the rule rather than the exception. He was coming home later and later, often after Leah had fallen asleep.

Johnny was moderately successful in the initial years, the difficult years of building a clientele. But his "geld" was still limited, a pittance in comparison to the extraordinary success of his father. By that measuring rod and the canons of Sam Slocum, he was still a schmuck. He wanted the big time, the mega-bucks that spelled success, financial liberty, and community respect.

At the end of the decade of the sixties Johnny added mutual fund speculation as a sideline. He acquired a broker's license and plunged into a scheme of accelerated riches that was quite legal. He learned the ploy from a New York friend who drove around Long Island in a Fleetwood limousine with a personalized license plate with the initials, OPM.

It was the license plate that piqued Johnny's interest. In the cocktail lounge of Arronomink Country Club after a round of golf Johnny asked the man about it.

"Hey, Hank, what's with the OPM on your license plate? That is your car out there isn't it? I mean 'Hank' is a nickname for Henry. Your real name isn't Orin Patrick Manion is it?"

Hank Manion laughed. "No, Johnny. The license plate is not my name, it's my game. OPM stands for Other People's Money."

"Other People's Money? What's that supposed to mean?"

"It means that I bought the Fleetwood with other people's money. I bought my house with other people's money. I bought my boat with other people's money. And I bought my condominium in Florida with other people's money."

"What are you, Hank, a cat burglar? An international jewel thief? How could you buy all those things with other people's money?"

Hank spent the rest of the afternoon explaining in detail the scheme he operated that had made him a fortune in mutual fund speculation. He got in the game early when the funds were taking off. The mutual fund system offered the twin virtues of moderately high yield of investment with low risk diversification. It was like betting across the board at a paramutual track. The mutual fund corporations specialized in diversified stock and bond investments. The assets of a mutual fund were made up strictly of the value of their large portfolio that included a stock and bond value of up to a 100 million dollars or more.

The managers of the fund would buy and sell stock to increase the total value of their portfolio. The small or middle income investor was attracted to these funds in the early sixties because they could in effect buy a small piece of a large basket, minimizing risk. Instead of the investor buying $5,000 worth of shares in a single corporation like Sperry or Pennzoil, risking the full $5,000 on the fortunes of those individual companies, the investor purchased $5,000 worth of shares in one company that managed a portfolio of hundreds of different stocks. Here massive diversification was achieved, taking a ride on the professional coattails of investment managers who daily monitored the market as a whole.

In the decade of the sixties the growth of mutual funds accelerated. The investor's return on several of them was often between 10-12 percent, beating the rate of inflation and returning over twice the rate of a savings account in a local bank. Shareholders had a double opportunity for selecting options for income or reinvestment. Income distribution paid to the mutual fund shareholders from earnings in stocks and bonds could be taken or reinvested in more mutual fund shares. In addition, and most importantly was, the capital appreciation of the fund itself. As the mutual fund companies grew, so did the value of their shares. The net gains of the shares of the fund were passed on to the shareholder.

Because of the growing economy of that era the mutual funds were able to give margin limits of up to 70 percent. Margin buying was profitable as long as the capital appreciation of the fund covered the spread between equity and interest payments.

The bull was snorting heavily for the mutual fund companies in the sixties and they were experiencing phenomenal growth, attracting new investors every day. The danger for margin investors, as always, was that the bull might meet a bear in the woods and get mauled to death.

Johnny knew all about the risks lurking in the shadows of margin buying. What he was hearing from Hank was a twist he had never heard of which was getting his excitement level brewing. Hank posed a question. "Johnny, when you buy a car do you pay cash or do you finance it?"

"I finance it, naturally."

"OK. Let's say you buy a $6,000 automobile, put $1,000 down and finance the rest at 6 percent. What happens to your capital investment?"

"Well, I know the car depreciates a thousand bucks the first time I turn on the ignition and the damn thing ends up costing me six grand plus 6 percent on the $5,000 I borrowed. But listen, pal, I never buy cars for investment purposes. They're the lousiest investment in the world."

"Here's what I do, Johnny, to turn a lousy investment into a gold mine. I make the deal for the car, right? I go to the bank and borrow the five grand at 6 percent interest. But instead of paying the car dealer I buy mutual funds. Then I borrow five grand from my mutual fund account at 6 percent interest and pay off the car dealer."

"What's so hot about that? It sounds like you're just borrowing from Peter to pay Paul. Why don't you just borrow the money from the mutual fund in the first place? Why do you have to make it so complicated?"

"Johnny, that's the way most people think. That's why they throw away their money on cars and other bad investments. The point of OPM is that every expenditure becomes an investment, the more money you spend the more you make. It's the capitalist's dream. The key is leverage."

"I still don't get it. But if you can tell me how I can make money every time I spend money I want to hear about it."

"Look, it's really simple. Remember the five grand borrowed from the bank to buy the car? First I bought mutual funds with it, then I borrowed it back from the fund to pay off the car. The car is still costing me 6 percent interest but I make 10 percent on my mutual fund investment. So I lose 6 percent on the interest I pay but make 10 percent interest on my investment. I have my car plus a 4 percent net gain on the money I borrowed. The difference is that I earn 4 percent on my car loan rather than lose 6 percent on it, a neat little profit-loss swing of 10 percent in my favor. Remember I can borrow up to 70 percent of my share value in the fund at a lower rate of interest than the fund is paying out.

The more money I can leverage into the fund, the more profit I make. I buy everything on credit and buy mutual funds with the credit money first. I refinanced my house and did the same thing on the boat, the condominium in Florida, and even the washing machine in the basement."

"But what happens if the interest rates rise and the profit of the fund shrinks?"

"You've got to watch it like a hawk. You have to get out of the fund before that ever happens. But I've been doing this for years and nothing like that has come close to happening. What I've been able to do, in effect, is to buy mutual funds on 100 percent margin and earn 10 percent on the full amount, which I simply reinvest in the fund. It's like betting the track's money. It's a parlay, man, a golden parlay. I'm using other people's money to make a fortune. My own profit stays in the fund to keep me within my borrowing limits."

Johnny came home from New York with stars in his eyes, or more accurately, dollar signs. He didn't breathe a word of the scheme to his father or to Leah. He got into the game by mortgaging his home, the home Jack Kramer had purchased with cash. Johnny mortgaged it to the limit and invested the equity into the fund. He made this move at the very moment the spiraling rise in mutual funds went into decline and the real estate market took off flying.

Within six months Johnny received his first margin call. He borrowed the money from the bank on a demand note to cover the margin, sure of a quick rebound in the fund's growth. Within a year he was forced to sell, leaving him with a net loss of $20,000. He still had his house and his car and was able to make the payments, but his grubstake was gone and the dream had evaporated in smoke. It was his money he had lost, or Jack's, but he didn't dare tell Jack about it.

Johnny continued to live beyond his means. To keep up appearances he entertained lavishly at the country club and spent a small fortune to keep his liquor cabinet well stocked. He was a big spender at the Red Fox Lounge, always buying drinks for his comrades at the bar. His insurance business held its own but it required the full measure of Leah's added income to meet the monthly bills.

It was during their fifth year of marriage that Johnny began calling Leah "Mama," despite the fact that they were childless and that Johnny's real mother lived less than a mile away. The first time he used the term Leah was not disturbed by it, taking it as one more word in the litany of terms of endearment he used with her. But the name stuck, being used with increasing frequency, unconsciously reaching first place in Johnny's use of nicknames for her. It began to nag at her, especially when he used it during their lovemaking, which was diminishing at an alarming rate. Leah silently wondered if she had assumed a role with her husband that was part nurse, part buddy, large part mother—everything but wife and lover. Something was missing. Her doubts were mixed with feelings of guilt for not being able to bear children. The latter she sought to remedy.

One evening Johnny came home earlier than usual. Leah had a fire burning in the fireplace, bouncing a shower of sparks off her own soul, each ember reflecting a glow growing within her. It was time to discuss it with Johnny, to put the idea out in the open, suspended in the air where it could be examined from every angle, vulnerable to pinprick of criticism. That was the risk she had to take. It was time.

"Johnny, we need to talk." She set a fresh drink beside him, then whisked across the room, her bathrobe loosely hugging her, to the overstuffed chair by the hearth. She curled up in the chair with one leg crossed under her, half Indian style, her knee exposed to Johnny's view.

Johnny sank into the soft cushions of the sofa, legs spread out, his tie loosened at the collar, and picked up the drink, nursing the mellow fluid. The first sip seemed to have an immediate narcotic effect on him as the taut sinews of his arms and legs released a hidden inner spring and relaxed. He was in a good mood.

"I closed on the Walker policy tonight. It's a biggy. I've been chasing him for months," Johnny said, ignoring the somber invitation to a deep discussion thinly concealed by Leah's opening gambit. Johnny played hide-and-go-seek whenever Leah tried to interject heavy conversations into their marriage. "How was your day?"

"My day was fine, and I'm glad the Walker deal went well. But I must talk to you about something important." Leah had

rehearsed her speech thinking how she would lead into it gradually, coyly, warming Johnny to the subject. She couldn't wait.

"I want to have a baby," she blurted out.

"I know you do, Mama. So do I. But we have to face it. It's
just not possible. You don't want to go through another round of
tests. We both know what the results would be."

"We can adopt, Johnny." Then the carefully rehearsed speech
came out, in bits and pieces, building a case, marshaling an argument to elicit his agreement.

Johnny panicked inside at the suggestion. He knew it would
come to this sooner or later and had sought to stiff-arm any earlier
hints at the idea. He couldn't make it without Leah's income,
especially if there was another mouth to feed.

"That's a great idea, Leah. Maybe next year after we have
some money saved we can look into it."

"No, Johnny, not next year, or the year after that. Now, I'm
talking about right now. If we wait any longer we'll be too old and
adoption agencies won't let us have a baby. I talked with Charlie
about it earlier tonight and she was ecstatic. She wants us to apply
right away. She can't wait to be a grandmother."

Oh no, Johnny thought. *That's all I need, the two of them ganging
up on me.*

"Please, Johnny. Our home needs a child. We need a child.
We need more than rosebushes. Please say it's all right."

"Sure, Mama. I'll look into it right away. If it's a baby you
want, that's what we'll get. Now let's go upstairs and pretend
we're making our own."

Leah sprang out of the chair and threw her arms around him,
almost spilling his drink on the rug. Upstairs she gave herself to
him with a measure of abandonment he had seldom experienced.

The next day Johnny wracked his brain to figure a way out.
Leah was full of baby talk at the breakfast table, rushing ahead
with her plans like a high-speed train. Johnny was searching for a
brake, an emergency pull cord that would bring the train to a
blistering halt. He was feeling trapped, locked in a room with no
exit, guarded by two women who held the keys in their aprons.

His game plan was to stall her, to go through the preliminary
applications, pretend that he was interested, until her ardor

waned and she became more reasonable. A strong flight impulse
was building up inside. He wanted to walk out of his office, get in
the red Corvette and drive—anywhere—but drive. He reached
for the phone and dialed a number with an exchange listed in
Millport.

"Racquel? Can you get to the apartment? In an hour—I'll
leave here in a few minutes. Good, OK. Bye."

It was time for a late afternoon in Millport, another visit to the
cheap efficiency apartment he rented there under an assumed
name. He needed Racquel.

Johnny had met Racquel Del Greco almost a year earlier. He
thought it would be another one-night stand, harmless and easy to
hide, like the game he had been playing since the first year he and
Leah were married. It started in New York when Jack Kramer
sent him away from his bride for six weeks to a management
training course with the home office. His fidelity was unblemished for the first two weeks of his absence. He called Leah every
night and even sent flowers to the house on Windy Tor. But two
weeks of celibacy was his limit. For the remaining time he left his
wedding ring in his briefcase and spent his free nights cruising
the single's bars in New York.

It became a pattern with him, carefully concealed from Leah.
It was an addiction, a manic rage inside of him he was unable to
quench. His game had one cardinal rule: never get involved.
Never the same woman twice. No strings. No emotional entanglements. With this rule intact his conscience could survive. These
were harmless flings, a simple matter of biology having nothing to
do with marriage, mere zipperless encounters.

Racquel broke the rule. It was her fault. Johnny didn't want it
to happen, he didn't mean for it to come to this. She was the one
who called him the second time. She didn't buy the phony name
he gave her the first night. Racquel went to Millport High School
too, three years behind Johnny Kramer. She remembered him.
Johnny Kramer from Briarwood. It was easy for her to find out
where he worked. It was even easier to entice him into "one more
meeting." Now it was a full-orbed affair. She was his mistress,
meeting him regularly at the apartment he rented, further draining his income, another expenditure hidden from Leah and the
probing eyes of Jack Kramer.

During the day Racquel worked in a stenographer pool at the

management complex of Millport Steel Works. She tormented the men of the building with her voluptuous body and teasing smile. She was a free spirit, a spirit kindled by the latin fire in her genes, a walking goddess, but not of the vestal virgins. She was the embodiment of a transported *la dolce vita*, enjoying the discomfort of the men around her. She paid attention to her dress, walking the thin line, the razor's edge between adopting the costume of the office slut and merely being stylishly provocative. She was clever enough to avoid the crude and the cheap. She cultivated the tantalizing. She had a quiet understanding that it was only the gift of her body, a gift bestowed upon her by the Holy Mother for whom she lit a candle every morning at Saint Stanislav's on her way to work, that was her ticket out of Millport. She invested heavily in her precious gift from the Immaculate Virgin using her paycheck to build a wardrobe to rival the costume department of a Hollywood movie set. She shared an inexpensive apartment with two girls, foregoing extravagant luxuries to keep her wardrobe fresh and in fashion. She jogged and did daily exercises, took an eight-week course in cosmetology, and read self-improvement books by the score. She was investing in herself, in her future, in her femininity. Johnny Kramer was the prize.

She left the office at 4:30 and went straight to the secret apartment. She saw the red Corvette already parked down the block, a safe distance from the entrance to the building. When she entered the room she could sense Johnny's agitation. Their time was short and none could be wasted. But time was never so short to allow her to break her own cardinal rule: never be rushed. To allow a hurried encounter was to be used, to surrender to the finality of the permanent status of mistress. That was an unacceptable goal. She slowly removed her stilleto-heeled shoes, a consummate act of seduction, each shoe removed one at a time, her hands fondling the leather straps, a move she memorized from an old Marlene Deitrich movie.

She refused to submit to Johnny's impatience. The drama had to be enacted scene by scene lest her role be violated and her womanhood spoiled.

At 5:45 it was time for talking. Johnny unleashed his frantic story. "Leah wants to adopt a baby. She's hellbent on it and I don't know how to stop her."

Racquel tried to remain calm, to suppress her own panic at

the news. This couldn't happen. It would be one more link, a powerful link, in the chain that tied him to Leah.

"What are you going to do?" she asked calmly but with a slight hint of warning in her voice, a hint that said to Johnny, "Be careful, Johnny. If you let that happen I walk. No more meetings, no more thrills. Watch it, mister."

"I don't know. I'll think of something . . ."

Five years of seminary teaching matured Scooter. He was able to finish his graduate work by flying to Amsterdam for the summers, working there from mid-May to mid-September, taking advantage of the lengthy summer break on the seminary school calendar. He was Dr. Evans now and elevated to the rank of associate professor. He learned the ropes of the publishing world, first by publishing a popularized version of his doctoral dissertation, and then by publishing two books written especially for laymen that received wide circulation and sales.

He was catapulted to the national speaking circuit, appearing on the platform of conferences, first in the Northeast and, as his reputation spread, all over the nation. He flew to Dallas, Chicago, San Francisco, Atlanta, wherever Christians gathered for special conclaves. The seminary gave him special permission to be gone for these events, capitalizing on his growing fame. Wherever Scooter went, a portable display booth advertising the Philadelphia Institute of Classical Theology went with him. The enrollment of the Institute mushroomed due in large part to Scooter's charismatic appeal. He became the drawing card that lured young students to Philadelphia for their seminary training.

During this time, Scooter learned some other things. He was a financial neophyte having little knowledge of monetary magic and even less concern about it. When his mother's estate was settled he put his financial affairs in the hands of Albert Bernstein, trusting him to manage the inheritance. He lived primarily within the limits of his income as a professor, choosing a modest brownstone apartment on Delancey Street as his dwelling place. The white Thunderbird was aging but not showing signs of overuse. It still had low mileage since he walked to work and to nearby stores, using the car only for brief excursions to the coast, to the beach at Barnegat Bay where he stayed the weekend at the home of his cousin, Dr. Bob Evans, now chief of staff at the local hospital.

Scooter drew only as much money from his inheritance as he needed to pay for his summer junkets to Amsterdam, and to indulge his weakness for Brooks Brothers clothes and his addiction as a bibliophile. His mania for books was creating a musty smell in his apartment and threatening joists with imminent collapse. Apart from these indulgences he let his inheritance ride, getting quarterly reports on his net worth from Bernstein, Crawford, and Schwartz. He was initiated to the recondite world of the pecuniary arts by experiencing the magic of the Eighth Joyful Mystery, the law of compounded interest. In the five years since his mother's death his fortune had swelled to over one million dollars, rapidly approaching the million and a quarter mark. The pittance he drew from his annual yield hardly slowed the tide of exponential growth.

He came to love the institute even more than he had loved Witherspoon. The students were more advanced, the city more exciting, the faculty more stimulating, the atmosphere more cosmopolitan. The building on Broad Street was as charming as Dr. Barton had described it. From its entrance, looking south, one could see the brim of William Penn's hat, proudly adorning the top of his statue high above City Hall. It was indeed palatial. Every time Scooter walked through the large entrance hall with the balcony that once held a brass quintet that played for guests of the former owner at special dinner parties, he paused to admire the exquisite mosaics and fine antiques, smiling to himself thinking, *Yep, they're all in situ.*

Scooter's Sundays were spent preaching as a guest in the pulpits of the city and teaching adult classes in theology, usually followed by a late brunch at the Philadelphia Athletic Club. He took his Sunday afternoon rest time seriously, capping it with a brisk rubdown under the skillful hands of the club masseur, a bona fide native-born Swede. Two nights a week he played squash, more than enough exercise to keep his body trim and to accuse him of the folly of cigarettes.

The adult lay-classes were a special delight to him. His students were not cloistered seminarians but citizens of the real world who were forever asking practical questions. They insisted that theology be an applied science and looked to Scooter for principles of application. This was disconcerting at first. Scooter was trained in the theoretical disciplines and was accustomed to the pedagogical method by which the professor explained the content and let the student figure out the application. The bankers, lawyers, doctors, and business people attending his classes wouldn't let him get away with that. They were hard-core pragmatists and demanded that once in a while he come down from the ethereal plains and touch his toes in the dirt. The earthbound corner of Scooter's heart took secret delight in these forays.

Some gradual changes were taking shape in Scooter's aspirations, helped along in part by the enthusiasm of his Sunday morning class. His grand passion, like most young theologians, was a modest one. He simply wanted to change the world, to be a catalyst for a new reformation of society where the triad of the good, the true, and the beautiful would gain the upper hand over the evil, the false, and the ugly. His strategy had been fixed in his mind; win the war of academia, capture the flag of the university world; restore the dignity of classical values at the theoretical level and the rest would take care of itself. Slay the hydra heads of existentialism, secularism, and a host of other isms, and allow the wind of the ages to bring in a new rush of classical truth. But trying to make an impact in a university world so allergic to all things classical was like trying to stop a jet plane with a butterfly net. Besides, he was now past thirty and the generation gap was starting to tell with his students. He was spending more time with adults, more time in the marketplace and wondering if the universities were, after all, the real power structures anymore. Maybe the church door at Wittenburg was no longer the place to start a movement. Martin Luther King's ninety-five theses were scribbled on the back of a bus.

For the first time since his college days Scooter allowed the possibility in his own mind that his destiny was targeted for some place other than the parochial confines of the scholarly world. He was starting to get an itch for the grass roots.

The summer of 1971 brought people to Philadelphia ready to scratch that itch. They were a delegation of members from the pulpit committee of a large church near Phoenix, Arizona. The three-thousand-member church was without a head minister, and the chairman of the committee had drooled when he heard

Scooter speak at a conference in Los Angeles. Scooter was preaching this Sunday morning just blocks away from his brownstone at the historic Tenth Presbyterian Church, filling in for their dynamic preacher who was on vacation. Scooter considered Tenth his home church now, the site of his adult classes. He had become close friends with Dr. Burbick, the head pastor, who was a graduate of Harvard University and Princeton Theological Seminary before he went to Germany for his doctor's degree. Burbick was a kindred spirit, another Presbyterian who loved all things classical.

Scooter preached a moving sermon that morning on the "Mantle of Elijah." He wove a dramatic narrative of the glorious departure of the prophet Elijah carried to heaven in a chariot of fire, leaving behind his young understudy Elisha, and his mantle, the symbol of his prophetic mission. Scooter recreated a mystical scenario that had the young Elisha, the prophet-in-waiting, spellbound, paralyzed by fear as he stood trembling before the fallen mantle. Scooter looked away from the congregation, lifting his eyes to the ceiling as if he were staring at the vanishing chariot. Then he looked at the ground, mesmerized by the garment, like Marcellus before the sacred robe of Christ. He shouted at the imaginary garment, a garment the hushed congregation almost believed they could see lying in a heap in front of the pulpit. "Pick it up!" he shouted at the invisible Elisha. "Pick it up . . . put it on. It is your mission . . . ."

Chills tingled the spines of the hearers as they lived the agony of Elisha's moment of truth. Scooter built the tension so masterfully that members of the congregation were ready to forget their Bible history and believe for a moment that Elisha might actually walk away from the hideous mantle and let it rot in the dust; that he might forsake his mission, deny his calling and go back home to let God find someone else to do His dirty work. The congregation exhaled a collective sigh of relief when Scooter stuck to the script, following the biblical text to the pregnant moment of heroic decision when Elisha picked up the mantle.

At the door Scooter enjoyed the ritual of shaking hands and exchanging warm greetings with the people of this church. How different it was here from the same ritual repeated two or three times a month when he spoke at other churches where he was a stranger in their midst. Here every face was familiar and he could greet most of the people by name. He failed to recognize the last group that approached the door, a small clique Scooter noticed lingering at the rear of the sanctuary. The man who was clearly their leader stepped forward to introduce himself.

"Dr. Evans, my name is Curtis Siegel and I am the chairman of the pulpit nominating committee of the Camelback Community Church in Scottsdale, Arizona. I wonder if you have a few minutes to speak with our delegation?"

Scooter had been through this scenario before on numerous occasions, learning an adroit method of polite refusal. Today there was a chink in his armor, a willingness at least to listen.

"Sure, we can meet in the office for a few minutes."

The office meeting expanded into further discussions over lunch where Scooter learned the details of the fast growing church.

Siegel's enthusiasm kindled a warm response from Scooter. The man was at once jovial and ponderous, mixing a love of theology with a passion for sports, a blend that touched the right buttons in Scooter. He owned and operated an executive golf course in Scottsdale. The portly Siegel was rubicund, with a squatty frame that befitted the role of a green grocer more than that of a professional athlete. Yet Siegel had once graced the ranks of the touring professionals and now supplemented his income by giving trick-shot exhibitions for pro-am golf clinics.

Siegel's chief companion on this occasion was Patrick Rolfe, a multimillionaire toy manufacturer whose avocation was oil painting. His paintings of western art were displayed in several posh galleries in Scottsdale.

Siegel and Rolfe were accompanied by John Rock, an economics professor from Arizona State University whose favorite economic maxim was "If it works, use it," and Joan Ruffner, a platinum blonde member of Scottsdale's jet set.

"We are looking for a minister who can communicate, someone strong in the pulpit and teaching. The sermon is broadcast on the radio in Phoenix and we have a weekly television program aired on Sunday nights on our local CBS affiliate."

Scooter's interest increased and the conversation grew more serious. He agreed to visit the church for an interview before the whole pulpit committee.

The flight from Philadelphia to Phoenix was smooth; the crystal sky afforded an excellent view. The vista over the Rockies was spectacular. The desert floor took on hues of pastels and purples in the shadows of the mountains. Touchdown was on time and Scooter walked the ramp to the new terminal building at Sky Harbor Airport. Curt Siegel met him at the gate and escorted him through the main terminal toward the luggage area. Scooter stopped abruptly in the main terminal staring at the huge mural of painted tiles covering one wall. The mosaic was of a gigantic Phoenix bird, rising out of the ashes; the pagan symbol of resurrection, of rebirth, of a new life springing out of the dust. The Mexican-Indian art form told the story of the city, a town springing up out of the barren desert inhabited once only by scorpions, vicious desert rattlers, jack rabbits, road runners, and cactus plants.

The ride to Scottsdale followed a highway blasted between small mountain buttes. Scooter saw his first saguaro cactus soaring thirty feet into the air, its uplifted arms formed by centuries of growth. Curt noticed Scooter's wonder at the rare and endangered species of cactus.

"They are majestic, aren't they, Dr. Evans? The Southwestern desert is the only place in the world where the giant saguaro grows. No one knows why they thrive here within a scope of two hundred miles on this entire planet. They take about a hundred years to grow one arm. They're protected by the state. There's a heavy fine for cutting them down or for transplanting them without a permit."

"What about transplanting preachers? Do you need a permit for that?" Scooter asked.

Scottsdale was a charming contrast to the declining area of Phoenix proper. It was a playground for the wealthy, a long way from Butler, Pennsylvania, a lifetime removed from the belching steel mills of western Pennsylvania. The buff-colored California-Spanish buildings all looked alike. It was difficult to detect the difference between a bank building and McDonald's. The community church was built in the shadow of Camelback Mountain, so named because, from a certain angle, the silhouette of its ridges forms the comical shape of a two-humped camel. This was the resort section of Scottsdale surrounded by country clubs and hotels.

Scooter fell in love with the desert. He discovered a part of nature's design that held a mystical quality rivaling the sea. To Scooter the desert conjured up images of the traditional meeting place between God and His people, a miniature holy land with dry gullies where water flowed once or twice a year. The desert was where Moses saw an emblazoned bush on the edge of the Midianite wilderness; where a pillar of fire guided the Israelites on a serpentine route from Egypt to the Jordan; where Elijah fled in exile and where David sought refuge from Saul. It was where the bearded John the Baptist subsisted on locusts and wild honey and Jesus withstood the hellish assault of Satan in the wilderness of Judea. The destiny of the human race was drawn in its sliding sands. The supreme law code was delivered from the barren rocks above the desert floor where fools danced about a calf of gold.

The desert is at once nefarious and holy, foreboding and promising, arid and parched, yet capable of exploding in color with the wild flowers of the spring. It can heal the wounded spirit yet kill without warning; give sanctuary to the fugitive and a shallow grave to the unwary; offer solitude for the harried or insanity to those whose brains were fried by the sun. Those living from childhood on the rim of its vast expanse have skin like leather and eyes with a strange vacant look in them. They are like people who have seen too much, watching ghosts romp in the purple-black shadows of twilights made surreal by sunsets that looked as if they were painted by an angry god hurling his pallet at the horizon wall, splashing paint in every direction. These things had Scooter quickly in their grasp.

There was no debate within the ranks of the pulpit committee. They were seduced by Scooter's charm, voting unanimously to extend a call to him to be their spiritual leader. The only reservation was that he was single, bringing with him no Mrs. Evans, no first lady of the church or hostess of the sanctuary.

Scooter shocked the faculty of the Philadelphia Institute by announcing his resignation with the news he was going into the pastorate. The presbytery of Philadelphia gave him an honorable dismissal to labor in the Scottsdale parish, which was affiliated with no denomination, connected to no ecclesiastical hierarchy. Scooter was now on his own, a maverick from the herd, an orphan of Holy Mother Church.

The autumn move to Scottsdale forced Scooter to make a decision. The church owned no manse, dispensing with the antiquated tradition of providing the minister with a house the church owned and maintained. Following the new trend made popular by the Internal Revenue Service's generous exclusion clause for clergymen, the church gave Scooter a nontaxable housing allowance making it possible and desirable for him to purchase his own home. His salary package was two and a half times what he earned as a seminary professor and the affluence of the congregation demanded that the senior minister be capable of walking with his head in the ozone of their social climate.

Scooter purchased a Spanish-American style ranch house perched on the slopes of Camelback Mountain, a hacienda type villa with stucco walls and tile roof, creating the illusion of a frontier Spanish mission. The inside featured high ceilings with iron lattice work and deep rich parquetry. Scooter furnished it with Spanish-American antiques purchased at a boutique on Scottsdale's Fifth Avenue. A crescent-shaped pool was guarded by a high wall and illumined at night by spotlights built into the sides of the pool, sending an eerie blue-green glow into the night. Outside the screened porch was a Jacuzzi that shot jets of hot bubbly currents of water against his back and legs to relieve the nagging pains of his football injuries.

Scooter celebrated Christmas with a decorated cactus plant. He missed the pageantry of Wanamaker's and the lights of Philadelphia's center city. The elderly women of the church were already competing with each other for motherly rights over their bachelor minister. Scooter was inundated with Christmas cookies, Christmas pies, and Christmas dinner invitations. The Christmas season also brought Pamela Green into his life.

He was doing some Christmas shopping at Goldwater's Department Store. As he was discussing a Wedgewood vase in the gift department with a salesclerk, a stunning woman walked in. Immediately the clerk broke off her conversation with Scooter and walked over to the woman, leaving him standing with his mouth open, staring at the stranger who was commanding the clerk's immediate attention.

The woman was regal, filling the space around her with an unmistakable air of confidence. She moved with a delicate grace that failed to conceal an imperious posture of authority. As Scooter watched, other sales personnel gathered around her, fawning over her, scurrying around to show her whatever merchandise she indicated interest in. Finally, the woman smiled, uttered some grand announcement of departure, and whisked away as abruptly as she had entered. Scooter found himself staring at her hand as she passed him, taking note of the fact that she was not wearing a wedding ring. She glanced at him in passing, her dark eyes not lingering, but dismissing him with a perfunctory look. The clerk returned to Scooter, suddenly embarrassed for keeping him waiting.

"Who was that?" Scooter asked, assuming that she must be a movie star, but he couldn't place her.

"Oh, that was Mrs. Green. She's the chief executive buyer for Goldwater's."

Scooter took pains to conceal his disappointment at hearing the words, *Mrs.* Green.

Without coaxing from Scooter the salesclerk went on gushing admiration for Mrs. Green.

"She's only been in Scottsdale for two years. She started to work right here in this department as a clerk. I never saw anybody move up an organization so fast in my life. Within a year she was the top buyer in the whole company."

"Where's she from?" Scooter asked.

"She moved here from Colorado Springs. Her husband was killed in a freak accident."

Scooter purchased the vase and filed away the information about Mrs. Green in his mind. That night he drifted off to sleep without thinking about Patricia.

The day after New Year's, Scooter went to the Scottsdale Civic Center for an art exhibit. He walked the galleries, moving quickly through the Andy Warhol section to find the Rouault. Though Scooter was disdainful about fauvism he had developed a strong admiration for Rouault. Though Rouault had, early in his career, exhibited with the Fauves, he had arisen above the "wild beasts," expressing at last the Christian's assurance of the ultimate triumph of grace over despair. Scooter loved the poignant suffering expressed in the Seated Clown, but his favorite was The

Old King. Here he saw a modernized stain-glassed Rembrandt style breaking through.

He stopped suddenly in the Warhol section. Pamela Green was standing in the gallery, staring intently at a Warhol silkscreen of Marilyn Monroe. He casually sauntered in Pamela's direction and took a stance beside her, feigning interest in what he really considered artistic waste. He peered at the pop art display, thinking its repetition of the movie sex goddess boring and only a step removed from Warhol's mechanical representations of Coca-Cola bottles and Brillo cartons.

Pamela did not seem to notice Scooter. She was absorbed in contemplation. He interrupted her thoughts. "You don't consider this art, do you?" Scooter said, using his professional tone.

Pamela stiffened and glared at him. "I certainly do. What the man is saying needs to be heard."

Scooter laughed. "What's he saying? Hummm-mm, good. That's what Campbell soups are . . . Heavy stuff. M. M. and Coca-Cola. Who cares?"

"I care," Pamela shot back, obviously annoyed at Scooter's dogmatic dismissal of Warhol.

Scooter softened the repartee, assuming the attitude of a school boy open to the teacher's instruction.

"I'm sorry. I guess I was just trying to cover up my ignorance of modern art. I really don't know what it's all about. What *is* Warhol saying?"

Pamela softened too at the momentary surrender. Truce was in her response.

"Look closely at the silkscreen. What do you see?"

"I see Marilyn Monroe, over and over again. It's the same picture repeated about thirty times. What's that supposed to mean?"

"Look closely. I mean very closely. Look at the first image and then the second."

Scooter studied the images in the artwork with fierce concentration. "The second image is minutely different from the first and the third differs slightly again. They're not the same!"

"Exactly. Warhol is trying to tell us something about the philosophy of the second glance. I think he wants us to look at things more closely, more deeply. It's kind of a protest."

"Protest against what?" Scooter asked.

"Against superficiality—the very thing you're accusing him of. What he's saying is that in our popcorn culture everything is instantaneous. Anybody can be a media star for five seconds. We move so quickly we don't take time to reflect. We want everything quick, easy, and cheap. Real talent takes time and pain to develop. You don't get a gourmet meal in five minutes from a soup can, and you don't get the Mona Lisa from a Xerox machine. The television commercial offers solutions for all our problems in thirty seconds. It's like bumper sticker theology—salvation in a nutshell, four words or less."

"I get it. Instant salvation, instant dinner, instant success, instant everything. Kind of like shooting to the top of Goldwater's in one easy year or less."

Pamela raised her eyebrows. "How do you know me?"

"I don't really. I was in Goldwater's the other day and the salesclerk dropped me like a hot potato when you walked in. I was intrigued by the mystery woman that had everybody falling all over themselves to accommodate you."

"You followed me here?"

"No, no. I just happened to be in the gallery. I was looking for the Rouaults and saw you here. I was curious."

"But you're not a cat, I trust."

"God forbid, Mrs. Green. I'm not looking for a feline sort of demise."

"Touché. And what, may I ask, is your name?"

"Richard Evans."

"And what do you do, Richard Evans, besides accosting innocent women at art exhibits?"

"Oh, sometimes I marry them and sometimes I bury them."

"What are you, Bluebeard the Pirate?"

"No, I'm Richard the minister. I'm the pastor of the Camelback Community Church."

"I see. You must be the new minister in town. I've heard about you."

"Don't believe anything you've heard. Look, I've heard about you. You've heard about me. All secondhand. Let's get acquainted over lunch."

"Sorry, I don't date ministers."

"Oh? That's a great rule. First time I ever heard that one. C'mon, I'm hungry. A lunch break doesn't have to be a date. You can keep your rule sacrosanct and I promise I won't give you any bumper-sticker theology. We can have a real sit-down lunch. No fast food. Plenty of time for reflection."

Pamela laughed. "OK, pastor. Maybe you can explain Georges Rouault to me."

Scooter and Pamela walked across the park to the Doubletree Inn. Scooter felt self-conscious that Pamela was taller than he and wondered if the match might be evened out if she were not wearing heels.

The maitre d' seated them by the window.

"Well, Mrs. Green. What looks good to you for lunch?"

"Please, Reverend Evans, don't call me 'Mrs. Green.' It sounds so matronly. My name is Pamela."

"Very well, Pam, but please no 'Reverend Evans' either. It sounds ecclesiastical. Call me Richard."

"Fine, Dickey. My name is Pamela, not Pam."

"Seems like we can't get beyond introductions before we're jousting. Let's call a cease-fire."

"Fine. But you've just mixed your metaphors. You don't have a cease-fire with lances."

"Right. And you just picked yours up again. Tell me. Why the 'no minister' rule? What do you have against us? Are you an atheist or something?"

"Not at all. I just had a bad experience with one, that's all. I was dating one in Colorado Springs. I moved out here to get away from him. He thought he was Noah."

"Noah? Why, was he in the ship building business?"

"No, he just liked everything in twos. I was dating one of him, but he was dating two of us. When I found out, I left. No more compassionate clergymen, thanks."

Over lunch Scooter probed into Pamela's background. Growing more relaxed, she opened up and recounted the tragic death of her husband which she had witnessed.

"I was a church member before the accident. In fact I was heavily involved in church. My faith went through a deep change at the cemetery. Suddenly it was more real. It had to be. I found out what the Bible means when it says, 'It is better to go to the house of mourning than to spend your time with fools.'"

"Yes," Scooter agreed. "I'm a Herman Melville fan. He once wrote, 'Not until we learn that one grief outweighs a thousand joys will we understand what Christianity is trying to make us.' I think that was Rouault's message too. You can't put that on a bumper sticker."

As the conversation progressed they spoke about grief and of bitterness and self-pity. Scooter insisted that grief was a virtuous human response to tragedy but the others were destructive. While they talked, he sensed a rapport different from a counseling session with a bereaved widow or a theological gabfest with an eager student. He was acutely aware of a male-female transaction taking place. He was both moved and excited by it.

When the waiter brought the check, Pamela announced that she had to return to Goldwater's.

"I must get back. I skipped out most of the morning to catch the exhibit. Thank you for lunch, Richard. I thoroughly enjoyed it."

"So did I. I hope you enjoyed it enough to give thought to discarding your rule. My name is not Noah."

Pamela laughed, making no commitment, yet stopping short of repeating her vow.

Scooter saw Pamela again. And again. His excuse was that it had been so long since he had dated he no longer understood the meaning of the term. Pamela could relax her rule since they weren't "dating," but merely seeing each other. Within weeks she began attending the Camelback Community Church and carefully followed Scooter's midweek lectures. By March the mothers of the church had stopped trying to introduce their daughters to Dr. Evans.

It was Saint Patrick's Day, 1972, when Scooter's intercom buzzed, disturbing his labor of sermon preparations.

"Dr. Evans, you have a call on line 3."

"Do you know who it is, Mrs. Frances?"

"It's a woman named Mary Gregg and she sounds very distressed, almost hysterical."

Scooter's throat constricted. *Mary Gregg! Something's wrong with Patricia.* "Put her through," Scooter barked, his voice carrying a tone Mrs. Frances had never heard from him.

One night Leah was waiting up for him when Johnny came home. He was barely in the house when she bubbled over in a torrent of excitement. "Johnny, I got the names of two agencies today where we can apply for adoption. We can get the process started right away."

Johnny tried to keep it light, "Gee, Mama. That's great. But take it easy, you're sweeping me off my feet. Give me a little time to think about it before we rush off and sign papers. I know you're eager, and so am I, but I need a little time to get used to the idea of becoming a father. Most guys get nine months to think about it."

"Oh, c'mon, silly. Nobody gets nine months to think about it; even the woman doesn't know that quickly. Besides, the process takes a long time. It isn't like going down to the store and bringing a baby home by dinner time. I just want to get started, OK?"

"Sure, Mama. Just give me a couple of days to think it over. Is that too much to ask?"

The days of delay tactics and stalling fattened into weeks and months, turning the once placid Kramer house into an imbroglio. Charlie Kramer summoned Johnny to her kitchen table where she held her matriarchal court. Jack was in New Orleans preparing to officiate the Sugar Bowl game. Charlie roughly grabbed two bottles of Budweiser from the refrigerator, popped the caps off and handed a bottle to Johnny.

"What gives, John? Leah's a wreck. You've been telling her for months that you would adopt and as soon as push comes to shove you get cold feet. What are you running from?"

"I'm not running from anything. I just don't want to adopt a baby, that's all."

"Why not? You promised her you would."

"I know it. But I changed my mind. Is there anything wrong with that or is that only a woman's prerogative? Look, Mom, I'd love to have kids but I don't want somebody else's baby. Can't you understand that?"

"No, I can't, as a matter of fact. That's the only way you'll ever have any kids. The stork doesn't stop at your house, boy. It's somebody else's baby or nothing. Besides, you wouldn't have the baby home for five minutes before you felt like it was your own. If you raise the baby, it's yours. I can see a woman feeling like you do, but not a man. It's not the man who misses all the things that go with the pregnancy and the delivery, it's the woman."

"You sound just like Leah. You two are crowding me. You just don't understand how a man feels about things like this. Think of the responsibility I'd be taking on."

"What's the big deal? That goes with the territory. You can afford it."

Johnny finished his beer in silence, feeling the walls closing in on him. In the middle of the week the phone on his desk rang. Johnny stopped its shrill scream in mid-ring, picking up the receiver, annoyed by the interruption.

"Johnny?"

"Racquel," Johnny whispered a seething reply. "I told you not to call me at the office. Where are you? Are you calling from the plant?"

"No, Johnny. I'm on my lunch break. I'm sick. I have to talk to you."

"What's the matter? What kind of sick?"

"I'm pregnant sick. We have to talk. Meet me at the apartment at 3:00." The line went dead.

Johnny slammed the receiver in its cradle almost shattering the plastic armrest. He glanced at his appointment calendar and saw he had no afternoon appointments. Storming out of the office he told his secretary to take his calls and didn't say where he was going.

Route 51 was wet but clear. The edges of the road were piled with stale snow streaked with grime, with ugly gray slush covering the berm. He stopped for a drink to kill time before the meeting. He felt like a rat in a corner.

I've been had. The bitch trapped me. The oldest scam in the world and I let myself get suckered.

Johnny was at the apartment early, pacing the cheap rug in fury. He heard the key click in the lock and glared at Racquel when she walked in. She looked pale and was shivering. She burst into tears sobbing, "I'm sorry, Johnny. I'm sorry. I know what you're thinking."

"You bet you know what I'm thinking, you little gold digger. It's the oldest trick in the book, Racquel. I may look dumb but my mother didn't raise any stupid kids. If you think I'm going to divorce Leah now and you and I are going to ride off in the sunset, you're crazy. No broad pulls this on me."

Johnny's eyes were menacing. He began taunting her with

caustic mimicry. In a falsetto voice he shrieked at her, "'Oh, Johnny, don't worry. I'm on the pill, Johnny. Nothing can happen, Johnny.' I suppose the kid should be called Houdini. He's the great escape artist beating the system of modern science."

Racquel was dazed by the attack, trying to find words to fend off the assault. "I was on the pill. I was always on the pill. Except once. One time was all, Johnny. You have to believe me."

"When?"

"Right after Thanksgiving. One of those days you called me at work and told me to meet you here. I forgot to take my pill that morning and didn't remember until that night."

"It doesn't matter. We can take care of it."

"What do you mean?"

"You're going to get rid of it, that's what I mean. Don't worry. I'll pay for it. You can go to New York. It's legal there."

"Oh, Johnny, I can't do that, it's a mortal sin."

Johnny spat in disgust. "Mortal sin? What do you think we've been doing in this apartment all this time, saying the rosary?"

"That's different, Johnny. That's between you and me. Besides I promised the Holy Mother I would never do *that.*"

"You know what the Holy Mother can do. Let *her* have the kid."

Racquel made the sign of the cross on her own body. "Johnny, that's blasphemy. Leave me here alone if you want but don't you ever talk that way in my presence again. Get out."

Racquel's tears were gone, suddenly replaced by vehement sparks, her face contorted with rage.

Johnny sighed deeply and sank down in the chair. "I'm not going anywhere. We have to cool off and figure this out. Look, you can take a leave of absence. Sick leave or something, get out of town for a while. Have the kid and put it up for adoption. Maybe Leah and I can adopt it."

She came across the room at him like a banshee, fingernails aimed at his eyes. He grabbed for her wrists to block the attack. She was spitting in his face. "You rotten pig. You want Leah to have my baby? You filthy scum, I'll rot in hell before I give up this baby. It's mine you hear, mine!"

"All right . . . all right . . . Take it easy. Keep the baby. Do what you want with it. Just leave me out of it."

"Right, Johnny. I just stop working, have the baby and quietly leave you out of it while we sit here and starve to death."

"That's not what I meant. You know I'll take care of you and the kid. You won't have to throw a paternity suit at me."

After Johnny left, Racquel mixed herself a drink and sat down in the dingy apartment and began talking to the embryo taking shape within her. She patted her stomach and said, "It's you and me, little darling. We have to stick this out together. You'll have a daddy sooner or later. As long as my womb is fertile Leah doesn't have a chance. One thing for sure, we aren't going to live in this rat trap. Your daddy's going to have to do better than this."

Scooter braced himself, half rushing, half halting to pick up the phone. "Mary?"

"Scooter . . . I was afraid I wouldn't get you . . ." She lost control of her voice, breaking down into inarticulate sobs. She tried to speak but her words were undecipherable. Scooter tried to calm her, to soothe her with gentle, controlled speech.

"Take it easy, Mary. It's all right. Just try to tell me what's wrong. Take your time."

Scooter listened through the silence punctuated by convulsive heaves until he finally heard a regular breathing rhythm.

"That's fine, Mary. Now tell me what's wrong." His voice was having a tranquilizing effect on Mary, but his stomach was in knots and his hands were shaking. He wanted to scream at her, to reach his hand two thousand miles across the wire and slap her into coherence. *In the name of God, tell me what's wrong.*

"Patricia's sick, Scooter. Real sick. She's in the hospital and they won't let her out. Over a month now. She won't eat. She wants to die."

"What does she have, Mary?" Scooter feared the worst, a fatal form of cancer or some other dreadful terminal disease.

"A nervous breakdown. She's in the psychiatric ward. They're giving her shock treatments."

A sense of relief mixed with horror swept through Scooter. People recover from nervous breakdowns. Sometimes.

"Why, Mary? What triggered it?" Scooter was going through a check list in his mind. *Trauma? Depression? Severe neurosis? Psychosis? Schizophrenia?* What was it? He knew the term *nervous breakdown* covered a multitude of crises, a euphemism that is nonspecific, undifferentiated. It was not a literal diagnosis. He knew that nerves don't break down, the nervous system doesn't suddenly atrophy. People break down.

Mary rehearsed the ugly story that triggered Patricia's collapse. Months earlier Robert had walked out on Patricia, leaving her for another woman. He used his power to harass Patricia with a battery of attorneys seeking to pin the blame of the marital breakup on her. When she collapsed and was rushed to the hospital screaming, she was placed in the psychiatric ward. Robert got a custody order from the judge, placing the children in his hands. She was powerless to stop him as the attorneys built a case of *non compos mentis* against her.

"Scooter, can you come? Please, dear, I know you can help her. You're the only one who can."

Scooter glanced at his calendar. He knew without looking what it would say. He was sure he could get a few days emergency leave but it would be complicated with his schedule.

"What's the name of Patricia's doctor? Will he let me see her?"

"I'm sure he will. His name is Dr. Phillip Woodhouse."

Mary relayed Dr. Woodhouse's phone number and Scooter promised to call him right away and get back to her.

"Mary, you take it easy. I'll discuss this with the doctor and we'll figure out how to handle it. I'll call you as soon as we have a game plan. OK?"

"Oh, Scooter, I knew I could call you. Please don't let them use those horrible shock treatments on her anymore. Please take care of my little girl. I love you, dear. You know that don't you?"

"Yes, Mary, I know it, and I love you too. Now you relax and I'll call the doctor."

Mary poured out a few more maudlin terms of endearment, the kind of expressions Scooter found it difficult to field, usually committing errors born of embarrassment. He gently guided her to terminate the conversation so he could get on with calling Dr. Woodhouse.

Scooter reached for the intercom switch to have Mrs. Frances make the call, but withdrew his hand deciding to place this call himself. In her office Mrs. Frances noticed the light on line three blink off and then come on again alerting her that Dr. Evans was immersed in something important enough not to be disturbed. Her only clue to the drama unfolding in his office was the flicker of bulbs on her phone.

A switchboard operator announced to Scooter, "Oceanside Hospital. May I help you?"

"Yes, this is Dr. Evans calling. I'm calling long distance for Dr. Woodhouse."

Scooter knew the magic of using his title *Doctor* to get past the barricades of switchboard operators and waiting room nurses to direct contact with physicians.

Dr. Woodhouse came on the line. His voice was a rich baritone, exuding a tone of confidence and compassion. Scooter wondered in a tragic-comic instant if psychiatrists took voice lessons in medical school.

Woodhouse seemed genuinely pleased that Scooter had called. He sounded like an old friend.

"Yes, Dr. Evans, your name has come up frequently in my sessions with Patricia. You play a large role in her psychological history." It was a statement of fact, not an accusation.

Scooter laughed and said, "You should have me on your couch for a while and see how many times her name comes out of *my* mouth. You could write a textbook. Listen, is there any way I can help or would I merely add to her trauma?"

"I'm sure you can help if you're willing."

"If I'm willing? I'd crawl over glass to help her."

"Yes, I'm sure you would. But it's a delicate matter we have here. You are a very important key to her recovery. Your involvement is critical. But there are risks. She's in a severe depressive state at the moment. She is vulnerable to excessive transference, to locking into a heavy dependence on whoever is treating her. Those risks would be exaggerated in your case. She has an idealized fixation on you already."

"I quite understand that, doctor. I am neither a psychiatrist nor a psychologist but I'm not altogether ignorant of these mechanisms. I've spent hundreds of hours in counseling sessions, as I'm sure you can imagine. This case, however, would be difficult for me. I'm already deeply involved with her emotionally. To be honest, I've been in love with her."

"Have been, Dr. Evans, or are now?"

"I'll let you be the judge of that. For several years I was in love

with a phantom. Now the phantom is materializing and I don't
know what that will mean. I certainly don't want to hurt her or
complicate matters for her. But I want to help if I possibly can.
Am I making sense?"

"Of course you are. Her mother insists that you are exactly
the tonic she needs. There is nothing in my evaluation of the situation that would refute that. I think it's worth a try."

"All right. I can see two possibilities. Two options we can
explore. I could come to Florida for a day or two or, if you think
it's better, I can make arrangements to have her transferred to a
hospital here. What do you think?"

"Let's explore for a moment a variation on your second
theme. The more time you can give her the better. A quick visit
here would have limited value. If she can go there it would be
better. I can send her records there but I think it would be better
if she were with you rather than in a hospital. The hospital syndrome itself can add to depression. We know that. Sometimes
keeping a patient like this hospitalized is the devil's choice. She is
not violent or wildly deranged. Hers is an acute depression
brought on by prolonged trauma in a messy divorce case. She is
not psychotic and there is no evidence of suicidal tendencies. But
she does need attention, a strong support system which I'm sure
you can supply. She needs medication and we can take care of that
for a couple of weeks. If you can swing it, I'd like her to go to you
for that period."

"I'm sure I can work it out. I'll have to think through where
she'll stay. We can't put her up alone in a motel and it would be
disaster for me to have her stay at my house. The tongues would
be wagging all over Phoenix."

"Yes, I gather that would be touchy. Still, if you could have a
nurse or chaperone or something it would be better for Patricia to
be under your roof."

"I'll work on that angle. When can she come?" Scooter
asked.

"As soon as you're ready to have her. I can have her on the
airplane tomorrow or as soon as you give the word."

"Look, our church elders meet tonight. I'll go over a game
plan with them and get back to you in the morning."

"Very well. I'll look forward to your call."

That night Scooter presented a plan to the elders calling for

Patricia to be housed with him under the supervision of an elderly woman from the church who was a practical nurse. Curt Siegel was outspoken on the matter. "We can't let the critics determine our agenda. If the doctor's recommendation is that she stay at Dr. Evans's house then that's what we do. We are not going to be intimidated by the threat of gossip-mongers."

The vote was unanimous and Scooter arranged with Mrs. Riley, a practical nurse, to prepare for the one-week assignment. He contacted Dr. Woodhouse from his office the next morning and phoned Mary Gregg to fill her in on the plan. As Scooter left his office he paused at the door and said, "Mrs. Frances, I won't be in the rest of the day. I'm going out to Pinnacle Peak to see Curt."

She nodded in understanding.

Scooter drove through the entrance of the Pinnacle Peak Golf Club past twin giant saguaros that today leered at him like two menacing gargoyles. He slipped his car into an empty space near the Pro Shop. Curt was sitting in a small cubicle at the rear of the shop, his feet propped up on the desk while he perused the latest issue of *Golf Digest*. He looked up to see Scooter framed in the doorway.

"Richard? Am I being treated to a pastoral call?"

"No," Scooter shot back. "I was looking for the grocery store and got lost. Let's go hit some balls."

Curt recognized the telltale signs of Scooter's inner agitation. He had been to the practice tee with a thousand executives who were beating balls instead of clients, allowing their pent-up frustrations to travel from their bodies, through their arms and be released through the club head as it lashed at the ball. He gave no hint that he recognized the syndrome in Scooter, but adopted a mein of professional concern for a student seeking a serious lesson.

On the way to the practice tee Curt focused the conversation on golf. "How're you hittin' them?" he asked.

"Fair, Curt. I've been pulling some and coming off the ball a little. I keep fighting the problem of spinning out."

At the tee Scooter reached for his seven-iron and began warming up. Curt could see his muscles tensing, strong cords bulging in his neck and upper back.

"You're not gripping the club, pastor, you're choking it. Relax. You can't make a smooth pass with a stranglehold on the club."

Scooter hit a few seven-irons and quickly moved down to a five-iron. He was lost in his ritual. He hit shot after shot, hard and crisp. He got into a groove, sending the balls flying high to their apogee before they settled to earth with a slight draw. About every sixth shot Scooter pulled the ball to the left.

"There! There it is, why am I doing that?"

"Two reasons, Richard. First, you're getting flippy with your wrists at the top and you're casting. Second, you're overpowering the shot. Irons are for finesse, not power. You need to think of them as instruments, not clubs. Now try it by keeping 10 percent of your power in your pocket. Tempo, tempo, tempo."

Scooter quickly got his swing under control and settled into a fluid pattern. Perspiration beads dotted his forehead as the Arizona sun was drawing the liquid from his body. Abruptly he stopped and turned to Curt.

"What am I going to tell Pamela?"

"You're asking me, pastor? How about the truth for starters?"

"How much truth? The whole truth and nothing but the truth so help me God? It's not always that easy. I don't have to lie, but do I have to reveal all my feelings about Patricia?"

"I think she needs to know the score. Besides, she deserves it. What are you worried about? She's a big girl. She can handle it," Curt offered.

"No doubt about that. She's as tough as they come. But on this one we're hitting smack up against a supersensitive point."

"What do you mean?"

"She has a sore spot about ministers. She was two-timed by one before she moved out here. How can she read this except as an instant replay?"

"Is it? Are you in love with Patricia?"

"I don't know. I mean, no, of course not, I'm in love with Pamela. My hang-up with Patricia was kid stuff."

"I think you need to tell the whole story to Pamela. She trusts you, Richard. She'll understand. She'll see that this whole thing was dumped in your lap. It's not like you've been chasing after another woman. You can't erase the past, but you can deal with it. This is probably the best thing that could have happened to you and to Pamela. What if you married Pamela? You'd be haunted by Patricia the rest of your life."

"Whoever said anything about marrying Pamela?"

"C'mon, Richard. It's written all over you. You'd better get into Scottsdale and see her right away."

"Just when I got my swing clicking!" Scooter jibed.

"Yeah. Now get moving."

Curt walked Scooter to the car, shoring him up with words of encouragement.

"Thanks, Curt. I'll let you know how it turns out."

"Fine. You owe me one."

"Don't worry. I'll bury you for free some day."

"Ah, Goniff! You'll probably steal my golf clubs at the funeral."

"Better yet, the next time your parents are in town, bring them over to the church. I'll marry them for you."

"Get out of here before I put a slice in your swing."

Scooter was tense during his drive back into Scottsdale. His steps were heavy as he approached the front entrance to Goldwater's from the parking lot. Once inside he saw Pamela before she noticed him approaching. He hesitated, feasting for a moment on her classic beauty. High cheek bones, velvety elongated neck, erect posture, impeccably dressed in a shantung skirt and silk blouse.

Pamela broke into a flashing smile and moved toward him the instant she saw him. "Richard! What are you doing here at this time of day?"

Scooter's face was locked in a serious frown, like a doctor about to announce grim tidings to an anxious patient. "Can we talk?" Scooter said, ignoring the niceties.

"Yes, but what's wrong?"

"Let's get out of here and I'll tell you."

They left the store and walked in silence to a bistro on Fifth Avenue. Pamela respected Scooter's sullen mood, repressing her acute anxiety while walking beside him in cool composure. *Inwardly she was bracing herself for some horrid news. It's another woman. No, he's sick. Terminally ill. No, he's been called to the mission field. He's leaving Scottsdale. It is another woman! That's what it is. I'll kill him. Stop it, Pamela. Be calm. Just take it as it comes.* She noticed that Scooter was walking with his jaw jutting into the breeze. His fingernails were digging into his palms as he kept clenching and unclenching his fists.

They sat across from each other in the bistro. Scooter's gaze kept dropping toward the table. He was struggling to find words to start. "Uh, Pamela, something's come up and you need to know about it."

It is another woman. I can hear it in his voice. "Yes? What is it, Richard? You're obviously exercised about something."

Scooter told the whole story. The call from Mary Gregg; the discussion with Dr. Woodhouse; the whole history of his besetting fixation with Patricia. "She arrives tomorrow morning. She's looking to me for counseling. It will be a therapy support time. Strictly ministry. Nothing else. It's not like I'm chasing another woman."

Pamela smiled deeply and winsomely. *Therapy! These men are all the same. He's got himself believing it.* She used her most assuring tone of voice. "Of course, Richard. What do you think I am, a jealous shrew? How could Patricia's mother do anything other than call you?"

Pamela reached across the table and took Scooter's hand in hers. Gently, she stroked it with both of hers. "Look, this was meant to be. How could our relationship ever go anywhere unless this Patricia business were resolved once and for all. It's providential. I can go to Chicago tomorrow and then on to New York to the garment district and get some business out of the way. I'll be away for a week. It'll be a perfect interlude."

She felt Scooter relax. His fingers let the tension dissipate. A boyish excitement came into his voice. "I knew you'd understand. I'll call you every night and let you know how it's going."

"You'll do no such thing. We're not eighteen years old. You need this time alone with her without worrying about me. I need you to have this time alone." *Like I need a headache!* "It's only a week. We'll see how things stand then. I'll call you as soon as I get home."

"No dice. I'll meet you at the airport and drive you back here."

"Fair enough."

Scooter got the flight information from Pamela and the two

parted after lunch. That night Pamela had difficulty sleeping.
Her last thought before she slipped over the edge into unconsciousness was, *He's building an ark.*

Scooter had trouble getting to sleep too. He battled the
witches of insomnia until 2:00 A.M. He knew his efforts to sleep
were futile so he got up, dressed and walked into the crisp air. The
night was an Arizona high sky with crystal clearness giving the
stars a vivid, piercing sharpness. Scooter walked to the church
and unlocked the door, stumbling through the blackness to the
sanctuary. He moved quickly along the edge of the front pew to
the chancel steps. He walked up the steps and sank to his knees
first, then plunged face downward on the rug, his hands stretched
out grasping the woolen loops of the rug with his fingertips. He
wanted to pray but all his throat would allow at first was inchoate
groans. He lay there for minutes, feeling the texture of the rug on
his face before he could form intelligible words with his lips.

Oh, God. You know who I am, and what I am. You
know my feet of clay and my frame of dust. Right now I
don't even know how to address you . . . or what I should
say. You are too holy for me. Too awesome . . . too majestic. I can't argue with you, so let me plead. Let me beg. If
I knew what promises I should make I would make them.
Please . . . please . . . please . . . let Patricia be all right.
Help me to know what to say to her . . . how to help her. I
feel so helpless. You said that perfect love casts away fear,
but I am afraid. I can't get rid of the fear . . . please help
me, I beg you.

Oh precious Christ. You alone are my priest, my great
High Priest. Speak to the Father for me. Carry my prayer
to the Holy place. Intercede for me now. Come to Patricia
as the Son of Righteousness with healing in your wings.
Have mercy upon me, oh, King of Israel. Touch me as
you touched the horrid leper. My soul is rotting like a
leper's skin. Only your hand can cleanse me. Oh sweet
and excellent Saviour . . . That is what I need tonight. A
Saviour. Please save me in this hour. As Patricia comes to
me I don't know what to do. Please be with me. Don't
abandon me. My faith is so fragile and you are so strong.
Forgive me of my sins. They insult your glory and I am

ashamed. Hide my sins. Throw them in the sea of forget-
fulness. Restore my soul. Give me peace. Help me.

Oh blessed Holy Ghost. Fill my empty words with
power. Help me form my prayer. Interpret my groans to
the Son that He might carry them to the Father. Be my
Comforter. Anoint me with holy unction for this task.
Rape the soul of Patricia and heal her spirit. Sanctify me
for tomorrow and let me sleep in peace.

There, at the center of the chancel Scooter began to weep
softly, letting his heart trickle out of his eyes onto the rug. He
began to breathe evenly and fell asleep at the foot of the great
wooden cross. He didn't twitch a muscle until the sunlight of
dawn stirred him once more into consciousness.

When his head cleared he scrambled to his feet, his clothes
speckled with lint from the carpet. He looked like a man who had
been caught in a scarlet snowstorm with the particles giving a
comic splash of red to his blue pants. He walked quickly back
home, and began preparations for the day, feeling a surge of
strength mixed with excitement. The fear was gone, buried
deeply within the pile of the carpet at the chancel steps.

It was Scooter's day off. He set the timer on the Jacuzzi for ten
minutes and stepped gingerly into the swirling hot tub. Leaning
back against the side he closed his eyes and opened his body to the
pulsating jets of water, letting their turbulent needles massage his
back and legs. The blurbing sound of the water had a peaceful
cadence that covered the hum of the motor. When the timer
clicked off he rose from the steam and toweled himself dry enough
to walk to the shower for a second lavation. From childhood days
the shower stall had always been a cubicle for more than soap and
shampoo. It was his basin of ablution entered mostly at night for
ritual as well as physical cleansing. This day the rite was celebrated in the morning.

Scooter went out for breakfast, trying to kill the clock, to force
its hands into $6/8$ time by keeping himself occupied if only by the
simple task of ordering sausage and eggs from the menu. Patricia's flight was scheduled to arrive shortly after noon, the gods of
the time zones working in his behalf.

He left for the airport early, succumbing to the superstitious
folly that given a strong enough will the watched pot might

indeed boil. He drove west along Camelback Road and then turned south on Forty-third Street toward Sky Harbor. When he entered the parking lot in front of the terminal his dashboard clock told him he was an hour early. Inside the terminal building he glanced at the schedule board, relieved to see the words ON TIME beside Patricia's flight number. He exchanged some dollar bills for quarters and went inside the amusement arcade to the pinball machines. He felt an eerie sense of *deja vu* when he inserted the quarters in the slot that promised three games on the machine. There were other people in the arcade, but only one in a Hart-Schaffner-Marx Country Gentleman beige three-piece suit was popping quarters into a pinball machine while a three-quarter inch ash suspended tenuously on the edge of the cigarette resting on top of the glass.

His thoughts began to assail him. *Generations come and generations go, but the earth remains forever. The sun rises and the sun sets. There is nothing new under the sun. It's all vanity. Cut it out, Scooter. There is something new, Pamela. It's time to exorcise the demons. Patricia can't hurt you. Not anymore. But how will I feel when I see her? O dear God, get me through this.*

When Scooter heard the P.A. announcement of the arrival of Patricia's flight he had four free games left on his machine that he promptly turned over to the nearest player. He quit the arcade and walked briskly to the arrival gate. He scanned the faces of the disembarking passengers riding down an escalator toward the waiting area. He saw Patricia before she picked his face out of the crowd of people waiting for arriving passengers.

She looked ghostly, her face pale and wan. She was bone thin, an emaciated shadow of herself. Her skin appeared sallow and the cat-like fire was gone from her hollow eyes. But her hair was finely coiffed and she was wearing a stylish suit. Her eyes came to life with the sparkle of recognition, and a smile, parsed half with delight and half with embarrassment, crossed her face when she spotted him.

Scooter used his fading athletic agility to squeeze through narrow openings in the crowd to get to the front of the mob surrounding the turnstiles giving access to the waiting room. He met her at the front and whisked her aside from the traffic flow and in the same fluid movement pulled her to his chest in an embrace. He could feel her trembling as she buried her head in his shoulder, weeping. He stroked her hair saying, "It's all right now, Patricia. Everything's fine."

His own eyes were moist as he stood next to the turnstile staring into space but seeing nothing. She was clinging to him with desperation; he could feel a wisp of her hair tickling his nose; the fragrance of her perfume was filling his brain. He stepped back from her and clasped both of her hands holding them at arms length.

"Let me look at you. Don't move. Just let me look at you."

The first words she spoke were, "I hate for you to see me like this. I look awful."

"Patricia, if you got run over by a Mack truck you would still look terrific. Let's get out of here."

He held her hand while they walked to the baggage area. She was unsteady on her feet and Scooter noticed that her once delicate fingernails were now ragged and chewed to the quick telling him more than the gaunt appearance of her face. "You're on vacation now, Patricia. We're going to relax for a week and get your strength back and some color in your cheeks."

She had a death grip on his hand, squeezing it like a vise, as if she were afraid that if she let go she would fall into some hellish abyss. Scooter didn't mind the pressure. He used his thumb to lightly massage her fingers, sending a message of strength and protection into her hand. By the time they retrieved her luggage and walked to the car there was already a noticeable change in her mien. Her steps were more certain, her posture more erect, and a glimmer of light was igniting in her eyes.

They stopped for lunch on Indian School Road. Scooter explained the housing arrangements and the role Mrs. Riley would play as nurse and chaperone.

For the first time Patricia laughed. "Chaperone? We're grown adults. Scooter, this isn't the age of Queen Victoria."

"It's a minister's house. We can't have our bachelor minister hosting a beautiful woman as his house guest. Don't worry, Mrs. Riley is a jewel. We'll have plenty of time to be alone together. I've kept my schedule as light as possible this week."

Patricia found Mrs. Riley as kind and friendly as Scooter had promised. She helped her get unpacked and her clothes hung on hangers and piled neatly in drawers. She checked over her medication schedule and took charge of monitoring it. Scooter waited impatiently in the living room for Patricia to reappear. She came out dressed in sports clothes looking more relaxed.

"I can't believe this house, Scooter. It's breathtaking. Here I imagined you living in some poor parsonage with chintz curtains and no rug on the floor. You must have a wealthy congregation to get a manse like this."

"It isn't a manse, Patricia. It's mine."

"Yours? How in the world did you get it? I mean, you know what I mean. I thought ministers were poor."

"I hit it big in the numbers, Patricia."

"You always said that some day your ship was going to come in," Patricia said.

"I know, I always thought my ship was the *Titanic* but it turned out to be the *Queen Mary*."

The week was spent like a teenager's summer vacation. They ate out every night going to the Emperor's Garden for Chinese food, to the old west steak barbeque at Pinnacle Peak Patio, to the costume bazaar at Bobby McGees where the waiters and waitresses dress like Superman, Zorro, Wonder Woman, Cinderella and a host of other fictional characters. They had Sunday brunch at the Phoenix Country Club and danced till midnight at the Arizona Biltmore. One afternoon they went to the zoo and another was spent at the Botanical Gardens getting a mini-lecture on the varieties of cactus plants indigenous to Arizona.

The days passed like lightning. Mrs. Riley was ecstatic about Patricia's visible improvement. The elders reported that the rumor mill was quiet save for the ladies who were titillated by another prospect of a serious romantic interest in Scooter's life.

The night before Patricia was scheduled to return home, they splashed in the pool in a moonlight swim and then went to the Jacuzzi for one last immersion in the steaming cauldron.

"Scooter, we've talked about everything in the world this week. My illness, my divorce, my children . . . everything but us. What about us? Am I just a counseling case or do we have a future? Tell me the truth. No pastoral platitudes."

"I've always wanted a future with you, Patricia. I've been waiting all these years, hoping against hope, being afraid to hope for some kind of invisible hand to bring us together. Now it happens, but there are obstacles in our path."

"What obstacles?"

"Apart from the fact that you are not divorced yet there is an obstacle that no law court can handle. I'm a Christian, Patricia, and I can never marry someone who doesn't share my faith."

"That's no problem, Scooter. I can't wait to join your church. I love to listen to your sermons. The one you preached on Sunday was just for me wasn't it?"

"Yes . . . I guess it was pretty obvious," Scooter said.

Scooter had preached from the Old Testament. His text was Jeremiah 31:15, "A voice was heard in Ramah, lamentation, and bitter weeping; Rachel weeping for her children refused to be comforted for her children because they *were* not."

"But you don't get faith simply by signing on a dotted line. The evangelists of this world to the contrary, you don't get it by making a decision either. You can decide to dedicate your life to something or decide to join a church, but you can't just push a button and decide to believe something unless you already believe it in the first place. Neither can you borrow from someone else's faith. Real faith must be your own."

"I understand that, Scooter. And I know you're afraid that I'm believing in you instead of God. Maybe I am. But right now you are the one who is showing God to me. Maybe the faith I have isn't quite pure, but I'm close. I know it doesn't measure up to your faith but you have no right to judge me."

"You must be feeling better. I see those cat's eyes shining again. I'm not trying to judge you. It wouldn't surprise me if you had a more pure faith than I do. If you tell me that you have faith I would not deny it. I just don't want to push you into something that you're doing merely to please me. That does happen, you know. But faith is too precious to get all mixed up with feelings of romance and all that. I am not Jesus. I would let you down, disappoint you, make you mad and cause your eyes to blaze."

"Look, Scooter, this is no rebound thing. We've been at it too long for that. Now tell me, do we have a future together or not?"

Scooter's chest tightened. Something inside wanted to burst forth saying, "Yes. Yes! We have a future. The rest of our lives. This is my dream come true, my fantasy realized." Scooter repressed the impulse. Instead he said, "There is another obstacle. After all these years . . . I have fallen in love. Really fallen in love. I can't deny it. Not to you, not to myself, not to anyone. Her name is Pamela Green. I want to marry her." Tears flooded

Scooter's eyes as he made the painful revelation to Patricia, and to himself.

Patricia's face clouded. Her lower lip began to tremble and a twitch in her face made her words sound distorted, strained. "Oh, Scooter. Scooter. I should have known. I felt something strange, something distant in you since we met at the airport. I should have guessed. I assumed it was just an awkwardness about being together. It's been like you've been with me, but not all the way with me."

She started to laugh. First a nervous giggle, then a belly laugh that tottered precariously on the edge of hysteria. "This is a good one. But it's OK—really, it's fine." She tweaked Scooter's nose and said, "I love you, you dope. I've always loved you and I'm sure I always will. But I know—and I've always known—what you're just finding out. We couldn't be married for five minutes. But I can still love you and you've got to promise to be my own special minister."

"That's an easy promise to make."

"Great. Now let's get out of this hot tub before it turns us into a couple of lobsters. You can put me on the plane tomorrow and grimace, saying, 'Here's looking at you, kid!'"

Patricia boarded the plane the next morning looking and acting like a whole woman. Even her fingernails were growing back, showing little sign of being gnawed in nervous anxiety. Scooter visited the sanctuary that night in the cover of darkness, again prostrating himself on the chancel rug, this time to offer a trinitarian prayer of thanksgiving.

The flight from New York was late. Scooter paced back and forth in the waiting room, checking the monitor screen overhead for changes in the estimated time of arrival of United flight #357. Finally, the digits changed and the screen announced that the plane had landed.

Pamela took her time getting off the plane. She stayed in her seat when the L10-11 pulled up at the gate while the other passengers crammed into the aisles, jockeying for position to deplane. She was anxious about her meeting with Scooter and masochistically prolonged the moment of encounter. She was no stranger to disappointment and had passed the week in New York bracing herself for whatever awaited her. Finally, she let out a sigh, clutched her purse and rose to leave the plane.

Scooter was counting the passengers as they came into the building. Already he was in the nineties, growing alarmed, panicked inside at the thought that Pamela might not be aboard. *Where is she? She always flies first class. She should be out here by now.*

Scooter saw her. She was casual, walking nonchalantly into the building. Forgetting his public demeanor as a clergyman, he broke into a run, rushing toward her and sweeping her from her feet, swinging her around and around like a madman. When they stopped whirling, he kissed her; not a gentle touch of the lips, but a strong, passionate, prolonged kiss.

"Richard!" Pamela gasped. "What will people think?"

"They'll probably think there's a crazy minister running around Sky Harbor like a thirteen-year-old kid in love. Who cares? I love you, Pamela. I don't care if the whole world knows it. I want the whole world to know it!"

That evening Scooter made reservations for the two of them at Gregory's. He spoke privately with the maitre d', making special arrangements ahead of time for dinner. The restaurant featured a delicate continental cuisine with an ornamental European decor complimented by a strolling French violinist. The violinist sang the patrons' requests with a lilting air, his accent softening the harsh edges of American ballads and adding his own charming mystique to the lyrics.

As soon as Scooter and Pamela were seated, the man strolled by and began singing "The Song from Moulin Rouge."

Pamela blushed at the merrymaker and said, "Scooter, how did you arrange that? It's my favorite."

"Should I squint my eyes and put a tic in my smile and say, 'Play it again, Etienne?'"

They ordered Carre D'Agnean Provencale for two, garnished with mint jelly and spinach souffle. The maitre d' sent the wine steward with a bottle of Puligny Montrachet Bouchard per instructions. During the main course the musician strolled by again and did a gallicized version of "Mona Lisa." Again Pamela blushed.

"What's next on your surprise list, Scooter?"

"Just wait and see what they sing during dessert."

Scooter ordered chocolate mousse and insisted that Pamela have strawberries Romanoff. When the waiter brought the desserts to their table the violinist started moving in their direction. Scooter's romantic nature was plainly visible in Pamela's dessert dish. Atop the most prominent strawberry, the capstone of the lot, was a glittering ring, the platinum band planted in its center. The gesture made a pauper of Prince Romanoff and his exotic strawberries.

Scooter reached over and plucked the ring from its mounting and dried the band with his linen napkin. He slipped the ring on Pamela's finger at the precise moment the violinist began to play the "Anniversary Waltz." By now the patrons at nearby tables were gaping at them and at the end of the song burst into spontaneous applause. They urged the newly engaged couple to dance. Again the violinist played, this time a medley of the three songs the maitre d' had earlier instructed him to play. The patrons were on their feet watching Scooter waltz Pamela across the floor.

Scooter hadn't counted on public participation in his carefully orchestrated engagement, but now it was too late. Already a champagne toast was being made to them by older patrons reaching back into their own nostalgia, experiencing a fresh vicarious rekindling of faded romance.

When they left the restaurant to the smiles of the other patrons, the maitre d', the waiters, and the violinist, they had the first conflict of their betrothal. Scooter wanted to drive to the desert and sit in the moonlight, prolonging his enchanted evening come true. Pamela wanted to rush to her apartment and call her mother and father. "We can drive to the desert after we talk to them."

The debate was over. The hen started to peck and Scooter had to adjust the scenario of the play he had enacted on his pillow the night before. He had not planned for a commercial break in the drama but neither had he figured on Pamela's having her own script. Already she was the producer and Scooter merely the director.

Racquel's swollen stomach was a nagging reminder to Johnny of increased financial pressure. She would not be able to continue working much longer and every time they were together she talked about a new apartment. Johnny had to make more money. A friend had planted the idea of opening an independent insurance agency with Johnny, inviting him in as a full partner. The venture was rich with promise and high in growth potential but it required a capital investment from Johnny of thirty thousand dollars.

He approached Jack on the matter. "Dad, I have a golden opportunity. Kenny Barker wants me to open up an insurance agency with him here in Briarwood."

"What's wrong with the job you have?"

"It's fine, Dad. But there really isn't much chance for me to move up in the organization. I'd like to try it on my own."

Jack Kramer was attacked by mixed feelings, an ambivalence born on the one hand by his desire to keep Johnny in his own organization, and on the other hand by his admiration of his son's spirit, his desire for independence.

"John, you know I admire the entrepreneural spirit, but get to the big question, what's the ticket? Give me the numbers."

"Thirty thousand. For thirty thousand I'm a full partner and there's no chance we'll be under-capitalized."

"We'll see what kind of an entrepreneur you are. I'll tell you what I'll do. I'll put up half. Fifteen grand. You get the other half."

"That's terrific. Fair deal. More than fair, Dad. I'll come up with the rest. When can I get the fifteen from you?"

"As soon as you show me your fifteen."

Johnny's task was cut in half but his prospects were all but eliminated. He couldn't think of another person in the world to ask, except one. He boarded a morning flight for Chicago and exactly one hour and ten minutes later the stewardess was intoning their arrival at O'Hare. Johnny took a cab to the merchandise district, making a futile attempt at conversation with the surly cab driver. "How are the Blackhawks doing this year?"

"Dunno, I don't follow basketball."

Johnny sat back in disbelief. How could a Chicago cab driver not know that the Blackhawks were Chicago's entry in the National Hockey League, he wondered. The petulant cabbie flipped the meter off in front of the office building and mumbled the fare. Johnny's appointment with Leah's father was scheduled in twenty minutes.

Frank Labans's secretary announced Johnny's arrival.

"Mr. Labans, your son-in-law is here to see you."

Johnny's father-in-law appeared at his office door and gave him a warm welcome.

"Johnny, it's good to see you. I'm sorry we don't get together more often. This business really keeps me hopping. Sit down. How's Leah?"

"Leah's doing great. Everything is copacetic."

"Copacetic? I trust that means something good."

"Sorry," Johnny laughed. "I guess that's a bit of Pittsburghese. Just an expression we use like 'hunky dory.' It means everything is A-OK."

"What can I do for you, Johnny?"

Johnny settled into a lengthy explanation of the business venture stressing the potential of the partnership to advance their income so that Leah wouldn't have to work. He appealed to a father who was suffering guilt pangs for neglecting his daughter, but he was careful not to suggest such an explicit accusation. Johnny told him of Jack's offer to put up half the capital, subtly weaving a net of male competition. If Frank declined he would look like a piker to his daughter. Johnny was scoring heavily on Frank's bruised conscience.

Frank retained a remarkable composure of paternal dignity outwardly, though inside he felt like he was being psychologically mugged. "Sure, Johnny. The fifteen thousand is no sweat. It's a great idea. Give me a couple of days to liquidate some things and I'll send the check in the mail. Tell Leah it's a gift from her father."

"No gifts, Frank. I'm asking for a loan. I'll pay you back."

"Not this time, Johnny. This one's a gift. Nothing but the best for my daughter."

Frank's sudden gesture took Johnny by surprise. It took Frank by surprise too but his impulsive statement was the only way he could turn the tables on Johnny. It was a fifteen-thousand-dollar salve for his conscience, an expensive investment to repurchase his pride. Now Johnny was psychologically, if not financially, in debt to him.

For the return flight to Pittsburgh Johnny exchanged his coach ticket for first class. He drank his scotch without giving a thought to psychology. He had his grubstake and it was buying him independence.

The check came in the mail five days later. Leah shared in Johnny's celebration. They went out to dinner and recaptured a few hours of love. Leah liked the new spirit she saw in her husband. Thoughts of adoption had receded with the more urgent task of salvaging a stagnant marriage. She viewed this night as a turning point, a new beginning, with Johnny a free spirit again, out from under the shadow of Jack Kramer.

Racquel saw it in much the same way. It meant a new two-bedroom apartment and a paramour who was breaking free of the ties that were binding him.

In April Johnny received a letter from Scooter.

Dear Roomie,

It's time for you to return a favor. I'm calling in my marker. I crossed the Atlantic Ocean to be best man at your wedding. Now it's your turn. I want you to be the first I invite to my wedding. Yes, your old buddy is going to take the step. All things come to them what waits. My bride is Pamela Green. It's a long story and I can't wait to tell you all about it. If you can make it I'll fill in all the details by phone and send your plane tickets. This is really not an invitation but a mandate from heaven. Get you to the church on time. I'm sending an invitation to Jack and Charlie. Tell Charlie she was wrong, I did find a woman dumb enough to marry me. Tell her I said our secret romance is off and to eat her heart out.

Love,
Scooter

Johnny showed the invitation to Leah. His eyes were welling up with tears. "Isn't it something? After all these years he asks me to be his best man. Mama, we're going on a trip to Arizona."

Arizona was unbearably hot in the summer of 1973. Scooter hardly noticed. The church was buzzing about the wedding and all the arrangements were made. A small army of volunteers were attending the reception details. The reception was to be held in the large fellowship hall in the building adjacent to the sanctuary. Scooter's ladies corps had the menu planned, the punch bowl and the hors d'oeuvres orchestrated. Everything was in order for what the women regarded as the church's answer to the Cinderella ball. Pamela's parents flew into town a week before the ceremony. The Kramers, four of them, arrived two days before the wedding. Scooter had reserved rooms at Camelback Inn for them.

Scooter had hoped for a small intimate wedding but the excitement of the congregation made that impossible. The day of the event saw over a thousand people in the sanctuary craning their necks for a glimpse of the new first lady of the church. When Pamela appeared there was a ripple of sighs moving through the congregation. She was radiant in her pastel dress standing next to Dr. Evans. The wedding ceremony was expanded from the standard brief liturgy into a full worship service, including two choral anthems and a homily from Dr. James Burbick who flew from Philadelphia to perform the ceremony.

Later, at the reception, Scooter had a chance to speak privately with Leah. "How are things in Briarwood, Leah?"

"Sounds like an Irish ballad, Scooter. The next line should be 'Is that little brook still leaping there?'" Leah answered. "But to answer your question; things are fine at home. It hasn't all been rosy, we've had our ups and downs but we're making it all right. Since Johnny is opening the new agency things have gone much better. We had a couple of stormy years and, to tell you the truth, I was afraid for a while that maybe Johnny was involved with another woman."

Scooter's eyebrows arched, "Another woman? Did you ask him about it?"

"No, no. Oh, Scooter, I shouldn't have said that. I've never said that to anyone. For some crazy reason it just popped out of my mouth. Please don't breathe a word of it. Johnny would have apoplexy if he thought I was running to you about these things. He just kept coming home at night later and later and was acting funny. And he started drinking too much. He said it was just business pressures, and it probably was, because since his new job he has been his old self again. I'm probably just paranoid because we can't have children."

"Have you thought of adopting?" Scooter asked.

"Yes, that was the center of our trouble. I was pushing hard for adoption but Johnny ended up refusing. He simply doesn't want any children."

"Would you like me to talk to him about it, Leah?"

"Oh, no. Please don't ever bring that up to him. It's a hot spot with him. I've said way too much already. I sound like a typical fretful housewife. Things are really fine, Scooter. Please don't give it another thought."

"OK, but if you need help, you holler. Will you promise me that?"

"Sure, Scooter. I will. I really will. I promise."

Scooter had a month's vacation. The first two weeks were given to a honeymoon cruise. The couple went directly to Sky Harbor Airport after the reception and flew to Tampa, Florida. Their wedding night was spent in the bridal suite of Don Cesar resort hotel at Saint Petersburg Beach. The next morning they sailed out of Tampa bound for Cartagena, Colombia, the San Blas Islands, Cristobal, and Balboa in Panama; then on to Acapulco before sailing into port at Los Angeles.

The second part of the honeymoon followed a transcontinental flight to Boston. Scooter rented a car at Logan Airport and drove to the North Shore. He had rented a cottage on the peninsula jutting out from Ipswich, looking across the water to Plum Island, just a few miles from Pamela's family residence. They had lunch in Gloucestor savoring the fried smelts that had just arrived on the Italian fishing boats. They watched the salty old-timers mending their nets on the pier next to the restaurant in sight of the cold, unseeing eyes of the statue of the sea captain leaning into the pilot's wheel attired in a "Sou' wester." They spent a day in Boston and boarded the U. S. *Constitution*. Scooter indulged his fancy for Melville with a side trip to New Bedford and Martha's Vineyard. The whaling museum at New Bedford sparked visions of Queequeg sharpening his harpoon and Starbuck pleading with Ahab to abandon his maniacal and ungodly quest.

Their whirlwind trip ended with a flight from Logan Airport to Phoenix where they spent the remaining days of Scooter's vacation opening wedding presents and transforming the bachelor residence into a home.

Johnny's business continued to prosper and he managed what few men are able to do, he sustained a life of the bigamist, keeping two women satisfied, maintaining two residences, living two lives.

In August the baby was born. Johnny was not with Racquel when she delivered. She still had no husband, but she had a son. She christened him Joseph.

Racquel took some of the financial pressure off by leaving Joseph at a day-care center while she returned to the stenographer pool at the plant. She loved the apartment and doted on Joseph but was less than satisfied with settling for the permanent role of mistress. Joseph needed a full-time father and Racquel was determined to secure one for him.

As the seventies were passing, Racquel's frustration level accelerated. Johnny's promises to divorce Leah were no more substantial than his earlier promises to Leah to adopt a child. In the fall of 1978 Racquel turned once more to her only potent weapon, her fertile womb. She threw away her pills and prayed to the virgin that her lucky number might show up on the wheel of Vatican roulette. The rabbit died in November giving her opportunity to brighten Johnny's Christmas holidays with a new announcement.

The week before Christmas Johnny stopped at the apartment. He was in a festive mood, laden with packages for under the tree. Joseph hugged him, beaming with pleasure at the wrapped boxes on the floor. "Uncle Johnny! Gee whiz, so many presents. Are they all for me?"

"No, Joey. Some of them are for your mother, but there are plenty there for you." Johnny tousled the boy's hair and wrestled him on the couch. "You'd better be good though or you'll get a lump of coal in your stocking."

"I'll be good, Uncle Johnny. Will Santa bring me more presents?"

"Sure, if you listen to your mother."

Racquel enjoyed the sight of the two of them playing. This was her moment, while Johnny was in such high spirits, to make her announcement.

"Joey, you go on and play now. I have to talk to Uncle Johnny," she said.

When Joey left the room Racquel spoke to Johnny.

"It looks like you're stuck on him a little bit."

"I am. I'm really glad we had him. It's super to have a son. I just wish we could be together all the time and we could stop this 'Uncle Johnny' crap."

"Would you like to have a daughter too?"

"The king's choice, huh, Racquel? Sure I'd love to have a daughter but you know that's out of the question."

"Is it, Johnny?"

Johnny squirmed, noting the glint in her eyes.

"Now don't start getting any funny ideas. We can't have any more kids."

Racquel managed a coy smile, "Too late, Johnny."

Johnny stiffened. "What do you mean 'too late'?"

"I mean there's one on the runway and one in the hangar. You know, one on the table and one in the oven. It happened again. I'm pregnant, almost three months."

"Don't joke around. You know better than that."

"I'm not joking. I've had the test and everything. I don't know how it happened, but it did. Don't worry so much. We managed before and we can do it again. Think of Joey. You don't want him to go through life an only child. He'll be thrilled to pieces."

This time there was no angry scene. Racquel had guessed right. Johnny was settling into his role as father and quasi-husband. He left the apartment in good spirits, secretly proud that he was going to be a father again.

His business was now established, and even the thought of Racquel's taking another leave of absence did not trouble him. His cash flow was solid and he had stayed away from high risk investments. He had even recovered much of the original equity of his house, steadily erasing his tracks which Jack had not discovered.

Leah was not so naive as to miss the signals around her. By this time it was almost common knowledge in Briarwood that Johnny had another woman. The rumor was widespread that he had fathered a child by a mistress in Millport. It was a juicy tidbit, chewed and swallowed with delight at bridge parties, the bowling league, and whispered between husbands and wives in the bedroom community.

Leah noticed an abrupt hush in conversations when she walked into rooms. She could feel the people whispering about her behind her back, but she fought an inner war with herself to dismiss such telltale signs as the work of an overwrought imagination. Johnny had been sweet, even suggesting that she quit working so they could have more time to do things together.

Again Racquel's stomach began to swell, and her courage grew with it. She could feel the baby kicking inside her and took it as an omen to put her bold plan into action. She had seen it done in the movies and on television countless times. She spread out an assortment of magazines on the table along with construction paper, scissors, and paste. She added a bit of melodrama to her work by donning plastic gloves from the kitchen. She was, she was certain, going to commit the perfect crime; her ultimate act of revenge against Leah, a woman she had never met and had only seen from a distance. Racquel's view of Leah was colored by Johnny's chronic complaining about her nagging and her lackluster performance in the Briarwood boudoir. She conceived of Leah as a wicked woman who had a stranglehold on Johnny. Racquel's act would be heroic, a noble gesture designed to liberate Johnny from his chains. She had to think of it that way.

She began snipping letters, large block letters from various space-ads in the magazines. When she found the letters she needed she pasted them on the construction paper until they spelled out a message.

YOUR HUSBAND HAS A
MISTRESS AND A
CHILD.
A FRIEND.

She trimmed the construction paper to fit inside a plain envelope and drove to Briarwood to post it. She had already addressed the envelope to Leah, using a typewriter from another department at Millport Steel. She dropped it in the mail slot of the Briarwood post office knowing that the act was irretrievable. It was done, finished. Now she could sit back and await the flying sparks.

The next afternoon Leah Kramer turned in the driveway after work, pulled on the emergency brake, reached for her purse and stepped out of the car. Her mind was still on a problem she had with a patient at the hospital. She walked to the front door with the house key in her right hand while she lifted the top cover from the mailbox with her left hand. She carried the small bundle of mail inside the house and placed it on the dining room table. Without thinking, she went through her ritual of changing clothes and fixing herself a cup of coffee before sitting down to open the mail. She never tired of the daily task, seeing the mail as a kind of surprise package waiting to be opened. She savored the routine, holding off a few minutes like a child saving a delectable piece of candy.

Today, as always, she sorted through the stack, separating Johnny's business letters, bills, magazines, and junk mail. She saw a letter addressed to her in the familiar handwriting of an old friend bearing a Racine, Wisconsin postmark. She also noticed a plain envelope with her name typed on it with no return address. It bore a Briarwood postmark. She opened the letter from Racine, smiling to herself as she read the breezy epistle from her girl friend. Still smiling she picked up the other envelope and slit it open with her sword-replica stainless steel letter opener. She looked at the message printed out in the cryptic letters and froze.

She dropped the crude construction paper notice like it was something alive, something that could sting. She put both elbows on the table, her arms rigidly upright with clenched fists shaking convulsively. The thing before her was obscene, a vile and loathsome piece. She let out a primal scream and began pulling her hair.

She jerked herself to her feet shouting hysterically, "No! No! No!" She grabbed the paper savagely and started ripping it. She carried the torn pieces to the bathroom and flushed them down the commode. Watching the wretched block letters disappear into the hidden sewers below, she grasped the edge of the sink, stumbling weakly, weaving back and forth over the basin, whimpering now in measured sobs, her eyes shut to blot out the nightmare.

When she opened her eyes she saw her reflection in the mirror. She was revulsed by her image—her hair wildly askew, eyes puffy and bloodshot. She looked half-crazed like a wounded animal. She began talking to the image in the mirror, panting heavily: "Con—trol your—self, Leah. Get—control—now—" She grabbed a washcloth from the towel rack and held it under the cold water tap until it was saturated. She pressed it to her face feeling a mild shock, then dabbed at her cheeks and eyes to restore color to her pallid face.

The regular rhythm of her breathing returned and she composed herself, running a comb through her hair. She could still feel her pulse racing and the nauseous stab in the pit of her stomach provoked by the malignancy she had flushed down the toilet. Her thoughts were jumbled, scattering in every direction by a wild, chaotic stream of consciousness. One lucid thought kept registering in her brain. *I must talk to somebody. I must talk to somebody.* Without human contact she feared she would slip over the edge of uncontrolled hysteria, into hopeless insanity.

She walked to the bedroom and picked up her address book and began leafing through its pages.

The intercom in Scooter's office buzzed and Mrs. Frances said, "Dr. Evans, you have a call from Mrs. Leah Kramer on line 2 and it's collect."

"Put it through, Mrs. Frances," Scooter said, his stomach going rigid with alarm.

"Scooter . . . ?"

"Yes, Leah, what's the matter?" The tone of Leah's voice confirmed Scooter's alarm, revealing instantly that something dire had happened.

Leah was unable to answer. She tried to speak but all she could manage were unintelligible sobs. Scooter let her cry, whispering words of consolation into the phone.

"It's all right, Leah. Don't force it. Take your time."

Finally she gained control of her voice. She began relating the story, first slowly, then in rapid bursts of words.

"What do I do, Scooter? Do I confront Johnny with it? What if it's just a crank letter? Oh, Scooter, I know it isn't. It's true. It's all true. I've been lying to myself and I feel like a complete fool."

"Think about it, Leah. If it's true, Johnny will surely deny it. If it's false, he'll deny it as well. You have no hard evidence. Even the note is gone now. I know it is real and terribly incriminating on the surface. But there is still that slim thread of hope that it could be a cruel joke, a crank letter from somebody acting on unsubstantiated rumor. I get letter from crazies all the time, from people who give me inside dope on the time and place of the return of Christ and things like that. Some of my mail sizzles with hate. There are lots of people out there with nothing better to do than to send hate mail to their 'pen pals.' Maybe that's all it is. I know it's serious, very serious, but we can't leap to the worst of all possible conclusions."

"You're right. But still I have to know. One way or the other I must know for sure."

"Would you like me to call Johnny and hit him with it head-on? I can usually tell when he's being straight with me."

"No. I appreciate your willingness to get involved but I want to know *before* there is any confrontation. I don't want Johnny to have an inkling of an idea that I suspect anything. I'll find out. I'll figure out a way. Maybe I'll follow him in the car or set up some kind of trap for him."

"I'd advise against that, Leah. Playing private detective on matters you're intimately involved with can put scars on your soul you'd never dream of," Scooter said.

"But what else can I do? I have to know."

"I understand that. You probably won't like what I'm about to say. It will sound cheap and crude but I'm going to ask you to trust me for a minute. This is not the first time I've had to deal with something like this. I have a rule, Leah. If I need information or any important job done, I go with the pros. The do-it-yourself route is usually a ticket to bungle-ville. I soberly and seriously recommend that you hire a private investigator. This is messy business and they're the pros in delving into this sordid type of thing. Let them handle the cloak and dagger stuff. You don't need it. If Johnny has a mistress and a child somewhere, a detective will come up with hard evidence, evidence that will not only answer the questions you need answered, but if worse comes to worse, could be very helpful to you in the long run."

"It makes sense, but frankly it sounds tacky. I never heard of a minister who called in the dirt mongers."

"You've heard of one now, Leah. Again, they're the pros. They're not dirt mongers. Dirt-merchants? Perhaps. Dirt-tracers? For sure. It may sound tacky, but not nearly as tacky as someone sending you that letter. Not all private detectives are seedy characters trying to come up with the money to pay the light bill. There are competent professionals who are quite respectable. If you'd like, I can check my sources here to see if they know someone reputable in the Pittsburgh area."

"I'd feel better about it if you would do that."

"OK. Call me back tomorrow afternoon. In the meantime I'll

see what I can find out. And, Leah, call collect again, unless you want Johnny asking questions when the phone bill comes in."

"OK, and, Scooter?"

"Yes, Leah?"

"Please pray for me."

"It's already on my list. You can count on it."

Scooter traced the name of the Pendleton Associates, Private Investigators located in Pittsburgh and passed the recommendation on to Leah. Leah looked up their ad in the Yellow Pages and noted that the agency specialized in civil and criminal surveillance, accident investigations, and industrial security. The ad promised "Coverage by former F.B.I. agents." Her telephone call was handled by Rusty McAllis who scheduled an appointment with Leah for the next day at the hospital.

Rusty McAllis was in his late fifties, his once sandy hair now peppered with gray. He was stocky with a granite chin and bull neck, his body still showing signs of years of rigorous physical conditioning. He was not particularly warm but he was polite and well-mannered. His shoes were cordovan, buffed to a high gloss on the toes. He questioned Leah about the particulars, asking for the photograph of Johnny he had instructed her to bring, plus details about Johnny's office location, a description of his car, his habits, the establishments he visited frequently, and other matters. What impressed Leah was his obvious thoroughness. She was fidgety and impatient to get the investigation under way.

"When will you start?" she asked.

"I already have," McAllis replied. "The more accurate data I get from you the easier my surveillance will be. The more information I can gather here the less time and money, your money, my time, will be wasted in the field. The better the plan the easier the task is my motto."

Johnny made it easy for McAllis. On the first day of the surveillance Johnny left the insurance office at precisely 3:09 P.M. McAllis noted it on a clipboard sheet resting on the front seat of his nondescript sedan. His partner for this task was Shirley Chichester. McAllis liked to do surveillance work on a team basis so that he had one set of eyes fixed on the mark at all times. He preferred a female partner because a man and a woman riding in a car together arouse less suspicion than two men.

For a surveillance operation, the first five minutes after contact is crucial. Which way will the mark go? Will he be walking or taking a car? Will he drive fast or slowly? Are there distinctives about his car—a unique fingerprint like a cracked side window, a bumper sticker, a weird antenna? Most importantly, does the car have a right hand outside mirror? Are the driving habits of the mark erratic? Does he weave in and out of lanes in traffic? Leah had supplied the answers to most of these questions anticipating for McAllis which direction Johnny would move if he were headed for Millport from the office.

She was right. Johnny pulled out of the parking lot in his 1978 Pontiac Grand Prix and headed south toward Millport. McAllis was relieved to note that the Grand Prix had no right-hand outside mirror. The first five miles posed a minor problem. Johnny was driving the back way to Millport over a country road where McAllis had to lag far behind to avoid suspicion. A rubber magnetized decal was attached to the side of McAllis's car bearing the printed words Corps. of Engineers.

Avoiding detection was not McAllis's problem on the country road. The problem was keeping Johnny in sight. He knew the winding road by heart and had a heavy foot, taking the curves like a race driver. He maintained a half-mile lead over the surveillance team, which McAllis tried to close when they came closer to the intersection of Route 51. The team was lucky that a heavy flow on the four-lane strip kept Johnny hung up for over thirty seconds at the stop sign. Rusty and Shirley pulled up right behind him, careful to avoid looking at Johnny lest eye contact in his rearview mirror gain him a foothold of recognition. Johnny pulled out onto Route 51 and McAllis was behind him a few seconds later.

Johnny reached a traffic light, pulling into the left lane preparing for the turn-off of the four-lane highway onto the ridge road to Millport. McAllis stayed in the right lane almost next to him but one car behind and to the right. Rusty anticipated that Johnny would be turning left and he needed a bird dog, at least one car between Johnny and himself for the drive over the ridge. When the light changed green McAllis accelerated slowly, waiting for Johnny and two other cars to pull ahead of him in the left lane, then he swung over and fell in behind them. With the two-car shield momentarily in procession Rusty and Shirley both donned hard hats, metal helmets worn by engineers and other workers at Millport Steel.

Johnny had his left-turn signal on and made his move onto the ridge road. The car behind him did the same. The second car behind Johnny continued south on Route 51, leaving McAllis behind Johnny with a single bird dog between them. At the traffic light entering Millport the road ended in a *T* intersection. Johnny's left turn signal was blinking but the bird dog was turning right. For a quarter mile until the road widened to four lanes on Millport's main street McAllis was directly behind Johnny, hanging back from his bumper. Johnny took the right lane on Main Street giving McAllis a chance to pass him on the left and assume a front tail procedure.

McAllis saw Johnny's right turn signal blinking in his rear view mirror and watched him make his turn onto a side street. Now was the moment when McAllis's instincts and his cunning took over. He turned right at the next corner and followed the parallel street accelerating hard to the intersection. Shirley spotted Johnny cross the intersection continuing on the same street a block to their right. McAllis raced to the next stop sign and waited a few seconds. Johnny's Grand Prix didn't appear so McAllis made a right turn and moved to the next intersection. Shirley spotted Johnny's car across the street from an apartment building and Johnny walking toward the front entrance. McAllis drove through the intersection and parked the car at the curb, out of view of the apartment.

Rusty and Shirley took off their hard hats and removed the magnetized Corps. of Engineers decal from the car door and continued their surveillance on foot, separating before coming in view of the apartment. Shirley walked alone to the front entrance of the apartment and followed the arrows to the manager's office. She pretended to be inquiring about renting an apartment. The manager gave her a guided tour of the complex and showed her printed floor plans of one-bedroom, two-bedroom and efficiency apartments. She took her to the laundry area and to the garbage-incinerator. Shirley asked if she could see the inside of a two-bedroom apartment assuming that if Johnny's mistress had a child they would be renting a two-bedroom. She also made inquiries about restrictions against children. The manager was talkative, giving a full sales pitch of the advantages of the neighborhood, of the friendliness of the tenants, and "Yes, of course, children were permitted in the complex."

Rusty scouted the area across the street searching for a vantage point to snap photos of Johnny leaving the building. The street was lined with small commercial businesses. There was a shoe repair shop, a drugstore, a dry-cleaning establishment and a lunch room. He killed some time browsing in the drugstore and then went into the luncheonette, carrying a newspaper and a briefcase containing a camera with an adjustable long-range lens. The lunch room was at an angle from the entrance to the apartment, not more than fifty feet away.

Rusty took a seat at the table closest to the plate glass window looking out across the street. He looked at his watch. It was a few minutes after four and he was the only customer in the building. The waitress came to the table and asked if he wanted to order. "Can I still get a late lunch?"

The waitress smiled and said, "Sure, but it's almost time for an early dinner."

He ordered a bowl of soup, a hamburger, fries and coffee, spreading out the newspaper while he waited for his food. When he finished the meal he asked the waitress if he could sit there for a while and work on some business papers explaining that he had an appointment in Millport later that evening. She said it was fine and cleared the table. Rusty opened the briefcase and brought out a ledger book, yellow legal pad, and a calculator, arranging them on the table. He scribbled meaningless figures on the yellow pad and punched the calculator buttons for effect.

Again he called the waitress over and showed her the camera. "Have you seen one of these?"

"Looks like a camera to me," she said.

"It's Japanese. I just got the thing and I'm not exactly sure how it works."

Rusty picked up the camera, playing with it and talking about its mysteries to the waitress, all the while maneuvering it to a spot where it would be aimed directly at the apartment entrance. Once it was set up where he wanted it he changed the conversation and, ordering another cup of coffee, went back to the yellow pad and the calculator.

He saw Shirley leave and walk briskly up the street and around the corner to the car. A half hour later he hit paydirt. Johnny emerged from the entrance with a raven-haired woman dressed in a maternity smock, followed by a young boy. Rusty quickly pushed the shutter of the lens, silently clicking a series of shots. The woman took the little boy by the hand and followed Johnny across the street to his car. Rusty surreptitiously adjusted the angle of the camera, still playing with the calculator. Johnny opened the car door and leaned back to give Racquel a good-bye kiss. It was a short peck on the lips, but McAllis captured it on film.

When Johnny pulled away from the curb and Racquel and Joey disappeared back into the apartment building, Rusty casually closed the ledger book and returned his working articles to his briefcase. He folded up the paper, paid the bill, thanked the waitress and walked out. When he got back to his car he opened the door and said to Shirley, "Score!"

The next afternoon Leah called the detective agency and asked for Rusty McAllis. McAllis came on the line:

"We have it, Mrs. Kramer. I've got pictures of the meeting. Mr. Kramer, the woman—who is very pregnant, and the boy. We are gathering information on the woman and data on the child as well. We can continue the surveillance if you'd like, depending on how much hard evidence you want. Why don't we meet today and I'll show you what we have. You can decide then if you want us to continue."

The meeting was at 4:30. Rusty spread an assortment of pictures out in front of Leah and handed her a file folder containing the information he had gathered so quickly. Leah's shoulders slumped heavily. As she examined the photos her lips were pressed tightly together. Three of the photos were enlarged, blown up to show all of the details.

"I'm sorry, Mrs. Kramer. I'm sure this isn't pleasant."

"It's not your fault. I needed to be sure. Look at her, the slut! A cozy couple aren't they?" Bitterness dripped from Leah's lips. "I think this is enough. May I have this one to take with me?" Leah asked, selecting the enlarged photo of Johnny kissing Racquel by the car door.

"You can have them all. I have the negatives on file."

"Just this one is all I want for the present. I'll contact you if I want anything else done."

Leah extended her hand to Rusty McAllis and said, "Thank you, Mr. McAllis. You are certainly a professional. I respect that a great deal."

Rusty shook hands with Leah and she left, clutching the photo that confirmed her fears.

Rusty felt a good sense of accomplishment, a sense of pride within. There were two things about his work that gratified him in the midst of the sordidness of it. He enjoyed the thrill of the hunt, the sense of satisfaction of tracking his quarry, getting information and pictures, and sneaking away with the mark having no idea he was caught. The second point of satisfaction came when he saw justice done. At heart Rusty McAllis was a cop, a man frustrated by too many arrests that failed to yield convictions. He took special delight in turning the tables in domestic cases like a man suing his innocent wife for divorce, kicking her out of the house and then conducting secret trysts with his lover. When McAllis had been able to nail these types he had the double pleasure of vindicating the innocent and catching the guilty, a combination all too rare in this world for his blood.

Leah went straight home, hid the photo, opened her mail and went about the methodical task of preparing dinner. Johnny came home a few minutes after six and greeted Leah warmly.

"Hi, Mama, how was your day?" Johnny was in a good mood, animated, and completely unsuspecting. He fixed himself a scotch to be downed hastily before dinner.

"I had a good day. How was yours?" Leah smiled.

"Great! Super! I closed another group account. We ought to celebrate this weekend. Go out to dinner or something."

"Let's, Johnny. It would be fun," Leah purred, carrying on the grand performance of her lifetime.

Johnny went out to the Red Fox Lounge around eight o'clock, announcing, "I'll be home early. How about a little party in our playpen, Mama?"

"No, tonight is definitely not the night. I have a big day tomorrow and I need to get to bed early. But, Johnny dearest, tomorrow night is the night. Your little Leah will become Lolita. I've got special plans for you for tomorrow night. I'll be the red-hot mama, the vamp of Briarwood. Tomorrow night we howl, OK?"

"OK? Are you kidding? What bug bit you? I can hardly wait."

"Don't worry, Johnny. I've been reading a very interesting story and I have some new tricks up my sleeve. I promise you that you won't be disappointed. My motto for tomorrow is 'everything goes!'" She smiled sweetly and watched him leave with stars in his eyes.

After breakfast the next morning Leah got up from the table to leave first. She kissed Johnny on the cheek, then darted her tongue in his ear saying, "Be ready for tonight, lover boy. It will be the night of delicious surprises. Think about it today. When you come home I want you to have horns like Mephistopheles."

"You keep talking like that and I won't be able to wait another five minutes."

"Good-bye, Johnny. I really have to go. You just wait for tonight."

Leah pulled out of the driveway and headed for Pittsburgh, but not for the hospital. At 9:00 A.M. she met with an attorney and initiated divorce proceedings. At 10:20 she was at the bank withdrawing every penny from the Kramers' joint savings account. Next she returned to the house and packed three suitcases full of clothes and her jewelry. She taped the enlarged photo of Johnny and Racquel on the headboard of their bed and added a one-word sign underneath it. "SURPRISE!" At 1:15 she was completing the concealment of her car in a rented garage. At 2:10 she arrived at Greater Pittsburgh Airport by taxi. At 2:45 she was in the air, winging her way to Chicago.

At 3:45 Chicago time Leah checked into the Palmer House and was led to her room by a bellhop pushing a hang closet on wheels bearing her three suitcases. As soon as she unpacked she reached for the phone and called her father's office filling him in on all that had happened. He insisted on meeting her for dinner at the hotel.

At dinner Leah's father was distraught, gushing with sympathy and fatherly words of advice. "What are you going to do, baby?" he asked.

"I'm going to nail him, Dad. I've arranged a two-week leave of absence with my supervisor while my attorney works on the preliminary papers and on getting Johnny out of the house. I never want to be under the same roof with him again. Never!"

"Do you need any money?"

"Not at the moment. I cleaned out our bank account this morning and tomorrow I go on a credit card shopping spree. But thanks for asking, you're a dear."

Mr. Labans was fuming inside, thinking of the fifteen thousand dollars that was surely down the drain.

"What about Johnny's business? Do you own any of it?"

"No, Dad. That's in Johnny's name. He insisted on that and dazzled me with a lot of legal talk about it that I didn't understand. I guess he was thinking ahead."

After Mr. Labans walked Leah to the elevator and said goodnight he went to the registration desk and arranged to have her room billed to him.

Leah entered her room and sat beside the bed and made a long-distance call.

Scooter and Pamela were just ready to step into the hot tub when the telephone rang.

"I'll get it," Scooter said, "it's probably for me." He walked inside the house and picked up the receiver, ending the strident ring. "Hello?"

"Scooter? It's Leah."

Leah rehearsed the events of the past few days thanking Scooter for his advice about hiring a private investigator.

"There's no more doubt, Scooter. I have pictures and everything, even of the little boy."

"Whew, that's a rough one, Leah. I'm sorry. Does Johnny know that you know yet?"

"I don't know. Probably. I'm in Chicago at the Palmer House. I left this afternoon and taped the photo on the bed. I never know what time he's going to come home, but I suspect he has already been there. He was eager to come home tonight. I made sure of that."

Leah promised to keep in touch with Scooter and ended the conversation.

Johnny stopped at the Red Fox Lounge on the way home. He was feeling good, buying drinks for his friends at the bar. At 5:45 he left saying, "Got to go, guys. The little mama is waiting for me."

Johnny turned the Grand Prix into the driveway and pressed the automatic garage door opener. He was surprised to see an empty space where Leah normally parked her car. He was not alarmed, assuming that she had gone to the store, maybe for a bottle of wine for their special evening together.

He picked up the *Pittsburgh Press* from the front stoop and entered the house. He went directly to the dining room and opened the liquor cabinet, selecting a bottle of Johnny Walker Red. After breaking the seal he poured himself a drink, fetched a single ice cube from the freezer, went into the living room and sat down in his favorite chair to read the paper. The thought struck him that it was odd Leah had nothing cooking in the oven for dinner and the table wasn't set. He brushed off the thought growing more excited at the idea that it was simply part of Leah's surprise. He kicked off his shoes and settled back to read the paper. He read the funnies first, a habit left over from childhood, then turned his attention to the sports section. The Pirates were in their usual spring slump that Johnny was certain would end with the hotter days of summer. *They'll be ready in the stretch,* he thought.

By 6:20 Leah was still not home and Johnny was getting hungry. He put the paper down and reached for the remote control box, switching on the television. He watched Bill Burns wrap up the news and turn it over to Bill Curry for the sports. At 6:30 he switched off the TV and headed for the bedroom to change.

He saw the photo as soon as he entered the room. He stood in place, stupified, the SURPRISE! sign leering at him. He inched slowly toward the bed as if the photograph would materialize if he startled it. Staring at the vivid print of Racquel and him he kept thinking, *How? Where? Who?* For a second he thought of ripping it from the bed, fast, before Leah came home and saw it. His mind repelled the obvious conclusion until he gazed again at the leering sign.

He turned abruptly and rushed to the closet door and opened it. It was empty. He was staring at a metal cylindrical bar that was naked, save for a few dangling wire hangers. Next he checked Leah's jewel box that was also empty except for a cruel scrap of paper that read, "Surprise again."

"My God. She's gone. She took off. She planned the whole thing," he said aloud. He went back to the photo and removed it from the headboard. "Geez," he said, "that was taken the day before yesterday." He realized instantly that Leah couldn't have followed him and done this. It had to be a professional. "Damn! She hired a private dick."

He took the picture and the sign and went to the garage and got in the car. He sat behind the wheel, thinking before turning on the ignition. *I've got to find her before she runs to Jack and Charlie with this. Dammit, she's probably already there.*

He started the engine and screeched out of the garage leaving a trail of burned rubber on the cement floor. He drove the short distance to his parents' home and slowly cruised past their driveway looking for Leah's car. *She's not there. Where the hell did she go?* He drove past the residence of Leah's friends and saw no sign of her car. Next he cruised the shopping center but still saw no trace of her.

His fear was turning into anger and he cursed Leah for her spiteful actions. "The hell with it," he said to the dashboard and turned his car toward Millport.

Racquel was surprised to hear Johnny's key in the lock at this hour and walked toward the door. Johnny entered the room, his face still ashen with shock.

"Johnny! What are you doing here? I didn't expect you. Joey, go in your room and play."

"It hit the fan, baby. Leah found out."

"How? When? What happened, Johnny?"

Johnny lifted the photograph for Racquel to see. "Here's what happened. Take a gander at this beauty."

"How did she get that? What did she say?"

"She didn't say anything. I haven't seen her since this morning. She took off. Cleaned out her closet and split. I don't know where she is. She taped the picture to the bed with this stupid sign." He held up the sign for Racquel to see.

A sudden bolt of fear sliced through Racquel. The similarity of style between the SURPRISE sign and the block-letter warning she had mailed to Leah was immediately apparent to her.

"Why in the world would she do a strange thing like that? Why all the dramatic props?" she asked.

"Who knows? I guess she wanted to make me suffer. She played it real cute. She must have already known last night. She was very cozy, teasing me about the great surprise she was going to give me. I wonder how she found out about us. Someone had to tip her off."

"Oh, Johnny, don't torment yourself about it. It could have been any one of a number of people. We honestly couldn't expect this to go on forever without some busybody getting wise. There must be scores of people here in Millport who know about us, and it's not like Briarwood is clear across the country from here. Some people just live to poke their noses into other people's business. It's a miracle we've gone this long without her finding out."

"Yeah, I guess you're right. I guess it really doesn't matter who it was. Unless . . ."

"Unless what, Johnny?"

"Unless it was someone I trusted. You know, already I find myself suspicious of my best friends."

"See what I mean about torture? You can't do that to yourself, sweetheart. Who knows, maybe no one tipped her off, maybe she found out all by herself."

"No way. That photograph is a professional job. She had a private detective," Johnny said.

"Maybe that's the answer. Maybe she was just getting suspicious and decided to hire a detective. Or maybe she followed you over here herself once and then hired a guy to check it out. It doesn't matter, baby. What matters now is you. You must be worried sick about your parents."

"That is going to be grim. Jack's going to have my butt in a sling."

"You poor dear. Johnny, you know that whatever happens I'll stand with you. You can depend on me. I love you, baby."

Johnny spent the night at the apartment. The next day he packed a suitcase and moved in with Racquel. That night, Charlie Kramer, with no knowledge of what was going on with her son, was admitted to Mercy Hospital, gravely ill.

The following morning Johnny's phone rang at the insurance office.

"John, what's going on at your house? I called ten times last night and again this morning and no one answered. Is your phone out of order?" It was Jack on the line.

"No, Dad. What's the matter?" Johnny asked.

"It's your mother. I had to put her in the hospital. She's very sick."

"What's wrong?"

"We don't know yet. They're running a lot of tests on her."

"Where is she?"

"Mercy Hospital. I'm going over there right now. You'd better come into town and meet me there."

"Sure, Dad. I'll leave right away."

Johnny's foot was vibrating on the accelerator. He was unable to get his nerves under control. He was terrified at the prospect of facing his father's questions at a time like this. *How am I going to tell him now? Where is Leah?* No answers came to him.

Jack was in the waiting room at the hospital, his face etched with grim lines of concern.

"How is she, Dad?" Johnny asked.

"It's bad, John. I just spoke to the doctor. The preliminary diagnosis is cirrhosis of the liver."

"What's it mean? How bad is it?"

"It means there is a hardening of the liver. There is too much connective tissue or something, a kind of fibrosis. They don't know how much damage has been done. The liver is a vital organ. This is very serious."

"Is she awake? Can I go up and see her?"

"She's out like a light right now. The nurses will call down here when she comes around."

Jack had forgotten Johnny's phone for the moment and didn't raise any more questions about it. Charlie regained consciousness for a few minutes just before noon. Johnny talked to her, then left her alone with Jack and waited in the hall for his father.

When Jack came out of the room Johnny was waiting.

"Let's go out and get some lunch, John. She'll probably stay asleep most of the afternoon."

At lunch Jack mentioned the phone again. "Where were you this morning?" he asked.

"I was out."

"At 6:45? Since when do you leave that early?"

"Dad, I don't know how to tell you this." Johnny's face flushed.

"Tell me what?" Jack said.

"I'm in big trouble. Leah left me."

"Leah left you! For God's sake, John, why?"

"It's my fault, Dad. There's another woman."

"You stupid idiot. You'd better get rid of your other woman fast, boy, and get Leah home."

"It's not that simple, Dad. And I'm not a boy. The other woman is pregnant, and I already have a son by her."

Jack dropped his fork. His face contorted into a mask of rage. He struggled to subdue the impulse to come out of his chair and smash his fist into Johnny's face. He spoke, finally, through clenched teeth. "Is this other woman married? Are you messing around with another man's wife?"

"No. Look, Dad, I never meant for all this to happen. The girl got pregnant and insisted on having the baby. I felt obligated to take care of her."

"How noble," Jack said. "Where is Leah?"

"I don't know. She left day before yesterday. When I got home she was gone. Her closet was empty and so was her jewel box. I haven't heard a thing from her."

"You will. You can bet on that. Well, you know what your mother would say, 'You played the music and now you dance to the tune.' "

"Yeah, I know. 'Go tell your troubles to a policeman,' " Johnny added.

Jack assumed an authoritarian air. His rage was dissipated and he resorted to his role of commanding officer and pragmatic problem-solver.

"Three things, John. One—you'd better get yourself a lawyer. Fast. Two—not one word of this to your mother. Three—if Leah divorces you, she gets the house. I paid for it. She deserves it."

Johnny rose from the table and extended his hand to his father as if he had just closed an agreement with a client. "It's a deal."

Jack shook his hand making them partners in the plan. It was more, by far, than Johnny had hoped for.

Johnny's lawyer advised him to move out of the house peacefully, aware that Leah had the upper hand on that aspect of the divorce settlement. Johnny cancelled his credit cards, but not before Leah ran up $3,000 in charges. Leah returned after two weeks. Johnny's things were cleaned out of the house and the two of them had no personal contact except at the divorce hearings. Johnny was docile throughout, not contesting the divorce suit.

Jack visited Leah at the house.

"Leah, you are still my daughter-in-law and Johnny is still my son. I know I can't undo what he has done to you, but I want you to know that I'll stand with you as much as I can. I have already insisted, and Johnny has agreed, that you get the house."

"I won't have any trouble making the mortgage payment."

"Mortgage payment? What mortgage payments? I paid for this house in full," Jack declared.

"I know. I just found out myself. I guess Johnny needed some extra money so he mortgaged the house several years ago. We still owe $10,000 on it."

"What about your share of the business?" Jack asked.

"I don't have a share in the business; Johnny owns it all."

"No, Leah. That can't be. I gave Johnny half of his capital investment and your dad put up the other half, didn't he?"

"Yes. He gave the money to me and I gave it to Johnny. Johnny put the business in his own name though."

"So. He stuck you with $10,000 on the house and your dad with $15,000 on the business. We'll see about that."

The next day Jack called Johnny to his office and confronted him about the $25,000. "What do you propose to do about it, John?"

"I guess I can keep paying on the mortgage until it's paid off. There's not much I can do about the other $15,000. That's all tied up in the business."

"You'd better think again. I don't care where it's tied up. That was Leah's money and you have to pay her back. It's part of the music, John. If you want your freedom it's going to cost you. One thing's sure. Leah is going to get the fifteen grand if I have to write her a check myself. But I'd advise you not to let it come to that."

The Camelback Community Church was growing fast. The membership swelled to over thirty-five hundred people under Scooter's ministry. He continued to publish popular books and his radio program was syndicated nationally to 150 cities. He was in great demand on the conference circuit and traveled with Pamela extensively.

On Easter Sunday, 1979, Scooter and Pamela were standing together at the church door after the service greeting the congregation. There were always scores of unfamiliar faces filing past him at the door since Scottsdale attracted so many vacationers. Easter added to the number. A lanky gentleman crowned with a white mane, obviously at least in his seventies, paused at the door and introduced himself. Scooter instantly recognized the name. It was a household word. The man was the chairman of the board of one of the few family-owned and family-controlled Fortune 500 megabusinesses.

"I am in town until Wednesday, Dr. Evans. I wonder if you would have time to meet me for lunch tomorrow or Tuesday."

Scooter agreed to meet him, feeling a familiar chill at the invitation, his mind snapping back to a lunch date with another white-maned lanky gentleman, Dr. H. L. M. Barton. Restaurants and church doors seemed to be the favorite site for the Invisible Hand to tap him on the shoulder.

They met for lunch at the Biltmore. Scooter's mysterious visitor got to the point quickly. "I know you are a busy man, Dr. Evans, and so am I, so I'll get down to business. My company spends millions of dollars each year for advertising, most of it for television commercials. I'm an old man, sir, and I'm also a Christian. Frankly I'm turned off by the electronic church with its tawdry programming and endless appeals for money. Don't get me wrong. I know air time is expensive and it's the only way for most to get the Christian message on the air."

"I think you're right," Scooter added. "The media is controlled by the secularist. The church doesn't seem to be able to compete."

"Yes. And in order to raise the money, these programs have to appeal to a broad base. It's just like secular television, if you want the ratings, which the sponsors look at, you have to buy the KISS principle, 'Keep it simple, stupid.' What I think we need to do the job is a quality program on prime time on the secular networks that will be both educational and inspirational. Everybody says it can't be done but I think it can."

Scooter was impressed with the man's boldness. He listened intently.

"You are old enough to remember the "Catholic Hour" with Bishop Fulton J. Sheen. His program was an enormous success. He proved that the concept will work if we have the right sponsor, the right format, and the right teacher."

"That was a long time ago, sir, and the public mood has changed. Programming has changed, and don't forget, Bishop Sheen was a Roman Catholic. The Catholic church is still by far the largest Christian denomination in America. When they elect a new pope the networks give detailed coverage. When the Presbyterian elect a new moderator there's hardly a peep."

"That's all true, Dr. Evans. But you are overlooking one thing. Need. There is a need for such a program. If you fill a need that people are feeling, and you do it right, there will always be a positive response. Now, as I was saying, we need three things: sponsor, format, and the man. I can take care of one of them. My company will be the sponsor. The format can be handled by a competent director. My problem has been to find the man. I've been studying this for over a year. I've gone to conferences, watched miles of videotape and hundreds of speakers in action. There is no doubt in my mind. You are the man."

The words rang in Scooter's ears provoking a weird connection to Nathan's indictment to King David, "Thou art the man," with Pilate's infamous *"Ecce Homo,"* pronounced over Christ, "Behold the man."

"I don't know," Scooter replied. "That's a major undertaking. I'd have to run that by my elders and know a lot more of the details, the time involvement, and that sort of thing before I could give you any kind of decision."

"Fair enough. I'll get back to you with all the details by June 15."

On July 4, Independence Day, the day commemorating the nation's birth in the north and the fall of Vicksburg under the siege of U. S. Grant in the South, Racquel Del Greco gave birth to a six-pound-fourteen-ounce baby girl. That same evening Charlie Kramer died, not knowing that she was twice a grandmother, not knowing that her prediction about the stork was only half right. The pointed-beak bird never found the Tara Wood house so he dropped off his packages in Millport. In the space of less than twenty-four hours Johnny experienced the birth of his daughter and the death of his mother, the cycle of life hitting him between the eyes.

Johnny spent most of the day driving between hospitals. He was in the room at Mercy Hospital when Charlie gasped her final breath and her mouth froze in an open position. Johnny kissed her on the forehead and left the room. He drove to McKeesport Hospital to break the news to Racquel.

Racquel was sitting up in bed watching television when Johnny came in. Dinah Shore was being interviewed by Barbara Walters on the screen. Johnny told Racquel the news and started to cry. "She never even knew she was a grandmother," he sobbed, while Racquel squeezed his hand.

"I never met her, Johnny. But I have the feeling we would have loved each other. She must have been quite a woman."

Johnny brightened. His emotions were on a roller-coaster ride. He started to laugh. "She was a pistol. Hard as nails on the outside, soft as mush on the inside."

Though it was after hours the nurse let Johnny have one more peek at the baby girl in the nursery. He peered at her through the glass partition. It was different from seeing Joey for the first time. This was his little girl and an enormous surge of pride and affection swept through him. He walked back to Racquel's room.

"There's no name on her bassinet. I thought we decided to name her Helene. What happened?"

"Oh, Johnny. When they asked me today I said we weren't sure yet. Helene just doesn't sound right to me somehow. I was fine before I saw her but she just doesn't look like a Helene."

"What does a Helene look like?" Johnny asked.

"I don't know but we'd better come up with a name." Racquel glanced at the television. "How about Dinah? I think that's a pretty name."

"Oh, no you don't. I knew a girl by that name in college and she was teased all the time. The guys kept saying, 'Someone's in the kitchen with Dinah. Someone's in the kitchen I know . . .' We don't want to pin that on her."

"That won't happen. By the time she's grown up nobody will

even remember Dinah in the kitchen. Please, Johnny, I think it's perfect."

"OK, hon. You're the mother. If you like 'Dinah' then Dinah it is."

Johnny got back to the apartment near 10:00 P.M. He was exhausted and a wave of depression came over him. He picked up the phone and dialed long distance.

"Pamela? Johnny Kramer. Is Scooter home?"

"Yes, Johnny. I'll get him right away."

Scooter came on the line. "Johnny! How are you doing?"

Johnny said nothing about the divorce proceedings. He was unaware that Scooter knew anything about it.

"I'm OK, Scoot. I just called to tell you that Charlie died today. I thought you would want to know."

"I'm sorry, Johnny. I know the feeling. It's awful. When is the funeral?"

"Uh, I don't even know. I left the hospital right after she died. I haven't talked to Dad since. I don't know what arrangements he made."

"It will probably be the day after tomorrow or the next day," Scooter said. "I'm glad you called, Johnny. Are you all right?"

"I'm hanging in there like an Oriole, pal."

Scooter and Pamela talked about flying to Pittsburgh for the funeral but decided against it. Pamela was sure that Scooter's presence would just make Johnny uncomfortable. They sent a large basket of roses and a sympathy card to Jack.

During the summer the news of Leah's divorce suit and Johnny's philandering rose from the nether region of whispered gossip to the level of common community knowledge. Johnny's reputation was severely marred and the impact was being felt at the insurance agency. Kenny Barker began dropping hints about buying Johnny out. He was becoming a liability to the partnership. Jack kept up the pressure on Johnny to come up with the $15,000 he owed Leah from the original investment. The confrontation came at the end of August.

"Look, Johnny. No hard feelings but your name is mud around here. It's the kiss of death. Face it. You're finished in the insurance business in Briarwood."

"You're just panicking, Kenny," Johnny answered. "It'll blow over and everybody will forget about it."

"Not as long as Leah stays around. Everywhere she goes people whisper behind her back. 'Poor Leah Kramer. Look what that dirty husband of hers did to her.' We're losing clients like water through a sieve, Johnny. You've got to let me buy you out."

"You don't understand. If I sell out I have to give $15,000 off the top to Leah. That won't leave me with much to build on. The divorce is cleaning me out. I'm losing the house and if I'm out of the agency I won't have anything to fall back on. I can't go back to work for Jack. You know that."

"I know it's tough, Johnny. But the longer you stay here the less the business is going to be worth. I'll tell you what I'll do. If you get out now, get out clean, sever the ties, I'll buy you out for fifty grand. You put thirty in to begin with. You'll come out with fifty. You pay off Leah and you'll still have thirty-five thousand to start up somewhere else."

It took Johnny four days to decide. He finally agreed to the terms and cleaned out his desk. He turned over his clients to Kenny and sent Leah a check for $15,000 and a photocopy to Jack Kramer. He was out of his marriage, his house, and his job. He still had a grubstake for a fresh start with Racquel. He was able to find a job to tide him over while he thought about getting into a new business. A friend in Millport who owned a Buick dealership had a vacancy in his used-car department. He gave Johnny the job as manager of the used-car lot.

By October, 1979, Scooter's portfolio had climbed over the two million dollar mark as a result of Albert Bernstein's shrewd management. Bernstein employed a coterie of investment managers and brokers. In October he called Scooter in Arizona.

"Scooter, I'd like to run an idea by you."

"Shoot, Albert. What do you have in mind?"

"Up to this point we have been rather conservative in handling your portfolio. But you see what's happening with inflation. I think it's time to get more heavily involved in commodities. What would you think if we put, say $100,000, into precious metals?"

"Hey, you know the game better than I do. Go ahead . . . I'm sure you know what you're doing."

"I appreciate that, Scooter, but this is a speculative move and I didn't want to do it without clearing it with you first."

Albert Bernstein purchased the $100,000 worth of silver at $5 an ounce. It took off immediately like an Apollo space shot climbing to $25 an ounce by December. The New Year brought a further rise as gold and silver reached unprecedented heights. When it reached $35 an ounce Bernstein got out and converted the cash into diversified securities. He earned Scooter a gross profit of $500,000 in less than five months.

Johnny was watching the silver and gold market too. Gerald Ford's WIN campaign didn't and inflation was still spiraling upward. The OPEC crisis and the invasion of Afghanistan made matters worse. People were turning away from the real estate and stock markets to put their money in commodities. The fear factor drove the prices of precious metals higher and higher.

Johnny met Bill Kay at the Red Fox. Kay was a longtime friend and valued financial advisor.

"I've been thinking of getting into precious metals, Bill. What do you think?"

"It's only going to go higher and higher, Johnny. Silver and gold are tied to inflation. When inflation rises so do they. People are jumpy about double digit inflation. The rest of the world is laughing at us. Look at Argentina and Israel. They're both running over 100 percent annual inflation. That's triple digit, Johnny. With the national debt where it is, and the Fed printing funny money, the inflation rate can only go up. I think it's just the beginning. I'm convinced silver will go over $100 an ounce within two years and gold will go over $1000."

"What's your advice?"

"Personally, I prefer silver. I know it's harder to handle and all that, but right now the silver/gold ratio is all out of whack. Gold is running too far ahead of silver and the gap has got to close. I'd put my money in silver. In fact, I already have."

"What's the best route to go?" Johnny asked.

"You know, there's basically only three approaches. You can go into the futures market, either buying long or buying short. Or you can buy on margin. The margin rate is unbelievably low, it's only 19 percent. You can buy a lot of silver with that kind of leverage. But if the market gets volatile, that can be real dangerous. That's the high risk way. You already know that. You can make a lot of money or you can get slaughtered. The safest way to buy is by taking physical delivery of the silver. That way you don't ever have to worry about making margin calls."

"How do you do it?"

Bill smiled. "I leveraged the whole load, but I got in at $12 an ounce. I wouldn't do that now. It's too risky."

"But you said that you thought it would keep climbing to at least $100 an ounce," Johnny said.

"That's right. And I think it will but I don't know that. I've been keeping a chart on it every day. As soon as I see a sign of a downward trend, not just a little dip, I mean a trend, then I'm getting out."

Johnny went home and figured it out. He had $35,000 to invest. It was not enough to buy into the kind of business he wanted. He estimated that he needed at least $50,000 in investment capital. He didn't want to wait two years to get it. He calculated that with the $35,000 he could buy approximately $175,000 in silver. It was now at $48 an ounce. If it rose to just $54 an ounce he could sell with a gross profit of over $20,000 that would give him the $50,000 he needed. He got more and more excited as he played with his calculator. He finally realized that if silver rose just four more points to $52 an ounce that would do it. It had already risen forty-three points in just a few months. Four more points and he was home free.

The next day Johnny bought his silver contract, leveraged to the hilt. He made his own chart and watched it like a hawk. Silver kept climbing, inching to $50 an ounce. He was halfway home.

Scooter's television program aired nationally for the first time. His animated, upbeat style was winsome. He kept the program catholic in scope, appealing to a broad-based audience. He was at once humorous and articulate, interpreting art, music, movies, the whole culture from a theological perspective that was fresh. The ratings registered a high share of audience participation and the network was pleased.

The popularity of the program was live evidence that religion was far from dead in the United States. A portion of the program was given to teaching, and a segment was given over to interviewing guest personalities. Famous people from the world of politics, sports, show business, and big business appeared on the show discussing their faith openly. Scooter repeated an aphorism that became a household phrase within months. He introduced the interview portion of the program with the statement, "Faith is personal, but never private." The personal-but-not-private motif became a catalyst to urge closet Christians, the spiritual underground, to surface and let their faith be seen in the marketplace. Within months Scooter became one of the most recognized religious figures in America.

The Camelback church experienced growth they weren't expecting or prepared for. It was unsettling for many, including Scooter. He never realized how valuable human privacy was until he lost it. It was one thing to be known, quite another to be famous. Scooter and Pamela felt as if a television lens was aimed at them twenty-four hours a day. Talk-show hosts besieged Pamela as well as Scooter. They couldn't go to a restaurant without having their meal disturbed with persistent requests for autographs. What appeared so glamorous to others was becoming a nightmare for the couple. Scooter's comments were rehashed in editorials, his marriage to Pamela was sensationalized by the *National Enquirer*, they had to get a security system at their home and an unlisted phone number. Within a few months, they had become prisoners of fame. Scooter hated it and began feeling inward tugs to get out. He had signed a one-year contract and he was beginning to wonder if he would make it through a full year.

Scooter slipped out of town on an early morning flight to Atlanta. From Atlanta he flew to Charlotte, North Carolina. In Charlotte he rented a car and drove to Montreat for a private meeting with Billy Graham. He was greeted at the Graham house by Ruth who graciously escorted him into the family room and summoned Billy. Scooter relaxed in a rustic setting, enjoying the roaring fire in the fireplace, an experience he missed since moving to Arizona. The mantel was a large rough-hewn beam of wood with the first line of Martin Luther's hymn, "A Mighty Fortress Is Our God," carved into the wood in the old script of German.

"Dr. Evans. I'm so glad you were able to come." Billy's eyes flashed and a warm smile was on his face.

Scooter plunged into his topic headlong.

"I appreciate your giving me this time, Dr. Graham. As I mentioned in my letter, I need your counsel. In the past few months, as you know, I've been catapulted into the public eye in a way I was not quite prepared for. I keep hoping it will go away but it doesn't. You've had to deal with this for years and I thought maybe you could give me some advice."

"There is really not much I can tell you. People react to this differently. The most important thing is always to remember who you are. I told George Wilson that if he ever sees me trying to be anything but Billy Graham to let me have it, hard and fast. Apart from that there are only two other pieces of advice I can offer, one spiritual and the other practical."

"What are they?" Scooter asked.

"When you start feeling sorry for yourself because people won't let you alone, or when the critics jump on everything you do or say, you must pick up the Book and read it. It says, 'You are not your own. You have been bought with a price.' If the One who has purchased you decides to call you to this task, you do it. It's as simple as that. What we owe Him is far greater than what He asks of us. The price you and I pay is a pittance. Don't ever forget that.

"The second point is practical. You can't give up your privacy entirely. Even our Lord had to get away from the pressing multitudes. You must have a place of retreat. For Ruth and me it is here at Montreat. People are kind to us here. We've been here for many years and they respect our need for privacy. If I lived in Scottsdale I would get myself a hideaway in the desert. Maybe around Palm Springs. The nice part of that area is that there is a whole colony of famous people living there and they tend to protect each other. Think of it. Frank Sinatra, Gerald Ford, Bob Hope—they all live out there. It's like a miniature Beverly Hills. If I went to a restaurant where Frank Sinatra was eating nobody would bother me, they'd all be staring at him."

Scooter laughed. "I doubt that. At least they wouldn't be afraid that you would jump up and deck them."

They spent the rest of the meeting discussing family, friends, and ecclesiastical matters. Scooter left Montreat walking on air, encouraged and humbled by his time with Dr. Graham.

The phone rang in Johnny's apartment. Johnny moved to pick it up. The caller did not identify himself. His opening words sent terror into Johnny. "Disaster." There was no "hello," no "This is Bill Kay," just a single word, *"Disaster."*

Johnny squeezed out a question from his panic. "What are you talking about, Bill? What kind of disaster?"

"Johnny, the silver market just collapsed. You'd better get over here right away."

"How bad, Bill?"

"Disaster. Get over here fast."

Johnny slammed the receiver down, grabbed a jacket and raced out of the apartment leaving Racquel looking at him wide-eyed. His hands were trembling on the steering wheel during the drive to Bill Kay's house. When he got there Bill led him into his private study and sat him down. "It's not a trend, Johnny. It's outright collapse. In hours the price of silver dropped from $50 to $34 an ounce."

"Why? What happened?" Johnny asked.

"I don't know. Something wild is going on. I can't figure it out. But this isn't a simple fluctuation. The thing has gone haywire."

"What should I do, Bill?"

"You have two options. You can liquidate, take your losses and lick your wounds or you can come up with the margin payment and hope this is just a temporary lapse and the thing will jump back. Now it's a question of how far you want to chase the rabbit down the hole. I don't like it. I'd get out, fast."

Johnny went after the rabbit. He made the first margin call. The news media was full of sensational reports of a grandiose scheme by Dallas's Hunt brothers, Herbert and Bunker, to corner the silver market. Bunky Hunt, especially, was buying up massive amounts of silver. The New York based Board of Commissioners put a moratorium on buying silver, limiting the number of silver contracts a person could buy. The equity percentage was raised from 19 to 50 percent and ultimately to 75 percent. The rules were being changed in the middle of the game.

Johnny frantically asked around for advice. His friends in the business all said the same thing. "Hang tough, Johnny. The pros are just playing rough. They're rustling the bushes trying to shake the amateurs out of the market. It's a scare tactic to force guys like you to sell low so they can buy in before the market rises sharply again. The amateurs are panicked. They're all selling. If you can, ride it out. You'll make a killing."

To ride it out meant making what amounted to double margin

calls. He was fighting a two-front war. Not only was the price of silver declining but, at the same time, the equity level was climbing. Johnny's head and shoulders were squeezed tightly into the burrow and his fingers still could not reach the rabbit. He hocked or mortgaged everything he could put his hands on. He got loans he should never have been granted. It became an obsession with him. He was being controlled by things he had no control over. He kept watching the paper and staying away from telephones. When he did hear a phone ring he broke into a cold sweat.

Silver kept plummeting. Its downward spiral showed no sign of leveling off. When Johnny was finally forced to quit, the bank was pulling his legs and the rabbit was scampering down a hidden underground tunnel. He was ruined. His $35,000 investment was gone, wiped out, and he now owed an additional $20,000 in loans.

Rumors were flying on Wall Street that Bunker Hunt was merely the eastern establishment's scapegoat, a smoke screen conveniently used by members of the Board of Commissioners to conceal a monumental financial scam. The gossip columns were hinting that a real live sting had been engineered by New York heavyweights who were buying low in the futures market. By changing the rules in midstream they were able to manipulate the collapse. While the guns were pointing at the Hunt brothers the New Yorkers made two billion dollars virtually overnight. The smoke screen protected them from long-term residency in Leavenworth. Whether the rumors had substance or not had little interest for Johnny. He had hit rock bottom.

TWENTY-FIVE

In the autumn of 1981 a letter crossed Scooter's desk that bore the return address of the Briarwood Community Church. It was written by the Rev. Dr. Lucius Staley, the new senior pastor of the church.

> Dear Dr. Evans,
>
> It has recently come to my attention that you are a son of this church. I was shocked to discover that you had never been invited to speak in this pulpit. I would like to take steps to rectify that. We would be highly honored if you would accept our invitation to be our evening speaker on Ash Wednesday, March 4, 1982. If you could be our keynote speaker for the spring lenten series it would be a noteworthy occasion for our church.
>
> I personally have admired your ministry from a distance. The people of this church are very proud of you. You are indeed a prophet with honor in your own country. Many people have proudly proclaimed to me of their remembrance of you and of your growing up in this church. We would be delighted to fly Mrs. Evans also, so that she might participate in your homecoming.
>
> We know you are frightfully busy and that your schedule is burdensome. Yet we earnestly pray you will be able to return for a visit and grace our pulpit on Ash Wednesday.
>
> Sincerely yours,
> Lucius Staley

Scooter was moved by the letter of invitation. He felt like an exile receiving a safe-conduct pass to return to his homeland. He flipped the pages of his calendar to see if he was free on the date.

Without even consulting Pamela he dictated an immediate response of acceptance to Dr. Staley.

Scooter was exuberant at lunch, effusive in his excitement to tell Pamela the news.

"Guess where we're going in February."

"Hawaii?" she guessed.

"No."

"Where?"

"Keep guessing. You get twenty questions. You have nineteen left."

"Come on, Richard. You know I'm not good at guessing games."

"We're going home. We're going to Briarwood. I've been invited to preach at the Community Church. I never thought I'd see the day."

"You mean Dr. Franklin invited you to preach in his pulpit?"

"No, honey. He's not there anymore. The new minister invited me. He said the people were eager for me to come."

Pamela started playing with Scooter's hair, running her fingers through it and teasing the nape of his neck. "This means a lot to you doesn't it?"

Scooter reached back and squeezed her hand. "I really didn't know how much it meant until I was invited to join the club where I'd been blackballed for years. I'll get a few extra days so we can sightsee and visit old friends."

"Does that mean a pilgrimage to all the stadiums where you used to play ball?"

"Only a few, hon, only a few."

By New Year's day of 1982 Johnny was reduced to scratching out a meager living in the used-car business. He was learning the rules of the game of dealing at the auction sales. He stayed away from late model cars because the risks were too great in the bidding. He stuck with the clunkers, preferring the low risk, low profit side of the business. Racquel was back at the plant, and between their two incomes they were able to keep their apartment and make regular payments on the balance of Leah's mortgage and on their other loans.

Johnny stayed away from Briarwood. His divorce was long since final. Jack Kramer retired, sold his home and bought a beautiful home on the Gulf Coast in Naples, Florida. Johnny had no contact with Leah or with their former friends. Occasionally he bumped into people he knew at the shopping centers or fast-food restaurants but he kept his greetings brief and his conversations elusive. He closed the book on that chapter of his life, settling in with new friends in Millport. He got along well with Racquel and doted on Joey and Dinah. Every week he promised Racquel that someday they would be free of their debts and they would move out of Millport and start over somewhere else.

Trouble was brewing for the town of Millport. Race riots had made the high school a focal point of national news coverage. Racketeers were controlling local politics, and bad news for the steel industry was filtering out of Youngstown, Ohio, and Alliquippa, Pennsylvania. Layoffs and cutbacks were already starting at Millport Steel. The new-car business was in troubled times and getting worse every day. Johnny's business was starting to pick up as people were buying used cars rather than new.

In February Johnny made a quick stop on the highway passing the edge of Briarwood. The one store he still frequented within the boro limits was Ted Branowski's shoe repair shop. Ted was a fixture there, always friendly to Johnny, remembering him from his high school days. It was Wednesday, March 4.

"Hey, Johnny, guess who's in town?"

"Who," Johnny asked while handing Ted two pairs of shoes that needed new heels, "O'Sullivan?"

Johnny liked to tease Ted by calling him O'Sullivan. Ted wore a ragged, black-stained green apron provided by the O'Sullivan Company that manufactured rubber heels for shoes. Their slogan was, "O'Sullivan, the World's #1 Heel." Johnny made use of the pun by calling Branowski, Ted O'Sullivan.

"No, O'Sullivan's always here. He stands proudly behind this counter every day," Ted said.

"I give up. Who's in town?"

"Your buddy, Scooter Evans. He was here about an hour ago. He was asking about you."

"What's Scooter doing here?"

"He's preaching tonight at 8:00 at the Community Church. Don't tell Father Manyak, but I'm going. I've never been inside a Protestant church in my life, but I'm going tonight. I'll bet there will be a lot of other Catholics too. You'd better be there, Johnny."

"Hey, I haven't been in that place since I got married. You know I can't show up there. Leah will be sure to be there. She wouldn't miss seeing Scooter for the world."

Johnny drove back to the lot. He was in a quandary debating all day if he should go hear Scooter.

Scooter was pacing up and down in the motel room. Pamela said, "Don't you think it's time we went out and had dinner? You have to be at the church at 7:30."

"I guess so. You must be hungry but I can't eat a bite. Where would you like to go?"

"You know I can wait until after the service and eat a late dinner. My stomach is still on Arizona time. I was thinking of you. You can't preach on an empty stomach."

"Honey, my stomach is going to be empty whether I eat or not. I'd just as soon wait until after the service."

"What's the matter? You're a nervous wreck."

"I've never been so nervous in my life, hon."

"Why? You speak to millions of people every week."

"Yeah, but they don't know me. These people watched me grow up. To them I'm still a little kid."

"No, you're not. These people have television sets. They've already heard you speak. You don't have to prove anything to them."

"I'm not being very spiritual am I? I'm more worried about my performance than I am about preaching a sermon."

"Cut it out. It's perfectly normal to worry about your personal reception in your hometown. I'll bet Jesus was nervous when He preached at Nazareth."

"If He was nervous it wasn't because He had a problem with His ego like I'm having."

"Stop flagellating yourself. Are you forgetting who you are? These people will allow you your pound of flesh. Relax, honey, this is supposed to be a good time for you. Besides, you know that as soon as you open your mouth and start your sermon you'll forget all this nonsense."

"The King is dead . . ." The words hung in the darkened sanctuary, their somber declaration suggesting an aura of mourning. Dr. Evans went on.

"Not David. Not Saul. Not Herod. This king was not so famous. His name was Uzziah—a monarch who brought a measure of stability to a nation torn apart from civil strife, a nation made cynical by court intrigue and bloody coups. During the reign of Uzziah old wounds had healed and the people gained respite from treachery in high places.

"Isaiah ben Amoz heard the decree; the black-draped proclamation was posted at every inn, heralded in every city. Jews ripped their garments, put ashes on their foreheads, and wailed in the streets. Isaiah went to church. What he saw there is not what you see tonight.

"You've left your homes this night in the middle of the week to observe the beginning of Lent. You stare at me this moment, and what do you see? Perhaps tonight you look at me and see a boy playing in the schoolyard next door or a lad dressed like a cherubim sitting over there in the choir loft dressed in a white surplice and a black bow. You laugh to yourself as you see me in your classrooms" (Scooter looked toward his grade-school teachers), "in your barber chair, your hardware store . . . You look at me and you know you have nothing to fear. I am flesh and blood like you and you know from where I came. Some of you are smiling and you are saying to yourself, 'I knew you *when,* Scooter Evans.'"

Johnny smiled at the reference, a guilty smile as if Scooter had just read his mind.

"Isaiah could not say that. His lonely vigil in the temple of mourning was interrupted by a presence that was not flesh and blood. His was a vision of God. Isaiah came, stabbed in the heart by grief, fearful of the future of his nation. The king was dead and the throne of Judah was not vacant, Uzziah's crown had passed to his son Jotham. The king had died, not in the regal splendor of the palace but in disgrace, in the house of lepers, cut off from the house of God because of sin that blemished the later years of his reign. Isaiah was there to pray, to pray for the throne of Judah.

"Without warning the Temple began to quake, the doorposts started to move—the room was filled with smoke and Isaiah had the scales removed from his eyes. He suddenly saw behind the veil, the drape that covers all of our eyes from holy things—the drape that shields our souls from instant death lest we peer inside its forbidden chambers. 'No man . . . No man shall see God and live,' the Scriptures say.

"The presence became visible, and in that awful moment Isaiah was suspended between heaven and earth, transported over an unbridgeable chasm, lifted into ether plains where his eyes beheld what no mortal dared invade—the sacred space, the holy ground of the Most High God. The vision unfurled before his eyes in dazzling splendor. He saw the Lord. He saw *Adonai,* the Sovereign One, a vision of God Himself seated upon a throne, high and exalted, His royal train filling the Temple, its folds engulfing the chamber.

"Stop. Think . . . "Scooter held a pause. "What would you do tonight if suddenly I vanished from this pulpit, if the congregation around you instantly disappeared, and in the twinkling of an eye the chancel began to glow with divine iridescence and God appeared before your eyes. Suddenly you see Him face to face—not just a vague shadowy concept, not merely a stained glass window or a fresco painted on the ceiling. You see God sitting in the seat of cosmic authority surrounded by the blinding glory of the heavenly host. What would you do?

"Isaiah was confused. As confused as you would be if you gazed into heaven, as dumbstruck as I would be if I peered into the inner sanctum. He saw strange creatures, bizarre creatures, creatures called seraphim, flying about and singing the Trisagion."

Scooter changed the tempo, momentarily breaking the spell. He smiled and began to reminisce about his childhood in Briarwood.

"I remember winter in Briarwood. Behind our house we had a bird feeder. Each morning before I left for school I sprinkled bird seed on the feeder. Sunflower seeds were preferred by the bigger birds. We kept a little book by the window to help us identify the varieties of birds that came to feed. They came in all shapes and sizes; brilliant scarlet-chested cardinals, pompous chattering blue jays. There were finches and woodpeckers, sparrows and mourning doves. As the seasons changed so did the birds that visited us. It was always a thrill to look out there toward the end of March and see the first robin of spring. We have different birds in Arizona, and none are so comical as the desert road runner. I've seen lots of birds . . . but I've never seen a bird with six wings. Have you?"

The congregation chuckled at the thought of a bird with six wings.

"Why would God make a bird with six wings? A bird needs only two to fly. Yet Isaiah saw six-winged creatures flying around the throne of God. Their extra wings were not superfluous; they were not vestigial appendages or malignant growths of an aviary freak. They were given these appendages by their Creator for a purpose. They were not chance mutations but were functionally necessary. They used two wings to cover their faces and two to cover their feet. These winged creatures required special equipment. They were in the presence of God. The effulgence of His glory was too brilliant to perceive directly. They must have their eyes covered. Their creaturely feet could not tread on this holy ground, they must be covered.

"What would we use to cover ourselves if we were exposed to such a sight? Sunglasses would be impotent, blindfolds utterly useless. Would we scream to the hills to fall upon us and to the mountains to cover us?"

Johnny was starting to feel uncomfortable. He slouched down in his seat seeking refuge in the shadows. He didn't like the sermon. It was distasteful to him. He thought about leaving, about quietly slipping out of the pew and into the fresh night air. The heavy atmosphere in the sanctuary was suffocating him and he wanted out. But he could not move.

"Do you hear the seraphic song, the hallowed hymn sung in the sacred place? You sing it all the time here in this sanctuary. The thrice stated hymn of adoration. 'Holy, Holy, Holy.' Isaiah caught its meaning. He was a Jew. He didn't fail to grasp what we are wont to overlook. Why the repetition? Why the three times holy? Why not merely, 'Holy,' or 'Holy, Holy.' It was the third exclamation, the triplicate stanza that pierced the soul of Isaiah.

"We are Americans, not Israelites. We speak English, not Hebrew. If we want to denote emphasis we use the exclamation point; we underline; we set our words in bold italics. The Jewish method was by repetition. When Jesus was about to tell His disciples something extra important He prefaced His statement by the words, 'Truly, truly, I say unto you.' Their ears perked up when the Master repeated the word *truly*.

"It is rare. Very rare. Indeed very, very rare that the Scrip-

ture repeats anything to the third degree, to the superlative degree. Only once is an attribute to God elevated to the third
degree. How we wish that the song of the seraphim was love, love,
love, or mercy, mercy, mercy, or peace, peace, peace. Each of
these describe the character of the God we long for. But who can
bear the unveiling of the divine majesty with the transcendent
accent of the choir singing, 'Holy, Holy, Holy'? That is why we
flee from Him, searching the darkness for shelter from His countenance. That is why we curse Him . . . He is Holy and we are
not."

Johnny felt a bead of perspiration drip from his temple and
cascade down across his cheek. He wiped it away nervously hoping that Scooter would change the subject. He felt frightened,
a kind of cold terror he had never known before. He was at
once repulsed and fascinated by the story he was hearing. It was
foreign to him yet he sensed a vague kind of understanding of it.
Isaiah was from another world, yet somehow he was from
Johnny's world too. He was feeling sorry for Isaiah, secretly
rooting for him to get up and run out of the Temple, away from
the dreadful vision.

"Some say Isaiah was the most righteous man in Israel. He
was no murderer, no thief, no adulterer." The last word stung
Johnny.

"But what did he do? Did he sing out in exaltation, praising
God for revealing Himself in such a spectacular display of majesty? No, my friends, he did not. He did something also unheard
of in biblical history. He made a prophetical pronouncement. He
opened his mouth and spoke, nay, screamed an oracle. His oracle
was not a benediction—it was a malediction, an oracle of doom
pronounced not upon his enemies but upon himself. 'Woe is me,'
he screamed, putting the curse of judgment upon himself in fear
and trembling.

"Ordinary people don't do that. We curse and sometimes
even curse at ourselves. We call ourselves stupid and dumb and
use all sorts of self-deprecating language when we become disgusted with our own actions. But none among us has ever know-
ingly spoken an ultimate divine oracle of judgment upon our own
heads. Isaiah was on the edge of insanity. The instant he saw
God, Isaiah also saw Isaiah in a way he had never seen himself

before. The sight was unbearable . . . 'Woe is me for I am undone.'

"Isaiah was coming apart. His self-image was disintegrating. He was being shattered to pieces. He cried out, 'I am a man of unclean lips and I dwell in the midst of a people of unclean lips.' "

Scooter's voice began to rise, filling the sanctuary, reverberating from the walls. "Did you hear that?" he shouted from the pulpit. "The prophet Isaiah had a dirty mouth. His tongue was filthy, contaminated by lies, by slandering his friends, by empty prayers to God, by dishonest boasts of his own achievements. And he knew he was not alone in this. The whole nation suffered from the dirty mouth, mouths full of cursing and bitterness, mouths with the poison of asps under the lips, mouths leading to throats that were like open sepulchres. Is your mouth any different? Is mine? Are we the first generation of mortals who have escaped this malady? You know better."

Johnny was being crushed. Scooter's words fell on him like hammer blows. It seemed like he was alone in the congregation and he was in a dark tunnel that connected with Scooter at the other end. No one else was listening. It was as if Scooter were talking to him alone, reading his mind, stripping off his clothes, laying him naked at the foot of the altar. Each word had special meaning for him. His mouth tasted sour and bitter. His mind accused him of the things he said, the lies he told, the promises he broke.

"What happened to Isaiah, dear friends? Did God leave him there groveling on the floor cursing himself? Did he say, 'Come now Isaiah; you are being melodramatic; you are on a neurotic guilt trip; don't take yourself so seriously'? Never! Listen . . . hear Isaiah tell it in his own words:

> Then flew one of the seraphim unto me, having a live coal in his hand, which he had taken with the tongs from off the altar: and he laid it upon my mouth, and said, "Lo, this hath touched thy lips; and thine iniquity is taken away, and thy sin is purged."

Scooter described the purging of Isaiah in vivid terms. He spoke of a glowing coal being applied directly to Isaiah's mouth, his flesh seared by its touch. He spoke of the fiery pain of authentic repentance of a man honest for a moment in the presence of God. He remembered his own midnight pacing in the dormitory hall years before, the excruciating battle for his soul. He knew grace was not cheap. The pain of judgment had to be felt, not merely contemplated or recited as doctrine. The wound had to be cauterized with the blistering coal before it could heal.

Johnny recoiled from the narrative as if an angel were standing in front of him ready to put fire in his mouth. He closed his mouth tightly to resist the touch. He felt it anyway. It spread from his mouth to his throat and surged through his body in a blaze of white heat. It was over so quickly he was sure he imagined it. But inside he knew. Nothing could ever be the same. Something ultimate was settled for him.

Scooter was finishing his sermon.

"Dear friends, I look around this sanctuary and do not see God. I detect no smoke. The doors are not moving. I have no vision of the splendor of God. But I know this: He is here. We may see no ladder bridging the gap between heaven and earth as Jacob saw in his midnight dream, yet we can say . . . we must say, 'Surely God was in this place and I knew it not.'"

Johnny smiled to himself. *No, Scooter. This time you're wrong. Surely God is in this place and I know it well.*

Scooter closed his sermon in prayer. When he finished, Dr. Staley rose to his feet and announced, "I think it is fitting to conclude our service by standing and singing 'Holy, Holy, Holy.'"

The choir broke into a spontaneous descant on the fourth and final stanza. Shivers went up Scooter's spine. He glanced down at Pamela. Her face was radiant, transfixed as she sang the final chorus. Her eyes met his and she grinned like a small child on Christmas morning.

After the service Scooter stood at the bottom of the chancel stairs hugging his third-grade teacher, embracing his baseball coach, and shaking hands with old friends. He turned and saw Scotty McTavish with tears lining his cheeks. Scotty moved forward and embraced him. His tears were dropping on Scooter's shoulder. "Please don't write me off, coach," Scooter muttered. McTavish pushed him to arm's length and placed both hands on his shoulders. "Never, Scooter. I never did write you off and I never will."

Scooter saw Leah. She rushed up and added her tears to his

chest. While he was holding her he looked over her shoulder and saw Johnny standing alone in the shadows of the corner of the church. He was waiting.

For a half hour Scooter and Pamela stood greeting his old friends and strangers who stepped forward to introduce themselves. After Leah left, Johnny inched closer, moving up the outer aisle, away from the people leaving by the center aisle. As the last person left, Scooter walked to the side to see his friend. Johnny still looked boyish save for the wrinkle lines that were etched on his face. His clothes were disheveled and he looked harried. After they embraced Scooter looked into his eyes and said, "Are you making it?"

Johnny didn't flinch. He looked straight back at Scooter and said firmly, "Yes, Scoot. I'm making it. Don't worry."

Scooter got Johnny's telephone number and new address. Johnny turned to Pamela and gave her a bear hug. "I love you two." He turned to leave.

"Where are you going, Johnny?"

"Home. It's time for me to go home."

"OK, roomie. And let me hear from you."

Johnny looked back over his shoulder and said, "You will. I promise."

Scooter watched him walk toward the back of the church. When he was almost to the door he called to him, "Johnny!"

Johnny turned and looked back.

"One last thing," Scooter said. "May the Lord watch between me and thee, while we are absent, one from the other."

Johnny nodded his head and walked out the door.

Coming Home

Out there
In that "far country"
It looked good
It felt good
It seemed good.

But from here—
From home—

I see with a
Different eye.

Out there
All I had to
Judge by
Was amateur attempts
By Others in the same
Stage that I was.
We all were coping
Well—
Apparently . . .

But then the Call
Began—
The Call that I was
Wanted
At home.

Unclear, indistinct,
Even fuzzy—
The Call persisted.
I followed my instinct
And began that
"Long journey home."

Not by miles, but by
Years was it measured,
Side trips,
Long lay-overs
Were many
But still the
Persistent Call—
"You are wanted
At home."

Slowly that "far country"
Lost its glamour
Lost its appeal

Lost its hold
What once appeared
Good and wholesome
Began to look
Shabby, tawdry,
Cheap.

I was rediscovering
A new standard
Not amateur this time,
But truly professional
And pleasure became
Exchanged for Pain—
Security for Risk—
Control for Trust
And I began to be
Afraid.

But I was getting
Closer to
Home
And my vision
Was being
Corrected.

The facade of the
"Far country"
Melted away
Leaving behind
Nothing.

These new eyes
See through the
Home facade
As well.
What appears to be
Pain,
What appears to be
Risk,

What appears to be
Trust
Are *really* Life.

"Those who have eyes
To see
Let them see."

Roberta Carlson

MISSION STATEMENT

for Wolgemuth & Hyatt, Publishers, Inc.

The mission of Wolgemuth & Hyatt, Publishers, Inc., is to publish and distribute books that lead individuals toward:

- A personal faith in the one true God: Father, Son, and Holy Spirit;
- A lifestyle of practical discipleship; and
- A worldview that is consistent with the historic, Christian faith.

Moreover, the company will endeavor to accomplish this mission at a reasonable profit and in a manner which glorifies God and serves His Kingdom.